MW01275599

CHARISSA'S SHOES

A Novel

by

David Gay

This is a work of fiction set in the future. The characters and events are products of the author's imagination. Certain surnames are taken from seventeenth-century English historical figures; otherwise, any similarities among characters in this story and real people living or dead are coincidental and unintended by the author.

TABLE OF CONTENTS

PART ONE

PART TWO

For Bill

Part One

PROLOGUE 1

Prison Island, February 2050

The sun rose like blood above the Atlantic waves. Hungry clouds scudded above the horizon's baleful haze. The ocean seemed ready to boil. It was barely dawn, but the temperature was already 37 degrees Celsius.

Charissa Dryden-Burnet, Canada's most notorious eco-terrorist, awoke from a troubled sleep. She sat up and rested her head against the cinder block wall of her hut. She brushed some straw from her bare feet. She planted her soles firmly on the hot concrete floor. She watched the two other women who shared her cell. Ruth turned over on the straw, opened her left eye, then fell back to sleep. Sadma lay on her back snoring gently.

She stood up and opened the door of the hut. When she walked into the compound, two guards in two towers fired two bullets four metres from her feet. This practice was known as "calibrated cautionary handling" among the guards, who were all women. She wasn't afraid. She knew they fired their guns to pad their weekly reports.

She stopped twenty metres from the perimeter. A wall of flaming gas four metres high served as a fence. The prison commandant told prisoners that the flames burned gas from pipelines on the sea floor. The lines, he claimed, connected Cuba, Australia, Japan, Ireland, Venezuela, Newfoundland and Vancouver Island. The underwater junction of the lines was a kilometre beyond a rusty scow moored just off the beach, the commandant insisted. The scow encouraged prisoners to think about the fossil fuels needed to keep them in jail. Prisoners needed to know that the flames would burn forever. If the prisoners could learn to blame themselves for the flames, and show some common sense, they might gain a very faint hope of re-joining the family of civilized nations. The prison commandant, Stuart Otis, read this information from his penal manual through a deafening bullhorn – an *Ogresso Messenger* X-11 – twice a week.

She placed her hands on top of her head to make the shooting stop.

"Morning Izzy!" one guard shouted, holding her fire.

Her parents and everyone from her childhood up called Charissa "Izzy" for short. Now her guards and fellow prisoners called her Izzy too.

She gazed briefly beyond the wall of flame to the round blue ocean. She remembered a poem she memorized when she was seven.

Why hurry, little river,

Why hurry to the sea?

There is nothing there to do

But to sink into the blue

And all forgotten be.

It was the first poem she memorized in school. It was not a favourite poem, but it was hard work at the time. Now she would gladly trade it for one of her father's robust heroic couplets. Simeon brought a tear to her left eye.

She was tired of dreaming the dreams of the world's captors. Simeon told her there would be poetry for everyone someday, even for the undeserving, the diabolical and the stupid. She hummed a few bars of "Feet Fall on the Road" by Bruce Cockburn. Noah, her other father, hummed this song to her whenever Simeon's extemporaneous couplets grew too abstruse.

Suddenly the compound's loudspeaker blasted a jumped-up, fast paced, hard rock version of *Swing Low Sweet Chariot.* The tune exploded the dawn every morning of the week. Commandant Stuart Otis appeared on the veranda of his hut, as he did every morning at dawn. He wore bright white shorts and a white T-shirt with large silver epaulets, as he did every morning. He held an antique, non-functioning boom box on his shoulder as a prop. It helped him keep his balance. He jerked, swayed, circled, walked backward, walked forwards, walked sideways and did stride jumps around the compound, emphasizing his starts and stops like bad punctuation in a run-on sentence. It was time for inspection. The prisoners lined up.

Ruth and Sadma dragged themselves out of their hut and rubbed the sleep from their eyes. Ruth squinted into the light through her light brown eyes, and pushed her shoulder length, honey wheat hair away from her freckled face. She gripped the bark of a makeshift bannister as if her willowy, twenty-seven year old body might collapse at any moment.

Sadma Blandina Martin was a tall black woman of forty-three years. Her hair was short and straight, her bright eyes wide and brown. She whispered the names of her missing children as she moved purposefully to the assembly line. Twenty-one women emerged from other cells in groups of three or four. Otis performed two clumsy backward moonlaps around Izzy to pass the time while the stragglers lined up. He sometimes belched out some improvised lyrics in a low voice, conscious of his raspy monotone. He believed his made-up words would stimulate prisoner rehabilitation. Izzy could smell the farmed crayfish and cheap Chablis on his breath from five feet.

"Good morning, eco-terrorists!" Otis exclaimed. "For eco-terrorists you are, and eco-terrorists you must remain. Convicted by the evidence of truth, outlawed from the family of civilized nations, condemned to penal servitude, I welcome you once again to your place of incarceration!"

Izzy grinned at Otis's grammar. She sprinkled gaffes through his weekly reports to Ottawa, which he ordered her to "peer review" and edit. The fun was wearing thin.

Her prison job placed her in the "Stuart Otis Communications Centre." The SOCC was an aluminum lean-to next to the commandant's personal latrine. Ruth typed the thoughts of his brain from Sadma's rough notes on a large, antique, battleship gray Sutton X1, built in 1984, featuring 20 MB hard drive, 3.5 inch floppy disc port and a daisy wheel printer. Izzy edited the final copy. Prison Island was a "black zone" for communications. It had no wireless connections, no Internet, no satellite links, no e-mail, no 21st century computers and no e-phones. Communication was strictly limited.

Journalists had some clues to the island's location, but none ventured there because of its primitive communications.

Some toyed with maps apps on their laptops to see if the prison really existed. The apps were misleading. The original island was known as Putmania, and was owned secretly by Senator Fitzputman Otis. A vocal skeptic of global warming, Senator Otis nonetheless donated Putmania to the Canadian government as a potential prison in exchange for a tax write-off and Senate appointment. He knew the island was shrinking. Putmania was the size of greater Edmonton at the turn of the century. It was now the size of a small Edmonton neighbourhood. Maps apps no longer noticed it.

Some journalists tried to get government workers to admit to the prison's whereabouts off the record. None did. A volunteer organization called the "Spirit of the CBC" showed up off the coast of Putmania in a small fishing boat. They wanted to keep the CBC tradition of stellar investigative reporting alive even though government cuts had diminished it. They tried to start an interview with signal flags. Otis bellowed at them through his *Ogresso Messenger X-11*:

"Infiltrators! Doomed to be disbelieved, I order you to vacate these waters," he bellowed.

When the group refused to leave, Otis turned on the shore battery flamethrowers to persuade them further. Fresh water was strictly rationed, but there was never any shortage of flammable gas on Prison Island.

* * *

Otis received his appointment from the Prime Minister's Office. His father, Senator Fitzputman Otis, a wealthy donor to the ruling party, vouched for his son's steadiness and discipline. In fact, Otis could not sit still in the mornings. Like many boys from well-to-do backgrounds, he grew up with an e-phone and an e-pad and a giant game console with baseball, hockey and an en suite hologram fantasy closet. Now he was in a constant state of blue light withdrawal. A paediatrician in Montreal invented a special "patch" for such cases. The patch released small hourly doses of photons to appease the brain, and slowly wean it off the salvoes of unnatural light. The patch worked best with both eyes covered. This caused the product to flop on *Businessaurus Rexes,* a popular TV show featuring new entrepreneurs pitching deals to established business magnates.

Otis tried to cultivate his inner life to compensate for life in the black zone. He secretly wanted to be a novelist. In his spare time, he invented titles for future bestsellers: *Island of the Imprisoned Women! Criminal Women, Sand and Surf! Confessions of a Stranded Eco-Warden!* He was good with titles, but not quite as good with narrative. His stories got stuck, often on the first page, their minimalist plots mired intractably in exotic settings. Well, what need of words? Perhaps film was Otis's real gift. Movies were mainly visual. He began to produce and direct movies in his head. With film, he felt he could take characterization for granted, but plot and dialogue remained problems. He felt frustrated. Whatever the medium, he couldn't ask Izzy or Ruth or Sadma to type his stories at taxpayer expense. And, being criminals, they would be sure to steal his ideas, he believed.

Sadma took pity on Otis. She recognized his symptoms. She knew Otis needed endorphins to make it through a day. Chablis was no use. Vigorous dancing would manufacture endorphins. So she decided to teach him to dance.

Sadma was a Natural Republican, the nationality that superseded "American" after the breakup and realignment of the United States of America. One night, when she was thirty-four, she called the police to quell a disturbance in the apartment next door to her. Her three sons – Malcolm, Emmett and Langston – had tests at school the next morning, and were trying to sleep. The neighbour's TV was tuned to *Real Life Dropouts.* The volume was way too loud. Police arrived. Sadma explained the situation. The police promptly shot Sadma's pet cat Mavis, killing her in a long, withering crossfire. Sadma protested, so they placed her under arrest. They charged her with resisting arrest and threatening police officers. They dispersed her sons into a moonless night because men's prisons were overcrowded. Sadma had not seen them since.

Sadma spent her entire trial in a state of shock. She said nothing. In a memorandum of guidance to the Grand Jury, police described her as a "combative subject justifying the discharging of firearms prior to said combativeness as caused by discharged firearms." The prosecutor imputed righteousness to the officers, then rested his case. Sadma's lawyer argued that she suffered from PTSD. She could not afford an expert witness to support her, so her trauma was declared hearsay. This was her first offence, but the judge was in no mood. The way he saw things, her stress was a result, not a cause of her crime. He gave her twelve years in the Women's Facility of the Natural Republic of Northeast Central Carolina.

Serious overcrowding in the facility helped to lift Sadma out of her shock. Overcrowding inspired her to start a dance program for inmates there. WFNRNECC officials frowned on it. Interpreting a new free trade agreement, they traded her to Canada's Prison Island for one Wall Street trader and future considerations. The trade included two other women, who were serving mandatory twenty-year sentences under the republic's "one strike" rule. The two women were guilty of stealing gluten-free organic baby food for their children. Gluten-free products were natural commodities, and Sadma had mentored the two women through dance.

These facts made Sadma an accessory to eco-terrorism, satisfying the needs of Canadian officials and smoothing the way for her transfer to Prison Island. Prosecutors called the constellation of facts a "slam dunk." The two young women died of burst hearts *en route* to Prison Island. Sadma understood why, and wondered if she would die soon too. Officials were confident Sadma would find few dancers in a Canadian institution. Dancing was not the purpose of music on Prison Island.

* * *

Ruth Keren Boudica was the leader of the notorious Blue Light Brigade, a group of three eighteen-year-old grade 12 students from Anne's River, New Brunswick. They set out to avenge their friend Tamara, who swallowed her mother's tranquilizers after a spammer posing as a dating service executive producer posted graphic photos of her on the Internet. Tamara fell into a coma. Ruth developed a strange condition while Tamara lay in her hospital bed. She began to fear cameras. She could not stand to have a camera pointed at her. But she also began to hate screens, and violently. Her weapon of choice for smashing screens was a shovel, preferably a short-handled spade that she learned to wield like a samurai sword.

The carnage started in Fredericton. Ruth and two friends, Mona and Monique, flung hoes and rakes and swung hammers at computer consoles in the inter-city bus station. They whipped their short spades like whistling scythes that smashed the windows of a six-story computer superstore in Moncton. Shattered glass fell like rain. They made for Truro, Nova Scotia. They hijacked a truckload of e-phones while the driver was peeing on a bush. They drove the truck to a bridge over the Salmon River. They bailed out as the truck careened down the bank in flames.

Mona and Monique surrendered to police in Truro after tearful online facechats with their parents. Two weeks later, police captured Ruth in Halifax as she was about to board a cruise liner, but not before she smashed video cameras in an airport, shattered laptops with a crowbar at an eco-recycling centre, and split open the ticketing console of the cruise line while the agent cowered under the counter. She knocked the bullhorn out of the hand of an arresting officer from thirty metres with her last short-handled spade. Her friends got six-month suspended sentences after posting remorse statements on the Internet, and naming Ruth as their leader.

Ruth's father hired a lawyer named Joel Roley, who specialized in medical claims. He once presented a defence of "Afflatulenza" for a wealthy freshwater commodity trader who had tried to suffocate a homeless man chosen at random. Roley took a similar approach with Ruth. He named her aversion to cameras "Runtsmin's Blephositis," after his mother's maiden name. He did not believe Ruth had a medical condition, but it was not his job to believe. During the trial, a specialist from Alberta called, offering to testify to the facts about "MacPherson's Misoscopohobia." He warned Roley not to plagiarize his disease.

In court, Ruth refused to cooperate with Roley's medical defence, despite her father's pleas. The attack on the eco-centre gift-wrapped a charge of eco-terrorism for federal government lawyers, who celebrated Ruth's conviction with a Saturday of family skiing at Gatineau's Mont Bisque Fantasy Executive Vacations for Less Resort and Spa Place.

Ruth was now in the ninth year of her twelve-year sentence. She had no way of knowing that Tamara had awakened from her coma after two years and was studying journalism at college. Therapy and good parents helped her to get back on her feet. Meanwhile, time was stuck on Prison Island. The judge sent Ruth to Prison Island where no screens or blue lights could distract her. Typing memos to a steady beat was somewhat therapeutic for Ruth. She soon realized that Commandant Otis was tone and beat deaf: he couldn't discern Ruth typing his memos to the beat of *Swing Low, Imagine, Hallelujah* or *Four Strong Winds*. She liked to type to the beat of different songs. It felt like dancing.

Music was not the main purpose of music on Prison Island. An official in the *Bureau of Social Justice, Human Privacy and Political Hygiene* in Ottawa had assigned songs to Otis for practical reasons. Music was intended to deprive selected inmates of sleep, not provide a basis for Otis's exercise routines or Ruth's finger dances.

Sadma liked the melody to *Swing Low.* The government provided the fast, hard-rocking version for sleep deprivation purposes, not as a morning wake-up call. A slower version with prescribed government lyrics accompanied solemn ceremonies. Sadma liked the fast version. She had persuaded Otis that the fast version version would make a fine anthem for the compound, getting folks lively, happy and fired up every morning. And sleep deprivation, from a management perspective, made no sense. It would lead to typos and gaffes in the SOCC, making it difficult for Otis to get his message out. This last argument persuaded Otis. He chose, by executive order, to use the slow version for ceremonies and the fast version for dancing at all other hours when prisoners were not asleep. He permitted prisoners to sing the original lyrics or make up their own lyrics for the dance segments only. Music became music again. And Otis became a dancer.

* * *

"Attention!" Otis barked.

The prisoners stood lazily at attention. The guard in the southwest corner climbed down from her tower, put down her rifle and picked up her accordion. She played the slow version of *Swing Low* during the flag-raising ceremony. Her interpretation was part hymn, part dirge. She kept pace with a taped bass voice that sang the government lyrics through the loudspeaker:

"Eco-terr-orists. Try not to think about home."

Two guards unfurled the flag and hoisted it up a blue pole, hoping to make it reach the top in exactly two minutes, 28 seconds: the time the accordionist required to complete her rendition. The flag usually arrived early, often waiting another ten or fifteen seconds for the final tug. Dancing was permitted in this interval.

The flag reached the top early and hung limply in the hot

air, waiting to complete its servile copulation with the accordionist. A light gust of wind spread the flag out, displaying FACINAT; against a light blue background. FACINAT stood for "Family of Civilized Nations." The semi-colon was a mystery. At the bottom of the flag, a yellow lightning bolt lay on its side like a deflated condom.

"At ease, eco-terrorists," Otis barked. "Closer to the equator than Canada, here where nature registers no signs of seasonal change, uncertain even of the time of day or day of the week, owing to the sameness of our day length, and forgotten – yes, forgotten! – by history itself, I demand that you orient yourselves to your tasks at hand. Try not to think about home and you will surely find peace."

Izzy had managed to orient herself. The signs of the seasons were abundant. Some trees beyond the compound went dormant once a year. She had seen a flock of frigate birds angling down from the north the week before. They flew over the water to the south and west. Izzy guessed that Cuba, or even the Florida might be to the west, given the long range of the birds. She remembered them from the *Earth Still Alive!* documentaries she watched as a child. Cold fronts passed over, but hurricanes were months earlier. The steps of the sun inclined to the south. Average winter temperatures were climbing from the high twenties of the distant past into the thirties. It was a winter morning.

* * *

Otis reviewed the formation of prisoners. He wore mirrored sunglasses to affect the look of a soulless taskmaster and to replicate the one-way mirrors of interrogation rooms.

"Criminally reckless enough to commit eco-terrorism, I order all of you to begin your day's work. Or tasks. You have thirty minutes to prepare. Dismissed!" These ritual denunciations helped Otis to manage his withdrawal symptoms. His forehead turned strawberry red when he strained to secrete commands.

Izzy, Sadma and Ruth trudged to the communication centre. The prisoners wore plain white floppy sandals. The floppies all looked the same. They adjusted for size with Velcro strips. The women lined their floppies up carefully to avoid confusion. She avoided wearing these regulation sandals. Her own pain was sufficient. Her feet had toughened in her seven years in this prison. For once in her life, no one could accuse Izzy of stealing other people's shoes.

That afternoon, the gravel compound was so hot that Izzy had to slip on a pair of floppies to go to the latrine. Three pairs rested against a cinder block. She chose one pair, and hoped they were hers. She stepped into them.

A sharp pain convulsed her brain. She felt her body morph into a band of light struggling in the grubby blue hands of a giant who tried to hold on to her like a slippery fish, who wanted to pin her down and pound her with an antiquated camera as a stone pounds grain. Each time the camera flashed, Izzy's body seemed to divide in half. It kept dividing into smaller and smaller grains.

The floppies belonged to Ruth.

Chapter One

MACPHERSON'S PAPOUTSIOSIS

Edmonton, September 2030.

Charissa Naomi Dryden-Burnet was the only child of Noah Albert Burnet and Simeon Herbert Dryden. Everyone called her Izzy for short. Noah was an internationally renowned environmental scientist specializing in fresh water. He had worked on water supply projects in Africa and South America and India and the Canadian north. He had taught at universities in Europe, Africa and the Middle East. Originally from Camrose, Noah was happy to return to Alberta when a position opened at the University of Alberta. He loved that Edmonton still had so much green space. But the lakes were feverish, and the rivers were writhing. He wanted to cure the lakes and rivers across the west and beyond. He knew Albertans to be hopeful people. He believed he could make persuasion do the work of fear.

Simeon was the son of English missionary parents from the Lambeth district of south London. He retained his London accent. He grew up in different mission fields from Bolivia to India. He developed his vocation for cleaning in response to the poverty and illness he witnessed. He remembered his mother Rita pouring warm water over the soapy heads of giggling children. It looked to him like the meaning of life. Cleanliness to Simeon was not a compulsion. It was a sacrament.

Noah and Simeon met in the Negev desert where Noah was working on a desalination project to supply a desperate refugee camp, and Simeon was a volunteer janitor and orderly in a field hospital. Simeon liked to compose limericks. Noah pushed him towards heroic couplets. Poetry, beautiful and worthy in itself, brought order to the chaos he saw.

The University of Alberta offered spousal laboratory facilities to Noah and Simeon. Noah was Director of the Fresh Water Research Institute. Simeon was laboratory custodian and an adjunct member of the university's interdisciplinary water institute. He held a bachelor's degree in English poetry. He planned to infuse poetry into the institute's seminars.

Noah set to work. He wanted to find a way to supply fresh water to everyone in Canada as a matter of scientific ethics and human rights. Noah's first research proposal was ambitious: he planned to develop water filtration systems designed for the microclimate of needy communities in the north. Harnessing the North's long summer daylight and winds, he hoped to power local water filtration systems through a network of magnifying lenses and wind turbines. Source water would be quarantined from zones of orthodox economic activity, where water served fire in the process of oil extraction. Noah wanted fire to make water for people to drink. Elements should dance, not toil, he felt.

In the first three years of his tenure, Noah won international grants to protect lakes and rivers from inflammation and bring balance to Alberta's intake and output of water. He fought to end price-per-barrel trading of Canadian water on international *CAP* (commodities and plastics) exchanges. He warned Canadians that damaging nature would damage entrepreneurship. He worked hard to keep his hopes up amid a mass of indifference and contradictions. He had to order solar panels from China, which produced profitable green energy products in foggy factories. He refused to participate in nuclear modified rain or hyper-tar-suck technology or CO2 subterranean hermetic monasticism or deep smog freezer bags or aquatic carbon outfall rectification, all current favourites of the federal government.

The next stage of Noah's research stirred controversy. People thought criminals were products of their own choices. Noah thought otherwise. He wanted to see if clean drinking water could lower the crime rate in Canada. The right to clean water would change the self-image of children, but it would require serious collaboration among government, industry and the research community. Above all, it would require a constitutional amendment to be viable. He organized an international symposium called *Eco-Rights: End Crimes, not End Times*. He invited scientists to join philosophers, sociologists, literary critics, political scientists, poets, painters and dancers. The event offended the new Prime Minister, a staunch Solid Retentivist who had no desire to open constitutional negotiations. The PMO tried to divert the flow of Noah's energy. It invited him to chair a prestigious national roundtable on the renaming of extinct species. Noah declined.

Opinion writer Jonah Flambo smelled eco-hypocrisy in this so-called scientist. He called Noah a "soft-on-crime phony." He accused Noah of "non-transparent, non-accountable treachery" for purchasing solar panels from China. Information about the purchase was on public record in Noah's publications and expense reports. Unimpressed, Flambo claimed to have exposed Noah. The Prime Minister's Office described Noah's research as "off message." His funding was "under review." The PMO assured the press that such reviews were routine. The university assigned a staff member to support Noah through the inevitable audit his science beckoned. Noah had periods of depression. He found professional help across the river. Through it all, Simeon kept Noah from despairing while keeping his laboratory clean and bright.

Finding themselves in their late forties with much to be thankful for and much to share, Noah and Simeon adopted Izzy. She was seven months old at the time. Hours after her birth, on a dark winter solstice night at three a.m., an unknown person placed Izzy inside the sliding doors of the emergency room at Mercy Hospital on the Edmonton's north side. A trail of blood drops led up to the shoebox that held Izzy, and then away from the box into the inky black night. The bearer of the box had been bleeding. Nothing was known about Izzy's biological parents. Her ethnicity was uncertain. Her hair had streaks of black and red, as if something had been left undecided. Her skin had a slightly dark tone. People who met her thought she was beautiful in some unconventional way. They could not say what exactly. Some asked if she was Inuit. Some asked if she was from Palestine or Lebanon or Asia or South America. Some asked if she was Irish. Her eyes caused much of the uncertainty. Her eyes were a sharp green.

Noah and Simeon brought her to their modest Crescentdale home in a state of joy. They had lived in five different countries on three continents before moving to Edmonton. As she grew, Izzy loved to see pictures and hear their stories about different places. Digital slide shows of past adventures followed dinners with ingredients from faraway places. Simeon loved to cook. Noah was a wine expert, but his culinary skills were inferior to Simeon's, so he poached eggs and fed Izzy's cat on slide show nights.

They bought her a black kitten when she was eight, and asked her to name it. Noah and Simeon were alarmed by her choice. Noah tried to veto the name. Simeon said no: the child is the decider in this household. Izzy chose the name after learning about sea nymphs in Greek mythology. Simeon had read Milton's "Lycidas" to her at bedtime one night:

Where were ye, Nymphs, when the remorseless deep

Closed o'er the head of your loved Lycidas?

So Izzy named her cat Nympho.

Noah continued to object. Surely it was the role of the parent to flag and correct verbal gaffes. Simeon would hear none of it. Choice would empower the child and build her self-esteem, giving her a bright executive future. By the time the debate ended, Izzy had been calling her cat Nympho for two weeks.

"Did you argue this much over my name?" Izzy asked them one night.

"No, Charissa," said Simeon. "Come to think of it, we both loved the name from the beginning."

"And waiting for you to decide would have been impractical," Noah added. "Wouldn't you agree, Simeon?"

"Not entirely," Simeon answered.

* * *

Edmonton was divided into northern and southern halves by the North Saskatchewan River. The river flowed into the vast northern parkland from the great Columbia Glacier in the Rocky Mountains. The city followed the historical pattern of many western cities: the Indigenous civilizations of time deeper than money time encountered fur traders in the eighteenth century, and railroad builders in the nineteenth century, and city builders in the twentieth century.

Crude oil was the elixir of the arts of peace and the science of wealth. But the fusion of earth and fire in the oil sands to the north mixed wisdom and hubris unevenly, exposing hope and fear to ups and downs. Noah was among those who feared the dangers of tearing fire out of earth with water and air. Whatever dies was not mixed equally. He hoped his research would bring hope.

Edmonton imagined its past in the historical buildings of Fort Edmonton Park on the south bank of the river. Visitors strolled through past decades and centuries in mere hours. An old locomotive with a powerful whistle still worked like a time machine. Its cars rumbled with playful children. A York Boat, once used to move supplies up and down the river, lay moored in placid water close to shore.

In the later twentieth century, the city expanded rapidly and built a giant mall. For a time, shoppers came from far away places to share the mall experience. The mall was a pastiche of time and water. Especially water. Galleons lay anchored in its artificial lakes, while submarines lurked beneath its surfaces. Fires flickered from comic book war zones and Cajun grills and waterslides among the lagoons. Dolphins once dreamed restlessly of flying in the cold wind and the white wake of the galleons at full sail. But the galleons never moved. And the wind never blew. Then they set the dolphins free.

The glory of Edmonton was its green space: the North Saskatchewan River Valley. The long valley, part long-live-the-wilderness, part trimmed-for-picnics, could change a viewer's perception in an instant. In places, the entire city disappeared, presenting a pre-human past. In others, local actors wove cloud-capped towers against the sunset and the stars (for this was a great theatre city).

Golf courses helped to buffer the wilderness in the city

core. A golfer trekking the Victoria course might see a palimpsest of conifers and Maples framing the early LeMarchand Mansion. The city raised statues to musical citizens, and parks for feminist leaders. On bright heights, it honoured police officers and politicians who gave their all.

The city lived through dark undercurrents of violence and counted its missing people. Its charity shone like a bright cut diamond in every crisis, from dark tornadoes to horrific wildfires to vast migrations. In more normal moments, Charity wandered the streets of the inner city keeping an ear out for her sister Wisdom, and their daughters Truth, Justice, Mercy and Peace. Charity longed for that six-fold sisterhood, but these sisters found it hard to reunite. Someone was always too busy. Someone was always away.

* * *

The family settled in a small bungalow in Crescentdale, a neighbourhood on the city's south side. After the Second World War, Crescentdale rose in rows of cozy cloned structures called semi-bungalows. The neighbourhood supported great spruces, many planted by parents celebrating a child's graduation from grade one. It embraced the irrepressible maples that tangled its back alleys. It praised the elms that seemed to hum Vivaldi and make graceful symmetries for summer streets.

In the middle of the neighbourhood was a large village green with a school on its west side. This feature attracted Simeon and Noah. Noah saw the right balance of subtle wilderness and manicured park, and a communal vegetable garden managed by "The Diggers."

Simeon saw children tumbling in colourful water features, and wondered which day was garbage day. To Noah, Crescentdale seemed like a miniature Manhattan, an urban peninsula with a central park. Simeon estimated that the neighbourhood was roughly the size and population of

Jerusalem in the time of King David. Noah liked to think of himself as living on Crescentdale's upper east side. Simeon liked to breathe the psalms of birds and hear children singing in the gathering dusk.

A large soccer field stood beside the school, Crescentdale Elementary, built in 1952. There, on luminous June evenings, parents cheered on children in forest green jerseys. Most of the cheers were communal. A few parents implored children not their own to pass the ball to children who were their own. Izzy never heard her name called from this parental cauldron. Her parents stood placidly on the sidelines. Noah might bring along a dense scientific paper to study, but never look at it; Simeon might steal critical glances at the school's dumpster and downspouts.

It was here, in the autumn of Izzy's grade six year, that Noah and Simeon first noticed Izzy's condition. Izzy liked to play hard. She had a scorching shot whenever she got a chance. On this night, she noticed a girl on the opposing team from Blue Quill neighbourhood loitering alone in the corner of her end of the field. She looked forlorn and friendless to Izzy. Her team-mates needed her help at the Crescentdale end. They shouted at her: "Hey kid! What's-your-name! Get down here!" So Izzy surmised the girl was new and lonely.

Jill Bender of Crescentdale stripped the ball from a Blue Quill attacker and moved up the field. She teed up a pass for Camrose Keillor, Crescentdale's dominant scorer. Suddenly, Izzy swooped in on the ball just as Jill was about to kick it. She scooped it up in her hands, ran to the forlorn girl and laid the ball at her feet like a spice box. The forlorn girl turned her back in embarrassment. Parents moaned. The referee called hand ball and stopped play.

Camrose's mother approached Simeon on the sideline.

"Listen! Camrose would have scored with that pass."

"And she will yet," said Simeon, smiling and nodding. "She'll get a pass in no time. Just look at her go!"

"Possibly," the mom said. "But not the pass she should have had a minute ago. Now, how are we going to resolve this?"

"I'm not sure I take your meaning," said Simeon.

"Do you not? I tell you I want resolution. Your child needs to understand the damage she caused and its impact on Camrose. I seek closure. So should she. I suggest a meeting."

Simeon mused on this for several seconds. Camrose bonged one off the crossbar, then headed in her own rebound. Her mother's eyes stayed fixed on Simeon.

"No malice in her handling of the ball," Simeon proclaimed. "But liberty and justice for them all! There you are – closure!"

Camrose's mother walked away. Still, Simeon and Noah were quite worried about Izzy.

* * *

The incident was the first sign of a more serious problem. As the days grew colder, the children removed their boots and lined them up outside the classroom door along the corridor wall. They kept inside shoes, dance shoes and gym shoes in cubbies at the back of the classroom. After school one snowy December day, Izzy put on a pair of boots, placed her knapsack on her back, and turned down the hall toward the exit doors.

"Get back here, clueless!" The voice belonged to Barton Squirrel, whose charisma commanded a small following in the schoolyard. The teacher, Ms. Quinn, told Squirrel to stand still and *close-his-mouth.*

"She took my boots goddammit!" Squirrel whined. Ms. Quinn looked at Izzy's feet. It was true. She was wearing tattered, leaky Wellingtons, with the initials "BS" scrawled on the sides in nail polish, or possibly nicotine. The boots were too big for Izzy. Ms. Quinn was mildly disappointed to see that Barton was right.

"Charissa Dryden-Burnet," Ms. Quinn demanded. "Why are you wearing Barton's boots?"

"I didn't know they were his."

"Pass the bullshit, please!" Barton screamed.

"That will do, Barton! Izzy: why?"

"Honestly," Izzy pleaded. "I was hoping they were mine."

"Hoping?" Ms. Quinn asked Izzy. "Do I hope my overcoat is mine when I put it on? Do I hope my lunch is mine when I eat it? Take them off and find your own boots – now."

Izzy removed the boots and handed them to Barton. He demanded that she put them down, refusing to take them from her hands. She looked down the long row of boots. She could count them. There were twenty-four, making twelve pairs. Some were brown; some were black; some were red. But she could not tell them apart. Izzy had no ability to find her own boots. She had been hiding this problem for months. On rainy days, she loitered after school. When all the children had collected their boots, hers would be the last pair standing. The first snowfall forced a crisis. Squirrel and his colleagues had been serving long detentions for uttering curses in recent days. She didn't want to wait an extra half hour to discover her boots. So she started to gamble.

"You know, Ms. Quinn, I should let the others go first," Izzy said, evasively.

"She's fucking with you, Quinn!" Squirrel warned.

Izzy burst into tears. Ms. Quinn shook her head. But Izzy wasn't crying for herself. She was crying for Barton. Her problem was much deeper than mistaking boots. When she wore Barton's boots, she felt her her body morph. The shoulder of a dark city street invaded her bones. Her back became the edge of a dark road, her spine the long white line. Hot rain poured from the night sky. Headlights passed in soporific waves in the evening rush hour. A pair of headlights made of whisky and beer swerved across the white line. Her body sprang upwards, becoming a crowded bus shelter. When the car struck, her body flew out of the shelter like coughed blood spraying unbearable daylight on a bed of spring flowers. All the flowers wore Barton's face. White clouds were hands of brothers resting on his shoulders. This pain sink in Barton's soul worked its way through her body and out again in two minutes.

* * *

Ms. Quinn decided to dismiss Barton. "Put on your boots and go home, Barton. *Now.*" Then she turned to Izzy. "What exactly is *your* problem, Izzy?"

"I can't tell shoes apart."

"I see. You can eat, drink, read, spell, draw, throw, catch and run. But you can't tell shoes apart."

"I'm afraid to put on the wrong ones. It hurts. Once I put shoes on my hands, sort of like oven mitts, to check to see if I could find my own. But it didn't work. It's like the shoes pick me. Or maybe it's all random. I'm not sure if you know this: Barton's life has been really hard!" She burst into tears again.

Ms. Quinn texted on her e-phone.

"Did you hear me?" Izzy begged.

"Yes. I know. And obviously so do you. Now I'm texting, Izzy. I think you can guess who."

"Mr. Blowflough?"

"Mr. Blowflough."

Arthur Blowflough was the school principal. He nodded gravely as Ms. Quinn explained the situation.

"Tantamount to some new pathology," he opined.

"Or a hoax, Arthur," Ms. Quinn remarked.

"To be sure, Darlene. But I'd like to sequester the charge sheet for the moment. Let's let science decide."

"Alright, Arthur – but know this: I'm texting Alvin Boneslaw right now."

Blowflough proposed a series of "blind tests." He asked Izzy to study his brown galoshes for several minutes, and then describe them to him after he concealed them in his closet. Izzy had no difficulty passing this test. But when he placed his galoshes beside the white golf shoes he kept in his desk drawer, Izzy panicked. She couldn't tell them apart.

Blowflough tried a version of a police line-up. He lined up seven pairs of different shoes, some women's and some men's. Some were high heels. Some were hiking boots. He asked Izzy to pick her shoes out of the line-up. She couldn't do it. Wherever two or more pairs of shoes were placed together, she could only guess. When she guessed wrong, her body became a conduit for childhood traumas, nasty quarrels, failed investments, lost jobs, broken hearts, addictions, regrets, assaults, betrayals, time leaks, dark secrets and worse. Izzy never spoke of it, and never complained. She suffered with those she saw suffer.

* * *

In marched the district school counsellor, Alvin Boneslaw.

"I've tried some blind tests, Alvin."

"No thank you Arthur, and call the parents right away."

Noah and Simeon arrived. They were of two minds. Noah called for scientific investigation and medical specialists, and the sooner the better. Blowflough concurred.

"Specialists in what?" Boneslaw inquired. "Specialists in guess the shoe? Let's back up for a moment. Let's ascertain her truthfulness first. I'm not saying she's lying. But is she covering something up? Something in her own home perhaps?"

Blowflough offered a solution: "Extended detentions might do double service. Izzy would be suitably disciplined, and hers would be the only shoes left by detention's end. The problem might gradually go away."

"Enough from you, Arthur. This is a drug case."

Boneslaw pressed his palm methodically against Blowflough's forehead, as if performing an exorcism, and pushed him firmly towards the wall.

"Drugs here or at home, parents?" Boneslaw continued. "I want to know, and so should you. Well gentlemen? Anyone for closure?"

Simeon tried a different approach. "Neither of the above, but yes, we do need to learn more. Close supervision is the answer, surely. Arthur: what say you hire me as deputy school janitor? I'd be on duty after school, and I could help Izzy through this possibly brief phase of her development."

"Why you scheming opportunist!" Noah barked. "Do you know how hard it was to get you a spousal appointment in my lab? And what about that *pro bono* street sweeping you've been performing on Whyte Avenue? Oh, I know about it! Did you seriously believe I'd think you were having an affair? Ha!"

"This would be part time work," Simeon assured Noah. "I'll meet my commitments to the lab first. School dismissal is the critical window. We need to step up here, Noah."

"Step up to methylamphedrizone?" Boneslaw seethed.

"We don't use the word janitor any more," Blowflough added.

"It's an honourable word," Simeon stated firmly.

Noah scooped Izzy up while Simeon snatched her rightful shoes out of the line-up. They took her home and made hot chocolate and asked if she felt ready to talk about it. Together, they explored the experience. Izzy wept, but she persevered. Simeon helped her find words. Noah listened to every detail. He searched the Internet for headlines about the Squirrels of Crescentdale. Yes – a drunk driver killed Barton's mother at a crowded bus stop when he was four years old. It happened on a rainy night.

* * *

By week's end, Simeon was adjunct custodian *pro bono* at Crescentdale Elementary School. By month's end, through Noah's efforts, Izzy had seen several specialists in cognitive development, family medicine, brain science and psychology. All agreed that Izzy's condition was unnamed, unknown and undocumented. Dr. Julius Macpherson, a local private consultant, elbowed his way into the team and made himself its leader. He allowed that the team's findings should be published jointly, preferably in *Nature.* He insisted that his name be applied to the disorder as team leader. Others felt uneasy, but Macpherson's was a thuggish charisma. He opened his lap-pad and opened his translation app. He found that "shoe" in Greek is "papoutsi." The team agreed to call Izzy's condition "papoutsiosis," since there were no signs of inflammation requiring "papoutsiitis." Under Macpherson's guidance, they agreed to call it, "Macpherson's Papoutsiosis."

Major journals rejected the article, since it affected only one human being and showed few signs of research. Izzy was no doubt fortunate that the larger scientific community took no notice; nevertheless, her condition eventually went on record. "Macpherson's Papoutsiosis: Dermal Provocations and Para-Psychic Considerations: a Specialized Approach to Early Intervention," appeared in the *Northern Review of Western Reformed Medicine* (Spring 2032).

Noah received a complementary copy at his university office. He tossed it into his recycling box, but mentioned it to Izzy and Simeon at dinner that evening.

"Whatever name your condition merits, Izzy," he explained, "Macpherson's Papoutsiosis isn't it. You're condition is one of extreme, paranormal, even superhuman empathy. We may need to get you a thicker skin."

"If she so chooses," Simeon added. "Moreover, empathy is by definition human and perfectly normal."

"Animals empathize," Noah remarked. And the row was on.

Izzy grinned at the cumbersome name while her parents argued. The soccer game seemed like a lifetime ago.

Chapter Two

RICHMOND'S END

Edmonton, October 2030

Lucius Spukwell was also an only child. His family lived in a semi-bungalow in Crescentdale. Lucius and Izzy were the same age and attended the same school. His mother, Lady Cassandra Spukwell (nee Feenie) had a job re-shelving books and rebooting wi-fi terminals at the branch library in a nearby strip mall. Lady held a Master's of Business from the University of Alberta, specializing in real estate. But she bore a strange curse. Her financial advice was wise, sound and practical, but no man ever listened to her, and no man ever believed anything she said. So she became a quiet woman.

Lucius's father, Richie Spukwell, was associate executive road manager for a rock band called *The Storm Poodles*. He was often on the road. He made it home to see his son born in Mercy Hospital and to name him. Lady wanted to name him Naboth, after a just man and a property owner in the first Book of Kings. Richie did not believe her story of Naboth. He named their son Lucius Maximus Spukwell after characters in one of his favourite classic movies: *Gladiator*.

When the *Storm Poodles* weren't on tour, Richie worked putting up tents at music festivals from Winnipeg to Regina to Canmore to Grande Prairie to Slave Lake. He was away so much that he began to complain about Edmonton when he returned.

"What's with the numbered streets?" he would ask while making his "specialty" for dinner one night: wieners and process cheese slices broiled on toast. "Regina has some sweet street names: Victoria, Albert, Broad, Elphinstone."

"We studied city names in social studies," Lucius shared. "A girl in my class said it should never have been named Regina. Regina is an imperialist name. Its should've been named Wascana."

"Bro," Richie said. "dubya' TF? You've never even been to Regina. Someday I'll show it to you when you're ready."

"She knows a lot about names, and she sounds confident about it."

"Bro, dubya' TF is Wascana?"

"Pile of Bones, sacred burial place of the bison."

"Bro, that's so not up to date."

* * *

Lady Spukwell read books to Lucius every night. He tried to nudge her towards war histories. He did not care for fiction. If a musket ball crashed into someone's chest, or a town was incinerated, he wanted to know that it really happened.

Lady collected books on parenting boys for emotional health. She refracted her findings through art and literature to avoid being called a liar. She read biographies to Lucius. She avoided biographies of conquerors, tyrants, dictators and other historical nuisances. She did not want Lucius to identify power with self-proclaimed titles and flashy uniforms. She read biographies of Frederick Varley, Terry Fox and William Blake. She assured Lucius that the inner life can be more heroic than pomp and pageant. Lucius didn't believe her.

Lucius fell asleep one afternoon on the couch reading a new e-book on his laptop: *Scattered Seeds: The Psycho-biographies of Canada's Prime Ministers.* Ms. Quinn asked all the students to find a book on Canadian history and write a short report. Lady noticed the book. That night, she put away the biography of Frederick Varley, and turned to current events. She read Lucius Caleb Timson's feature article on the International Court of Justice in The Hague. Timson wrote for the *Edmonton Mercury.* The court was hearing a case brought by *Homeless Without Borders.* They wanted rights for the homeless who crossed national boundaries. The advocates cited the Dutch Constitution, and the Calgary proclamation of homeless rights in 2015. They asked the court to make an international law. Lucius asked to keep the article.

* * *

One afternoon, Lucius came home from school. His father had returned. His mother was in tears. Richie was wearing a black T-Shirt with bright white words emblazoned above a skull and crossbones: *Roadies for Open Marriage, Eh*?" He said he liked the acronym: ROME. Lady scoffed. Finally he admitted that he'd paid to join the ROME group.

"Membership is only $3000," he assured Lady.

"You paid $3000 for this?" Lady screamed.

"Relax. It's per year, not per month."

The group met in an Internet chat room. Its members claimed to have dynamic and fulfilling open marriages. Most avoided the term "open marriage," preferring to say that they and their wives had an "understanding." Their stories were impossible fantasies, glorious lies and absurd fabrications, which were the real joys membership gave these men. Richie believed all of them. He hoped to find true stories of his own. In the meantime, he decided the t-shirt wasn't worth such drama in the home. Richie took off the shirt and handed it to Lucius.

"Take this in the backyard and burn it," Richie ordered.

Lucius stood dumbfounded.

"Bro: burn it like a man!"

Lucius took his father's plastic barbecue lighter and went into the backyard. He was afraid to set the shirt on fire. What if the paint peelings on their old garage caught fire? What if the fire tore though Crescentdale? He went to the fence, leaned over the sagging rickety structure and placed the shirt in their neighbour's composter, pushing it down quietly under eggshells, apple cores, coffee grinds, yogurt containers, toilet paper and twisted condoms. He hoped the shirt would liquefy quickly in this ecological hellhole.

***

Richie could be firm and decisive at home, but he was treated badly at work. The *Storm Poodles* appreciated the hard work he put in on the road, but they all agreed that when it came to the music, Richie was a phony. His tendency to listen to blues or roots music on the bus had not gone unnoticed. Richie had ambitions to be more than a roadie. He wanted to write songs. If he worked for a folk group, he might try to write folk songs. But he was working in dronecult, so he wrote dronecult. *Szchwrerm's Encyclopedia of 21st Century Rock* defined dronecult.

> **Dronecult:** (drɔn-kʌlt). Dronecult emerged in the late 2020's as a rogue offshoot of late 20th century heavy metal. Rock scholars and culture theorists have called it metal's disinherited, addiction-prone great-grandnephew twice removed. Maintaining its cultural distance, Dronecult critiques mainstream music by emphasizing the general common denominators of human existence rather than particular characters, stories and situations. There are four denominators: death, taxes, sex and drones. Dronecult fixates on sex. Rock scholars consider *Whomworm* (active 2023-24) to be the first authentic dronecult band. *Whomworm* continues to inspire imitators, notably *Tax Rage* and *Rage Against the Touch.*

Richie tried to write two songs a week during the long hours on the tour bus. One night on the bus, he decided to show a song to the *Storm Poodles*. The group leader – Joey "I'm Joey Knotwad and you're not" Knotwad – crumpled the paper up and mimed wiping his ass to the delight of his band mates. When Richie switched to writing on his 6-inch lap-pad, Joey mimed wiping his ass with the device. He tossed the abused machine back to Richie with just enough care to make sure it didn't break. Joey feared legalities, and didn't like to pay for broken gadgets. He told Richie straight out that he considered him a poser in their midst. His pretensions to write songs were royal rock fakery.

* * *

One night while standing in the wings at D*C*FEST in Regina, Richie showed his song to Marcus Culvert, leader of

Hell's Velcro.

"I write from experience," Richie said. This rang false to Culvert. Richie tried other gambits to claim credibility. Culvert waved him off as he studied the song on Richie's lap-pad screen.

"Piss off, Richie. I really don't give a crap where it came from, so long as it didn't crawl out of Knotwad's ass."

Culvert loathed the unhygienic persona of Joey Knotwad more than anything else in rock. But he saw potential in Richie's song. He wanted it for *Hell's Velcro.* Richie would have to let Culvert have his way with it. But Culvert liked it, and not simply because he hated Joey Knotwad. He genuinely liked it as a song.

The group recorded it, offered it as a free download across the country, and declared it their signature piece, routinely playing it once in the main set and twice in the encores. It was a catchy little tune called "Mercy Hospital Blowjob." With droning chords pounding under every syllable, the song's brief narrative drilled into the consciousness of audiences through satellite radio, podcasts and live performances at *Hell's Velcro* gigs.

They debuted the song on a Sunday night at Edmonton's *Basejump* rock club near Jasper and 102 Street. Lead guitarist Saul Flatmince opened with a nattering hook:

nyananyananyananananananananana!

Culvert whined the lyrics in his piercing soprano:

Mercy Hospital blowjob!

I was on a gurney

With an i.v. line

My head was sore

But I was feeling fine

They took my pulse

The room was spinnin' round.

This elevator is goin' down!

Mercy Hospital Blowjob!

Culvert punctuated the last line by tossing his signature "drone" microphone high in the air, then catching it in his magnetized armour-plated signature crotch. Richie joined Culvert on stage in a black smock to suggest a tuxedo. He waved a drumstick in circles through the air to suggest an orchestra conductor. The crowd cheered the song on, and roared when the microphone glanced sideways off Culvert's high definition penis. The crowd unaccountably turned on Richie, hurling profanities at him. Someone tossed a small object that struck him on the back of his head. Richie looked down on the stage. It was a bullet.

"Get the hell off the stage, Richie!" Culvert screamed, away from the microphone. "You're done! Out! Now!"

A concertgoer overheard Culvert's command. He began to clap his hands in wide arcs above his head, chanting, "hell off the stage! hell off the stage! hell off the stage! hell off the stage!" Soon the entire crowd was clapping and chanting in unison: "phon-y phon-y phon-y phon-y." Richie's shoulders slumped. He bowed his head and made his exit, flushed with success and shame.

* * *

A lawsuit confounded the group two days before they released the single. Velcro Inc. sued them for wrongful use of their brand name. The group changed its name to *Six of Dicks*. Within hours, *Card On,* a Las Vegas casino chain that featured pornographic playing cards, poker chips and slot machines, sued them for plagiarism. The group finally settled on the name *Drone I.V.* in honour of Richie's hit.

"This should've been our name all along," Culvert remarked. He claimed the name came to him in a dream. The claim strengthened his position as group leader.

Culvert declared "Mercy Hospital Blowjob" to be the "anthem of a generation." Culvert knew how to "tweak" the reputation of a song using social media, and he tweaked this one high. He set up a page dedicated to the song on *Anthembook*. In an anonymous post, he wrote that the key to the song's meaning lay in its "complex rhythms" and its being "open to interpretation." With the press of one key, he asked all of his *Anthembook* co-anthemists to press the "anthemize" button for the song. For a fee, he used the push app to boost the consensus.

Feedback confirmed that the song was open to interpretation. Some were shocked by its stark pornographic suggestions. Four radio stations banned it. Others sensed some insult to overworked health care professionals. Others saw it as a direct attack on government mismanagement of the public healthcare system, with its long queues and wait times. Surprisingly, the song appealed to over-60 male doughnut shop regulars, a notoriously difficult demographic for *dronecult* groups to penetrate. These affable, angry seniors liked the song's "talking points." They knew that health care was broken. They wanted to be listened to on health care.

The Storm Poodles were furious. They demanded a song from Richie as compensation. Culvert already claimed right of first refusal to Richie's next song in a binding contract penned on a fast food serviette. Under pressure, Richie followed up with "Sex Is All There Is." This song tapped his deeper convictions. The title captured the heart of the song, while the lyrics offered a wistful indeterminism available to the sensitive ear:

> Don't make meaning where none of it is:
>
> Sex is all there is!
>
> Don't paint rainbows with fake promises:
>
> Sex is all there is!

Culvert set to work proclaiming the song the "new anthem of a generation." He encouraged sceptical fans to compare the chorus with "Mercy Hospital Blowjob." The denial of narrative made "Sex is All There Is" more authentically *dronecult*, he observed.

Emboldened by the health care system critics who embraced "Mercy Hospital Blowjob," Culvert sensed it was time to break out of the limited dronecult demographic. He told Richie to apply to the Edmonton Folk Music Festival for a main stage spot for *Drone I.V.* They had already widened the audience for dronecult; now they were riding the crest of a second hit. All of the roadies except Richie resigned in protest. They saw Culvert as a sell-out. Fans complained bitterly in e-mails, seeing Culvert as a bullshitting traitor to dronecult. So what? Culvert was ready to burn bridges. He ordered Richie to tell the Edmonton Folk Music Festival Director that *Drone I.V.* would close next year's event.

"A new song?" said the kindly EFMF Director, speaking on his e-phone to Richie. "An EP? Well, congratulations. We wish you all the best."

"Thanks, sir," said Richie. "And I'm authorized to tell you that *Drone I.V.* will close the festival next year."

The director had spent half an hour that morning on the phone with *Free to Be,* a Bruce Cockburn tribute band that agreed to close the festival. Still, he felt badly when rejecting the well meaning, the less talented or the merely ambitious. His wife kept telling him that people are responsible for their own emotions. He hoped Richie might prove her right.

"Closing is an honour, you must realize. And we have a closer for next year."

"OK," Richie replied. "How about if we open. We'll play 'Mercy Hospital Blowjob' twice in the opening set. As you know, the title refers to a long tradition in music."

"It might be called a topic. I don't see it as a tradition in folk, roots or rock. Nor as music's future. From what I've heard, your song is a hit with seniors."

"Gotcha, but you can't deny that sex is all there is."

"Can't I? What about environmentalism, peace, child poverty, human rights, truth and reconciliation, social justice? What about homelessness?"

"Think about it. This is your chance to replace 'Four Strong Winds' with 'Sex is all there is.'"

"I think not."

Silence passed between the two men for twenty seconds. Then Richie perked up.

"OK. Here goes. I'm hereby authorized by Marcus Culvert to accept a small stage workshop. Stage 6 will be fine. *Drone I.V.* will tackle the sensitive subject of open marriage. Cutting edge stuff. We'll expand our demographic. You'll expand your, um, traditions. Win-win."

"A workshop on open marriage is out of the question. Our festival is intergenerational. Kids grow up with us, people get engaged, even married on site, people grow old with us. Do you really wonder why I can't hire you? Let me assist you. For us, it's about the music first. Now, I don't want to be rude, but dronecult just isn't always like that. Sometimes it is, I grant you, but not always. It has its knockoffs, its imitators, just like everything else. There are a lot of wealthy under-achievers in the world of dronecult, and plenty in rock and roll. Meanwhile, there are plenty of underpaid, marginalized geniuses in roots and folk and classical."

"But that's the thing! 'Mercy Hospital Blowjob' *is* a classic. A lot of demographics like it. Marcus says it voices the people's anger, especially the older generation."

"Do you mean it's a protest song? Now you've lost me. 'Sex is All There Is' sounds angry, I'll grant you."

Richie felt desperate. He scrolled further down Culvert's list of demands on his lap-pad.

"I have a smock. We can be your emcees."

"No you can't. We won't host *Hell's Velcro* this year. Excuse me: *Drone I.V.* Isn't there some festival in Regina you could attend? Have you ever played at *Metal Case Fest*?"

Richie reported the outcome to Culvert. Furious, he ordered Richie to protest at the main entrance during the Folk Festival. Richie stood alone for four consecutive evenings holding a sign: "Folk Fest unfair to *Drone I.V.*" On a rainy Saturday night, a volunteer brought him tea and a sugar bun when the rain peaked. Richie clenched his fist and whispered "sex is all there is." Then he accepted the gift with a small tear in his right eye.

* * *

An independent Internet reviewer called "Sex Is All There Is" a "nuanced cry in an age without faith." Culvert muted her on social media, bearing down on her with his de-resonance app, and diluting her blog with a deluge of worshipful comments submitted under fake names. Secretly, he worried that she might actually be praising the song. How to be sure? He e-mailed the song and the review to Dr. Royal Starking, a celebrity neo-atheist based at Upchalk University in England.

Starking had abandoned research in favour of podcasting and public speaking. He promised the world a young adult fantasy tetralogy about an aging superhero named Yerrezun, who used the power of reason to vanquish evildoers and religious fanatics. He called his planned four-volume opus, *The Awful Building*. Volume one had yet to materialize. Starking needed time to sit down and write. Instead, he led podcast crusades to bring cosmologists and particle physicists to neo-atheism. He arranged TV interviews to ambush religious groups resistant to evolution. Their obstinacy made him incandescent with rage. They were the perfect foil for his reasoning powers. His doctor prescribed sedatives and a month's rest. Starking refused.

"Starking gets it," Culvert declared to his band mates when a positive e-mail came back from Upchalk. "He wants to open for us. I'm hereby naming him our special guest on tour."

Richie, now senior associate roadie for *Drone I.V.*, was confused. "Open for us? How? Can he sing?"

"Richie, dubya' TF? Are you talking back?" said Culvert. "Here's the deal. The lights go up. Starking is sitting in an armchair with a reading lamp. Maybe there's a side table and one of those Persian rug things, a fake one. It's super peaceful. Soothing. The crowd relaxes. He invites them into his conversation. His major point: sex is all there is. I'm sick and tired of all the knocks against Dronecult! Starking is going to give us serious intellectual chops."

Starking signed up to open for *Drone I.V.* as special guest on their upcoming tour of Kamloops, Grande Prairie, Edmonton, Calgary, Lethbridge, Medicine Hat and Red Deer. He planned to teach ticketholders the reasons for the evolution of human brainpower. Intelligence, to which we owe our quality of life, is, in point of fact, a point of sexual attraction for mating in humans and human precursors. Sexual attraction is the wireless signal of evolution, like a lap-pad seeking a network and getting five bars. No wonder we got smarter and smarter. Females selected mates based on intelligence more than strength or looks.

Starking joined the tour in Calgary because the city had a direct flight from Upchalk. He offered his first conversation at Calgary's *Hydraulic Saloon.* There were five hundred people in the audience. But were they listening? Starking was unsure. Even with a microphone, he had to strain to be heard above the crowd noise.

"Is sex all there is, ladies and gentlemen?" he shrieked from his armchair. "No, not really, what with art, books, music, and what not else people attempt. But yes! In a very real way, sex is all there is! You see, sex was a selector for human intelligence. The smarter you were in the days of *homo habilis* and *homo erectus,* the more likely you might be to receive a gold-plated invitation to breed. For that simple reason, I believe we have been slowly getting smarter ever since. And so, this evening, I bring you tidings of good news. Soon and very soon, I believe, we shall all be too smart to take religion seriously!"

Glass rum bottles, smuggled past security personnel, smashed into dangerous shrapnel around Starking's feet.

"You there!" he yelled, pointing at an intoxicated fan. "How did you get a bottle of intoxicant through security? It's forbidden!"

"Cuz' of my big brain, Starking. Now – invite me to screw!"

Starking recoiled in horror. "Try to see reason!" he screamed.

Then he saw a strange light emerge from the dark well of the crowd. It was a gin bottle hurtling towards his face. He should have ducked, but years of practice on the soccer pitches of Upchalk fired up his reflexes. He tried to head the bottle out of bounds. It struck his left temple, leaving a deep gash. Staff at the General Hospital ER stitched the wound as Starking booked his flight back to England. He failed to reclaim costs from *Drone I.V.* for the dry cleaning of his bloodied tweeds.

* * *

After the unexpected success of "Sex Is All There Is," Richie decided the time had come to lead the life of a rock star. Acting alone, he sold the family's semi-bungalow in Crescentdale and purchased a vacant former McDonald's restaurant. The vacant restaurant stood on a small, grassy island in the middle of a busy traffic circle on the edge of Crescentdale. Richie surprised Lady and Lucius with the news.

Lady wept. Lucius was stunned.

Richie sat them down. He showed them an online coffee table book featuring large country estates owned by rockers past and present. His favourite was *Tittwield Abbey*, owned by Sir Billy Boiler of *Eel Rage.* He showed a picture of *Montedellaeuro*, a Tuscan villa owned as a time-share by members of *Tax Rage.* Richie promised to plant a spruce tree for each family member on the grounds. After the landscaping and renovations, they would officially name the estate. "Richie" was short for Richmond. Richie thought of *Richmond Abbey,* but that title was already taken. So he searched names of books based on stately houses and experimented. *Richmondshead Revisited* appealed to him, but it seemed hard to utter. He finally chose *Richmond's End* because it was based on a work of fiction in the public domain.

"The kitchen and toilets will stay as is, of course, but we'll still order out sometimes. I'll get a stand-alone bathtub. White will give us nuances, I think. We'll keep the bolt-down eating tables so Lucius can study. What say you to that, bro? I'll get room dividers for maximum privacy. And guess what – they left a whole tank of cooking oil full to the top. There's gotta be ten years worth. Score!"

Richie painted the McDonald's royal purple inside and out. Royal was fitting for a prince of rock, and the colour would deter motorists still looking for a fast drive-thru meal.

"This building is designed for fast-food production," Lady moaned. "Where will we wash our clothes? In the river?"

"Damn," Richie muttered. "OK. I'll think of something."

"And the house you sold – our house – was bigger. This place has no basement."

"I'm prioritizing intimacy, Lady."

"And why did you buy in a traffic circle? What about all the quiet countryside properties outside Edmonton?"

Richie was stunned by Lady's ingratitude. He half believed there might be such estates.

"The grounds are ample," he replied sheepishly. "And I have to stay intimate with my fans."

"Fans? You have no fans. No one cares who *wrote* the songs."

"We both know that's not true," Richie stated. "Besides, the guys gave me an on stage moment. I got to conduct 'Mercy Hospital Blowjob,' just like we were the Boston Pops."

"Or like a trained monkey? Why don't you just take up the accordion?"

"Lady, we both know you're not serious. The accordion is so not *dronecult.*"

* * *

They moved in. Richie stencilled the front windows with dronecult logos and proverbs for privacy. The dark stencils also helped to keep the eastern sunrise from waking him up. He spray-painted "nuanced cry" on the parking lot. He had a compact washer and dryer installed in the women's washroom.

All day and for much of the night, the traffic circle shunted traffic from all directions. In the darkness of his new bedroom, Lucius watched the swirling headlights that never let up flashing on the ceiling. The swirls of cars stopping and starting at the lights made him drowsy. Cars that mistook his home for an active McDonald's woke him up when they honked their horns for service. Traffic would lull him slightly to sleep. Then, like a sudden storm, a police siren or a road rage incident would awaken him with a shock.

He eventually believed that all eyes in every car were trained on him. His window was small, but he felt he was living in a giant glass fish bowl lit up in front of paying spectators. He wondered if people took e-phone photos of him through his window. He felt humiliated when he walked to school in the morning. A painted crosswalk made the journey to school possible, but it had no flashing light, and so he stood waiting with his head down until one motorist politely stopped, making all the scores of cars bumbling through morning rush hour stop to let him pass. He sped up as he crossed the circle, certain that the motorists were glaring at him, certain they were conveying children to his school. He felt the eyes of motorists stick to his body like burrs.

He began to meditate on sound. He tried to accept the hum of traffic around him. He wondered if waves of sound moving in a circle cancelled or reinforced each other. He thought about Doppler effects when he couldn't sleep. He built an inner zone of solitude.

His parents' fights escalated, if daft schemes explained to a patient listener count as fights. Fantasy and falsehood, optimism and indignation contended for supremacy across a fast food table. Richie could say that money was flowing in from his two hits. Money made him feel in control, but freed up time for other conflicts. He tried to change the subject to provincial politics. Lady hoped to see a change of government in Alberta, preferably to the left. Richie cheered for whichever party planned to stand up to China and keep him from being bombed in an air raid or burned by eco-terrorists. And sex? Surely he had earned more through the sweat of his songwriting brow.

"Lady, I don't want to be rude, but it seems as if this house has become a metaphor for our marriage," he began, reading from notes on a flashcard. "Did you know you can get the exact same burger anywhere in the world in a fast-food franchise? Is that all there is?"

Lucius listened carefully from the confines of his room. He knew this was rehearsed. Richie never used the word metaphor. Had he been reading magazines again?

"How dare you?" Lady cried. "First, this is no longer a restaurant, appearances to the contrary. Second, we've lived here less than a year. Third, you're the one who wrote 'Sex is all there is'? Now you say there's more?"

"Not *more*, exactly. I'm talking about, you know, a spectrum. A spectrum is like a broad range of a variety of different kinds of sex."

"Well eureka! Why didn't you raise the subject before? You never asked me for anything like this. If there was a problem, we could have talked, or read books on the subject, or sought professional counselling."

"I hate saying this, Lady, but I simply don't believe you.

Why do you make me have to say it?"

Certain there was assorted sex out there somewhere, Richie paid off the mortgage on the converted McDonald's. He left all of his royalties to date from his two hits in Lady's bank account: $40,000. He kept enough for air travel and some good hotels. He was officially "on hiatus."

Lady wept.

Richie took Lucius for a walk around the estate for a man-to-man talk.

"Bro: I'll always be here with you. I'll be in the wind and stars, in the moonlight you feel on your head as you study to be the man you will be." Richie strained to be heard above a noisy black pickup with a blaring internal sound system idling in the traffic circle. "But you must understand. Your mother is a strong, dignified woman. No – don't try to understand. You'll understand when you're older. We'll understand all things in time."

* * *

That night, Lucius felt a burning pain in his stomach. He was never more certain than now that every car in the traffic circle was heading to Crescentdale School. The firemen blaring past them in the opposite direction must know all about his crazy family. No one ever listened to Lady. No one understood what Lucius wanted. He wanted what everyone else seemed to have in abundance. He wanted to be normal.

What to do? He needed to decode his parents' quarrels as they filtered through the makeshift room dividers. He would dissolve them in his imagination, and recreate them at a respectable distance. He would tell people that the man they may have seen was a homeless person who had received a research grant from his father's foundation. He would claim that his father worked at the World Court of Justice in The Hague. "Hague" calmed his mind like a mantra. The word felt like a home.

He turned on his side and thought of the girl with green eyes in class, and drifted off to sleep in green thoughts sheltering him from the heat of the sun.

Chapter Three

THE RUN FOR THE CURE

Edmonton, November 2030

On Friday nights, Izzy, Simeon and Noah liked to order Szechuan takeout from the *Happy Village* and watch a movie in the basement. They began by making a shortlist of movies to watch. Noah thought they should elect a movie. One person – one vote. No thank you, Simeon opined. He felt Izzy must learn to make decisions without adult pressure. She was allowed to see the first two minutes of each movie on the shortlist, and no more before making her decision. This process often took until bedtime.

Noah put some old films on the list. He and Simeon avoided *Cinderella* because of Izzy's condition. They also thought *The Little Mermaid* was too invested in finding a man.

Getting legs and feet was extreme cosmetic surgery. Izzy liked *The Little Mermaid.* She did not care about the romance plot. She liked watching fish swim around.

Izzy had clear video tastes. She ignored new kid favourites like *The Golden Goose.* The show presented the animated adventures of a Canada goose named Gus who solved crises by passing pure natural gas straight into disabled aircraft, hobbled tankers or frozen homes. Gus's bladder never let up when lives were at stake.

She also liked the *Earth Still Alive!* documentary series. Noah was delighted, but the series took a toll on Simeon. He could not stand to see oil gushing beside coral reefs, or wine bottles drifting aimlessly along shorelines. He once left the couch in a rage. Noah looked for him after ten minutes, and found him scrubbing the bathtub with baking soda. He tried Milton's *Paradise Lost:*

> Forthwith the sounds and seas, each creek and bay,
>
> With fry innumerable swarm, and shoals
>
> Of fish that with their fins, and shining scales,
>
> Glide under the green wave, in schools that oft
>
> Bank the mid sea: part single, or with mate,
>
> Graze the sea-weed their pasture, and through groves
>
> Of coral stray.

"Show off!" said Simeon. "And rhyme isn't bondage!"

"He was describing a world before human beings," Noah remarked.

Izzy watched fish dart and glide in the golden waters. She imagined being a creature without feet. No feet, no shoes. No shoes, no stress.

Noah and Simeon returned to the couch.

"And stop calling her *your* scientist," Simeon said. "This child was born for wonder. And shoe-pain."

"Fine, poet-scientist," said Noah. "

Izzy was too engrossed in fish to listen.

* * *

Simeon spent his mornings in Noah's lab at the university. He cleaned test tubes, swept the floor and polished the benches. He fired off e-mails to the Provost recommending a no shoes policy in all science buildings. He wanted hand sanitizer placed in student orientation packages.

From two to four p.m. on Tuesdays, Wednesdays and Fridays, he volunteered at Crescentdale School. He stood with Izzy, ready to intervene while other children put on their boots or shoes. He made Izzy feel awkward.

One afternoon, Simeon stayed home with a bad cold. He asked her to livestream the row of shoes to him at home on her phone so that he could supervise selection. As usual, she had left her phone at home.

She waited anxiously. Then she tried a pair of boots. She put them on. Her body dissolved into billions of grains of brown sand. A strong hot wind blew the grains across the sky, and Edmonton became an empty desert. A voice ordered her to count the grains of sand in her body or perish in the desert. Her grains were already dissolved into the larger desert. The sky grew dark. She could not count fast enough. So the voice poured sand down her throat.

She was wearing the boots of a girl named Farida. Ms. Quinn had told the class about Farida in a quiet voice. She was a Muslim girl, and a refugee from the horn of Africa. A gang of twenty teenage boys, kidnapped by a charismatic murderer with a yellow beret, killed her parents and burned her school. The murderer gave himself the title of rear admiral. He proclaimed himself the leader of a new religion. He declared people who could read to be his personal enemies. He killed people who could not tell him the page number of any edict he read aloud from his sacred paperback. So Farida and her uncle made their way to a refugee camp in Ethopia.

So Izzy understood why she felt sand in her throat.

When she got home, she opened the fridge and poured some of Simeon's Mount Boucherie Chardonnay into a coffee mug. She drank it quickly. It made her feel dizzy, then ill, but it still felt better than Farida's shoes. Simeon came in and found her asleep on the kitchen floor. There was a halo of dry white vomit around her head. Simeon smelled notes of lemon and mint. The fridge door was still open. Her mug was on the kitchen table. He could see the Chardonnay was two thirds gone.

Simeon and Noah helped her to her room and put her to bed. They held an emergency meeting.

"It's this damned shoe thing. It's too much," Noah said.

"Well what do you suggest? An alcohol support group?" said Simeon.

"No."

"What then?"

"An aquarium. It won't solve the world's problems, but it helps. We both know why she likes *The Little Mermaid*, and it's not about getting a boy. I find fish calming, quieting, peaceful. Aquariums are naturally anti-depressive."

"True. But it has to be her decision."

"No it doesn't. We're buying one and it will be a surprise and that's that. We'll do all the work at first, but she'll gradually take over."

"Ha! I'd like to see that."

One week later, Izzy came home from school and found the luminescent universe of tropical fish lighting up before her eyes. She looked into the watery glass, filled her cheeks with air and exhaled. She asked to have her supper in front of the tank.

* * *

One afternoon, Simeon was late for dismissal. A collision between a teacher and a pupil had left an appalling *mélange* of applesauce, white bread and paper clips on the lunchroom floor. No one had the sense to inform Simeon until minutes before the bell. He wanted to clean it up.

Izzy stood alone in front of the row of winter boots. It was late October, but a blanket of snow had fallen the night before. Barton Squirrel was holding Card Dilbey, a boy with thick glasses, red hair and strange oracular powers, in a full nelson.

"So tell us Card, what would happen if women had six breasts, all turquoise and all permanently exposed?"

"Happen?" Card asked in his low, gravelly voice.

"Yeah, you know. What would life be like?"

"Well, you probably wouldn't notice it, because then it would be normal." This was Card's answer to every what-would-life-be-like riddle posed to him. The questions always seemed to be about breasts. Card always answered carefully, and with the same inevitable answer.

Izzy surveyed the row of boots and tried a pair on. Bad

luck. They didn't belong to her. She turned into a block of ice. A man was stuck up to his waist in the block of ice crying for help. A woman wept scalding tears on to the ice, but the ice didn't melt. Each tear froze. A boy hovered above the man, his body the centre of a turning carousel of fire engines and horses and buggies and log cabins and bronze statues.

Lucius Spukwell was pinching her elbow and demanding she give back his boots. Simeon arrived. "There now young fellow. Kindly remove your talon from my daughter's arm."

"Your dad's the janitor?" Lucius asked.

"I have two dads," Izzy answered.

Lucius swayed on his feet. Simeon grabbed his arm gently and propped him up. "There now, young master. Steady on. Having two fathers is hardly unheard of. You'll find your sea legs." Simeon studied Izzy. She was often upset after experiencing wrong boots. This wrong pair brought no tears to her eyes.

Ms. Quinn arrived, informing Blowflough and Boneslaw on nano-text. Simeon gently placed his hand like a blanket over her texting device.

"No need for that, seriously. Let me walk these children home together if you please." Normally, Ms. Quinn never heard anything while texting. Simeon, however, spoke in a cultured voice that delighted her attention.

"Alright. Since you're Izzy's father, please do!"

"Right you are!" Simeon beamed.

Simeon picked out Izzy's boots to avoid delay. When he looked around, Lucius was already gone. He let Izzy lead him to the schoolyard. In the falling light, they could see Barton and his lieutenants interrogating Lucius.

"Admit it!" they yelled at Lucius. "Admit it!"

"There now, youngsters!" Simeon bellowed. "Enough of that."

"We don't need your advice, freak man!"

Izzy wanted to throw a handful of snow in Barton's face. But she knew him too well.

"Love justice, do kindness – and go the hell home," Simeon told them.

Barton and company withdrew.

"What was that about?" Simeon asked.

"Nothing, sir," Lucius replied. "Just a disagreement about my living arrangements. As if they would know. They're actually looking for Card."

The three continued to cross the wide, snow crusted field following pathways cut by the boots of many children. Simeon walked behind like a shepherd, listening as the two awkwardly interviewed each other.

Izzy had seen Lucius walking home from a distance in days past. He was always alone. If crowds of schoolboys swirled around him, beckoning him or jostling him, he simply gathered his jacket collar tightly in his fist, as if it was starting to rain. Izzy felt she understood his body language. When she played with other girls during recess, she enjoyed their voices and energy and humour. But she was also afraid of the deep, uncharted, Barton and Farida fathoms of life or death beneath the waves of their voices. The noisy schoolyard felt like an anti-aquarium at times. She wondered if it might be that way for Lucius.

"What do your parents do?" Izzy asked Lucius.

"My mom works in information science," Lucius

answered. "My father is a diplomatic lawyer at The Hague, specializing in homeless law, so he's never home."

Simeon's ears perked up.

"A fine place! We enjoyed our time there. Mind you, the court itself always makes me think of St. Pancras Station, London."

Lucius froze. He thought of spraining his ankle or having a coma, just to change the subject. Izzy touched his elbow. "They lived there before I was born," she whispered. He watched the thin cloud of her breath swirl in the cold wind. Her breath called him back to his own breathing. He felt a small warm glow inside. He relaxed.

"I've never been there," he said. "My dad's going to take me a.s.a.p., probably the summer after next."

"Great," Izzy whispered, noticing a pair of blue jays sitting on the metal fence. Lucius paused and watched her favour the birds. He felt rapt for a moment in the profile of her deep green eyes and the studious frown on her lips. He cleared his throat and resumed.

"The Hague is home to many international organizations. The Hague is associated with the United Nations, as is Geneva and as is Vienna. It plays host to the International Court of Justice. Five Canadians have served on the court in the past. It hosts many important meetings and conventions, and maintains some light manufacturing of goods and several important minor industries."

"Peace and justice," Izzy replied. Lucius felt his body stir, and his dark mood lift. One blue jay settled on the ground and pecked a frozen crab apple.

They reached 109 Street, and turned south towards the traffic circle. The former McDonald's was now a royal purple island. It might pass for an art deco home despite the large parking lot. Inside, they could see Lucius's mother sitting at an eating table. There were papers scattered on the tabletop. Her lap-pad was open. Her face was buried in her hands.

Access seemed impossible. City Hall had erased the crosswalk when the structure ceased being a restaurant and became a single-family dwelling. Lucius said he could manage. He didn't want them to come any closer.

"Sorry about taking your boots," Izzy said.

"Sorry I got mad," Lucius replied.

Simeon and Izzy headed home.

"This appears to solve the mystery of who's been living in the old McDonald's," Simeon observed.

Izzy was quiet.

"What troubled you when you put on his boots, Izzy? Do you want to talk?"

"I was thinking that The Hague might be a symptom of papoutsiosis, or something like it," Izzy confessed. "He might have paterosis, or puerosis or fastfoodosis. I don't think his father works at The Hague."

"I agree, my dear. And I'm not sure you need papoutsiosis to see that. Poor soul. Introverted, is he?"

"He's an island," said Izzy.

* * *

At home, Noah sat in the living room grading papers. A fire blazed in the hearth. Nympho curled up and purred in the warmth. The aquarium glowed in last light of the winter dusk allowed by the window. Simeon and Noah argued quietly about wine. Izzy read an e-book in her room. She was reading a short history of American folk music. She read a chapter about

Appalachia. She liked to know where things came from. An hour later, during a dinner of tilapia chowder and spelt bread, Noah made a suggestion.

"Simeon says you're worried about your new friend, Izzy."

"I wouldn't go that far. I hardly know him. He's pretty creepy."

Her eyes studied the swirling patterns of butter and light cream in her bowl, and the gifts of fish lumps beneath the floating wreckage of broccoli and corn.

"Why do you say that, my dear?"

"Well, take last week. We had to give short speeches in class. Ms. Quinn gave us three topics to choose from. She made sure we spoke extemporally."

"Extemporaneously."

"Right. Extemporaneously. No screens, no texts allowed. I chose 'My favourite invention.' I talked about our aquarium. I called it the greatest screen on earth. Barton Squirrel talked about 'if I was Prime Minister.' He said he would fire all the chauffeurs and pilots, and drive or fly himself to meetings."

"And Lucius?"

"He chose how I would make the world a better place. And he was really cool at first. According to his research, humans are spending way too much money on things that do nothing. Porn, diet soft drinks and guns topped his list. He said we need to end homelessness, and that means shifting money. He wrote an equation on the board. J = mc2. Justice = money times considerations. He called it 'The Hague Equation.'"

"Why, he's an ethicist!" Simeon said. "A Plato banning inflammatories from his ideal republic!"

"Barton put up his hand and said Lucius met his father's definition of a communist. Jonas Morley called Lucius a leftard. Marchand Verde told Lucius to spare him the bleeding heart BS. All three said they were glad he would never be Prime Minister, and did high fives. Ms. Quinn told them all to shut up, but it was too late. Lucius turned red. I put up my hand and said I liked it, but why not let c = change? He gave me a mean look. He said we should all just leave it up to The Hague. I felt sorry for him, but I also thought he was seriously weird."

Noah paused for several minutes. "I know how to show consideration," Noah said. "Food! What if we have him for a meal?"

"Invite him?" she said.

"Precisely."

"I want to invite Farida." Farida moved suddenly to Fort McMurray when her uncle, a carpenter, found long-term work in construction. He was helping to build a new library, a new theatre and a new mosque there.

"Farida has seen the deep end. This young man at least has the advantage of being, shall we say, of a certain depth at the moment."

"Can we at least think about it?"

"Sure."

Izzy was frustrated by the exits of promising new female friends. A girl named Kati-tie befriended her when she was getting used to her diagnosis. One day, she slipped on Kati-tie's shoes. Izzy morphed into a flimsy door in a walk-up apartment basement suite. Two giant men made of concrete kicked the door down. Both men had barbed wire eyes and gray concrete ponytails. They found a beautiful princess inside, young and alive. But she owed them money. So they loaded their gold-plated guns with their own teeth and shot her to death. They left her newborn baby crying. They were never caught. So Izzy realized that Kati-tie was adopted just like she was. She kept this to herself.

Kati-tie's parents were aerial acrobats. They tied long ribbons to street lamps or tree branches and performed beautiful dances in mid-air. They came to Edmonton because of its many festivals. Kati-tie discerned that Izzy's feet sometimes hurt. So she taught Izzy to swing on silk ribbons in her bare feet at low altitude. She made Izzy feel as free as a bird in the air on the upswing, and free as a whale in deep waters on the downswing. Then one day, Kati-tie moved away. She went to Las Vegas with her parents to join the *Global Cosmic Circus.*

Izzy felt uncomfortable inviting Lucius. He never smiled. He avoided eye contact. She knew he stared at her from the side. Reluctantly, she agreed. Simeon and Izzy walked to *Richmond End.*

"Good evening, Ms. Spukwell," Simeon said at the door. "Forgive the intrusion. I'm Izzy's father. We hoped you might dine with us Sunday evening. The goal is thus: to meet the mother of her new friend. What say you?"

"The boy's father is away on business," she whispered.

Simeon feigned interest: "How true. The Hague! How delicious."

Lucius skidded into the room on white socks. He placed two hands on adjacent bolted dining tables and hoisted himself up, kicking his legs freely in the air. Lady Spukwell clutched her black shawl around her shoulders, as if Simeon's visit was a ruse to steal it from her.

"Let's put it this way," Simeon resumed. "Our modest table Saturday on you waits / Four hands bid fair to serve you tasty cates."

Lady Spukwell burst into tears and closed the door. The

door was the original sliding glass door to the McDonald's. Simeon could see her through Richie's dronecult stencils as she fell to her knees.

Simeon apologized to Izzy. He assumed she would be relieved by this total failure. Instead, she knocked gently on the door. Then she knocked harder and harder. She pounded the glass. Lucius could see that she wouldn't give up. They were watching each other through the thick glass. Izzy pointed her fingers at her face demanding eye contact.

"Come on, jerk!" she shouted. Lucius wanted to see the Dryden-Burnet aquarium. Some children bragged about seeing it from the street. Lady and Lucius conferred. Lucius opened the door and said: "Fine, relax why don't you – we'll come."

* * *

That Saturday, Lady and Lucius walked over to Izzy's home in the November twilight. The thin blanket of snow was gone. Winter was on hold.

"Make yourselves at home!" Noah boomed as the Spukwells crossed the threshold.

Lady Cassandra joined Noah and Simeon in the kitchen where they were preparing Basque stew and homemade rolls. Izzy and Lucius stared at the aquarium and fed the fish. His eyes followed three silvery fish with black stripes. "What are they?" he asked.

"They're called convict fish," Izzy explained, petting Nympho in her arms to maintain peace. "But they shouldn't be. It's a stupid name based on old prison clothes. They deserve a better name."

"How about zebra fish," Lucius suggested. He thought the aquarium was like a prison for fish. Izzy pointed to a fish that already owned that name.

"I call them Persephons," Izzy said. "For Persephone."

Lucius thought she had said "purse phones." They stared some more.

"What are those blue ones?" he asked.

"With the yellow bands? I call them Sannas."

"Meaning?"

Izzy took Lucius to the coffee table. She cleared away Noah's papers, and showed Lucius a small stone Inuit carving standing on the glass top.

"This is Sedna, an Inuit goddess. I pronounce her name 'Sanna.' She's the goddess of the sea and all that lives in it. She was very independent. She married a dog. This was an appreciation gift to my dad from Iqaluit Municipal Council."

Lucius studied the statue. Sedna's green stone eyes looked forward alertly. Her long hair appeared to wave backwards, as if from a strong headwind. Her legs disappeared into the base of the statue. The base could be a boat, or the whole sea in miniature.

"Cool!" he whispered. They watched the fish swim in silence.

"So do they just swim all the time? Or do they have homes?"

"They settle down at night," Izzy answered, "but there's no private property. By the way, I liked your presentation on the homeless."

"It's a critical cause," Lucius said, "especially in a cold climate. My dad's involved in homeless law. I'd like to follow in his footsteps, but maybe through politics or law. Those are spheres where you can make a difference."

"So why do you think homelessness happens?" Izzy asked, impatiently.

"Adverse circumstances, sure, but abnormalities mainly. The homeless need to normalize first."

"I saw Barton and his friends picking on Card Dilbey during recess yesterday. Barton asked Card what would happen if all women went permanently topless."

"I wasn't there."

"He said no one would really notice, because then it would be normal. So they asked him what would happen if all women had eighteen breasts exposed at all times, with orange fire coming out of their breasts."

"My mom says there's a kid like Card in every schoolyard. But my mom's a total liar."

"But what if your mom is telling the truth?" Izzy asked. "You wouldn't really notice, because then it would be normal."

Lucius struggled to connect all this to homelessness.

"What the hell is your point?"

"Normal is a sticky place, Lucius."

Noah interrupted the young people.

"Are you relaxing yet, Lucius? Nothing is more relaxing than watching fish swim. Do you think they mind living in a home surrounded by big moving creatures like us making strange noises? I don't think so. The dimensions of their aquarium make their universe. We partake of their grace when we relax with them. In their own way, they know that. Imagine being a fish."

This man doesn't talk like a scientist, thought Lucius. He must be a phony.

Simeon turned to Lady Spukwell. "So your day has been generally a good one?" he uttered loudly. He thought his question was rather a soft ball, but her face crumpled in silent grief. He waved his fingers gracefully, like a conductor guiding an orchestra through the hard part of a symphony. It was no use. Lady Spukwell felt the evening was another arrow in her midriff. She had dared to imagine Simeon a bachelor. Now look what she'd got herself into. Still, Lucius might find a friend.

"You must allow me to reciprocate your kindness," she said. "There's a luncheon at our church next Sunday. Come, won't you?" Noah certainly hoped not, but the thought of bussing tables, sweeping floors and stacking chairs after lunch was too much to resist for Simeon.

"We'll be there, Lady Spukwell," he said.

* * *

The church was the spectacular *Glass Cathedral of Normalcy* on the southwest edge of Edmonton. The Cathedral was founded by Marv-Johnson Marvelton, billionaire owner of North America's largest auto glass replacement company, *Marv-Johnson's Autoglass Eruptions.* Its massive central dome was a geodesic network of thick glass panels. Its apex contained tinted rear-view mirrors that created fiery effects.

To the north, downtown Edmonton appeared as a clump of buildings in the distance. To the south, a 27-hole golf course burrowed its way through long-lived weeds and wilderness. The course once belonged to Arson Digits, 50th and last President of the United States, and a longtime friend and associate of Marvelton. Digits swept to power with the campaign slogan, "Security For Me; Trouble For You." The slogan festooned jeans and t-shirts and bracelets and billboards throughout his time in office. Digits sold the course to Marvelton when creditors placed liens against his online gambling and family entertainment empire at the start of his presidential term.

Marvelton hired Sportsmaw Management Inc., a Vancouver development firm owned by Delta "Del" Sportsmaw, Digits' fourth cousin once removed. Sportsmaw built three layers of beige condominiums between fairways on each 9-hole section: Cathedral Breezes Executive Garden Homes, Cathedral Breezes Executive Plantation Homes and Cathedral Breezes Executive Manor Homes. High walls surrounded the developments. Tough, stainless steel netting covered their tops. Bowing to pressure from the congregation, Marvelton agreed to open the golf course at noon on Sundays to protect the Cathedral from ambient first-tee profanity.

The Cathedral's massive glass entrance hall featured a giant LED screen. A film of the "end times" repeated itself in an endless loop for twelve hours each day and eighteen hours on Sundays. The pendulum of a grandfather clock swung steadily above images of war, disease, famine and death. A translucent stock ticker showed the values of the ruble and yuan nearing zero. Tanks roared across desert plains. Artillery pounded Gaza, Syria and Venezuela under a triumphant fly-past of N-62 fighter jets streaming blue and white smoke. A gold cup fell from the hand of a raging woman dressed in scarlet. A tank flattened her cup. An aged, bearded prophet leaned on his staff on a windy mountaintop above what looked like Kamloops. The camera zoomed into his right eyeball, revealing U.S. Marines skimming the surface of his blue iris in landing craft that dodged the tentacles of a fire-spewing red dragon. Buff saints and ripped apostles de-mined underwater power lines. Families boarded helicopters with pilots giving crackling orders and call signs: *tango roger copy*. The choppers evacuated the families towards a brilliant yellow light in the distance, while radiant angels mopped up on the beach and interrogated enemy prisoners.

The Cathedral's curved glass bleachers reminded Izzy of a giant aquarium. When she looked up to the high glass ceiling, she saw leaves strewn by the wind and silhouetted by the sunlight. The Cathedral owned its own mobile hydraulic window-cleaning machine. The machine was the size of a house. Izzy saw human faces in the leaves looking downward, perhaps wanting to come in, bearing some unknown message.

The minister-in-charge was Reverend Augustus Phlap, a short, beefy, steaming ranter of an extrovert. The massed choir unleashed their voices in "On Golden Streets." Phlap bounced around the front of the stage like a beach ball passing through the waving hands of a crowd. A grim anger etched his face. His sermon title was simple and powerful: "The Lake of Fire."

"Oh the lake of fire!" he intoned. "It's real, friends. It burns forever, piercing and stinging with ongoing pain and misery. No man can tell its width or depth. But the stench can tell. Oh yes! The stench on the surface is the stench of sin. The fire is from above, but the Velcro that holds you down is a stench of your own making. But there's still time. And that's why I invite you all to run for the cure next Saturday!"

Lady Spukwell slumped forward when he mentioned Velcro. Afterwards, Phlap took time to sit with her party at luncheon in the hall.

"I must say," Simeon offered politely, "your sermon brought to mind that magnificent sonnet of Donne's:

> Pour new seas in mine eyes, that so I might
>
> Drown my world with my weeping earnestly,
>
> Or wash it, if it must be drowned no more.
>
> But oh it must be burnt!

"Donne captured it so well," Simeon continued. "The

fires of lust may gnaw, but a good marriage is a sanctified flame, a zeal for truth, the lamp we hold out against the darkness."

Phlap eyed Simeon suspiciously. Marriage? Poetry? Done? What the hell was he nattering about?

"Do you have any thoughts, young Lady," Phlap asked Izzy severely.

Izzy put down the gelatine-encased celery speared on her plastic fork, cleared her throat and said: "Yes. Hopkins: 'As kingfishers catch fire, dragonflies draw flame.'"

"Oh, good one, Izzy!" Simeon exclaimed, "'What I do is *me*: for that I *came*!' And now: another. I've wanted to set this poem to music. If I had a shred of talent for hymnody, and I don't, I'd call it 'Jesus is not normal.'" Simeon waved his fork like a conductor and sang to the tune of *In Excelsis Deo:*

He left his father's trade to roam

A wandering vagrant without home;

And thus He others labour stole

That he might live without control.

Glo-orororororororor-ia. Jesus is not nor-mal!

Phlap eyed Lady Spukwell. Why was she inflicting these reprobates on him? He assumed they were victimizing her, or living off her good graces, perhaps even blackmailing her. Phlap felt for her. Love – as he liked to scream until his vocal chords boiled into blisters each week – was the key to living.

Noah kicked Simeon in the shin. "I think Simeon means

that you've been, shall we say, descriptive, Reverend Phlap. Simeon sees science and religion as much the same: like most things in life, they're either good poetry or not. But let me ask you: do you like fire? I think you do. I'm a water person myself. But fire and water have a lot in common. A gentle flame in the hearth is one of the most relaxing sights. As you watch it, you begin to relax. Calmness comes creeping. Fire has an aquatic grace. The predictable patterns of the flames in gas fireplaces soothe. The stages of a wood fire, from beginning to middle to the inevitable end, tell us that change is delectable. The intimacies of fire are second only to watching fish swim, for me at least."

Phlap shook his head and rose. He waved Simeon off when he applied to help clean up. Phlap should have employed him. Idleness left Simeon available to mischief.

"If Jesus is the greatest man," Simeon posited, "then surely we should love him to the greatest degree, and not simply to a normal degree. Don't you agree?"

Phlap gave Simeon a cold look. If this was Elm Street Temple back in Texas, he could march this mega-bastard out of the building at the point of an assault rifle, with no charges and no worries. He missed that perfect freedom.

"Nothing to say, Lucius?" Phlap asked, looking back. Lucius shook his head, took a bite out of a biscuit, and stole a glance at Izzy. Phlap muttered "infiltrators" under his breath, then turned his massive back on them and left.

* * *

Noah kicked Simeon in the shin again. This one hurt. Simeon rose and walked to the bulletin board to straighten some lopsided notices. Some were schedules for weekend golf leagues: Moms and Tots; Misters and Missuses; Swingin' Swingtimers; Gone Fishin' Five Irons. Simeon reached for the magic marker to add one more golf team to the list: "Lovers in a Dangerous Time." Then he saw the notice for the run for the cure:

> Lifestyle choices can be cured. Oh yes! Evidence says so. But science needs dollars to stoke its way. That's where you come in. This Saturday, c'mon out and run for the cure! Let's get the right dollars to the right scientists. Sign up some sponsors. Meet new people too.

Simeon signed up for the run.

"Are you daft?" Noah demanded of Simeon in the car, after dropping Lucius and Lady as close to home as safety allowed.

"These people are as messy as the rest of us. I don't want their goddam plastic bottles strewn all over creation."

"And raise funds for quacks?"

"I won't be seeking sponsors. And speaking of cures, did you know the first clinical trial is in Daniel chapter one?"

"Yes – because I told you that."

"Oh."

"Fine," Noah said, "I'm going with you."

"Izzy will come to watch," Simeon said, "won't you, my poet?"

"Poet-scientist!" Noah snapped.

* * *

The Run for the Cure began at the John Janzen Nature Centre in the river valley. Simeon and Noah joined a crowd of 97 runners, many of them families or members of the Cathedral youth group. As they waited for starter's orders, some people drifted over to hear an impromptu lecture by a birdwatcher. Then some children asked to join a picnic table class on insects. Their parents reluctantly allowed them to exchange the run for the lessons. Then, a group of volunteers wearing yellow bibs appeared. They were cleaning up the river valley, picking up plastic bottles and paper. The teen runners defected to the bibs. Noah forbade Simeon to defect. By the time the race started, there were just 24 runners, with few under the age of forty.

Noah and Simeon won the race easily. They started off at a moderate pace, heading out in a loop around Fort Edmonton, peeking through the dense trees at the tall, weathered wooden palisades surrounding the fort, and the colourful tepees within its precincts. To their surprise, they were alone after twenty minutes. They paused and admired a York boat moored in the shallows. Still no runners came up behind them. They imagined borrowing the boat and drifting downstream, toes in the water, but it was far too big for toe dipping, and they wanted to win for Izzy. The wind stirred in the trees. They held each other and reminisced. And still they held the lead. So they set out again, running over the Quesnel Bridge and down into Laurier Park, then over the red iron footbridge to Hawrelak Park for a loop around the lake before doubling back to the finish line. They had time to sit down after passing the finish line and spend about twenty minutes together, so great was the distance to the third place runner, and the twenty-one runners in his wake.

"Would we have beaten them?" Simeon asked Noah. He pointed to a group of about thirty young, fit runners sitting in the sun at the nature centre. They were all in their early teens. Roughly half were from Phlap's church. They were picking up broken glass and plastic wrappers and putting them in a green box.

"No, I don't think so."

* * *

Three days later, the elders, over Phlap's objections, invited Simeon and Noah to testify on Sunday morning after the sermon. What did it take to win? Was it uplifting?

Simeon, Noah and Izzy sat on the stage with Lucius. Lady Spukwell sent excuses and stayed in bed.

Phlap's sermon was a five-alarm blazer. He brought every grain of his molten charisma to bear. He expounded the first chapter of Genesis: the six-day's work of creation. He explained why each day must be taken literally as a period of twenty-four hours. He defied anyone to find a place in the Bible that said otherwise. No proof – no truth, he screamed like a giant magpie. Dinosaurs? Sure, why not? They could have lived within the 6000 years from Genesis 1 to the end of time. Global warming? A falsehood trumpeting man's selfish pride, always on call to bear false witness! The only time that was running out was the end time! There was enough oil to see earth through the end times, particularly with Ecuador now in full production. Daniel foresaw oil fields in Ecuador.

* * *

After the sermon, Phlap managed a stern smile as he summoned Noah and Simeon to the podium.

"We finished first for a scientific reason," Noah claimed. "None of you can run faster than us!" A ripple of laughter spread through the congregation.

Simeon spoke. "Needless to say, we doubted the cure as we stood on the starting line. And since our victory shook not our doubt about there being no cure, that doubt failed not, nor waned in adversity, but changed into conviction, a true non-doubt if you will, growing stronger stride by stride."

Some people clapped tentatively. Some tried to parse his sentences.

"And so, without further verbiage, we want to introduce

you to our main source of inspiration. Our daughter Izzy!"

A swell of protest roiled through the hall.

"*Du calme, s'il vous plait*, said Simeon, pointing to his own head. "Izzy has a poem to read for you. It's her interpretation of Genesis 1, with a nod to Blake, a poet we happen to be reading at bedtime. Friends, this poem made straight our path."

Izzy came to the podium and cleared her throat. "Good morning ladies and gentlemen. 'Six Days' by Izzy Dryden-Burnet":

In the great vale of the North Saskatchewan

In the deep visions of Shaddai Elohim Jehovah

Spread like robes of starlight

Over Adam and Noah and Isaac

And Emanuel the human form divine

I looked and beheld the six day's work

Like six new pairs of winter boots

And I heard an angel bright who sang this song to me:

'Six times our souls must pass this way

Three times straight and three times gay!

Three times woman three times man

Across four rivers and five sands

Twelve on flowers twelve on stones

Six times across the plain of bones

And twelve shall rise to shining mountains

And wash off pain in seven fountains

And then all races ever known

Will dance in our eyes as I have shown!"

There was a silence in the room for thirty seconds. It felt like half an hour. Men with collection plates moved cautiously forward. This family would have to go.

An usher noticed Reverend Phlap writhing on the floor. His face turned from crimson to blue. Lucius merged into a row of spectators. Simeon took action, loosening Phlap's shirt collar, calling his name, and applying CPR before being pried away by the collection men. One of the men called emergency services. An ambulance was on its way. Reverend Phlap suddenly lay still.

Chapter Four

THE PULSATION OF AN ARTERY

Phlap's Singularity

Phlap awoke in a small, dimly lit room. Old blue paint peeled where the walls met. Spider webs grew from the edges of the peels. A vending machine glowed in the corner. Its loud fan grated sporadically. Dead flies stuck to the black grease coating the machine's ventilator. A rectangular fluorescent light buzzed noisily on the ceiling. Its cracked plastic cover was filled with moths and flies both living and dead. A pizza box and some old newspapers lay strewn on the floor.

Phlap hoisted himself to his feet and sat in a cold metal chair beside a wooden table. Old linoleum curled around his feet. Was this a lunchroom in hell? Fear gripped his chest.

"Do not be anxious," said a voice. A woman appeared in

the chair across the table from him. She had dark hair and dark fiery eyes. She seemed saintly *and* sexy, Phlap thought to himself. Both at the same time? I must be in hell!

"No, you are not," she replied, reading his mind. A small black dog curled up by her feet and snuggled his chin on her foot.

"Very well, where am I?" he demanded. This certainly wasn't Mercy Hospital, a place he knew from visits to the sick.

"What and where have no distinction here," she answered. "This is your grace period."

Was she a nurse? No. She wore a red summer dress of some satiny fashion. The Scarlet Whore! No. She was too petite. And the dress covered her knees.

"Who are you?" he asked.

"Why do you ask, seeing I am Servant?"

Something about her reminded him of the parts of the Bible that don't add up, factually speaking. He puzzled over them, but never dared admit it to anyone. Better just to brass it out, he thought.

"I know what you are. You're a demon!"

"We don't use that word anymore."

"Do you have a real name?"

"My name is Abdielle."

Her name was like the sound of a harp, but he could not admit it.

"What kind of name is that? Italian? Irish-Italian? Irish-Spanish?

"Abdielle is from your Hebrew language. My virtue is

zeal: the flame of holiness. My energy is desire: the flame of life."

Phlap hoped he was still on earth.

"I don't want to be rude," he said, "but as Earth places go, this is pretty crappy. Is this the health care my tax dollars pay for?"

"I have said: you are inside your period of grace."

"Well, I want a decent room. Now."

"This room is your own: the singularity of your imaginative universe in its present formation."

"I think not!" Phlap thundered. "And God said 'let there be pizza boxes'? No ma'am! Let there be junk and crap and bugs on the floor? Not in my Bible!"

"Both read the Bible day and night – but you read black where we read white."

He looked at the fluorescent light. The loud buzzing was getting on his nerves. Some living flies were eating the wings and legs off the dead ones.

"Pay attention, young lady. This is still a free country and I want out of here," he said. "Point the way, if you please."

"There is no way and no here yet."

"You're breaking the law! Never mind – I'll show myself out."

He raised the dirty, bent venetian blinds and found a cracked, filthy window behind them. The window was half open. Beyond the glass was a profound darkness. It was thick, heavy and visible.

"Is that outer space?" he asked.

"That darkness has no space. There is no outer, no beyond, no east of east, no west of west."

Phlap waved off her explanation. "What time is it, anyways?" he asked.

"None."

"Let's just see about that," Phlap seethed. He picked up the pizza box from the floor and threw it out the window, spinning it backhand like a Frisbee. It disappeared instantly, like a blade of dead grass hitting a dark fire. He looked down. The pizza box was back in its place on the floor.

"Why the vending machine? Why all this clutter and crap? And that infernal light won't stop buzzing! This place disgusts me."

"These are the totality of your imaginative efforts in the world you knew. All build mansions in eternity. This is yours."

"Eternity? Nobody can teach me about eternity. But nobody!"

Despite this conviction, his stomach was a churning habanero. He picked up some old newspapers from the floor and crumpled them. He tossed them out the window. Zap. They re-appeared on the floor. He threw them again and again. Then he noticed that the newspaper he kept chucking out the window bore his date of birth. It headlines spoke of wars and rumours of wars. He stopped and took six deep breaths.

"How long have I been here?"

"A moment. The pulsation of an artery."

"How long am I stuck here for?"

"A moment. Six thousand years."

He clenched his fists. He buried his face in hands. He

spread his fingers to cover his eyes and ears and nose all at once.

"I'm dead, aren't I?"

"Obviously not."

"Prove it!"

"Your feet are tired. That is a sign of life."

"OK. Then what am I, dare I ask?"

"In the body. There was unbearable pressure on your upper carotid artery."

"From what?"

"The voice of a child."

"That's right! I remember. That child spoke blasphemy! I thought my head would explode!"

"It did explode."

"So you know that child?"

"I do. I am pregnant with the child. Always."

Women! Phlap thought to himself. So manipulative!

"So this is not a dream and I'm going to die in my sleep. Fine! Have it your way. But I thought these near-death experiences would be a lot classier than this dump!"

"This room is the form of your imagination. One taste, one sound, one sight, one law for the lion and the ox and the infinite variety of life. This is your constricted, dimensionless singularity, unrenovated, unredeemed, but for a period of grace."

"This sounds rather technical."

"The room is you."

Phlap absorbed this for a moment.

"And the darkness?"

"Depth without Spirit. Void without voice."

"And the lake of fire – which way is it?"

Abdielle brushed a tear from her eye, smirked and shook her head. "I have said: there is no way yet."

* * *

They sat in silence for a period of 6000 years.

Abdielle spoke: "The moment the watch-fiends cannot find has come. Breathe it in and it will multiply. For in this period the poet's work is done; and all the great events of time start forth and are conceived in such a period, within a moment, a pulsation of the artery."

"Uh huh. You don't say. So when can I leave here? Never? I say again, you're breaking the law, young lady!"

"One law for the lion and the ox is oppression."

"What about laws for kidnappers?"

"You can leave any time you choose to leave. You can go back. But first you have to make your way."

"I see. And what will I tell people? Or will you make me forget all this with some kind of neural gadget?"

"It is as Charissa said in her imagination. You have six days to work. Tend to life and affirmation, and work will change into play. As you are now, you are working under the curse. Charissa's oracle will destroy you or bless you. Bring forth what you have within you to bring forth. Bring forth the wild child."

"In her imagination? Excuse me, ma'am, but I live in the real world."

"Charissa is a literalist of the imagination."

Phlap remembered parts of Izzy's poem.

"Fine. If there's any truth in what she said – and I doubt it – then I'm on day six, because I'm a man. God made man on day six! He gave Man dominion over the earth!"

"The good news is you can make your way back. Know, however, that this is your first day."

Phlap jumped out the window, and landed promptly back on his chair.

"So what are you proposing, young lady? Reincarnation? That's heresy!"

"We don't use that word. The pain was not yours alone. Pain knows many others."

Phlap bowed his head. So she knew about his pain. He felt ashamed of a tear on the edge of his left eye. He felt afraid.

"Alright, young lady. Show me the way. Now."

Abdielle stared at Phlap. Suddenly, his feet no longer ached. He felt energy in enter his toes like a holy flood.

"Please," Phlap said softly, feeling his feet almost rise from the floor. "I can't see my way from here. I need your help. Please."

"Do not be ashamed. Do not be anxious either. Imagine your way outward, like your pulse. This pulsation can go as far as forever, or no farther than the vending machine. Choose. This is the first instant of your stroke, the first near-fatal contraction of your artery. Now, imagine your artery expanding in the moment the poet's work is done. Build bridges over seas of cold abstraction. Carve minutes and hours into diamonds of light as a bird cuts the air with her wings. Humble yourself like the spider, the toad, the badger and the newt. Break the surface of space-time like Leviathan breaching the waves. Let the waves multiply around you. You must bless the myriad of the loving and the different. Choices are not all forks. Your choices will be concentric. Now choose."

As she spoke, Phlap dimly recalled the little girl with the two fathers. They seemed almost human to him now. The room began to change. The soft drink machine, fluorescent light, pizza boxes and old newspapers danced friskily in a ring, transforming into an albatross, a gorilla, a coelacanth (the dandiest dancer), a mosquito, a serpent and a giant land tortoise, all dancing in a ring.

Phlap wept for seven years.

"So, young lady, I can go back. Where do I go this time? How? I'll try to accept what you tell me. I will."

"The stroke has not killed you. You need only to stand up and walk."

Phlap saw a small light in the middle of the floor. It burned what remained of his birthday newspaper like a withered leaf, then moved outward into six rivers of infinite distance, multiple directions. Phlap turned to Abdielle and nodded politely to her with a faint smile. He stepped into one of the rivers. He set his feet on the sandy bottom of the light and began to walk.

Chapter Five

ON MOSS LAKE TRAIL

Edmonton and Elk Island Park, May 2038

Augustus Phlap spent eight years in his coma. When he awoke, he called for Izzy. He begged people to bring her to him. Two private nurses attending him, Destiny and Jasmine, listened to his ramblings seriously. A young girl read a poem, he said. He had a stroke. Was there a connection?

Destiny and Jasmine did not understand his fixation. Was he hoping to sue the child? Can you sue a person over a poem? He did not sound angry or vindictive. They tried to turn his attention back to his recovery.

"Put aside thoughts that make stress. You must realize that you've been in a coma for eight years," Jasmine reminded him.

"Eight years – a long time, surely, no?" said Destiny, with her Hungarian accent.

"Yes angels, eight years is a long time for the vegetable man. But that's the literal sense. In its eternal form, the duration of my coma was equal in its period and extent to 6000 years. It happened in a moment, a pulsation of the artery. I am weak in body, but not in mind and spirit. My real self, the eternal imagination, feels younger every minute. Now find me Izzy!"

So Jasmine and Destiny set out to find the child.

* * *

Much had happened in those eight years.

The elders of the Cathedral stripped Simeon and Noah of their victory in the Run for the Cure after analyzing Izzy's poem as a word cloud:

Mountains

ever Adam Emanuel

sands shining Across known

Shaddai **Three** Elohim

Sang place looked bones **seven** straight

North pass Jehovah Spread *GAY*

Human **four** boots winter Isaac man wash

Like Saskatchewan heard beheld

Bright Over song shown divine

Souls rivers races deep

Woman flowers Noah angel way

Stones starlight **twelve** form **five**

Dance rise new pairs

All robes day's great fountains

vale **Six times**

The signs seemed clear. They quietly transferred the crown of victory to the third place finisher, a self-employed kitchen renovator. But he was inspired to come out after listening to Izzy in church, and did so in the presence of the elders. So they transferred the crown to the fourth-place finisher, a young chartered accountant recovering from a prescription pill addiction. But she confessed she had taken a stimulant before the race. She tried to flush her pills down the toilet, but lacked the willpower. She wished she had a fraction of Izzy's strength. The elders thanked her for her testimony. They let her keep the crown, but thought it best to reconsider the annual run for the cure, then in its fortieth year. On the advice of children, teens and great-grandparents, they abolished the Run for the Cure. The youth group asked to run twice a year for Edmonton's Food Bank and for local homeless shelters from then on. The elders agreed.

* * *

While Phlap lay in his coma, Noah worked on water supply problems in northern communities. He warned Albertans that violent weather lay in the future due to global warming. He shared his expertise with resource companies, promising they would go down in history if they invested more in green energy alternatives. He spoke out against cuts to water projects in federal budgets. Having his suitcase searched and his body scanned every time he took a flight was a price he would pay for speaking truth to power.

* * *

Simeon volunteered for two more years at Crescentdale elementary after Izzy graduated. He was popular with the children and teachers, and found it hard to let go. They would all chant "one more year!" in the lunchroom whenever his departure seemed imminent. One autumn Thursday afternoon, Simeon leaned on his broom and contemplated leaving. Then he saw a man on school property. He saw a handgun in his back pocket. Simeon told the receptionist to call the police, and to lock the doors and windows and move all the children to the pre-school wing. He approached the armed man to lay down some ground rules.

"Good afternoon. We have one rule for visitors here," Simeon explained. "You must speak in rhyme so we can hear."

"What?" asked the man.

"If you do not speak in rhymes, we can't hear you, not even with the aid of limes. Now, who are you?"

"Who?"

"Let me walk you through this slowly, as your aptitude is lowly. Your character, sir, is much in doubt. Permit me, quickly then, to sketch it out." He cleared his throat and began a recitation from Dryden:

For close designs, and crooked counsels fit;

Sagacious, bold and turbulent of wit:

Restless, unfixed in principles and place;

In power unpleased, impatient of disgrace.

The armed man's pupils widened.

"That is you, sir, yes, as you might well guess," Simeon said.

The man teetered. Simeon pressed the business end of his broom against the man's torso, then tipped him over and took his gun. The man turned out to be the Arizona uncle of a Crescentdale pupil. As a member of *GLANS* (Gun Lobbyists for American National Security), he felt obliged to wear his gun at all times, even when it was not loaded. A judge fined him for public mischief. Simeon won a medal of courage from the Edmonton City Council for his brave action. His acceptance speech caused a stir when he vowed to "clean up the city." Was he planning to run against the mayor? Simeon had no political ambitions.

* * *

Izzy was now eighteen years old. She progressed from grade 6 to graduation from grade 12 at J. A. Boneslaw High School. Formerly known as Old Crescentdale High, the school was re-named for the counsellor who interviewed Izzy when she first presented symptoms of Macpherson's Papoutsiosis. When Izzy was in grade 10, Boneslaw interviewed a teen suffering from MacPherson's Kleptophosis. The student was Barton Squirrel. Boneslaw didn't dither with prefatory questions. He asked Barton if there were any issues in his family history before asking him his name. Without a word, Barton snatched Boneslaw's lap-pad and the principal's keys, fled the interview room and took off in the principal's late model Honda Civic. Boneslaw gave chase in his Volvo. Driving over the speed limit, Boneslaw took an e-phone call and got into a huge row with his realtor. Within 40 seconds, he was mortally t-boned by a large truck carrying a load of diet sodas. The sodas burst into flames on impact.

Barry Basewik-Quick, a new student at the school, happened to be standing at the intersection of 76th Avenue and 104th Street, e-phone in hand, when the truck exploded. He took still photos of the pillar of smoke and video of the carnage. Both appeared on the six o'clock local news that evening. He was disappointed that the newscasters called him "Basewik Quick." Despite this setback, he knew by the end of that day what he wanted to be in life: a journalist.

* * *

Izzy walked to school with Lucius whenever their paths crossed. She talked about her father's research on lakes. Lucius spoke of his father's heavy caseload at The Hague. Izzy told her parents. Lucius's lies disturbed her. Noah suggested a game.

"Here's what. Let's have them over for yet another dinner. We'll have a fire in the yard. The rules: everyone has to bring one object from their life for ritual burning. It will be a way for him to let go of the past, accept the present, and embrace the future."

"Pshhh," Simeon scorned. "As if therapy is that easy. And you know how I feel about burning trash. What if they choose to burn tires?"

"No tires, Simeon. Nothing a person can't conceal in a pocket. In fact, we'll call the game Conceal and Reveal. That will be rule two."

"Or Conveal!" Izzy screamed.

"Clever! And here's what Simeon and I will burn: a photo of me standing in front of The Hague City Hall. We were there a long time ago. It might give Lucius a little jolt, and help him cope."

It was a warm Saturday evening. Izzy talked while Lucius absorbed himself in his e-phone. He was playing Monopoly against the machine. Lady clutched her dark shawl about her shoulders. She asked Lucius to fetch a large, black case they had conveyed from *Richmond's End*. It was by the front door. Now was the right time, she assured him.

His face red from modesty and mild exertion, Lucius opened the case and wrestled a large accordion up onto his torso. Noah and Simeon watched from the living room couch in dismay. Lucius looked to Izzy for approval. Izzy looked at Lady and forced her best smile.

"Ladies and gentlemen," Lucius said mechanically, " I give you fever."

He launched into "Fever" by June Carter and Johnny Cash, a blazing instrumental version for solo accordion. His fingers danced like lunatic wizards over the black and white keys. He was so quick and so precise his audience almost forgot the oddity of the selection. Noah and Simeon couldn't help but tap their feet. Lady slumped at the parts where her mental singing mapped words of marital discord onto the blistering velocity of Lucius's accordion.

They sat down to a supper of lentil stew, wild rice and rhubarb squares. Simeon served blackberry banana yogurt shakes to Izzy and Lucius. Noah opened a bottle of Okanagan Merlot.

"I was planning to pair the stew with Cabernet-Franc," Noah told Lady, "but Simeon insisted on Merlot, given the balance of coriander and turmeric. I hate to admit it, but he's right. Look for hints of black pepper, toffee and red currant in this Merlot, Lady. It's more than a match for the stew. You must take a bottle back to Richmond's End with our compliments."

Elitist bastard, Lucius thought to himself.

* * *

After supper, they adjourned to the backyard, *sans* accordion. Noah hoped Lucius would play again, if some melancholy *Klezmer* was in the compass of his skills. Simeon thought otherwise. There was a slight chance of rain, he argued. Simeon did not want the accordion to get wet, although Lucius could choose to burn the instrument in the conveal ceremony if he so wished. Lucius had no intention of playing another tune. Fever was the one tune he had fully mastered.

Lucius and Izzy built the fire in the small brick pit. While the blaze took shape, Noah took the cloak off his telescope and showed it to Lucius. It was a white cylinder with a chrome star finder mounted on top. It stood on its tripod. Noah spoke of Bruno and Galileo and Herschel. He showed Lucius how to use the GPS setting and star finder app. Lucius observed the moon and Jupiter and Mars. Simeon joined them, and whispered part of a poem:

Turn away no more

Why wilt thou turn away?

The starry floor

The watery shore

Is given thee till break of day

Simeon pointed to Andromeda and Aquarius. They reminded Lucius of the Monopoly Man and the shoe token. They went to the fire and took turns convealing. Noah restrained Lady Spukwell when she tried to burn her black shawl. Since it was not concealed, it was not eligible.

Izzy carefully opened a napkin on the ground and

revealed the body of a convict fish that died in the aquarium two days earlier.

"This is all for the good," she explained. "Lots of people flush fish down the toilet. Never! Why should a fish end up in a water filtration plant? Now it will turn into something rich for the soil."

"Rich and strange," Noah remarked, relieved that Nympho was out and about that evening.

Lucius stood by the fire and pulled a piece of dark material from his trouser pocket. The material kept growing, like endless handkerchiefs from a magician's sleeve. He spread it out on the ground. It was a semi-rotten T-shirt. It was badly torn, but the words "pen marriage, eh?" were legible, like a fragment of some ancient hieroglyph.

"pen marriage?" Simeon inquired. "Is that like having a pen pal?"

Lady Spukwell cringed. The T-shirt had survived the neighbour's compost heap. The neighbour discovered it and returned it to the Spukwells at Richmond's End. He drove through the former all-nite drive-thru lane and tapped on the takeout window where Lucius was studying for a history exam. Lucius opened the window. "Didn't think I'd find you, eh?" said the neighbour, launching the fetid shirt into Lucius's face.

"Tell us what this is," Noah urged Lucius.

Lady Spukwell's eyes rolled back in her head. Lucius stepped to the fire.

"This shirt was worn by a would-be assassin who tried to shoot my father in The Hague. Dad was there working on homeless law. So it's ironic that his assailant was homeless."

Izzy's head slumped.

"And I've decided to drown the shirt, not burn it," Lucius continued. "If I drown it, it will be a fitting tribute. He spent his career across the ocean, after all."

"Ah! Your little world made cunningly! Exactly how does one drown a shirt, Lucius?" Simeon asked.

Lucius produced a balloon. "I'm going to throw it off the High Level Bridge, tomorrow perhaps."

Lucius stuffed the stinking relic back into his pocket.

Burning the photo now seemed pointless to Noah. Lucius did not rise to the occasion, and he would not embarrass Lady Spukwell with a cross-examination of her son. So he gave his photo of The Hague to Lucius.

"I want you to have this, Lucius," he said. "I hope it will help you when you think about The Hague."

Lady felt saddened by Noah's valediction as she and Lucius walked home. Lucius searched the Internet with his phone for "starry shore." The feel of the photo in his other hand divided his thoughts. The photo made him wonder where his father was that night.

* * *

At that moment, Richie was living in Quasipedro, California. *Drone I.V.* fired him when he refused to grant them full rights to his two hits. They asked too late. An agent for the background music industry had already approached Richie at a gig. "Mercy Hospital Blowjob" and "Sex is all there Is" were now heard without titles or words on elevators, in dentist's offices and investment banks. Some versions used Pan Pipes; some featured English horns; some used harpsichords. These soothing arrangements became popular in yoga classes, spas and to a lesser degree, day care centres. Royalties for the dronecult originals had long since dried up. Every melodious background play meant new royalties. Richie could not know how much this rising revenue stream would change the political landscape of Canada.

Richie was content to give up rock tours. He didn't want to die in a strange motel in questionable circumstances. He wanted an ordinary job in Quasipedro. He found work as assistant executive title writer to an executive producer of adult films. Working from the Internet, Richie adapted old, classic titles for random attachment to plotless interchangeable films: *The Grapes of Sex, Sex by Sexwest, The Wizard of Sex, Sexablanca, Sexual Indemnity* and *Citizen Sex.* The producer – whose grandmother was a legend in the industry for coining the 1969 title *Butch Assidy* – was livid to find *The Greatest Sex on Earth* on Richie's list.

"Not only are your titles awful, but most of them come from ancient times. And why do you use the word sex so much? This isn't a gym class, stupid. We don't use terminology here. What the hell is wrong with you?"

"But you said your grandmother won awards for adapting old titles."

"The film wasn't old in 1969, idiot! Look at this one: *There will be Breasts.* What kind of talk is that? Grow up! And what in hell is *Transit of Penis?* Or this one – *Vagincourt?*"

"The first is scientific. The second's a historical battle in a Shakespeare play."

"Is that true? Or is it you ripping off of our Pearl Harbour?"

"What about *Girl Harbour?*"

'Shut up! You don't support the troops. You're a damn phony!"

"No. Agincourt was all too real. Many died."

"Get out! And take your damned little factoids with you. If I find you in this building after fifteen minutes, I'll set the cops on you. My sister dates a cop. Oh yeah! Wipe your laptop clean, asshole! Now!"

So Richie was threatened with the police by a third-rate pornographer. This was surely the lowest point in his life, with the exception of breakfast that morning, when his latest girlfriend, retired pensioner Latrice Bomponce, chided him for his lack of sexual imagination. Latrice waited for her sons, Shaft, aged thirty-four, and Fargo, aged thirty-one, to be seated before beginning her graphic rebuke of Richie.

Richie was not sorry to be fired from his job. He had a bad dream one night after his day's work. He saw a field of healthy young people in orange swimsuits on the far side of a swiftly evaporating bridge. They were smoking, but their cigarettes turned into gun barrels and pill bottles. He asked Latrice to interpret the dream. She charged Richie $100. She said it supported her points about his woeful skills. He was sure she was wrong. The people in the dream seemed real.

As he walked the lonely streets of Quasipedro, he hummed a love song he used to play for Lady. He was no longer certain why he made this journey. He accidentally brushed against a policeman, knocking the officer's headphones askew. The officer threatened to ticket Richie for distracted walking, then replaced his headphones and continued his patrol. Richie sat on the curb. He dabbed a tear from his eye, and studied it on the end of his finger. He saw two faces reflected in the small, salty globe. He let the tear fall through a sewer grate. He imagined lush grass swaying in the soft evening light at Richmond's End, and his family waiting in the doorway with supper ready. Was it time to reach out to Lady and Lucius? In that instant, he decided to leave Latrice and make his way back to Edmonton.

* * *

In Edmonton the next day, Noah and Simeon asked Izzy to invite Lucius over yet again. Izzy was not keen. She did not want to hear the word Hague ever again. She relented, and asked Lucius to the Edmonton Folk Music Festival. At least they would not have to talk much. Lucius came. They all sat on a tarp the natural amphitheatre called the hill. Neon logos of banks and railways traced colourful signatures on tall buildings in the cityscape across the river. They watched the city lights sparkle in the falling dusk as bright candles appeared among people rapt by music.

Izzy was taken with a singer named Jen who sang at the side of the stage while the crew set up for *Free to Be*. She wore a long paisley skirt and had bare feet. Like most folksingers, she explained the history of her song to the audience. This was an old spiritual from the time of the Underground Railroad.

The old man is a-waitin' for

to carry you to freedom

Follow the drinking gourd

The stars in the heavens

Gonna show you the way

Follow the drinking gourd

Izzy shivered with delight at her voice. The words seemed so familiar. She was sure Jen must be papoutsiotic.

Noah and Simeon shared Chardonnay from a red plastic cup as *Free to Be* took the stage. Lucius stared into his e-phone. He refused to be distracted by the music industry. "If a Tree Falls" brought tears to Noah's eyes. Simeon remained critically detached, then recited Hopkins when the song ended:

O if we but knew what we do

When we delve or hew —

Hack and rack the growing green!

Noah narrowed his eyes and nodded, impatient for Simeon to shut up and listen. Izzy enjoyed seeing Noah happy. As the band played "Fascist Architecture," Lucius pretended to receive a text from The Hague. They closed with a rousing rendition of "The Trouble with Normal." Noah and Simeon helped Izzy and Lucius to their feet, and forced them to lock arms and sing the chorus.

On the drive home, Lucius asked Noah about the music.

"Why were you waiting for that group?"

"I thought about becoming a doctor, a dentist, an engineer when I was your age. Cockburn's music made me want to be an environmental scientist. I saw him play three or four times on both sides of the ocean when I was young."

Lucius thought three *or* four was imprecise for a so-called scientist. More evidence of phoniness.

Noah could see that Izzy was souring on Lucius. She no doubt resented her parents pushing a friendship. On the other hand, Lucius's question was a sign of hope. Noah asked Lady Spukwell if he might take Lucius on a hike through the Moss Lake trail.

Lady was grateful. She was certain Lucius needed men in his life. Her elder cousin, Ned Feenie, rarely came to visit anymore. And when he came, he spoke obsessively about his ill-fated political career and the burden of maintaining *Geogasm*, taking little interest in other people's news. Noah was a man worth knowing. Anxious to avoid being called a liar, she said nothing. After two minutes and some improvised hand signals, Noah interpreted her silence as consent.

* * *

The Moss Lake trail was once part of Elk Island National Park. It was an hour east of Edmonton on the Manchester Helmfloss Memorial Fireway, formerly known as the Yellowhead Highway. Prime Minister Juventus Helmfloss, son of the late Prime Minister Manchester Helmfloss, renamed the Yellowhead for his father. Juventus took power in 2025, and promptly privatized all of Canada's national parks and called for foreign investment to develop their wonders. He wanted to repurpose the parks towards their untapped economic potential. Potential at Elk Island meant two identical casinos competing with each other from a distance of fifty metres. Both showed deep cracks on their west side walls from fracking earthquakes.

The park, once a national darkness conservatory, was now host to brash neon lights and giant mirror balls promising 24-hour Texas hold 'em, unlimited slots and "sweet sweet liquor." The casinos shared a musical review to draw customers: "The Rock Stars that Time Forgot."

"It's sad to see these casinos on national park land," Noah said to Lucius.

"What's your objection? Morality?" Lucius asked.

"No. I see them more as symbols. They equate freedom with fracking."

Lucius was baffled. Noah's answer reminded him of Izzy connecting Card Dilbey's oracles to homelessness. The Dryden-Burnets seemed to be a family of non-sequiturs.

Noah followed a deteriorating two-lane road north to Astotin Lake. He pulled on to the shoulder of the road a kilometre before the lake and led Lucius into the bush. He had a compass, and an old trail map. They stood between dense stands of aspens and poplars backed by towering spruces. This narrow gauntlet was the relic of the old Moss Lake Trail.

An old rusty chain strung between two decaying posts blocked the trail. A small sign said, "Warning: No Park Staff." Noah unhooked the chain and threw it aside. They walked for ninety minutes through the long corridors of trees and broader vistas. The lake came into view to their right. Its still waters rested beneath a clouded sky. Charred stumps, remnants from a long ago natural fire, peered above the surface. A beaver dam stood like a silent altar near a dried up inlet. A solitary loon drifted in calm dignity close to the far shore.

"Lunch time!" Noah announced. He unzipped his backpack. Then he threw an orange tablecloth over the flat rock they had been sitting on. He unpacked pita bread and cream cheese and crabapple jelly, green grapes, almonds mixed with raisins and chocolate chips and a thermos of sweet potato soup. He passed his binoculars to Lucius.

"Try to follow that loon up close for a moment, while I set the table."

Lucius scanned the shore through the binoculars. He found it hard to pinpoint the loon. He aimed too high and then too low.

"Let me fix them for you," Noah said. Noah trained the instrument directly onto the loon in an instant. He held the binoculars in place while Lucius placed his eyes on the lenses and took over with his hands. The loon had a handsome black head with a black and white striped collar and patterned back. Its eye was a deep red; its beak was a rich ebony.

"It's a male," Noah said, " a teenager in fact."

"Does he mind us staring at him?" Lucius asked.

"I don't think we're a priority for him," Noah replied.

"Animals don't waste time or energy, except for humans, of course. Isn't it great to be out of the city?"

"Yes," Lucius said. He noticed the chorus of winds rippling through the poplars. A tiny orange flower at the edge of a rock seemed like a human face. He imagined Izzy rising out of the water and coming towards him like a nymph.

"If you're a scientist, you must know a lot about things like evolution or the big bang."

"Things isn't an ideal word, but let's say I'm in favour of finding things out, especially if they help us solve problems. Evolution was probably not looking for us, but it found us, and we found it. Now we like to claim kinship with the big bang. People imagine it as a ball of fire spreading outwards like a nuclear bomb. But I prefer this metaphor. Watch."

Noah dipped his hands in the lake and held some water in his cupped hands. He let all the water drain out, leaving one small drop on his fingertip. "Think of this drop as the universe. It's no bigger than a tear. It's actually enormous in its own way. But imagine it infinitely small, with no space and no time outside it. Imagine all of space and time folded up inside it by some enormous force. A space-time singularity." Noah flicked the drop from his finger into the lake. Faint ripples spread out.

"Not exactly a thermonuclear explosion was it? But where is that drop now?"

"It's gone," Lucius said.

"No, Lucius. It's the lake. All of it."

"How?" Lucius demanded.

"Big bang. Think about it. What part of it is the lake? What part isn't?"

Lucius thought about it. "So if you agree with the big

bang, where did the drop come from?"

"I don't know. It, or we, might have come through a black hole from a parallel universe."

"So can we go back?"

"No more than you can go back into your mother's womb. But all this could happen again."

Lucius decided to ask a question in a scientific tone.

"When did you know you were gay?"

"In real time? Six."

"No way!"

"I'm a scientist. I use my intuition. Sometimes you can see into the past, present or future. That's good science. And my parents helped me manage my fear."

"Fear?"

"Yes. It mustn't master us."

Lucius spread cheese and jelly on a pita. They drank their soup out of reusable cups. A ground squirrel saw crumbs fall. It waved its paws over its head in thanks.

"Why did you pick water?"

"It humbles me. It protects us from the heat of the sun, and it needs our protection, since, unlike other species, we give nothing back to the earth. We even wrap our corpses in nature-resistant boxes or burn them to ashes. I think I'd like my ashes spread on a lake. The elements are like virtues. With fire dominant, the four are out of balance, and water changes from solid to liquid. If we survive, future generations may speak of the fire age as well as the ice age. Our time is an age of fire."

They watched ripples lap the shore. Bugs flickered across

the surface. The earth seemed another sky in the lucid speculum of the lake. Lucius looked over the edge of a rock, and saw his own reflection in the water.

"His eyes fixed on the mirrored image never may know their longings satisfied, and by their sight he is himself undone," Noah said.

"Who said that?" Lucius said.

"Ovid."

"Oh yes. Izzy mentions him. But that's not scientific."

"Isn't it? The eye altering alters all, Blake said."

"Blake? My mom read me some of his biography. He didn't have much of a life."

"Outer or inner, Lucius? His inner life was vast and extraordinary. Remarkable outer lives often spell trouble."

"That's exactly what my mom said."

"She spoke true."

Lucius thought about the water drop while Noah packed up the lunch.

"Come you king of infinite space," Noah shouted when the packing was done. "Let's go home."

* * *

They hiked further up the shore, but the trail became impassable from years of neglect. They turned back to the car. After twenty minutes, they heard a sigh behind a barrier of fallen trees. Noah looked. An aged wood bison lay on his side, breathing and moaning heavily at the end of life. The bison were supposed to be gone. The government sent them to private ranchers and theme parks after the park was cut back.

This lonely creature had somehow survived alone in the woods for years. Noah stroked his head and ear. He was too fatigued to move. Noah saw his reflection mirrored in his gaping eye. He waved silently at Lucius to come and see for himself. Lucius looked. He saw dark fibres and vulnerable whites and fine blood filaments.

Wind blew dust and branches across their path as they reached the car. Lucius covered his face with his jacket. As they drove back to Edmonton, Noah was rapt in silence, and Lucius fell asleep. Noah felt that he had failed Lucius as he drove home. He wanted to out him about The Hague in the car. He was sure Lucius needed to have his walls breached. What better place than the intimacy of a car? Well, there would be another opportunity some time, he imagined.

Lucius awoke at a red light on 109 Street. He would be home in five minutes.

"The bison really shook you up, didn't it?"

"He did, yes."

"Is that what it's like for Izzy?"

"That's a good question. I'd say yes, only much deeper for her. We can't bear too much reality. Izzy has no choice."

They reached the traffic circle. As Lucius got out of the car, Noah saw a blood stain on his left sock.

"Lucius! Why didn't you tell me you were bleeding?"

"New shoes. I didn't mind. Who cares? Thanks," Lucius said, closing the passenger door forcefully and hurrying inside.

* * *

That night, Lucius dreamed about Noah. He waited in the office of the Dean of Science. He had something to report about Noah. He saw a "Wall of Shame" across from the receptionist's desk. The wall was decorated with framed pictures of men and women convicted of being off-message by a "People's Court of Conscience." They wore dunce caps coated with tar and feathers. Two were environmental scientists. One was a participant in a clinical trial on memory loss. One was a laboratory mouse. One was a poet. A ticker tape scroll at the bottom of each screen tweeted their names and offences. A live video feed from The Hague showed the offender's writings burning permanently in an eternal bonfire on the steps of the International Court of Justice. White bison the size of pickup trucks ran rings around the flames.

The receptionist summoned Lucius. A sign on her desk read, "honesty's the right policy." She asked Lucius to state his reasons for being there. Lucius said he had a proposal to change the name of homelessness. Homeless should be errancy; homed would be normalcy.

"That rocks!" the receptionist said, smiling sternly. Then she began to dance and sway, chanting, "homeless is errancy; homed is normalcy homeless is errancy; homed is normalcy homeless is errancy; homed is normalcy homeless is errancy; homed is normalcy!

Lucius woke with a start. He tried to recall his dream. He remembered wanting to report Noah. He held his throat and then rubbed his eyes. The bright red digits on his alarm clock read three a.m. Lucius knew he hadn't reported Noah. It was a dream.

He felt relieved.

He turned on his light. He made some notes about the dream on his computer before it vanished. Then he fed the notes into a word cloud app.

The word cloud appeared:

framed waited

THE HAGUE noticed Dean

complaint Eyes

she receptionist one dreamed lodging

decorated wall university ran

science Noah off green

I *ME* my court

Permanently flames eternal

Bonfire *phony*

offender's steps

It made sense now. The dream was about his future. It was a strategic dream. It told him to stick to The Hague, and don't let Noah or anyone stop you.

As he closed down his laptop, he studied his screen saver image: The International Court of Justice at The Hague. He searched for an image of the Centennial Flame on Parliament Hill in Ottawa, and pasted it on to the base of the court. He selected "animate" for the composite image. The flames swayed, licking the edge of the front steps.

Lucius was pleased with his interpretation. He closed his laptop. He tried to imagine infinite space. He soon fell back to sleep.

Chapter Six

SIX DAYS TO SUCCESS

Edmonton , June 2038

Barry Basewik-Quick was an only child. He moved to Edmonton from Fort McMurray in the summer before grade 12. His parents, Severus Quick and Talia Basewik, provided a shuttle bus service between the two cities and other points north. They called it "Tal's Trolley." Tal's Trolley gave sleep-deprived shift workers, teachers, doctors and volunteer fire fighters safe rides to and from the oil sands to prevent road accidents. The business was losing money.

Barry scanned his new school for friends. He studied Lucius's phone mannerisms from a distance. Lucius held his phone in a tight fist. His face descended onto his screen, his brow knit in concentration. Barry turned his screen outwards to cover the day's news. Lucius held his e-phone like a shield. Barry held his like a catcher's mitt. Barry thought he saw a kindred spirit in Lucius.

At the end of grade 12, Ms. Greenwell announced the "Six Days to Success" internship program for graduating students. She recommended Barry for a six-day internship with the *Edmonton Mercury*. Izzy asked Noah to open his water lab to an intern. He did so gladly. Card Dilbey spent a week with Noah, freed from the pressures of prophecy. Izzy applied to the Edmonton Fringe Theatre Festival. Lucius wanted no part of an internship. He told everyone he would gain plenty of experience at The Hague with his father. Privately, he asked Ms. Greenwell for help. She connected him to the Edmonton branch office of Maplenorman Resources.

Barry was becoming fascinated with election attack ads. His favourite ad showed the opposition leader, on a hot and humid Ottawa day, taking off his tie and unbuttoning his top collar button while leaving his office after twelve long hours of hard work. The ad zoomed in on his fingers unbuttoning his collar. The ad froze the fingers on the final button, then turned the button into a grainy black and white circle that resembled an eye. Then it superimposed the eye on young children playing happily on slides and swings. The children morphed into teen crack addicts and finally into homeless seniors. A narrator's voice warned voters: "The Leader of the Opposition: don't let him finish what he's starting."

A spokeswoman for the governing Solid Retentivist Party defended the ad to reporters in a scrum.

"No, we aren't saying that the leader of the other party is impulsive or irrational, nor do we believe he would ever consider peeing in a courtroom or masturbating in economy class on a plane or bus. By no means. As normal, hardworking parents, still less would we suppose that he delays his orgasm by using cannabis, paint thinner or methylamphedrizone. Nothing of the sort. To the contrary, we're pointing out that

Canada needs leadership. Is the Leader of the Opposition a Leader? You be the judges. Simple and transparent, that's our message."

Barry found the spokeswoman inspiring. He wanted to blend her job with journalism to create a new kind of messaging. And the *Edmonton Mercury* was no place to start, he believed. His *Six Days to Success* mentor was Caleb Timson, the *Mercury's* award-winning columnist on western affairs, and author of a celebrated memoir: *Caleb Timson Reporting*. Barry phoned to introduce himself.

"I'm delighted to take your call, Mr. Basewik-Quick, and very pleased to offer you my full support as your mentor," Timson said warmly. "Now, tell me a bit about your interests in journalism."

"OK. For example, did you see that recent attack ad against the Leader of the Opposition? I think that's state of the art journalism," Barry said.

"The one with malnourished seniors? I have to advise you that what you saw was not journalism. Make no mistake: that was an attack ad, and a nasty one at that!"

"So it looks like we have a difference of opinion – irreconcilable differences, as they say."

"May I quote Milton? 'all opinions, yea errors, known, read, and collated, are of main service and assistance toward the speedy attainment of what is truest.' Disagreement is no bar to working together. It's healthy, in fact. Even so, if you think that ad is journalism, you may not enjoy working with me, and I do want you to enjoy your internship."

"So you're saying we should probably dissolve this contract."

"What? No. I'm more than happy to be your mentor. From what I'm hearing you need to cultivate a more positive attitude, a more mature view of dissent and a more open view of the profession."

"Would you allow the government to use a quotation from you in an attack ad?"

"A political party can by law take anything I write and use it out of context in an attack ad. In my opinion, that law is stupider in practice than conception. I try not to let purloined fragments discourage me or compromise my integrity. But we'll have a good session on ethics when you arrive. I'll organize a *Mercury* roundtable on it while you're here. Our opinion writers will give you a grand tour on that subject. Right now, let's talk basics. At the *Mercury,* we start with objective histories. George Orwell insists that we hold to objective truth, that there is such a thing as history. Hold on to that, Barry! No journalist should be without Orwell on her or his shelf. I'll discuss Orwell with you over a hearty soup and bean salad lunch at the Edmonton Journalists' Mess. You'll be my guest on your first day! Next, we'll analyze sources, details, timelines, and we'll try to interpret their significance for our readers, respectful of their critical judgment. Now we come to the pith and marrow of journalism. I'll show you how to do a first-rate job of research, and how to interview people face to face over at City Hall. Then, we'll go to the Provincial Archives and Public Library for a day's orientation. Those buildings are worth a thousand e-phones to me. Chained to our desks? Not us two! You wait and see."

"Do *Mercury* journalists always take this long to say something?"

"I beg your pardon?"

"Listen, nothing personal, but I'm really looking to switch. Could you just please reject me? I have a form I need you to sign, or just call my teacher if that's easier."

"Is this your idea of success, Mr. Basewik-Quick? Well, not so fast. I haven't rejected you, much as you're begging for it, nor will I reject you. I'm not signing anything, nor will I speak to your teacher."

"OK. Could you tell her I'm working with you while I work somewhere else? I'd owe you one."

"I see. Understand that you alone have terminated this arrangement. Good day to you then. And if I find you've been taping this conversation, I'll bring on the police."

Barry felt cleansed. He now had a green light to contact the *Footman* group on his own. He knew exactly which journalist he wanted to work with: Jonah Flambo, writer of a twice-weekly national column called *Sincerely, Jonah Flambo*, and host of a nationally broadcast TV show called *Jonah Flambo's Tomorrow*. Footman Inc. dubbed the latter show into French and broadcast it under the title, *Jonah: la Menace Chez Nous.*

* * *

Barry hoped Ms. Greenwell wouldn't mind the change of plan. He texted the news to her as a courtesy. He wanted to avoid the unpleasantness of a face-to-face discussion. She had gone to some trouble to enlist Caleb Timson, and was likely to be annoyed. Well, so be it. He was ready to make sacrifices. Barry took the LRT and two buses to reach the *Footman* group offices in the far west end of the city. He met Jonah Flambo on a rainy May Monday morning.

"Welcome to *The Edmonton Footman*, Mr. Quick," Flambo exclaimed. "Do I call you Basewik? Or Base for short, I assume. Yes, of course I do."

Barry chose not to correct Flambo on his name. He was in awe. Flambo didn't offer Barry his hand. Instead, he clasped his hands imperiously behind his head. He walked solemnly around his office as he spoke, stopping occasionally to study the line of cars passing through a burger drive-thru across the street. His elevated elbows made him look like an inverted eggbeater. Some old perspiration stains on his underarms resembled the annual rings on an elm tree. The stains showed he'd paid his dues, Barry decided.

"So you think you might like journalism? Well, you're in the deep end here, believe me. Did you know that I have two thirds of my degree in pharmacy from the U of A? And here I am. Pharmacy and journalism aren't so very different if you see them objectively. Both thrive on finance. Both give people what they need for their day. Human body; body politic. It was pharmacy that tweaked my decision to go into journalism. Pills fix things fast. So do I. *Footman* began as a subsidiary of a drug chain. You didn't know that? Well, I'm not ashamed of it! If you like shame, the door is over there. We turn the power of shame on our enemies. And you know who they are, correct?"

"A spectrum of various kinds?" Barry ventured.

"Eco-terrorists!" Flambo thundered. "And spare me the sociology. We have MP's and MLA's, city and federal bureaucrats, teachers and students, and even tradesmen and retail sector workers who are soft on eco-terrorism. I've met waiters who are squeamish. Don't start me."

Flambo paused. For Barry, it felt like the pause dental hygienists permit for a swallow or a spit.

"We don't have jobs here," Flambo divulged. "We have a mission. And your first mission is simple: Caleb Timson is printing tons of stats and historical info in his pieces. Elitist bastard. Not that it matters: I'm the one talking straight goods to the Canadian people. I gather my news from live human experts. I observe what I see. Still, where does he get his shit from?"

"Research?" Barry asked, tentatively.

Flambo rolled his eyes. "That's slow. The Canadian people are in a hurry. News is a sprint not a marathon. Are you a sprinter?"

"I once covered a car accident fast with my phone. It happened one afternoon – ."

"Uh-huh. So you do understand me. Good. Now, I want you to infiltrate Timson – and fast. You know, gain his confidence. Maybe even be a mole intern." Flambo turned to the window and paused. "Did you know that I'm one year younger than Timson? That's right! He's 53. I think it bothers him."

Barry nodded.

"Are you aware that most *Footman* journalists despise me?" he asked.

"No," Barry said. In fact, Barry was aware of this. Serious *Footman* reporters saw Flambo as a pampered flake. They doubted his claim to have worked undercover to subdue a ring of eco-terrorists. Above all, they resented his claim to be the author of over thirty books. Flambo relished his colleagues' resentments. He said it put "daylight" between his journalism and theirs.

"Well, ignore them and they won't bother you. Have you read my books?"

The average length of a Flambo book was eighteen pages. People could read them for free online after enrolling with a secure password and pseudonym.

"I've read the best-seller posted on your web site."

"Which one?"

"*The Terrorist Terrorized, or a necessary unmasking of the scope and intent of environmental lobbying in our most exalted legislative assembly of Alberta, with thoughts appended on how best to deal with the perfidy of lobby.*"

"Good choice."

"Question, sir," Barry said. "What made you to decide to have really long titles and really short books? I ask out of emulation, of course."

"Short?" Flambo hissed. "Remember: interns come and go."

Flambo nodded towards a photograph above his couch. It showed him shaking hands with a stout gentleman with some kind of manservant standing beside him. The autograph was indecipherable. It appeared to say "Lassooc" or "Loodoz." Barry was losing his taste for asking questions. Lassooc would do.

"Me receiving the Consultant's Choice Award." Flambo tapped his own nose until Barry's eyes returned to him.

"Let them have their precious 'research,'" he said, wiggling his fingers to form quotation marks. "I talk straight goods to the Canadian people. And be warned: I never forget a face. Final questions?"

"If I may – why did they call the chain *Footman*?"

Flambo glowered at Barry with fierce pity: "Get your co-cubicle assignment from the receptionist. And keep your voice down out there."

* * *

On the first day of his internship, Lucius reported to Maplenorman Resources in a blue suit and tie. The company's motto was emblazoned in gold letters on a marble wall:

"Resourcefully Canadian." The receptionist invited Lucius into the office of Tim "Buzz" Nussdob, the Assistant Operating Officer, for his first briefing.

"Hello boy! Welcome to six days of honest work!" Nussdob beamed, throwing his meaty hand towards Lucius like a Frisbee. "Now boy, can I assume that you know all about our company by virtue of interweb research? Six days is a short time, and I want to get as much as I can from you. Needless to say, you will benefit in every conceivable way. Well?"

Lucius nodded, unsure of the question.

"Green light then? I like that! OK – here's the buzz."

Maplenorman and the government had signed a memorandum of intent to form productive partnerships in the areas of culture, heritage, history and memory. According to a government survey, Canadians had long dreamed of having a National Portrait Gallery similar to those in London and Washington. But where to put it? Absolutely *not* in Ottawa. Advocates argued that a portrait gallery should be located in the nation's capital, like those in London and Washington. Canadians should come to Ottawa. There, they could meet people from different parts of this vast country, and enjoy the gallery in each other's company. The Prime Minister bitterly opposed this kind of thinking.

"The PM is right," Nussdob scowled. "Put the gallery in Ottawa? Nothing doing. That's an elitist approach. Let the elites run some other country into the ground if they want. Ottawa has too long been favoured to the dismay of the rest of Canada. Our polls show it lowers nationwide morale and makes us less mindful. Why should people have to go there to see stuff? What? No choices? And no, the decision shouldn't be left to politicians other than the PM. No, boy – Ottawa's time is up. I'm making you a key staffer in this project. Your title will be *Assistant Fixer*."

Maplenorman owned one hundred and seven eighteen wheel tractor-trailer trucks. Nussdob assigned one for use as a roving National Portrait Gallery. He wanted to gauge public reaction to anywhere but Ottawa in random focus groups. So Lucius drove around the outskirts of Edmonton with Maxime Baxter, the chief driver and chief fixer for Maplenorman

Resources. They rolled the big white rig onto driving ranges at dusk, preferring private to public golf courses whenever possible. After dark, with floodlights, they assembled huge wooden easels that displayed portraits of nine influential Canadians hand picked by the government: Barbara Ann Scott, Isaac Brock, Laura Secord, Billy Bishop, John A. MacDonald, Lorne Green, Juliette, the Famous Five and Manchester Helmfloss. Max called it a "strategic corporate insurgency partnership," or *SCIP*. He pronounced it "ship" in order to "orally encrypt" the strategy.

"Aren't the Famous Five five people?" Lucius asked.

"Shut it!" Baxter seethed. "Fixing is all about action, not talk."

Maplenorman did not intend mobile displays to be the National Portrait Gallery. No – this insurgency was designed to *test* locations other than Ottawa with "multiple and diverse focus groups." What could be more diverse than a private golf course? Max asked. The final result, based on whatever feedback focus groups provided, was to house the gallery in the lobby of Maplenorman Resources' head office. For its part, the government would supply Maplenorman Resources with a new corporate tower with an elite gallery wing, and an annual operating subsidy, including full salary for a corporate curator.

Max and Lucius left the portraits up all day, out of the range of the best golfers. Lucius found the job left time to kill.

"When did you join Maplenorman?" Lucius asked Max as they drove. Max reached across to the glove compartment and pulled out a tattered Europorn magazine.

"I don't want to see you until noon," he bellowed, throwing the magazine at Lucius. Lucius left the magazine in the cab and watched the golfers from the shade of a maple tree, sipping a can of diet cola. Max tried to engage golfers in conversation about a possible National Portrait Gallery. They preferred golf.

At the end of the day, Baxter and Lucius packed the portraits up and moved to a new range.

* * *

Late one afternoon, Baxter and Lucius closed the gallery early under duress. Billy G. Alvarez, a celebrity professional distance driver touring the ranges, was hitting massive drives towards the portraits. Local golfers attending his distance clinic clapped politely when he punctured Sir John A's necktie. Max was furious. He circled Alvarez with his fists raised, daring him to damage another portrait.

"I'll fix you, you elite bastard!" Max screamed. He ducked and feinted, daring Alvarez to come to grips. Alvarez yawned, performed two shallow knee bends, and flexed his lengthy driver over his head like a riding crop, demonstrating its whip. Max abandoned the challenge.

"Let's haul ass out of here, kid," Max ordered, "before he turns Laura's blouse into Swiss cheese."

They loaded the truck and took the Anthony Henday Drive back to the city.

"Well, kid, you just came face to face with what the boss calls an elite."

"Alvarez? The sign says he's from New Mexico."

"Elite golfer! Quiet till you're spoken to!"

Lucius kept silent for the next twenty minutes.

"OK kid," Max said at a red light. "I'm supposed to ask if you've got any questions."

Lucius thought carefully about whether to ask his question. He knew it could be a waste of time.

"I was impressed by the way you offered battle to Alvarez," Lucius began.

"On guard for thee, kid," Max replied.

"Thanks. And yet here we are, in retreat. So, I was thinking we could take over the range in smaller increments. You know, plant a portrait one day, and let people get used to it. Plant another a day later. Before long, people would think the portraits had always been there. Also, increments would make people see how hard we work. It gives the impression that set up is a long process. Has Maplenorman given any thought to an incremental set up?"

"Duh – NO!" Max replied, biting firmly into the corner of a dusty brick of orange process cheese he seized from the glove compartment while waiting for the light to change. "And no more smartass questions," he added, through cheese-garbled teeth. "You should be asking about duty to country. Shape up, listen up, shove your dumbass questions up your smartass ass, call back to duty when she calls to you, and maybe – just maybe – you'll grow up to be a fixer."

"Will they add more portraits soon?" Lucius asked. "Eight seems limited."

"SCREW OTTAWA!" Max bellowed, with half a mind to kick Lucius out of the cab. He smacked Lucius's arm with the porn magazine.

Lucius kept his own counsel for the rest of the internship. The conversation was useful. He liked to think of himself and Max as curators. That would look good on a c.v. And the term fixer was growing on him.

* * *

Izzy joined the Edmonton Fringe Festival administration for a week. The festival took place in late August, but organizing this world-renowned event was a year-round job.

Day one: the Festival Director, Diana Bergen set Izzy to work thinking up catchy titles for the Fringe.

"We usually work with titles of classic movies, or familiar songs," the Director explained. "But unleash your imagination. Think outside the box, Izzy."

"How about 'Thinking Outside the Fringe'?" she answered.

"We'll check with you at noon."

Izzy roved the Internet, reaching back eighty years for adaptable titles: *Citizen Fringe; Fringe Side Story; Goldfringer; The Fringe on the River Kwai; The Great Fringeby, There Will Be Fringe.*

"Delightful!" Diana exclaimed. "Rank these, Andy, if you will." He handed the list to her assistant, Andy Caster who placed them in a brown envelope.

* * *

Day two: Diana made Izzy Special Assistant, Boyle-McCauley Neighbourhood Festival Liaison. The priest at St. Anne's Anglican Church had applied to the Fringe to put on a play. St. Anne's was on 96 Street on the north side of the river. Diana welcomed the prospect of a new north side production.

"You'll be an ardent fringer someday, Izzy. A new generation as it were. Scout it out with Andy – let us know how you feel about the venue and the plan. We need to know how it looks to generation Izzy."

"Generation Fringe!" Izzy replied, inhaling the praise like incense.

Andy nodded respectfully. He found Izzy's ideas for names jejune, a word that often appeared to him in his dreams. He could see Diana wasn't simply stoking Izzy's self-esteem. She really liked Izzy's titles. This worried Andy, but he was pleased Izzy had more ideas than their last intern. That intern managed only two titles: *Fringe is all there is* and *Mercy Hospital Fringejob.*

"Give me your e-phone number," Andy asked Izzy. "I may need to text you cues and prompts."

"I don't use an e-phone," Izzy said.

"What? You have a clone?"

"No."

"A knockoff?"

"No."

"Look – it's fine with me if your phone was 'borrowed.' Was it?"

"No. I have a phone, but it's somewhere at home. I don't know where."

"Well, do you have Mouthtalk?"

"No. My watch is a family heirloom."

"Faceview, eyespace, uslink?"

"No."

"Nosetime? Earplus? Mouthforce?"

"No, none of those. Sorry."

"Mibraine?"

Izzy shook her head.

"How the hell do you communicate?"

"I have an aquarium!"

"What? Is that an app?"

"It's a fish tank, full of water and fish. It's the most relaxing thing to stare at. Nice light. Real fish."

"Alright, forget it. A phone would be a distraction on Church Street. You'll be dealing with people who have no e-phones, except for the priest. Borrow his in an emergency. I'll handle Diana."

* * *

Day 3: Andy and Izzy drove to their meeting on 96th street. Edmontonians called it Church Street because of its many and varied houses of worship all concentrated in a five-block span. It was vital to the life and heritage of the inner city. There were Buddhists and Lutherans, Chinese Pentecostals and Ukrainian Catholics, and shelters and missions, and the great red brick Church of the Sacred Heart. Widened for the sake of parking, the street had a breadth that few back streets in Edmonton possessed. Andy noticed that one church had closed since the last Fringe. It now housed a law office and a Quaker reading room. Izzy observed the diversity of architectures lining both sides of the street. She imagined that all of the churches were shoes to mix and match.

She saw a group of men on the sidewalk through the passenger window.

"See any bottles?" asked Andy.

"Wine's very expensive," Izzy replied. She remembered a rhyme by Hopkins Simeon liked: "nor can foot feel, being shod." Their old brown boots once stood on construction sites. Their frayed, laceless sneakers once sprinted.

Then the men noticed her looking at them through the window. They waved and shouted "good morning!" The Hopkins blew up in her face.

"This is us," Andy said after parking the car.

When they stepped onto the sidewalk, Izzy realized she had been watching the street through the thick shell of the car. Now she felt intrusive, exposed, vulnerable to invisible connections she could only feel around her. No words came. No quotation prepared her. No poet could matter here if she hadn't breathed in this place. An old man in bright pink runners walked by carrying a rusty bicycle frame with one wheel. "Good morning!" he sang. He parked his bike at the health centre, where many people were smoking, chatting and waiting.

St. Anne's was a converted Thai restaurant. The parish was one hundred and one years old. The original church burned down on the night of Tuesday, December 1, 2037, when a sleep-deprived trucker bringing a load of diet soda to a downtown casino crashed into the front door. The sodas burst into flames. Bethlehem Lutheran Church offered St. Anne's interim worship space as the community faced rebuilding. Then they realized that they really wanted a full-service street-ready neighbourhood kitchen. So they took over the restaurant. The balance of the insurance money bought two in-from-the-cold mobile food trucks, which they named Raphael and Michael. Each truck had well-stocked kitchens and cracked windshields.

They built ten pews out of donated wood and kept three cozy dining booths for ambience. The altar was the former bar. A simple pine cross with colourful banners replaced the mirror-backed shelves of booze behind the bar. The banners depicted two images from Revelation: the Woman Clothed with the Sun and the Water of Life. A simple white altar cloth covered the altar. Two guitars stood on stands in a corner. A scratched cello lay on its side. The priest's office and coffee space were in a former storeroom at the back.

The priest, Nick Gidding, greeted them warmly at his office door. He was tall with thinning brown hair and dark, lively eyes. He wore a red plaid shirt and blue jeans, a clerical collar and a tweed flat cap.

"This restaurant's too small for a venue," Andy said.

"It's not a restaurant," Gidding replied. "Our Lutheran friends will lend us their hall. We'll provide the performance."

He invited them into his office. A pot of stale black coffee held in place by a bowl of powdered whitener sat on a hot plate. There were coffee rings on old service leaflets. Framed but frayed Eichenberg etchings hung on the wall: Christ of the Homeless; Christ of the Breadline. The quality was poor because they came out of Gidding's antiquated laser printer. Sharper versions were lost in the fire. Blake's "Glad Day," frayed badly at the corners, offered a big bang of colour in one corner. A worn desk was pressed against the wall beneath the picture. A gold communion cup singed by the fire and a wicker breadbasket with a linen cloth inside rested on its pine surface. Sounds of ground beef frying in oil and smells of herbs and tomatoes came from the kitchen where people were cheerfully preparing a vat of chili.

Gidding introduced his assistant, Barney, a seventy-nine year old volunteer. Barney wore an Oilers cap. Sitting beside Barney was a younger man, perhaps in his late twenties. He wore a rumpled green hunting shirt over a torn black t-shirt. A fly danced on his knee. He had a mane of jet-black hair tied in a short ponytail and thickened by infrequent washing. What made him seem different from the men on the sidewalk, Izzy wondered? His shoes? He wore firm but aging Kodiaks. His hair? No. Then she understood. It was resolute posture. His body language expressed no remorse, regret or failure of any kind. His green eyes blazed with kindness, confidence and courage. The aged clothes suggested that he should smell bad. He didn't. Izzy smelled cinnamon and spikenard and aloes and cedar and pomegranates reeking out of his trousers, especially his crotch.

"Andy, Izzy, permit me to introduce the man behind

our proposal," Gidding said. "Our executive producer, if you will. This is Jesseman Hexamer, a member of our community,"

"Jazzman?" Andy asked.

"No. Jess–see–man. Just call me Jesse." He rolled his eyes when Gidding named him executive producer.

"We're pleased to meet you Jesse," Andy said. "So you're the producers. Is it springtime for Church Street?"

"That's not funny," Barney said.

"Do you live around here?" Andy asked Jesse.

"Yes. I don't believe in the separation of church and street," Jesse replied. "You might say I'm an urban Erastian."

Andy thought he said Rasta man.

Gidding asked Jesse to begin the meeting with a short prayer for the success of the project.

"Creator Spirit, beautiful upon the mountains are the feet of your messengers," Jesse prayed. He then translated and pronounced the same twelve words in Hebrew, Cree, Mandarin, French and Ukrainian.

"Amen. Thanks, Jesse," Reverend Gidding said, "Now – to the agenda."

Jesse was creating a show called "Other Voices." The voices of street people often heard as intrusive solicitations or babbling manipulations are often not so, he explained. Many are oracular fields of light and darkness, praise and lament, if people listen. Jesse wanted to present three of the best street voices he knew. One spoke two languages. One spoke English that was hard to follow because of poor oral health. One was very quiet. Jesse would interpret their voices for the benefit of Edmontonians. Gidding assured Andy and Izzy that Jesse was more than qualified. He could speak at least six languages at any given moment.

"Jesse and I drive around on freezing nights in the church van," Gidding explained. "We work with police and other groups, trying to find homeless who are caught in a huge freeze and get them to safety. Jesse is like a deacon to me. He wouldn't like that, but it's true – deacon of the street. I've seen him speak in different languages to people who are close to freezing. It helps to bring them back from the edge, or coax them into the van. One night at about two in the morning, I saw Jesse pick up a big grown man and carry him like a baby. He died in the ambulance. But he got to hear Cree again right when he left this world."

Jesse frowned disapproval.

"Two in the morning is one thing, in the deep of a winter night. My talent is less valued in daylight," Jesse said. "If I speak three or four languages on the corner in daylight, especially in summer or fall, people tell me to go home, sober up, or get a job: cherchez un employ; znajdź pracę; Tìm kiếm một công việc."

Izzy and Andy let the words ring in their ears.

"Who'll write the script?" Andy asked.

"There'll be no written script as such," Gidding said. "You see, we prefer that –"

Jesse waved Gidding off. "Nick is trying kindly to cover my ass, as you say in English. The truth is, I can neither read nor write."

"What?" Andy gasped. "You speak six languages and you're illiterate?"

"Shalom, amen, it is so," Jesse beamed.

"We don't say illiterate here any more," Gidding added.

"Alright then," Andy decided. "Speak a dead language to me. Speak Latin."

"Latin isn't a dead language," Jesse replied.

"Well pick one then."

"That would be like picking an extinct flower. When they're gone, they're gone."

"I guarantee that Jesse is multilingual," Gidding said firmly.

A homeless guy? How is that even possible, Andy thought to himself? But if it's true, should a performance make a big deal out of his multilingualism to draw crowds? Or not?

"Not," said Jesse, reading Andy's mind. "We're an ensemble. If you play up my limitations, it will be like inviting people to see the world's tallest man or a contortionist. Try to relax. We call ourselves the *Infiltranslationers*. We work through mnemonic oral corporeality – body language and memory. Call it whatever you like. The name of our show tells it all: 'Other Voices.'"

"Hmm, I see," said Andy, his eyes narrowing. "Oh, and Guten tag, by the way?"

"Eine kleine blume ist das werk des alters," Jesse replied softly.

While the men discussed their ideas, Izzy carefully placed her right foot against Jesse's Kodiaks. She knew he would not feel it in such thick boots. A dark tree with stone fruit put roots down into her brain. Rough hands chained the tree to the back of a truck. The truck ripped it out and dragged it down a paved road. The road stripped away the outer branches of the tree, revealing bloodshot eyes on twisted boughs. The tree cried out in pain. When the tree caught fire, the sky opened and she and Jesse and Izzy stood on a beach watching stars with bright human faces fall into a dark, peaceful, healing lake. How could he stand it, she wondered.

Driving back, Andy expressed doubt about Jesse. "Such bullshit. Nobody can speak six languages and be a total illiterate."

"They don't say illiterate," Izzy replied.

"Well, pardon me – for being your supervisor! I want you to check this guy Hexamer out. He's got to be a phony."

"He doesn't like attention. And I'm sure he's not a phony."

"Check him out! Check him out!" said Andy, his knuckles whitening on the steering wheel.

"Fine," she said. She was glad.

Diana was comfortable with the production plan and the venue at Bethlehem Lutheran. She agreed that Izzy should return to Church Street, but not for Andy's reasons.

"Andy is a nervous soul," she explained to Izzy alone in her office. "He brought me a printout of 'Idiot Savant' from *Wikipedia* just a moment ago. Rule one: no snooping or prying. Build relationship. That's your mission."

* * *

Day Four: Andy drove Izzy back to St. Anne's.

"Diana won't always be Director," Andy mused. "You and I both know that. Some say the succession will fall to me. What can I say? There's talk around the office. I'm sure of it."

"This is a one-way street," Izzy snapped. "You're going the wrong way!"

Andy braked hard and turned into the nearest alley.

Eventually they reached the church.

"Thanks for the lift!" Izzy said, shutting the door firmly.

She sat down to a lunch of gherkins and bologna prepared by Barney. The members of Jesse's troupe attended: Madge Three, Samson Gleau and Johnny Bizck.

"Madge only whispers," Jesse explained. "She's Cree. Some asshole of a john raped her, beat her up years ago. Left her with about 10% vision in her right eye. Bastard pierced her eardrum with a screwdriver. Wrecked her plumbing too. For Madge, everything hurts down there now. And they never caught him. Johnny has mild Tourette's, so you have to be patient. To understand him, just relax and mind the gaps. Samson is eloquent, but his need for quiet is deeper. He's a navy vet with a business degree, but he ended up on the street because he's allergic to blue light. Seriously allergic. That's why he's always wearing sunglasses. He'd have been prime minister if it wasn't for that allergy. He talks with his face. You just have to listen. You have to put in the time."

"How do you know so many languages? Izzy asked.

"First, thanks for not asking if I'm an idiot savant. I've had specialized doctor savantistas, as I call them, push and poke and pinch me, all hoping to prove otherwise. One guy wanted a biopsy of the roof of my mouth. No thanks."

"When you were a child?"

"Secondly, thanks for asking if I was ever a child. It's hard to see us as former children down here. We didn't come out of flying saucers. The languages? OK. It started when I was fourteen. I went to a friend's Bar Mitzvah and heard the Cantor read, and I didn't need any translation. By the third reading, I just knew what he was singing. 'How beautiful on the mountains are the feet of those who bring good news!' It was like a poem made out of rain falling right on my face. I thought it was normal for everybody. But I kept it to myself. Soon I knew it was just me. And people would think I was abnormal."

Jesse paused.

"Later, when I was nineteen, I had a girlfriend whose parents were from Ukraine. They didn't like me much until I started talking Ukrainian to them. They loved me after that. I thought I might become a UN linguist. You know, a translating specialist. I supposed I'd get straight A's at the U in all the languages, even Greek and Coptic. Maybe be the first non-Catholic homeless Pope. But I had a deeper secret: I can't write. All these languages only come from my mouth when I'm face to face with people. Maybe I lost my writing ability, or maybe never had it. Or it dumped me, or it didn't need me. I can't text. I can't type. I came down here of my own free will. I talked on curb lips and in the mouths of alleys. People said I was drunk, especially during morning rush hour."

"Could it be lingualosis?" Izzy asked. "Maybe *Macpherson's* Lingualosis?"

"Macpherson's a dick," Jesse snapped. "He couldn't prove anything and he still tried to get famous off me. How do you know him?"

Izzy explained Macpherson's Papoutsiosis.

"Is that why you put your feet on my boots yesterday?"

Izzy's face turned crimson. He patted her hand to comfort her.

"You're lucky you didn't get inside my shoes. You might have lost more than your literacy, I can tell you. You might have lost your mind."

"I don't think so," she said.

"Alright. I believe you. But people like you and me have to exercise judgment. Especially you. I'm used to my situation.

You're still new, but you're getting older. You're pushing twenty, right? Your world is getting bigger."

"Why does it hurt?" she asked.

Jesse put his hand on her shoulder. "On account of the planet. This is a beautiful planet, with lots of life just being alive. When it comes to humans, though, this planet is a pain sink. Most planets are empty, with lots of still not-yet-humanized rocks and faceless gases, some red dust. They probably left a burger on the moon. Earth is one of maybe six pain sinks in the universe in my estimation. That's why people keep drilling into her. And it never goes well. They say they're looking to boost life quality, but deep down they really want to drain their pain, or blow it up. Sure, they work hard to minimize net pain, which they call 'environmental impact.' They just don't always get what they're doing. So this is a pain sink, maybe the first, maybe the third or fourth. I hope it's the sixth and last. And you and I are sitting on the drain. When water reaches the drain, it speeds up, right? It swirls, it blurs, morphs. Sound familiar?"

"Yes!"

"I thought you'd understand. And when the water speeds up it takes on more energy until it disappears into the drain. Take tap water, for example. Tap water gets filled with crap, then goes for shit, piss, speed, condom, pasta and valium cleaning at Gold Bar. Gold Bar doesn't hoard water; it cleans it. We don't know where our soul water goes. It's hard on people like you and me. It's less hard on others. They get more of the still waters. It takes faith. Pain is local. Suffering is big picture stuff. We're the sort that can't live inside the ratio of things. We're on the extreme edge of having to care. We're the real extremists, not those hooded assholes with guns. We process those dark visions. We do an important job in the spiritual ecosystem, and we don't cause pain. Often it's totally horrible. Many times it's a gift. It helps to know someone in a similar condition. So we've got each other, if that's any help to you."

"It helps a lot." Izzy struggled with his explanation. It sounded technical and poetic at the same time. She thought of her encounters with other people's shoes as a moment – a pulsation of an artery. The pressure builds, then drops. Time expands, then shrinks. Her brief moments were made of whole lives. She supposed Jesse's moments were made of centuries, epochs, days and years. But what could she call it? Maybe there was no name for his job.

"I like the name *Infiltrationers,"* she said.

"It's *Infiltranslationers.* We almost called ourselves *The Four Daughters of God,* but Samson thought it would stop us from adding more people. I disagreed – the more the better – but I prefer *Infiltranslationers* anyways."

Izzy finished her lunch, and visited with Madge, Samson and Johnny for an hour with the help of Jesse's translation skills.

* * *

Day 5: Izzy went to Fringe headquarters. Diana asked her to write a report on her activities. She headed home to work on it. Andy walked her to the door.

"Good work," he whispered. He handed her a copy of the *Bargain Finder.* There was a short advertisement in the lower left corner of a page he had circled in red: "Help with Verbal Syndromes. Don't suffer in silence. Fee negotiable. Call Dr. Macpherson's Communication Therapy Centre."

At home, she gave the *Bargain Finder* to Simeon to recycle. She sat down to write her report. Day 6 would be her final debriefing. She didn't put Jesse's name in her title. He wouldn't want that. She used the title of Jesse's theatre troupe: *The Infiltranslationers.*

* * *

Barry knew he had burned his bridges with Caleb Timson. So he spent day 2 in a doughnut shop crafting his first lie: security around Caleb Timson was too tight. When he tried to breach security, Timson's goons threw him out. Flambo wasn't surprised to hear this. It confirmed his suspicions about Timson.

"To hell with Timson," Flambo decided. "Let's out some bastards instead."

"Out?"

"Correct. One thing always trumps research in good journalism – a good outing. Investigative journalists like me probe beneath the surface. We rip the surface off like a bandage. Let's do this thing."

Flambo heard rumours of a family in Victoria that was sponsoring refugees. The father was an emergency room physician. The mother was a professor at a Christian college. Photos showed the couple, their children, some students and two refugees blocking traffic on Belleville Street to protest land development on Haida Gwai. Police arrested the mother for lying down on the road in front of a bus.

Sincerely, Jonah Flambo blared the headline: "Warm Welcome – MATS!" Flambo was livid to think that refugee sponsorship was fertile ground for eco-terrorist recruitment.

Flambo expected flak. He ordered Barry to dig in for a counter e-insurgency surrounding the article for the remainder of his internship. Coordination would be easy; Barry was the only person involved. But could he lead? The insurgency had offensive and defensive components. Offensively, Barry would register as a commenter on all news sites carrying reaction to the story. Barry received secret "code gold" status as a *Footman* commenter. He would monitor reaction to *Sincerely, Jonah Flambo* throughout the week. He would congratulate and "like" those who agreed with Jonah, and hose down dissenting voices with sarcasm. Flambo gave Barry fifty valid e-mail addresses for both purposes, which allowed him to register under fifty different pseudonyms.

"Make up good pseudonyms. Start now."

Barry began to work on pseudonyms: Voice0fthePeople99; Jonahr0cks!; Truthwill0ut; Truth13bomb; WTF?terror; dingleberry101; Strafingrun12; culvertman1a; Fottawa24; Harriet257. Seventeen of his pseudonyms, including "notrudo74" and "Ftxes91," turned out to belong to other readers.

Barry opened the *Footman* comments section and logged on as Harriet257:

Harriet257: What's wrong with new Canadians learning about dissent?

Jacuzziboy: @Harriet257: Fine! Let them block your car on your way to work. If you even work! Get out of your parents' basement why don't you?

Harriet257: I'm 57 years old. I have grandchildren. Look: protest is citizenship, not terrorism.

Sockpencil18: @Harriet257. Why are you reading this news site if you're such a bleeding heart butter-turd? Read one that agrees with your BS and leave us alone.

ruleoflaw77: @Sockpencil18B: You rock! The only clean environment is their brainwashed brains. Rock it Jonah!

Jackielong22: Harriet is right, bozos. Flambo is throwing gas and a match on this story. Wise up.

Jacuzziboy: @Jackielong22: Tell it to yourself! Make yourself useful. Pour acid in their gas tank while they're out protesting unless your bestfriends with them. Oh wait, they don't even speak English.

Jackielong22: 2 Jacuzziboy: Correct English: "unless you're best friends." Proofread young man!

Barry logged off as "Harriet257," satisfied that he had stirred up some Jonahphiles. He pressed "like" under all comments attacking Harriet. He repeated the sequence six times using different pseudonyms. And so this continued every day for six days. His internship ended. He hoped that Jonah might invite him for a windup lunch. Jonah had only one final request.

"I want you to log back on and tell Harriet257 she's full of shit."

"The moderator will remove it."

"Yes, but not for two hours. Remember: you're my intern. *Mine.* Tell her, Barry. Now."

Barry complied using a new pseudonym.

He took the bus home to Crescentdale with no farewell from Jonah Flambo. His head was spinning with ideas. Could he apply all that he had learned as an intern to the life of his local community? Yes! He would set up a blog. *Sincerely, Barry Basewik-Quick?* No – that was plagiarism. He chose *Barry, Out and About.*

* * *

Izzy looked for a summer job somewhere near Church Street. She became a skate lacer at a summer hockey camp near the arena. Lucius took a job at one of the driving ranges he had visited during his internship. He enjoyed driving around alone in an impregnable vehicle, vacuuming up balls, daydreaming, ignoring golfers who deliberately fired shots at him. Barry spent his summer in the bushes. He roamed Crescentdale taking videos and photos for *Barry, Out and About.* He left flyers in the bakery and community centre. The site was free, if anyone cared to look.

No one subscribed. Barry did not have the skills to put up a pay wall, or the money to pay for one. He needed subscribers for revenue. Simeon sent him a hard copy letter in fountain pen. He said he would be glad to review poetry for the blog, particularly oral poetry or found poetry. Frustrated, Barry applied to appear on *Businessaurus Rexes* to get seed money for his venture.

His pitch was simple. He proposed installing "video access features" in the one place they were still notably absent: porta-potties. He was surprised when he was chosen. He lied to his parents when he went to the downtown studio. They did not know about his blog.

Barry waited anxiously at the top of the stairs while the B-Rexes listened to the first pitch. A massive, bald, heavily tattooed man in a black t-shirt sought franchising expertise for his mobile emporium. He offered tattoos, body piercing and vasectomies in the privacy of his van. Purchase any two services – get a third free. He had one van on the road. He wanted fifty. He was summarily banished. His lower lip trembled – whether in rage or to salvage dignity wasn't certain – as he passed Barry on the way out. Barry took a deep breath and walked down the stairs. The four B-Rexes smirked compassionately.

"Good evening, B-Rexes," Barry said. "What do you enjoy most about an evening in a bar or a restaurant? Is it the food, the conversation, the atmosphere? Let's be honest. Your main experience is the bank of five, six or even seven large LED TV screens arranged around the room. You can focus on sports, news, stock prices, or all three at once while you're eating and drinking with friends or family. Where can you not do this? On the toilet: especially at special events. Introducing portablog! Enjoy the comforts of video while in the porta-potty at the Folk Festival, Big Valley Jamboree, Interstellar Rodeo, or anywhere potties are on duty."

"Let's see it," snapped one B-Rex.

"You can't. You have to imagine it," Barry said.

"How does it work?"

"Simple. Your investment will place pre-programmed e-phones in all porta-potties. The phones will be secured to the walls by those curly tungsten lines used for bicycle locks, making theft impossible. They'll be set permanently to my personal blog: *Barry, Out and About.* A captive audience! However, people will be able to see the stock ticker, sports scores and celebrity news headlines in words running across the bottom of the screen at all times. Best of all, you B-Rexes get to be code platinum sponsors. Every phone you sponsor will have your picture on it."

"Why aren't you aiming higher? Five star hotels, for example?"

Barry's eyes widened.

"Have you discussed this with the Folk Fest people?" a second B-Rex asked.

"No."

"If this proves popular, people will stay in the porta-potty for half an hour or more. Lineups will swell. Gravity doesn't care if it pushes piss or paint. Anarchy could ensue. What then?"

Barry winced.

"Have you patented the name Basewik? I assume that'll be the brand name of your laxative."

"Not at the present time," Barry said, squirming.

A fourth B-Rex intervened.

"Do you not suppose people might prefer to use their own e-phones in the facility?" she remarked. "Properly tethered to a safety line, of course. You might have done better to propose a wrist handle for the e-phone. Or perhaps a strong adhesive implant on the human palm, like Velcro. If it's a surgical procedure, it might be possible to patent it. Why not market surgical implants for e-phones for use in potties, on cliff faces, or while skydiving?"

"Because I want them to read my blog."

Three of the B-Rexes shook their heads and dropped out. A fourth said she was "out and about," and giggled. The fifth, silent until now, gathered his thoughts solemnly.

"Bowel evacuation is a moment of supreme intimacy for our species, whether it is manifested as pride or shame or simple indifference. And do I understand you correctly? You want to profit from it? I think you should be made to watch a video of a dog defecating 24/7. Or a fish. Would that satisfy your fetish? For shame!"

The other B-Rexes were taken aback. The B-Rex rolled up his note pad and made as if to swat Barry like a fly, offering chase when Barry tried to find the stairs. Once he was gone, the B-Rexes mulled a deal among themselves for the production of adhesive hand implants.

* * *

Barry was wounded. These events were on tape forever. He tried to phone Jonah Flambo for advice. The receptionist explained that Jonah could not remember Barry, if indeed they had ever met, which she doubted. Barry pressed her to check again. She returned to the phone a minute later with dark news:

"I'm sorry, Mr. Flambo has never met you."

"I'm the guy with the eyebrows!"

"Nope. Sorry."

The following days were torment for Barry. Then a letter arrived informing him that his episode would not air. B-Rex 4 had crossed a line. The CBC would not broadcast the ascription of a corporal fetish to a contestant. It could expose them to a libel suit. Barry was overjoyed. He was determined never to be naïve about his profession again. Rather than make the world converge on one outhouse, might it be better to focus on the neighbourhood and expand from there? Edmonton was a pond. Barry needed a journalistic rock to throw into it. He searched from behind various bushes and for rocks for weeks. He found two.

Chapter Seven

A FAMILY OUTING

Edmonton , August 2038

The Fringe Festival opened in late August. Simeon, Noah and Izzy prepared a supper of Cajun peppered tofu and basil bruschetta paired with a Gewurztraminer from the Naramata Bench. Izzy was now enjoying occasional glasses with her parents. The family had tickets to see *The Infiltranslationers* perform "Other Voices" at 8 p.m. at the Bethlehem Lutheran hall near Church Street.

At 6:30, a DATS bus pulled up in front of their bungalow. Simeon and Noah were having a loud row over wine pairings. Izzy watched the bus driver assist his exiting passenger. A short man with a plaid blanket over his shoulders descended the lift in his wheelchair. Two women wearing long coats, one a scarlet brandy, the other a metallic blue, held his hands and rubbed his back. The man wielded his arms impatiently as if the women were flies to swat. The bus driver turned off the engine. The women aimed the wheelchair straight at Izzy's front steps.

The man in the wheelchair was Reverend Augustus Phlap.

Simeon, Noah and Izzy walked out to the front steps to watch Reverend Phlap progress towards them. His leg muscles had atrophied in his coma, but he summoned effort from his large shoulders to help his companions propel him. He began to windmill his arms like small turbines. Apart from limited mobility, he hadn't aged a day. He wore a blue business suit under his blanket, and an Edmonton Eskimos toque to warm his head. Late August nights held the first hints of fall in Edmonton. He trained his eyes on Izzy. He knew her in an instant. He measured her new adult stature with wide eyes. He smiled brightly, then broke into sobs of joy.

"Simeon! Noah! My heart is full. Izzy! My brave girl! My precious girl! Blessings, honour, grace and peace to the house of Izzy!"

Simeon and Noah braced themselves for abuse. Izzy did not want to be late for *The Infiltranslationers.*

"Izzy! Phlap continued. "The place I've been. The thing I saw. Our life is a moment's fraction of grace."

Noah heard a sermon coming. Simeon thought the wheels on Phlap's chair could use a good clean. Both felt badly that the house had no wheelchair ramp, but not too badly.

"Reverend Phlap," Noah said, "We apologize for the lack of a ramp. Perhaps your daughters could help."

"Daughters?" yelped Phlap. "Ha! You're referencing Job, aren't you. I've been reading Job intensively. It's one of the greatest poems ever to spring from the human imagination. Did you know that the name of one of Job's daughters means box of eye shadow in Hebrew? Yes! Job was granted vision and so was I. This world is all vision! But no, these are not my daughters. These are my private nurses. This is Destiny and this is Jasmine. But there's more! They're also in love! That's right – a couple! And I blessed them – yes, I did!"

Phlap tried to read Izzy's reaction. Izzy's mouth looked tense. She wanted Phlap to finish so she could see Jesse.

"Yes, Izzy! I blessed them. Six times our souls must pass this way. Three times straight and three times gay! Izzy, you were right!"

Izzy did not care what he was on about. She looked beyond Phlap. She noticed a dark-eyed woman watching from across the street. She kept a small black dog on a very long silver leash.

Simeon intervened: "Are you referring to Izzy's Genesis poem? That was years ago. She's grown up now as you can see."

"My point exactly!" Phlap concurred. "Those years, that so-called ago, are a moment, a pulsation of the artery! A life of pure imagination awaits us, if we build mansions now. I must tell others in this somnolent vale. No, touch me not. I'll not be hoisted up the steps. When I take my final journey from this cloudy vale, my six pallbearers shall be three of each. No – six times six of everything – an ark! Child, you've grown. Yes, you're a young woman now. I bless the stroke. Destiny, Jasmine – DATS please! Au revoir, until we next meet, thou prophetess!"

Destiny gripped the handles of the wheelchair, taking care to protect her long, lustrous nails. Izzy liked Jasmine's silver seashell earring. Across the street, the dark-eyed woman smirked at Phlap. Phlap did not see her. Her dog – a frisky black cockapoo – bowed his head above a small pool of drool. Izzy whispered to Noah: "I want to go to the show. Don't drag this out."

Simeon and Noah walked Phlap to the waiting DATS bus. Simeon told Destiny to avoid a crack in the sidewalk, which might slow them down.

"Yes," Phlap cried all the while, "you are the pallbearers of my selfish self. Izzy, you are the midwife of my sixfold spirit. I will send news!"

Noah, Simeon and Izzy waved goodbye.

* * *

"Izzy: tell us what to expect this evening," Simeon said as they drove to see *The Infiltranslationers.*

"I told you already," Izzy said irritably. She pulled away from Simeon's hand and folded her arms.

"Relax. We'll be on time. Here's a question. What might happen if you sat in someone's wheelchair?" Noah asked,

"Wheelchairiosis? Isn't it obvious what people in wheelchairs go through?"

Noah was stung. "Phlap seemed to speak of angels."

""Zekiel saw a wheel; way up in the middle of the air," Simeon sang out. "Did Phlap?"

Izzy looked out the window. The woman with the dog was gone. Her life must be easy, Izzy thought irritably. Then she recalled the run for the cure. She thought of the times she ran or walked for causes over the years. She walked for AIDS, Alzheimer's, domestic violence, Pride, Edmonton's Food Bank, teen parents, missing Indigenous women and breast cancer. The constant in all these walks was Edmonton, with its lush nature trails and inner city streets. Walking is the way to know a place, but every walk makes a place seem real for the first time.

She recalled the summer when she was was fourteen. Noah and Simeon asked her if there was a special place she would like to visit. The summer before, they'd hiked through the Badlands around Drumheller. The coulees made her feel the salt embrace of prehistoric seas. The Royal Tyrrell Museum showed sea creatures evolving legs and moving onto dry land.

They stopped at an exhibit showing the Big Bang.

"The sign says the Big Bang was a tiny explosion in space," she observed.

"Yes," Noah said.

"What space?"

"Do you mean before the Big Bang?"

"No – during the Big Bang."

"Well, space could only be inside the tiny point, not outside."

"But we're looking at it from the outside through a pane of glass. What if we were inside?"

"We're all inside now, Izzy."

Izzy rolled her eyes and shook her head.

"Don't be rude, young lady," Noah said. "Fine, imagine an ice cream cone with a tiny point at the bottom and a circle wide enough to hold your ice cream at the top. If some ice cream dribbles down the cone, the drop will fall to the ground at the tiny bottom point. You could count the seconds until it fell. But what if there was no space beyond the tiny point or time to measure? A physicist would call that point a singularity. If we all came from that point, we are all still inside it materially. I suppose it may have been a fireball. I like to think of it as a ripple of water."

"Indeed," said Simeon, "'Old dark sleepy pool quick unexpected frog goes plop! Watersplash! Basho!'"

"Not just the surface, Simeon," Noah opined. "Imagine a point of light deep underwater. Imagine it opening fire air and earth."

"OK," Izzy whispered. "I sort of see it more like taking a deep breath." She walked backwards five metres in the corridor to the epoch before the dawn of feet.

When Noah asked her for a special destination, Izzy did not hesitate. She chose Thunder Bay. If she could try on anyone's shoes in all of human history, they would be Terry Fox's shoes. Noah thought of dissuading her. He was hoping for a wine region, like the Okanagan, Napa Valley or Tuscany. Simeon said nothing doing: her choice was final. They rented an RV, crossed the wide prairie into Ontario, saw ancient pictographs on rocky shores, stiff-breezed islands and the ruins of a freshwater research station, surrounded with wire and keep out signs. Izzy remembered watching her feet as she floated on her back in a sheltered bay.

They saw the statue of Terry Fox. She walked around it for half an hour. His face looked slightly to the sky. His right fist turned downward, and his left fist turned upward. She guessed this meant courage on the one hand and hope on the other. His t-shirt and shorts were creased with strain. He was poised to bring his right leg forward in a hop step. She admired the detail in his droopy sock and shoelaces. This was the only time Noah and Simeon saw Izzy take a picture with a phone.

* * *

They reached Church Street. Noah found a parking spot two blocks from the venue. They found seats. The lights dimmed. Strains from *In the Bleak Midwinter,* played by the *Goldbar String Quartet,* filled the space. A light projected an imaginary temperature onto the walls:

- 32C feels like -37

The lights went up. Madge Three stood at centre stage, eyes lifted, then lowered in benediction. Madge began with sign language in graceful movements. Johnny Bizck entered stage left. He welcomed the audience to Treaty 6 land, then asked the audience to translate Madge's signs. Audience members chuckled uncomfortably and shuffled their feet. Jesse entered stage right, wearing a t-shirt that said "AUDIENCE." He began translating Madge's signs.

"In the beginning, waste and void, words narrowed the spaces among themselves, languages danced in innocence, then stumbled in prides across the plains of darkness, towered upwards to seek pain where none was needed, while the wind spirit moved on, splitting time like cordwood for a sacrifice, uttering her lost children into new beginnings, wrestling with pain in their separate places."

Samson Gleau entered from a seat in the audience, and continued to translate: "High noon over the dark Atlantic waves is the time sunlight fingers touch Edmonton streets, low, angular, touching cold pavements, hushing pawn shop and hotel and herbal medicine windows that cry when the light hits their eyes."

"The light plays Cain to an old man's Abel," Johnny Bizck continued, "its blunt blow recalling him from some singular dream, rending the tissues of peace with the breath of echoes as he stares into a window at his broken face."

"While behind him," Jesse concluded, "cars churn and tilt their morning invasion, and the Flood called day begins."

The players presented four short skits touching on street life. All were in pantomime. All lasted roughly fifteen minutes. "The Grudge": a story of tragic misunderstandings among the homeless (musical score: *Quartet in C major, K465* by Mozart). "The Kiss": a homeless man seeking a friend who had died the night before (musical score: *Runes* by Keith Jarrett). "The Mattress": a warm bed that shut out the players with an invisible force field they could not break (musical score: *Koyaanisqatsi* by Phillip Glass); "Metamorphosis," a *tableau vivant* of *Laocoon and his Sons* with Jesse as Laocoon and Madge and Johnny as his sons suddenly morphed into a *tableau vivant* of *Christ with the Homeless* by Eichenberg (musical score: Bruce Cockburn, *Lovers in a Dangerous Time*). Samson Gleau read from Blake's *Laocoon Aphorisms* during the transformation:

Art is the Tree of Life.

No secrecy in Art.

Art degraded, Imagination denied,

War governed the Nations.

Then, the full ensemble joined hands and recited stanza one of "Vision and Prayer" by Dylan Thomas. Madge stood and smiled in the middle.

When the lights went down at the end of the performance, nobody clapped. Jesse came on stage and nodded. "Please, friends, give yourselves permission to clap. Be generous to yourselves." He clapped softly, encouragingly. Then he moved among some audience members, taking their hands gently and pushing them together. Applause slowly grew into a long standing ovation.

* * *

Jesse met Izzy at the exit. They embraced. Noah and Simeon exchanged concerned glances. Noah shook Jesse's hand. Simeon leaned closer to Jesse. He could smell cinnamon. Was it his breath, or a major cinnamon spill? Noah pulled Simeon back when he offered to find a vacuum. They moved on to allow Jesse to greet others. Outside, more people were waiting. Jesse more people were waiting. Jesse decided to make a speech.

"We're moved by your encouragement, ladies and gentlemen," he said. "And please, go and tell others. Yes, we face many challenges of body, mind and spirit here. But we hope you'll see these streets as places of revelation, not simply alienation. I'd like us all to sign our names in witness to this on the street. Here, I've got some coloured pastels."

Jesse repeated his speech in French, Polish, Arabic and Urdu, depending on whose eyes met his. Then the performers signed their names on the pavement under a streetlight. Gidding signed for Jesse. Jesse welcomed audience members to sign their names as well. Simeon and Noah watched Izzy sign her name.

* * *

"I'm thinking about the ending," Izzy said on the drive home.

"The ending? The Thomas was a wonderful touch of new birth," said Simeon. "The wild child! The whole thing was rich and vast. How did they manage it?"

"I'm not sure," Izzy said. "Jesse says abundance is a trade secret. The musicians volunteered for example. It makes me wonder: what happened when I was born?"

Noah answered instantly: "Into the dangerous world you leapt!" Simeon chimed in:

"Terror strikes through the region wide

They cry the babe the babe is born

And flee away on every side."

They gave each other high-fives. Izzy left them to their cackling. She thought about university: a BA in Creative Writing combining poetry with Biology, Urban Geography and Social Work.

"I'm not certain you can do all that," Noah said diplomatically at a red light. "You could take electives, of course."

Simeon elbowed him in the right shoulder. "Cease! Let her choose."

"Hey! I'm driving a car here!"

At home, she sat in the fireside armchair with Nympho. She looked into the cat's eyes. A glow from the aquarium reflected off Nympho's face. She wondered where Nympho went on her long rambles. Did she have close friends in Crescentdale? Enemies, threats, grudges, famines, insomnia and droughts? She closed her hands around Nympho's paws until she purred.

* * *

Izzy spent the next day searching for reviews of *The Infiltranslationers*. The *Mercury* reviewer gave it four out of five stars: "the sign language broke the fourth wall, challenging us to assess its inclusiveness within a shimmering soundscape. This is collaborative art that really takes it to the streets."

A junk message appeared in Izzy's inbox. Inside she found a link to a blog called "Fringing! with Base Quick":

Fringing! with Base Quick.

This column is dedicated to Jonah Flambo, Canadian hero.

The Infiltranslationers

An anonymous tip tells yours truly that Genesis, underlies the poetry. The Bible? Hello? Originality means new stuff. The only original sin in this melon is that it's soft on eco-terrorism! 1 star out of 5 for *The Infiltranslationers.*

Izzy printed it out so she could tear it to pieces. Simeon saw her agitation at breakfast. He checked her footwear. Izzy showed him the review online. He rubbed his chin as he read it. "Izzy, this is perhaps not a young man to cultivate."

* * *

Barry was home at that moment, preparing to go out for some morning videography. His parents, Severus and Talia, sat at the kitchen table with old laptops open and worried faces. Tal's Trolley was looking vulnerable.

Severus and Talia had a system to ease the tension between them in times of financial stress. If Severus rejected Talia's idea, Talia would give him a sarcastic standing ovation.

"Bravo, Smotherus. Bravo. But hey! Guess what? Our chequing account is still empty."

If Talia insisted on having her way, Severus would spring to his feet and give her a nazi salute. "Well, heil forkwad, Tal! But guess what? We're no closer to getting out of debt."

They would laugh together after these mirthful tiffs, then get on with it.

"I dropped off three passengers at Fort Mac at midnight, Tal, and brought two back to Edmonton at 3 am," Severus confided. "I counted forty-seven vehicles that passed me on the highway – in both directions! Thirty-three were pickups. How many people do you suppose were in those vehicles altogether?"

"Forty-seven, Sev?" Talia asked.

"Fifty, tops. I don't see how Tal's Trolley is going to take off."

"Why do people drive for hours alone after a hard day's work?"

"A sense of freedom I guess."

"Should we load 3D video games on the trolley, Sev? A virtual casino? Holograms? Karaoke maybe?"

"We can't afford it, Tal."

"Well, I insist. Entertainment attracts customers."

"Well, heil forkwad, Tal!" They shared a laugh.

They had an understanding. If they reached five heil forkwads or five bravo smotheruses in one meeting, the rules required them to stop work and make love. They were holding steady at four each when they realized Barry was standing beside them. Barry cleared his throat.

"I have good news," Barry announced.

"Oh?"

"Yes. I've decided not to sue you after all."

"Remind us please."

"Well, it's like I've tried to tell you for some time. Everybody thinks my full name is Basewik Quick. Teachers, soccer coaches, dentists, girls. I can't make progress sometimes."

"And?"

"And, like I said, I was going to sue you to change my name."

"When exactly were you going to sue us?"

"That's my point. I don't have to sue you after all. So that's the good news."

"Great. Thanks."

"I'm even using Basewik Quick for my latest project. It's my by-line for my entertainment blog. It resonates."

"Barry, did we tell you that we're in the middle of something?"

"Not yet."

"Very well. Barry-we-are-busy-at-the-moment-on-key-family-business."

Barry left the house.

* * *

At 10 a.m., Izzy found Barry loitering outside *True Dough.* Affable seniors loved *True Dough,* certain the name was an attack on the National Energy Policy of 1981. The baker was from Ecuador. He was puzzled. National Energy Policy? Why did old men ask to shake his hand and then purchase nothing?

"You bastard!" Izzy seethed when she spotted Barry. "Who are you to trash *The Infiltranslationers* in your ratfuck blog?"

"What do you mean?"

"Base Quick!"

"Base Quick sounded *un peu* classy to me, *un peu* about town. If people are going to call me Basewik, I might as well use it to my advantage."

"BASTARD! Is attacking the homeless classy?"

Barry reached for his e-phone with his free hand while Izzy pinned his right hand to the bakery wall. He inserted the password with the tip of his nose, and scrolled to *The Infiltranslationers* with the tip of his tongue.

"Oh that! I wasn't attacking anyone. It's just information."

Izzy applied pressure to his wrist.

"Stop! Look, I wasn't even there. I picked it at random from the Fringe web site. What's your problem?"

Izzy shoved him against the wall, then dropped to the pavement and tore off his shoes. She slipped them on quickly. Her body dissolved into a space bar. Millions of URL's spun around her head like rings of Saturn. The moon dropped from its sphere and rotated swiftly, revealing a strange face leering at her through tinted glasses as the revolutions quickened to a blurring speed. The hair was a fiery red. The left side of the face's mouth curled upwards towards a cheerful smile; the right side tipped downwards towards hell. With every rotation, the face grew wider until it began to deflect the planets and the galaxies out of alignment.

"Who the hell is it? Wide face? Red hair? Weird tinted glasses? Trying to decide whether to kill me or kiss me?"

"Jonah Flambo," Barry groaned.

Izzy removed the shoes and threw them at Barry's face.

"So that's it. You're schmoozing."

"We don't use that word. I'm networking."

"What's your middle name? Screwthepoor?"

"No. It's Talius, if you must know."

"Your feet reek!" she thundered, and marched home.

* * *

Barry followed her from a distance, hiding behind the brown dumpster behind the *Happy Village,* moving from shrub to shrub, lying prone in a patch of rhubarb, slithering behind a grade one tree.

Lucius was sitting on her front step. Izzy sat down with him. She listened and Lucius talked. Barry zoomed to *magnus maxi* on his e-phone and pressed video record. He still couldn't pick up their voices. Izzy seemed to touch Lucius's hand. Barry knew that he was missing something important. He had a decision to make. He could leave his e-phone in video record mode and miss what they were saying. Or, he could stop the video and open *Lipstick 7.2*, which let his phone read lips at up to seventy-five metres. He opened *Lipstick*. A dropdown menu asked Barry to choose two celebrity voices to channel the conversation. Four hundred celebrities were available. Barry had no time to waste. He pressed default. The broadcast began.

Voice of W.C. Fields: So you're still thinking about homelessness?

Default subtitles began to appear on Barry's screen in Esperanto. He swept them aside with his index finger.

Voice of Shirley Temple: Why shouldn't I think about

homelessness? It's in my family line of business.

W.C. Fields: Have you ever met a real homeless person, Lucius?

Shirley Temple: I'm creating an action plan.

W.C. Fields: Why not start by meeting someone who's really homeless?

Shirley Temple: You mean sociology? That's not action.

W.C. Fields: It's not sociology.

Shirley Temple: I don't need to meet anyone.

They were silent for a minute.

W.C. Fields: You once told me that your mom is a liar. I don't believe it. I never thought she was lying about anything.

Shirley Temple: You're so naïve.

W.C. Fields: Back in grade six, she said there's a kid like Card Dilbey in every school. Is there also one like me? Or you?

Shirley Temple: I put my mind to social problems!

W.C. Fields: OK. But I don't believe your mom's a liar. Still, thanks for your honest opinion.

Lucius seemed to brush his right eye. Izzy put her hand on his shoulder and patted him on the back. Lucius recoiled to one side. They were silent for a time.

Shirley Temple: Do you remember the time we walked

through the neighbourhood changing the letters on signs?

W.C. Fields: Yes! It was vandalistic. Taking the "f" off of "Prime Rib of Beef" at Sal's Bistro was brilliant.

Shirley Temple: I went back later and made changes alone, you know. I changed Lasagna to gas anaL. I changed truck dealership to epukerclashdirt. That night, I dreamed a five-star chef in a giant black truck tried to run me down.

They shared a laugh.

W.C. Fields: I have to tell you something. I think you're stuck in time. I worry for you. So do my dads. I might know a way to get unstuck.

The sound feed stopped. The screen told Barry that he was on reserve power. Too late. The phone died. He pulled his portable charger from his pocket and rammed it into the phone. Izzy was finished speaking. She and Lucius went into her house.

* * *

Barry wondered if Izzy was two-timing Lucius. Or were they even an item? If Lucius liked Izzy, Barry could brew up a scandal: the Crescentdale love triangle. He waited for his phone to recharge. Then he opened the video. He searched *Lipstick* for other voices to normalize gender in the audio. He tried to shop a boner onto Lucius's crotch with his *photo* app. He tried Arson Digits for Lucius, and Katherine Hepburn for Izzy. Strange, but at least the genders were correct. He replayed the interview. And this time he stopped at the end.

"I might know a way to get unstuck."

He replayed it. He wanted to know what Izzy said next. Just then, Noah and Simeon pulled up in their car. They went inside. Barry waited three minutes. He rang the doorbell. Simeon answered, and eyed Barry.

"Izzy. The gentleman from Grub Street for you."

Izzy scowled at Barry from the kitchen doorway.

Barry thought Monopoly would make a good excuse. A month ago, when Lucius's top hat token fell off the game board, Izzy picked it up for him. Lucius grabbed her finger and bent it backwards. He could not stand to have his token touched. Barry wanted to grasp the game board and toss its contents into Lucius's face like a bowl of dog piss. Instead he sat and watched.

"Monopoly?" Barry asked Izzy.

"Nope."

"Well, how about *Strikedown*?" he said, desperately.

Izzy rolled her eyes. Barry wedged his way past Simeon.

"You're going to take down that blog," Lucius whispered sternly.

"No way!" Barry whined. "Look, it's always better to change comments than remove them. I'll boost *The Infiltranslationers.* I'll stage a corrective intervention. I'll even insult myself. A counter-insurgency will set things right."

"Call it what you want," Lucius said, "But do it." Noah arrived and looked down at Barry's face, much as he would look at an unflushed toilet.

"If simplicity is on offer, Mr. Quick," Simeon said, "then you might simply apologize and delete your review. Or at least undertake a revision. Like trimming one's eyebrows, it can be hard work, but the results are worth it."

Barry was appalled. Did Simeon know the work that went into reviews? Of course not – he was a janitor.

"Without the review, the comment section makes no sense," he said. "It's been decided – I'm going to change the comments. I'll make them all positive."

Barry retreated to a living room chair, pulled out his comb and teased his eyebrows upwards. Simeon and Noah went into the back room. Barry was glad to have Lucius and Izzy to himself. "Monopoly? Strikedown?" he repeated.

"Counter-blog," said Lucius.

"Yes – and I'll do it *gratis*."

Lucius glared. "Now."

"On my e-phone? It would be easier on my lap-pad at home."

"I'm sorry," Lucius replied, pressing his index finger on Barry's collarbone, "but I don't trust you to do it at home. Here there will be witnesses. Now get on with it!"

"I only have two followers."

"Get going!"

Izzy drifted away to feed her fish. Barry opened his phone and logged in. He knew there would be no comments. Nobody cared. This would make the fix easy.

He scanned down to the bottom of *Fringing! with Base Quick*. He looked with satisfaction and horror. There were twenty-six comments:

Wolfbane21: One star – and all my tax dollars! They think they can tax and spend anything.

Jacuzziboy: @ Wolfbane21. Who said they had a grant? Nobody – yet. Stick to reality.

Nosenateforcanada325: these arts funding schemes are breeding grounds. Cut all the funding. Let them cry to their moms at public broadcasting.

Leftoverart989: people! My mom saw this play and said it was good. Homeless people wrote it, produced it, directed it. I'd bet money that Quick didn't see it. This review is total crap.

Mannudeandonfire2: Leftoverart989: What are you? A bleeding heart or a weasel-breath? Bleed your heart on your own tax return.

Nosenateforcanada325: Tax money? Not my taxes thanks! The homeless can put up shut up and or pay up.

Faitdodo112: @ Nosenateforcanada325: until you're homeless.

A new comment appeared as Barry read, then a reply to that comment. It was out of control. Barry tried counter-measures. He activated a filter requiring all commenters to conform to comment etiquette. He added a false addendum citing the commenting standards of a fictitious "Press Federation of the North." He couldn't risk citing a real organization without knowing Jonah Flambo's stance on it. He created a false account for himself under the name "sincerelynb27."

sincerelynb27: @everyone. The play is great. Just shut up.

Mannudeandonfire2: @sincerelynb27: you shut up. Obviously you never heard of our free speech rights. Say hi to your activist judge friends, by the way.

Barry broke into a sweat. He selected all comments and flagged them with one of two balloons: "Message regretfully withdrawn due to content requirements" or "PFN blogging standards regretfully contravened." He replaced the lot with a new effusion on *The Infiltranslationers:*

Kudos to *The Infiltranslationers.* Five stars out of five. Finally, a show that does justice to homelessness.

That was all he could think of to say.

Lucius snatched the phone from Barry like a bear seizing a fish. He scanned the page. He was impressed. He returned the phone to Barry.

"Can we play Monopoly now?" Barry asked. "We'll let you buy the old McDonald's, eh?"

Lucius grabbed Barry's index finger and pressed it backwards. The commotion roused Simeon and Noah.

"What's the matter, young people?" Noah boomed.

A circle of eight eyes converged on Barry. His eyes watered. He decided to show these people who they were dealing with. He called up some videos on his e-phone and held them out at his accusers. He moved it back and forth in a long horizontal arc, as if warding off vampires with garlic. He selected a video and held it towards Noah and Simeon.

"What's here, Master Quick?" Simeon asked, looking at a grainy image on the screen.

"You and him in a car. And guess what? You're not driving!"

"Shame on you," Noah whispered.

Barry flipped through his video archive and held a second luminous confection aloft.

"What's this?" Lucius asked.

"Hint – it's not The Hague! I took this exactly two hours ago – and you know who and you know where!"

Lucius strained to decipher the grainy picture. He was shocked to see his father, Richie, loitering outside of *Richmond's End.* He held his jean jacket close about his throat. Three strangers – Latrice Bomponce and her sons, Shaft and Fargo – were hurling profanities at Richie from an old orange Volkswagen van stopped on the traffic circle. They decided to hunt him down after he left Quasipedro. Now they found him. Angry motorists honked, but the Bomponces sat resolute.

"We don't take crap from Canadians!" Latrice screamed.

More honking.

"Why don't you just apologize, Canadian assholes?"

More honking

Latrice pushed a tattered U.S. flag out the window and shook it like an old rug in defiance.

Shaft and Fargo stepped out of the van and jogged towards Richie. They began to push Richie back and forth between them like an underinflated beach ball. Latrice pulled the van onto the grass. A soft rain began falling. She leaned her flagpole against the van, and shooed her boys off with her decrepit umbrella. She forced Richie through the door of Richmond's End at umbrella point. Shaft and Fargo loitered for a minute at the front door of Richmond's End. Then they saw

Barry in a bush across the street. Fargo pointed at the lens, and made towards it at a brisk trot. The traffic blocked them, allowing Barry to flee. The screen went black.

"What's this garbage?" Izzy demanded.

"Journalism!" Barry proclaimed.

"Basewik," Noah said in his teacher's voice, "have you been cryogenically frozen since 1968? You can't shame anyone here."

"Wanna bet?" Barry squealed. He flipped to a new video. "Now, tell me what you said about getting unstuck, or I'll play it."

Izzy shook her head. The video commenced. Izzy and Jesse were sitting under an elm tree. It appeared to be Paul Kane Park, with a fountain and in the background. They kissed and hugged. Izzy removed Jesse's boots and socks and washed his feet with her water bottle.

"And she lay at his feet until the morning," Simeon whispered to Noah.

"Boaz had a proper roof over his head," Noah remarked.

"Just keep watching!" Barry cried.

Jesse felt tickles from her touch. She spoke soothingly to him. She kissed him and sat on his chest and ran her fingers through his greasy locks. Barry fast-forwarded with his index fingertip. Izzy rolled up the cuff of Jesse's jeans and tickled his big toe.

"So?" Simeon asked.

"So? So this is a sex tape, people! It's what we call a genre. Don't blame me. I'm the journalist here," Barry said.

"They're wearing clothes," Simeon said.

"Ha! Maybe they're into clothes," Barry snorted.

"If you think this is journalism, think again," Noah said.

She straddled a bum!" Barry squealed. "She did a loser! Are you blind?"

"We don't use the word loser," Simeon said.

"Fine. She's 'seeing' a homeless man!" Barry said, wiggling his fingers to make quotation marks. "She's 'been with' him. And maybe they have a 'clothes' fetish. I'm just striving for accuracy. You can't technically 'date' a homeless man, can you? How the hell do they even get in touch?" He fast-forwarded again. Izzy rested her head in Jesse's denim crotch.

"How could you be with a man who looks and smells like hell?" Barry demanded.

Simeon whispered: "Your oils are fragrant, your name is perfume poured out."

"Simeon – enough!" snapped Noah.

Barry wondered what Simeon was babbling about. He switched on his voice record mechanism to catch what Simeon was saying, fumbling his phone in the process.

Noah faced Barry and Lucius sternly. "Lessons learned, gentlemen. Love is stronger than death. Now get out!"

"Just one minute more, professor, if you don't mind. Bear with me." Barry switched back to his video function. He fast-forwarded again. Jesse kissed Izzy. Two police officers approached from a distance. They were making towards Barry, not Jesse. The e-phone screen seemed to turn and flee before going black.

"Bastard!" Izzy flew across the room and shook Barry's throat. She punched wildly towards the side of his head, landing blows on a sofa cushion." Lucius grabbed Barry's e-phone and switched on the mirror mode. He stared at his own reflection for several seconds. Then he bashed the phone against the wall three times. A framed photograph on the wall fell, shattering the glass. It showed Angel Glacier in Jasper National Park as it was in 2014.

Lucius turned to Izzy and slapped her face. Her head snapped to the side.

"What did I do?" she asked.

"You know!" Lucius said.

"No. I don't," she said in deep pain. Lucius remained silent.

"Get out, gentlemen!" Noah shouted.

"Facts are facts!" Barry whined, "I won't recant!"

Lucius picked up the sculpture of Sedna from the coffee table. He slammed it into the side of the aquarium. The glass shattered, and the waters came forth. A traumatic tide of damaged and dying aquatic life spread across the living room floor. Sedna's head broke. She lay on the floor amid the ruins of the aquarium.

Everyone fell silent.

"Are you crazy? What did you do that for?" Barry whispered softly. The fish were dying slowly in front of their eyes.

Noah threw the boys out and slammed the door behind them. They jostled and shoved on the sidewalk, then parted ways, each heading warily to his home. Simeon started rescuing the fish in a large cooking pot filled with tap water. Izzy gently scooped fish into the pot with cupped hands. This was no time for tears.

* * *

Izzy, Simeon and Noah managed to save all the fish. Simeon put the tilapia he was planning to bake back in the fridge and made tofu paella instead. Noah and Izzy drove down to Church Street to look for Jesse. They found him and brought him home for dinner.

"It's a case of provocation," Jesse opined, as he studied a tofu triangle on the end of his fork. The tofu reminded him of a pencil eraser, but it was deliciously toasty and chewy. "I get provoked all the time. The world is full of grumps and grudges. It's normal."

"It would be better if it was provocation," Noah remarked. "Basewik seems to be some kind of imitator. He'll make himself miserable someday. But Lucius might make others miserable."

"So what now?" Izzy asked.

Simeon took a pen and a scrap of paper. He quickly wrote down some words, quickly, like a doctor writing a prescription. He handed it to Izzy.

"Give this poem to Lucius tomorrow, or in the next few days. It's urgent. His condition is getting worse. He needs this."

Izzy unfolded the paper. Simeon had written out Leonard Cohen's "Elegy" by hand. His penmanship was gorgeous as always. The poem transported her to a world a world warm and green and true.

"A.s.a.p.!" Simeon said.

* * *

It was getting dark in Crescentdale. Lucius walked its

streets for three hours. Two hours earlier, he ran into Card Dilbey who was walking his chocolate labradoodle Sybil. Card had thick glasses, red hair, and was now six feet three inches tall. Card walked past Lucius. Lucius called after him.

"Hey Card – what would happen if people could hear through their breasts instead of their ears, and delivered babies through their eyes. Would we all have to expose our breasts full time?"

"I dunno. Why are you shaking?" Card replied.

"You think you're such a freaking oracle, don't you? So what would happen if Canada had capital punishment by waterboarding or, say, beheading for all homeless people? On sight with no trial even, thanks to a special bill lumping them in with eco-terrorists. Answer me that."

"Well, you might actually notice that, because it would be judicial plagiarism assuming you like copying ruthless tyrants. Not to mention totally evil. And besides, I'm in law school, and I can tell you homelessness is not a crime in our democracy."

"I asked you what would happen. What the hell is wrong with you?"

Card moved closer to Lucius, placed his hand on Lucius's head, then moved his hand to his shoulder to show how tall he had grown.

"Nothing wrong with me," Card answered.

"Answer my question."

"What would happen? You'd probably be stuck in your time warp for good. You bullies never grow up. How come you never asked me about men with ten ice-cold dicks for heads?"

"I didn't bully you."

"Right."

"One last time. Would it be normal?"

"Sure. Whatever."

Exasperated, Lucius exchanged shoves with Card and walked away. He traipsed the streets of Crescentdale for two more hours. He peered into his old backyard. White foam was dribbling out of the neighbour's composter. He walked until dark, then he trudged towards the traffic circle. He started to cross, heedless of honking horns and whining brakes. Then he stopped. He turned back. He retreated into a grove of small pines that lined the road across from Richmond's End. This was the border of Crescentdale. He leaned his head against a tree, certain that he was in the dark. It was 8:30. He waited for the traffic to lighten, and slow, and cease. He waited in the pines, dozing on and off until 3:00 in the morning. Then he crossed the empty street.

He peered into his house through the takeout window. Lady Spukwell was visiting Geogasm. Barry said he took the video at 1:30 p.m. Had Richie really returned? Had he left? He sensed someone was inside. A police car entered the traffic circle. He pressed himself against the takeout window until it passed. The traffic circle was empty again.

He saw no signs of movement through the window. He could hear a buzzing sound. There was a burning smell. He found his key and opened the door. Yes: there was something burning. He looked into the kitchen. A body lay on the floor, its pants pulled down. A blow dryer was stuck on the body's penis. The blow dryer was on. Its motor struggled, smoked, complained. Lucius saw that the body was his father. Richie's eyes stared vacantly at the ceiling. Some dried blood stained his left nostril and upper lip. A tiny hole pierced his throat. An umbrella lay on the floor.

Lucius sat in a stall seat and buried his face in his

trembling hands. He thought of phoning the police. He imagined headlines in the *Edmonton Mercury*: "Fire in Traffic Circle Claims One. Investigation Underway." He imagined headlines in the *Edmonton Footman*: "Roadkill! Local Roadie Dies Fairly Young!" He thought of calling Mercy Hospital or 911. He saw a news headline. "Local Tunesmith Suffers Burnout." He thought of doing nothing. He saw another headline. "Rockicide! Foul play not ruled out!" The images would not stop.

Then he got angry.

He walked to the cooking oil vat. It was still brim full of oil. The family never used it. Lady said it was years past its best before date. Richie called that a lie. He had boasted of his fine oil vat when they first moved in; later he called it a waste of space. He once planned to convert the old grilling stations into guest quarters, using the empty oil vat as a theme bed. He never got around to it.

Lucius turned the crank on a spigot. It was stuck from lack of use. He pulled harder. A mass of cloudy, rancid oil spread over the floor. He saw his own dark form reflected in the spreading ooze. He looked at his father. Was that a tear on his face? Was Richie alive? Should he check his pulse? No. It could be a drop of oil.

He left the house and crossed to a vacant lot on the south side of the traffic circle. He took out his e-phone, opened the laser app, and aimed it at the swelling pool of oil. He scanned the street. No cars. A balloon on his phone screen asked, "Are you sure?" Lucius pressed "yes." The laser beam lanced the oil. After twelve seconds, flames engorged *Richmond's End.* Glass windows shattered. Tables buckled. He thought he heard a cry. No, it was the wind. He looked beyond the flames to the pines where he had waited.

Izzy emerged from the pines, holding Nympho in her arms. She stood frozen in the baleful glow, illuminated by a visible darkness. Horror widened her eyes.

Lucius withdrew into the shadows. Unseen, he watched Izzy dash across the traffic circle and into the parking lot of *Richmond's End.* He heard her shout his name into the fire. How like her, Lucius thought. Who else would come to a fire with no phone to call for help?

A lone car pulled to the side of the road. Alarmed, the motorist stepped out of her car, called the police, then held her phone aloft to film Izzy and the burgeoning fire. Izzy moved towards the take-out window. Still she called for Lucius. The motorist panned the scene in wide angle, then zoomed in on Izzy's face.

Two more cars pulled over. Motorists formed a circle around Izzy to prevent her escape. Lucius heard sirens in the distance. He turned away, and entered the intricate streets of other neighbourhoods. He walked briskly to the Southtown Shopping Centre. He saw a taxi sitting empty near Liquor Universe. He got in, and ordered the driver to the bus station. Dawn was faintly breaking. He bought a ticket to Henrymart. He opened his phone and looked at images of Izzy, her green eyes, her radiant smile. He narrowed his eyes and deleted all of them.

He realized he was famished. He looked forward to breakfast at Geogasm.

Part Two

PROLOGUE 2

Ottawa, July 1, 2050

Barry Basewik-Quick knelt on the observation deck of the Peace Tower. He was alone. The deck was closed to visitors on Canada Day. The time was 11:10. The Peace Tower clock was permanently set to 1 p.m. to commemorate the hour of "Spukwell's Propurgation." Barry had a bucket of fried chicken, a thermos of no calorie cola, and a black nylon duffel bag.

Barry felt the weight of the object inside the bag. He pulled his hand back suddenly. What if he accidentally set the damn thing off? The sound could break his eardrums! He pulled foam earplugs out of his right pocket and jammed them in his ears. He gnawed on a chicken leg – then dropped it. What if he choked on a bone? He might be caught dead on the deck with chicken, cola and his bag! He picked the leg up and sucked slowly on it like a lollipop. This seemed prudent. He resealed the bucket and wiped his greasy hands on his trousers. His hands were shaking.

Barry had no difficulty gaining access to the tower. One of the security men at the entrance remembered Barry from his brief time as a commissionaire at the *Ministry of Intimacy*.

"Good to see you, Base," he said, greeting Barry at the door one half hour earlier. He was glad to lead Barry towards the Peace Tower elevator. Few people came to see the view from the tower anymore. Tourists lined up to see the site of Spukwell's Propurgation in the former House of Commons. Tour guides offered several different versions of the event, keeping the story fresh and alive. Most tourists preferred the interactive hologram animations of the propurgation to live guides. Animations were available at the *Bureau of History* down the street.

"My name is Barry. Barry Basewik-Quick. Aren't you going to check my belongings?" He squeezed his duffle bag tightly under his arm.

"I will if he won't," said a second security man, chuckling. He pressed the tip of his nose against Barry's bucket of chicken, then guided his nose around the greasy rim. "Hmmmm – that's chicken alright. Check!" He repeated the inspection, this time rotating the bucket while keeping his nose in one place. Then he removed the cap from Barry's large bottle of cola with his teeth. He took a long swig, then fell to his knees grasping his throat.

"Arghh! I'm poisoned." Then he began to laugh heartily. "Heh heh – they're showing *Gladiator* this week on classic movies. Ha!"

"Such a kidder!" said the first security man. "Look Base, we read about the abuse you took at the Comedy Chute last year. Those were grave and manifold indignities to your physical person in my view. Did you sue?" Seeking to empathize, he offered Barry a bracing handshake.

"And this," Barry asked, stroking his duffle bag like a cat. "This is my photographic equipment, right?"

"No doubt," said the second security man. "You know damn well you can't take pictures up there you old salt. More likely it's the inflatable robot girlfriend the news sites talked about after the incident! Nice try!"

"Look, we're not here to judge you, Base," said the first security man. "The bag's fine. But tell me: can a plastic 'partner' support your weight? I ask purely hypothetically, of course. I'm married. Ha! I'll bet there's a pair of crutches in that bag, the eco-friendly kind that fold up and decompose."

Security man one went into a cloakroom behind the security desk and returned with a wheelchair. "Hand me your crutches, Base. Let us wheel you to the elevator."

Barry gave in, seating himself in the wheelchair. The massive, fast-growing eyebrows that dominated his face danced wildly above his gaping blue eyes, as they always did when events exceeded his expectations. His only backup plan, if caught with his bag, was to make an impassioned speech denouncing Lucius Spukwell to the security guards, since speeches were forbidden at sentencing hearings.

It seemed his backup plan would not be needed.

* * *

Security man one wheeled Barry past the display case containing Canada's Charter of Rights and Freedoms. Thirty years earlier, Manchester F. Helmfloss, the Prime Minister of the day, vented his legendary opinion of the Charter in robust oral cadences: "It is a cheap motel, nay lib-left spa, where ecologists and judges, all unelected, their nakedness uncover, each to the other, their fulsome coitus, brisk and brazen, churning defiance, at Canadian people. Nay, there it sits, a leaf of political correctness, covering such nudity, morally bankrupt." He broadcast this landmark address, nicknamed the "motel" speech, from the bridge of the houseboat in which he planned to be buried in a boat-sized mound off the shore of Burritts Rapids on the Rideau River. He named his houseboat the *Oval Base.* Distrustful of the media, he gave six prime ministerial addresses to the nation and three prime ministerial "national conversations" from his houseboat studio.

Helmfloss, who allowed his closest advisors to call him "Jay," read his speeches by candlelight. Viewers supposed the candlelight to be a nod to common decency, traditional values and a sense of history. As those closest to him did not know, Helmfloss secretly soaked the cushion he sat on during these addresses in premium gasoline. The overall sensation helped to focus his voice and body.

His will charged his followers to place the TV candlestick on his breast and burn his body on an open pyre by the lakeshore. Afterwards, they should load the *Oval Base* with such gems as might be found on board, and sink the boat. If the river was too shallow to submerge the full vessel, so be it. The boat's upper half would make a fine monument. He ordered his twin sons, Juventus and Arsenal, to reconcile with each other before lighting the pyre as one.

On the night of the motel speech, the PM left the soaked cushion on a chair in the kitchen of the *Oval Base.* Arsenal lit his hash pipe in the kitchen after his father had gone to sleep. Flames engulfed the houseboat. Arsenal escaped the carnage by wading the ten metres to shore. The Prime Minister died of smoke inhalation.

With the *Oval Basin* destroyed, officials organized a state funeral for Manchester Helmfloss. Pundits raved approval for his *de facto* farewell speech, which went viral on the Internet. After casting suspicion on his twin brother and main rival

Arsenal, Juventus easily won the party leadership, and swept to power on a wave of national sympathy. Years later, standing on the shoulders this giant, Spukwell declared the charter irrelevant under his new justice system, which relied on underqualified judges. The frayed, coffee-stained original document was now part of a permanent exhibit called "Landmarks in Democratic Missteps."

Security man one paused just beyond the exhibit to take a call on his e-phone. When he returned, he gave Barry his personal e-phone code. He told Barry not to hesitate to call if he needed any assistance during his visit. Barry was surprised they didn't offer him a "do not disturb" sign. Security had grown slack around this building since the end of parliament. It was the least visited tourist site in Ottawa.

Security man two rang for the elevator. "It's been great touching Base with you," he said. "Get it? Touching Base!" The two security men laughed heartily. "In all seriousness, we're glad to see you re-join the Canadian family," Security man two shouted as the elevator doors closed on Barry. "To be honest, we thought you'd be with all those protesters in the sequestration camp in Vernon. You know, Camp Carbon Capture. Of course, they have to pay do their yelling, in a black zone no less. Haters! Ottawa's free of charge. Happy Canada Day, Base! Don't mess up again. Stay real, guy."

* * *

Returning from these thoughts to the top of the Peace Tower, Barry looked out over Wellington Street. The street was like a short elastic band stretched to link the eastern and western municipalities of greater Ottawa. To the east were stone buildings with French provincial roofs, and stalls with flowers and vegetables for sale, and some venerable heritage bars interspersed with pristine bistros, venerable delis, and *de rigueur* craft beer dance pads. To the west, a long parkway shared the traffic with Lady Cassandra Boulevard, formerly known as Richmond Road, as it curved along the edge of the river, bordering art cinemas, moderately old churches of stucco or brick, miscalculated malls and big box hardware stores open for business. The shallow, white-capped rapids of the Ottawa River gushed around small islands, pushing forward a rare lost log that evoked the area's industrious, pre-digital past. The city basked in the lush humidity of summer, while the green hills to the north waited patiently to flame out in autumn and sparkle in mid-winter light.

Within its short span, Wellington Street embraced the great national buildings of Ottawa in its asphalt arms. The *Central Bank of Canada,* a renovation of a two-story fast-food outlet across from the National War Memorial, presented a lean and efficient countenance to the crowds. Its large front windows revealed a simple, push-your-tray cafeteria, reassuring Canadians that their dollars were well looked after.

One block west stood the venerable *Centre for Democratic Evolution*, where Prime Ministers kept their offices in times past. Further west, the sparkling *Ministry of Empathy* featured impressive mirror panels tinted blue to block the sun. The *Office of Sovereign Interpretation* occupied a refurbished Cathedral that matched the gothic stone of the Peace Tower. On the north side of the street to Barry's right stood the *People's Court of Conscience*, its broad green lawn and modern gray pillars implying common sense. Massive portraits of its current panel of judges – decent, male citizens who knew how to meet a payroll, stay on message and eschew activism – filled each of the six tall windows that towered above the main steps.

Beside the court, the *National Art Park* gave throngs of children scope to dream of a future, not dwell on the past. It featured sculptures and murals, fountains and graffiti, with old archival texts and rare historical manuscripts available for cutting and pasting into arts and crafts. There were automated booths with robotic arms for face painting and tattooing. Children ground up copies of Canada's defunct *Charter of Rights and Freedoms* in an old, hand-turned shredder. They produced colourful strips and confetti dots, and glued them to pictures of convicted dissenters. These "creative stations" focused on the theme of democratic reformation.

The art park lay in the shadow of the *Ministry of Intimacy,* a stainless steel tower that rivalled the Peace Tower in height. It stood on the former site of a cube-shaped building (rumoured to have been a library or an archive or both).

At the entrance to the *Ministry of Intimacy,* children played with consoles that let them unscramble and assemble a portrait of the Lord Protector on a giant 20-metre jumbotron. The jumbotron was called *MISHTHEFOP.* The *Office of Media Freedom* controlled it. An electronic inscription raced around the base of the jumbotron explained the acronym: "This **m**onument **is** placed **h**ere **t**o **h**elp **e**nsure **f**reedom **o**f the **p**ress." Quotations on the importance of a free press raced around the base. Children tried to read them in short installments as they whizzed passed their eyes.

Wellington Street, sealed off to traffic on Canada Day, thronged with families waiting for the party to begin at noon. A marching band blared "Taking it to the Streets," a late twentieth century rock classic, in brassy drum-filled blasts. Crimson maples adorned floppy hats, inflated sunglasses, disposable baby strollers and souvenir knapsacks. A young man was hustled away by two members of the Whistling Accountability Constabulary, a new security detail that wore the badge of the Atlantis Zone World Bank of Europe, its official sponsor. *WHAC* was the Praetorian Guard of modern Canada, specializing in the protection of Wellington Street and the Lord Protector on state occasions. The young man had bared his ass transparently but unaccountably to a family of five, revealing an orange maple leaf tattoo. He would answer for it.

WHAC officers carried *Ogresso* hand pistols loaded with orange paint bullets, and long plastic bayonets fixed at all times. The bayonets were twice as long and four times heavier than the pistols, making them impossible to handle in scuffles with hecklers in what *WHAC*s called "the red zone." The bayonets were part of a fast growing regimental tradition sponsored by the *Bureau of History*.

* * *

Barry took out his small binoculars and scanned the front lawn of the *Museum of Democracy*. A crescent road ringed the museum. The Centennial Flame burned at its centre near a stone wall that separated the museum grounds from Wellington Street. Beyond the wall, a statue of Sir Galahad stood on the sidewalk. Sir Galahad's cloak billowed, as if in a stiff, bronze breeze. His closed left hand touched his breast; his left hand gripped a sword that seemed to have been drawn by Galahad himself a moment ago from the broad stone pedestal beneath his feet. Beside the statue, two men scuffled with each other, until a *WHAC* Constable blew his whistle close to their ears. They shrank in pain.

A block away, Ottawa police officers waited beyond a restraining line, sipping coffee, ready to move in if needed. The *WHAC* mandate was ceremonial in theory. But they liked to interpret their mandate with latitude. They did not shy away from turf wars with real police.

Barry moved his lenses across Wellington Street. He fixed his gaze on the spires of the venerable *Chateau Populaire*, and then scanned left to the *Bureau of History* beside Rideau Canal. Inside the Bureau, a hologram tableau of Spukwell's Propurgation offered free admission to visitors on Canada Day. Visitors could follow the "propurgation narrative," from Spukwell's initial musings on democratic evolution, to his dramatic ultimatum to those sitting in the house. The exhibit was interactive, allowing visitors to alter the chronology and choose Spukwell's actual words from a limited menu.

Barry could not see the giant face of the Peace Tower clock above his head. He looked at his phone. It was 11:30. The Protectoral entourage was scheduled to leave Rideau Hall at precisely 11:45. It would arrive on Parliament Hill at exactly noon. He touched the duffel bag cautiously. The bag was hot from July sun. Would the heat affect his plan? Barry checked the current UV index on his e-phone. Had he put on enough sun blocker that morning? He bowed his head to shade his face from the sun.

A video game opened on his phone. It was a favourite game in his youth: *Strikedown.* The game invited players to launch drone strikes on cities of their choice, though the menu selection was limited: no North American or European cities were available. Precision bombs fell on fixed structures from great heights, blowing them to smithereens without a raising a single decibel. HQ buildings scored 1000 points. Schools scored -100. Would a few minutes of *Strikedown* calm his nerves? He started level one, but the glare of the noon sun made it impossible. It reminded him of school days in Edmonton, when he played the game with Lucius. He never beat Lucius, but never stopped trying. He put his phone away.

He closed his eyes and fell into the dream he had the night before. A man wearing a torn white T-shirt and faded blue jeans stood over him as he knelt in the tower. The man's hair was wispy, dark and thin. He was at most twenty-five years old. There was blue powder on both of his hands. He had a terrible injury. His right eyelid was massively swollen and fastened shut. It throbbed with a steady, tense pulsation, as if it might explode with blood at any moment. His left eye was wobbly and evasive. The young man tried to fix his good eye on Barry's bucket of chicken.

"We smelled that chicken," the man said.

Barry had to shield his eyes from the glare of the sun as he looked at the man's face. The man cast no shadow. The sunlight was blinding around the man's body, like the circumference of a solar eclipse. Softer light filtered dimly through his body, rendered smoky and opaque by his dingy t-shirt and worn jeans.

"What are you? Some kind of ghost?"

"No, sir. We aren't aware of any ghosts. No one has informed me I'm a ghost. No one has told me that or accused me of that. No sir, we're a specter."

"Isn't a specter just another word for ghost?"

"No, sir, I don't think so. That is not correct."

Barry studied the man's T-shirt again. Was he dreaming? He unsealed the bucket of chicken and inhaled deeply. No. He could smell the thick battered meat. He knew it was not a dream.

"What do you mean, 'we aren't aware of any ghosts'"?

"There's five of us, sir, last we checked. I have asked for someone to come forward and please assist us by counting. We need to get to six."

"Do you have names?"

"Yes sir. Booth, Harvey, Earl, Oswald. And then there's Princip. Boy did he set off some serious shit. Hey! Let's show you a trick!"

The specter splayed itself into five figures, and began a frenzied square-dance-in-a-ring of manic turns and molecular circles around the observation deck. All five foamed at the mouth: "Welcome be the sixth! Welcome be the sixth!" Barry realized that the dance was surrounding him, confining him, embracing him. He became the still, frightened point of a spinning whirl of locked hands and frenzied eyes, the nucleus of a demented atom. When the rotating figures reached the speed of sound, the moving sphere hummed "The Eyes of Texas" and "O Canada" simultaneously at high speed.

"Stop spinning!" Barry pleaded.

"Ain't spinnin'," the man said. "This is our singularity.

And yours too, we's hopin'.'"

"Singularity?" Barry asked.

"Yes sir. It's like a club for the like-minded. All singularities are. We get to keep all our similar beefs, gripes and pissed-offnesses, but we don't have none of the righteous context that made us feel important. And we need some bad. Take Booth, for instance. He needs to lose a civil war like a drunk needs a gallon of whisky – and the sooner the better. But there's no righteous cause like we hoped. So we're stuck in here and we're pretty damned cramped. Adding's the way to make it bigger, to get moving we figure. That's why we're lookin' for a new member with some new context to share. You look likely to us all decked out as you are. Join us happy few."

"We few!" screamed a voice inside the specter.

"Shut it, Booth. Joe Shakespeare there thinks the world's a stage. It's more like a sardine can."

"How did you find me?" Barry asked.

"The chicken. Nice ripe smell on it. The smell of noon drew us. Nice. Chicken tempts us. But mainly, we're here for you."

Barry pushed the bucket of chicken towards the specter. "Go ahead, help yourself. My apologies for not offering sooner."

"Ha! Hear that, James Earl? He's sorry. The nice man's apologized for not offerin' us chicken sooner. You Canadians kill us! James Earl holed up in Canada for a spell, you may realize. Hey James Earl – how was the chicken in Toronto?"

"Not as good as Memphis," a scratchy voice muttered. "Booth's nodding. He agrees. Peace at last!"

"Or Dallas! I chewed some in Dallas to kill time. I say

Dallas beats Toronto," said the specter. Another voice cried out in a language Barry did not understand.

"Fuck your mother's recipe, Princip! Pardon us, sir. We call him Joe College. Like I said, none of us caused the shit he did."

"Bullshit! I did!"

"Shut up! I'll handle this. Now sir, speakin' of our chicken beating Toronto and that of Canadians as a whole, isn't it high time you became like us? Americans I mean. Forget Joe College."

"Sic semper!" said a scratchy voice out of thin air.

"Shut your fat mouth, Booth! I'll do the talkin'!"

"You're even stupider than the history books say, Oswald."

"Pardon the interruption. That was Joe Shakespeare. Did I say that? Permit me to be formal, Base sir. You strike me as a man who likes quick results. You want a fast return on your amount of time spent."

"Do you want the chicken or not?" Barry demanded.

The specter plunged its bare forearm into the bucket.

"Yeah! Lemme see. I'm gonna choose a drumstick. Gonna give it something some folks in the state of Texas call it when you slip it entirely into your mouth like a smoking popsicle or a nice warm jumper cable. Gonna take it nice and slow. Nice and slow. Slow and comfortable."

Barry was surprised to hear the ghost call Texas a state. That was obsolete. He recalled the end of statehood all too clearly.

* * *

Texas sparked the breakup of the United States of America in 2043 when, with the nation embroiled in constitutional crisis, the citizens of Texas voted to renounce statehood, while keeping the U.S. constitution, rather than endure another gun-hating health-loving president in Washington. America began to unravel from within when its 50th president, Arson Digits, resigned the presidency after eighteen months in office. Digits inherited a promising national economy, but was stressed by overdue child support claims and a hostile takeover of his online family entertainment empire. He hoped to make history as the first sitting president to divorce and remarry while in office. Instead, he launched the break up of the country.

Digits resigned in a pre-recorded, nationally televised "people's conversation." He wanted to spend more time with his businesses, his children and his new fiancee. Texas legislators feared his more liberal vice-president would link needless health care and needless green energy to needless gun control once she took office, even though all three were obvious job killers in their eyes. The crisis came to a head when the seven members of C4 – the Congressional Constitutional Crisis Committee – opened fire on the seven members of the Texas Secession Delegation in an elevator on Capitol Hill after a heated Q and A session. One Texan, the only secessionist still moving, pressed the emergency stop button and gunned down what remained of the Crisis Committee with a maxi-pistol he kept in his left sock. It could fire 7200 rounds a minute. The carnage was such that engineers had to remove the entire elevator from the building with its thick gumbo of body parts still inside.

An honour guard bore the flag-draped elevator to Arlington National Cemetery on a caisson drawn by a black Humvee. At the graveside, ex-president Arson Digits delivered a stirring update on his business ventures and wedding plans. He then solemnly read out the names of twelve journalists he planned to sue for libel. A cannon sounded after each name.

Mourners interred the elevator beneath a single marker, leaving the puree of human remains inside united without regard to state, party or place of birth. The marker was a simple white cross with the numeral 2 nailed to its centre in affirmation of the second amendment. The crucified 2 soon became the hit bling of the year in parts of the country, adorning charm bracelets, necklaces and rear-view mirrors.

Gun lobbyists argued that all fourteen of the dead would still be alive if they'd used their God-given common sense to carry superior firepower. They called for armed marshals to ride on all elevators in all government buildings, and demanded more research dollars to put more rounds per minute into the hands of decent people.

Texas honoured its dead in a separate memorial. Then they voted to secede in a touch screen plebiscite. Texas renounced statehood and declared itself a "natural republic." It joined the G30. Other states scrambled to follow. Some stayed single; some amalgamated in pairs, trios or quartets with new names. The United States seemed to morph from an eagle into a hydra until The Network, a singularly massive corporate entity, assured citizens that the U.S. was really a phoenix. It rose from its ashes as the "Natural Republics of America," showing its spirit of innovation and resilience unfettered by federal government. The net size of continental bureaucracy quickly increased as republics scrambled to self-actualize. Most joined the G30, making it the G68. Smaller countries also joined, making it the G80.

A loyal remnant of the U.S. Navy established a U.S. federal government in exile on Nantucket Island, taking two U.S. patrol ships and a copy of the original constitution with them. The sailors took a quick census, confirming that their government was one third gay, two thirds male and one third white. The Natural Republics declared them lawless renegades. They decided to starve these scofflaws out. But they could not agree on a process. Some wealthy vacationers on Cape Cod formed a group called *Freedom Fighters For Patriotism and Order,* or F3PO for short. Using bullhorns and cabin cruisers, they stood off the shore of Nantucket and hurled accusations of treason and rebellion at the sailors. They set off fireworks at night to disrupt the sailors' sleep. They promised a war and soon. The sailors patiently erected barn board shelters, planted corn, squash and beans, prayed for rain and looked forward to Thanksgiving. When Thanksgiving came without war, they celebrated with roasted root vegetables with glazed cranberries, and a touch football game.

* * *

Barry turned his attention back to the specter.

"So, what do folks call this in Texas?" he inquired. He watched the specter turn a chicken leg like a screwdriver through the surface of its horrid purple lips.

"A South Dallas Valentine. Y'all ever heard that word?"

"That's three words."

"Don't get technical on us. In other words, you've not heard of it."

"You're lying," Barry replied.

"OK, sure, I'm lyin'. So what?" the specter replied, sheepishly.

"I know you're lying, and I'm not even from Texas."

"What's in there anyways? It looks lumpy. If it's a gun – and you've been touching that trigger – you get to be full partner with us."

"And what if it's not a gun?"

"Don't change the subject. If it's a gun, you'll change histories. Canada'll have a more colourful history. And your singularity will be set in stone. Come on. You wannabe like Americans. Admit it."

"Where have you been? It's Natural Republicans now."

"There you go, getting technical on us again. Open the bag. Is it one of those new donut triggers you read about?"

"You read about it?"

"Figure of speech."

"Fine. What if what's inside is a figurative gun?"

"Now you've lost us." The ghost tried, but couldn't touch any more fried chicken.

"Dammit to hell time's up!" he shrieked, dropping to its knees. "Shoot quick so we can stay! Chicken tempts us we tempt you! Win-win. Quick! Pretty please!"

The specter moaned in frustration. Its eyes congealed into burnt coal dust, falling to the floor like cinders on a fireplace grate. Barry squinted for the baleful red digits on his alarm clock radio. He must be dreaming. It must be 3 a.m. No. It was still now. Noon and daylight blazed.

Short of breath, Barry switched his e-phone to mirror function. He saw the lines of fatigue in his eyes, and worried curve in his eyebrows. There was a patch of gray in his dark hair, though he was just thirty years old. He tilted the mirror slightly, seeking some advantage. He was shocked to see his face transform into the face he had at ten years of age. It was eager, alive, curious. His blue eyes blazed with new enthusiasms. His dark black bangs hovered above his thick glasses frames. His massive eyebrows swayed from side to side with curiosity. Where had this reflection come from? Suddenly, he was oblivious to where he was, and what he had planned, rapt by his youthful reflection.

Then he felt faint. He grew dizzy. He stood. His knees buckled. He fell through the glass panels protecting the observation deck, shattering them and plummeting to the ground in terror.

Barry landed immediately on the observation deck at the top of the Peace Tower. The glass panels were intact. The chicken and the bag and the cola were not disturbed. His e-phone was not on mirror function. Its screen image was a picture of a bright full moon Barry had photographed near Edmonton in June. He thought he was dreaming. He began to pry his eyes open. They were already open. Above the tower, a lone pelican circled and glided towards the parade.

He took six deep breaths to calm down. He wanted to forget his dream. If he was patient, he was sure he would forget it in time. He turned his gaze back to the lawn in front of the Peace Tower. A father was conducting his wife and four children in a political chant: "Ten more years! Ten more years!" One of the man's children, perhaps ten years old, held a placard reading, "Normal Families for Lucius Spukwell." In fact, it would not be ten *more* years for the Lord Protector. He claimed the title of "Lord Protector of Canada" following his historic propurgation. Still, with Parliament permanently suspended, he magnanimously placed the option of renewable ten-year terms to the people in a national referendum.

Spukwell held the results of that referendum in a sealed envelope in his hands. This would be democracy's final curtain call. At some point in term one more permanent arrangements would be made for the future. Spukwell told his Minister of Memory to announce ten-year terms to reassure the public, to calm the markets, and to wean the people off parliamentary democracy. He ordered the Commissioner to restrict the flow of information to statutory and religious holidays, of which there would be plenty more in the future.

Barry looked east to the corner of Sussex Drive and Wellington Street. The landau would turn west at that corner.

He saw the commentators from the *Footman News* TV network perched on a scaffold near the corner. Spukwell favoured *Footman* news. They were busy interviewing some "special guests" supplied by the Lord Protector's Office. Chester Voxbrow, a newly elected member of the *Pan-Toronto Journalism Hall of Fame*, provided commentary and "historical background" for viewers. Now at the tender age of twenty-two, Voxbrow claimed to be under consideration for Chief Justice of the People's Court of Conscience. The appointment, even if true, would not preclude his working as a TV commentator in Spukwell's Canada. Spukwell's judges were allowed to keep their day jobs.

Barry cringed at the sight of the *Footman News* team in action. He looked down to the base of the Peace Tower. Barry pushed the chicken away and reached for his bag.

"Don't kill the messenger," he whispered to himself. Then he placed some earplugs in his ears.

Chapter Eight

THINK TANK

Geogasm, November 2038-40

Lucius Spukwell, Lady Cassandra Spukwell and Lady's cousin, Edward Feenie, whom Lucius learned to call Uncle Ned in respect of his age, sat back in brown leather loungers in the office of Feenie's lawyer, Malcolm Cuthbert, QC. They had adjourned from a lightly attended memorial service for Richie Spukwell, late of Edmonton, Alberta. Lady was touched that Joey Knotwad showed up at the service. In fact, Destiny and Jasmine spotted him on the roadside hitchhiking to Calgary as they drove Reverend Phlap to Geogasm. When Knotwad learned where the three were going, he wanted to go with them. Lady had told Phlap not to trouble himself by coming such a long way. Phlap believed her, but chose to attend and to speak.

"This world is not what it seems!" Phlap proclaimed from the podium. "Not at all! By some mishap, Richmond Moorhead Spukwell was consumed in the flames of this world's malice. Pity the world for it! Richie will pass through fire into a moment multiplied and expanded by every imaginative moment he has ever known, made or will yet know or make. And whether that moment is a stately palace or a humble cottage matters not. What matters is that it is genuine and inspired. Abdielle will attend him there, counselling him, giving him insight, precipitating *anagnorisis,* and the treasure of self-knowledge grounded in *caritas.* May the floors of his inspiration be diamonds, not dust, its shadows desire, not dung!"

Phlap recited the chorus of *Sex is all there is.*

"Listen *between* those lines, friends. They tell us Richie had a good heart. The words show us our vulnerability to life and love, the poverty of our bodies, the wealth of our energies. How I hope he knew Canticles, that richest of love poems! Richie had a longing, however malleable or misplaced, to reach out to others. We can hear that longing in *Sex is all there is.* Well, Richie – it's time for the extended play version. Mercifully, inspiration is all there is! You see, friends, like all of us Richie had a hole in his heart. It wasn't guitar shaped. It wasn't penis shaped or money shaped. It was shaped like his family, his dear son Lucius, his loving wife Lady Cassandra. I had a hole in my heart too, and a dear, wild, unusual child showed me that mine was gay and lesbian shaped. Like Saul I persecuted. Oh yes! Then I passed out. Abdielle showed me . . . . "

"Thank you Reverend Phlap," said Feenie, halting the testimony. The family withdrew to Cuthbert's quarters, leaving Phlap, Destiny and Jasmine to teas, cheeses and confections. Joey Knotwad paid his respects to Cassandra in a private conversation, then thumbed his way to Calgary.

* * *

Detectives from the Edmonton Police Service visited

Geogasm in September to question Lady and Lucius.

"The young lady we arrested at the scene was calling your name, Mr. Spukwell. She was distraught. She feared you were inside the restaurant."

"It was not a restaurant. It was my father's house. And yes, she might have thought I was there, incorrectly. I was at her house in the afternoon. But I decided to go to Geogasm to be with my family. The fire, from what I've read, started in the wee hours of the morning."

"What was your relationship to the young lady?"

"Acquaintances, I would say. We played Monopoly sometimes."

"She says there was an altercation during your visit."

"That is true. I'd be pleased to pay for the damage. She's befriended a homeless person, by the way, a subject close to my late father's heart. We quarrelled over hygiene. The homeless man can't pay for any damages. Still, he might be a person of interest to you. I say leave him alone."

The detectives were nauseated by Lucius's precise answers.

"We'll decide that, Mr. Spukwell. She says she came to, um, let me check the name – Richmond's End – to deliver a poem to you. Does that sound plausible?"

Lucius's head snapped to attention. "I suppose she might have, possibly."

"At 3 a.m.?"

"Her own poem?"

"That's not important. She threw it on the fire. How and when did you pay for your transportation to Geogasm?"

Lady intervened.

"I too thought it might be the homeless person," Lady said. "Lucius believes his father has a soft spot for the homeless."

"Believes?" The detectives looked sceptical.

"Let me put it this way," Lady said. "I think Lucius started the fire that caused my husband's death. Why? Perhaps he expected money."

The detectives exchanged knowing glances and shook their heads. They could tell she was lying. They closed their notebooks and put away their pens.

"Thanks, Lady Spukwell, but we're pretty sure we know who did this. Please accept our condolences. And stay out of this. If the perpetrator is convicted, you'll be called for impact statements, but probably not to testify."

* * *

Cuthbert called the family to order.

"Well, Reverend Phlap has delivered us from spiritual technicalities to legal practicalities," he said.

No one laughed. Lady reflected on Phlap's sermon. She often wept to think of how the lyrics seemed to impugn her sexually. Had she misinterpreted them? Lucius was inwardly disgusted but outwardly calm.

"Very good then," Cuthbert continued. "First, the Edmonton Coroner has determined that Richmond Moorhead Spukwell died by fire. It may have been by accident or misadventure. Foul play is not ruled out. Suicide is ruled out. For these reasons, we can now read the will."

Cuthbert unfolded a document.

"I have examined this handwritten letter left by Richie in his car," Cuthbert began. "And I'm pleased to say that it meets the standards of probate. Let me disclose the outcomes. Lucius Maximus Spukwell: you are the main beneficiary of the contents of this document. Lucius Maximus Spukwell: you own and control all royalties in perpetuity for the musical compositions titled by copyright and hereafter referred to as *Mercy Hospital Blowjob* and *Sex is all there is*. Copyright Richmond Moorcock Spukwell to be transferred to Lucius Maximus Spukwell, his son and heir. Lucius Maximus Spukwell: you are encouraged, but not explicitly required, according to the grammar of this letter, to, and I quote, 'see to your mother's well-being.' That qualifying phrase may be open to interpretation, provided it's not interpreted as having no practical force in law or in the actual world we now live in. I don't advise you to test it in court. I'll secure the claim to royalties and, of course, sue for any and all back royalties owed. Questions?"

"Don't sue," said Lucius.

"Pardon me? There may be several tens of thousands involved."

"Let's simply start from where we are. I don't want publicity. I don't want my mother hearing those lyrics again."

"A silent partnership in your own exclusive income? Unusual, yes, but possible – for a fee! But you're distraught. Will you at least take time to consider this decision?"

Lucius nodded contemptuously. He made a mental note to fire Cuthbert. "Get the revenue streams in place without publicity. Am I clear?"

Normally, Cuthbert and Feenie would be furious with the temerity of such a junior. Lucius's charisma had blossomed in a fireball of spoiled cooking oil. They nodded meekly.

* * *

The meeting adjourned. Lady Spukwell declined tea from Feenie's wife, Queenie. She went upstairs to rest. Feenie invited Lucius to join him at the peeing post at the end of his long backyard. The post was a decommissioned telephone pole sawed down to eight feet. The lopped end of the pole lay on its side, tangled in weeds by the fence. Feenie wanted to turn it into a monument to all who felt victimized by anti-fracking radicals. No local carver would take the commission.

A dusty, fly covered hand sanitizer dispenser was nailed to one side of the post. Feenie saw the post as an easy way to go green in the countryside. No flushes. No filtration. Acceptable damage to the grass. In his heyday, he hoped the post would give him real credibility among progressive voters. It bothered him that the eco-movement disliked him. It hardly mattered now. After leaving Parliament, he thought of taking the peeing post to the *Businessaurus Rexes*. But the PMO warned him to keep a low profile or face consequences.

Lucius swallowed his disgust and stood well back. Feenie removed the blue rhinestone ring the PM gave him when he was first elected to Parliament. Then he turned to the post, unzipped his trousers and primed the business end of his penis. It was time to talk politics.

"You've heard that Henrymart will be a federal riding in the next redistribution? They're naming it Central Geogasm. You'll be twenty-two when the writ drops. That gives you time to establish residency. In short, I want you to run for Parliament. Thoughts?"

Lucius was intrigued.

"Why me, Uncle? Why not you?"

"I'm damaged goods, Lucius. It's time to pass the torch at least two generations down the line. Remember: you'll be running as an outsider. Outsiderhood is a big plus in politics, so we'll play that card often. Still, the less history you have with me, the better. It'll take more than a pollster to sugar the shit I did. If we're careful, my banishment could actually tweak your outsiderhood. And that reminds me: your mother says you once gave a talk on communism in elementary school. Yes, I've been vetting you. I can tell she's lying. Still, how far from the truth is she?"

"It was a talk on homelessness, not communism."

"Good. Did anyone record the talk on video or social media?"

"No."

"Good. As soon as we announce, they'll shake your electronic life upside down. And we don't need any whiffs or stenches. I'll say this once: politics is about getting power and keeping it. Public policy? That's just the tin cans behind the wedding limo."

Feenie spiced the post with some final drops.

"Here's the plan," he resumed. "I envision a total makeover for Geogasm. Principles, mission statement, public intellectuals – the works."

"I was considering university," Lucius said.

"Consider going straight into the economy." Feenie advised. "That's what I did."

Feenie reminisced about the early days. He was elected to Parliament at the age of twenty-four after his father won some Solid Retentivist Party nomination papers in a game of Texas hold' em. Prime Minister Manchester Helmfloss signed off because the seat was safe, and cabinet was out of the question. The riding, known then as Coldblend-Foldville-Steerclear, never voted less than 78% Progressive Conservative, Reform, Conservative or Solid Retentivist in its history. When Feenie won the riding with barely 53% of the vote, he drew the ire of the PMO. He would have to work very hard to keep the nomination and redeem himself in the PM's eyes.

So he did. He used an accordion to disrupt questions that went "off message" at parliamentary committee meetings. He roamed the parking lots of Ottawa's two universities in his black pickup, and let air out of the tires of cars and bicycles parked near science departments. He joined debating panels on *Panels on Politics*, bouncing a softball on the desk when others tried to speak. He became the first panellist in the show's history to be removed during a commercial break.

One day, Feenie went beyond hard work. He brought a soccer ball to the House of Commons and joined the women sitting strategically behind the PM during question period. He jiggled the ball on his desk, mouthed "Helmflossforsoccermoms" silently, then performed some gentle "headers." He produced a second ball, and cupped both balls to his torso where he rolled them around while the PM answered a question. His goal was to bring the soccermom demographic decidedly to the side of Helmfloss. The CBC made this its lead story that night. The video went viral, reaching two billion hits worldwide. Doctored versions featured the PM singing a rap song in German, French and Japanese in a computerized voice while Feenie sported with his balls behind him.

The PM turfed Feenie from caucus and forbade him ever to call him "Jay" again. Then Helmfloss blamed the CBC for exaggerating the incident. The CBC angle raised Feenie's hopes for a comeback.

"How long an exile?" Feenie asked Hester Roo, Helmfloss's Junior Overall Chief of Senior Staff, and author of a bestselling handbook for political aides: *Be Your Most Feared Self Now*.

"Do you think the CBC thing means you can return?" she asked, her fingers dealing with other matters on the keys of her e-phone. "Jay is compartmentalizing two issues: you and his disdain for the CBC. Those of us who know Jay understand that. You'll not return. Now despair – and get the hell out!"

Feenie was political toast. His best option was a graceful exit without complaint, litigation, autobiography or dramatization. PMO potentates warned him to avoid fresh bids for disgrace.

* * *

Feenie decided a think tank was the right launching pad for Lucius. His plan was bold and expensive. It would be named the *Geogasm Institute of Political, Social, Moral, Ethical and Fiscal Accountability and Common Sense. GIPSMEFACS,* for short. The institute would sponsor an annual conference: the *Geogasm Conference.* Sops of dogmas would flow through *The Geogasm Quarterly Online* for the high-minded, and more playful blogs such as *Load Off My Mind, Piece of Mind* and *Tax This!* for the casual reader. Scholarly papers, podcasts and drink receptions would purify party doctrine. The thorn Feenie hoped to place in the PM's anus would also stimulate local voters. Win-win.

Lucius liked the plan. He went to sleep that night thinking about *GIPSMEFACS*. He had a disturbing dream. He stood in Feenie's massive backyard. A flaming sunrise glowed above a distant field of blue flax. A large stained-glass window hovered at the end of the yard. Two dark-shirted guards emerged from the window, leading Richie out with them. They marched Richie to the peeing post, tethered him to it with leather straps, and put a blindfold on him. The blindfold seemed to enhance Richie's confused countenance. Richie seemed to expect some benign explanation for his predicament. Lucius stood quietly. He could hear his father murmuring: "Lucius? Are you there, bro? If you can hear me, answer. Please, bro? Please?" The guards stood by with their handguns drawn, waiting for Lucius to give an order.

Lucius woke in that instant. He held his throat and took

slow breaths. What could this dream mean? He had to think. He jotted down details and began his analysis. Feenie's peeing post could suggest revenue streams from "Sex is all there is" to Lucius's subconscious. That was his inheritance. So the post was a positive symbol!

On further analysis, he was certain his father was not the focus of the dream at all. That much was clear! He went through it again. He quickly uncovered the dream's primary meaning. The foreground was irrelevant. The meaning lay in that distant sunrise. Yes! The dream was telling him to go ahead with the think tank. Lucius had burned his bridges with Edmonton. So Geogasm would ignite his political career.

He typed his jotted notes on the dream into a word cloud app. The cloud confirmed his interpretation:

Sunrise new day

BRIGHT*FUTURE*

GIPSMEFACS

brand Fire!

Streaming *ME*

Financially solid solidness

Accountability Blind justice

Leadership aims

Going forward Richie

He vowed that if he ever took control of the Normal Solid Retentivist Party, he would change the party's name. He would call it, *The Fireball Party.* No one need know that the name came to him in a dream.

* * *

The next day, Lucius talked to his mother, hoping to get her blessing for *GIPSMEFACS*. He would try to take her word at face value if he could, or ask her to blink twice for "no" if he could not. Next, he asked Cuthbert what protections and risk limitations could be built into to any investment he might make in the think tank.

Cuthbert compared his contract options to a pre-nuptial agreement: Feenie could die, desert, abscond, or evaporate – but he could never sue, embarrass or control Lucius under a properly worded agreement.

"Trust me," Cuthbert assured Lucius. "It will be like having Feenie's scrotum for your safety deposit box, and his balls for your key chain, and his ass for your – ."

Lucius raised his hand to halt the discussion. He instructed Cuthbert to invest.

Cuthbert shifted revenue from *Sex is all there is* to Lucius's covert political movement fund. He seized the residual flow going to Richie's former bands. Marcus Culvert threatened to sue, but his career was in decline and he couldn't rally his band to protest. So they accepted a settlement. Turnover in membership was high. Only Culvert was around in Richie's time. His attempts to stir outrage online simply boosted revenues for Lucius.

The revenues claimed from *Drone I.V.* and the *Storm Poodles* were small compared to the instrumental market. Richie did well by his family when he offered his two hits to the background music industry. Cuthbert was impressed. He clamped down on this gold mine. In addition to yoga studios, new age radio transmissions, big box pharmacies and elevators, *Sex is all there is* (*sans* lyrics) was now being heard on almost every telephone in the world. If you needed to cancel your credit card, you heard it while on hold. If you needed help troubleshooting a useless computer, you heard it while on hold. If you wanted to speak to a dentist, join the armed forces, give money to charity or purchase a bus ticket, you heard it while on hold. If you were on hold in Europe, the Middle East, South America or Africa, you heard it while on hold. Even sex therapists subscribed to it. Cuthbert was surprised to learn that it was playing in the waiting room of his own office. He negotiated a 25% royalty rate for Lucius. 25% worked out to 6.8 million dollars per year after Cuthbert's annual fee.

* * *

The next federal election was nearly four years away. Task one: get Lucius the nomination for Central Geogasm by 2042. Task two: roll out *GIPSMEFACS* in an inaugural conference in 2040. Feenie wanted to distance the think tank from the party. He hoped the party would come begging to him. So he coined an enticing conference theme: "The Fourth Way."

Feenie booked the Henrymart community centre for the summer solstice weekend. His plan was simple: titles of keynote addresses would "seep" into core principles for a reformed Solid Retentivist Party. He wanted "blue chip" speakers featuring "new blood" inclusiveness and "big tent" ideas. He tapped disgruntled former staffers and alienated former colleagues for six crackling plenary addresses:

- *Air doesn't Grow on Trees: Emerging Commodities and Free Market Common Sense.* Bryce Titharsh, Feenie's former campaign manager.

- *Reigniting the Canadian Dream: Countering Claims to Clean Water Rights while Hitting the Anti-Commodification Underworld Hard.* Sonya Sansdeak, Feenie's former image consultant.
- *Earth Science isn't Rocket Science: Normalizing Public Opinion on Climate Change.* Johnson Trojam, Feenie's former executive assistant.
- *Industrializing New Waters to the End of Red Tape: A New Normal for Canada's Remaindered Lakes and Rivers.* Franklin Dimson, Feenie's former speechwriter.
- *Elitist, Abnormal or Just Plain Dumb? Turning the Heat Up on Off-Message Climate Scientists who Hope to see our Freedoms go up in Smoke.* Deena Bluishin, Feenie's former public policy advisor.
- *Clothing the Truth: Bloated Science Journalism and the New Economy of Blame.* Charles-Lemon Forgage, Feenie's personal tailor.

Feenie also wanted a major keynote speaker with a common touch: Jonah Flambo. He wrote a flattering e-mail invitation. Flambo's secretary intercepted the e-mail in progress, and switched Feenie to her Liveface app.

"You there. Does Mr. Flambo know you?"

"We met in passing."

"Check that. Please hold." Feenie listened to an *allegro vivace* pan flute version of *Sex is all there is.*

"Confirm. Passing does not meet the threshold. Do you have a web site?"

"Affirmative: fourthway.Geogasm.ca."

"Check. Hold."

Six minutes of *Sex is all there is* for English horn and cello.

"Thank you for holding. Mr. Flambo will speak Saturday June 20 from 2 to 3 pm. His speech will be titled: 'Fire Times Four."

"Got it!"

"No. You need the long title: *Fire Times Four: wherein the execrable F's are squared in their infamy, and our claim to righteous ecology is expounded, with the claims of eco-terrorists and their celebrity friends expunged.*'"

Barry managed to jot it all down.

Flambo didn't disappoint. He drew about one hundred local farmers, hospitality workers, volunteer firefighters, restaurateurs and some tourists to Henrymart to hear the plain damn truth about eco-terrorism. Flambo collapsed after this effort, vomiting liberally at the edge of the stage. The firefighters made him lie down. They checked his blood pressure. He was severely dehydrated. A bystander offered him water, but he pushed it away. Drained and feverish, he made certain the audience would leave knowing the environmental underworld would murder them in their beds that night. It wouldn't be quick or painless either. It would be death by fire. Eco-terrorists would light each of their victim's four extremities – two hands and two feet – and watch the flames rise. Fire times four!

* * *

Strolling through the outdoor conference site, Lucius saw Barry Basewik-Quick sitting in a flimsy wire chair, filming the speech on his e-phone. Lucius looked away. Barry was dead to him. Lucius checked the registration list. Yes – Barry's name was down as a last minute registrant. He noticed Barry's title: Special Executive Assistant to Mr. Flambo for Cultural Memory.

Flambo begged off from the banquet citing mental exhaustion. He rambled on about needing a martyr's death as

Feenie and Lucius stuffed him into his car. They folded him into the passenger seat. Lucius ignored Barry, who was in the driver's seat. On Monday, a video of Flambo's speech appeared in the *Edmonton Footman online*. The transcript was edited down to 250 words; the two-hour video to 90 seconds, including preliminary advertisements. Lucius was disgusted with Barry's editorial evisceration of *The Fourth Way* keynote address.

Lucius wanted more control over future conferences. A livestreaming web site would override the elitist media. But what would be the theme? He went through the papers presented at the *Fourth Way*. He found an idea in Feenie's talk to a small group workshop on democracy. Feenie's paper was called, "Prorogation and Beyond." His thesis: prorogation of Parliament was a "baby step" on the road to democratic reformation. The party needed bold, new steps to lead Canada into the future. What would a bold step look like? Lucius wondered. Was there a name for going one step beyond prorogation?

In that moment, the theme of the next conference was born.

Chapter Nine

THE LAKE OF FIRE

Olam Lake, Alberta, September 2042

Izzy's life was hard after the fire at *Richmond's End.*

Police found her at the scene. By that time, twenty-eight bystanders observed her from a safe distance, filmed her with e-phones, and recorded her screams. Izzy saw a pair of feet engulfed in flames from the outside window. She thought it was Lucius. She tried to enter the fire and pull him out. Her hair and eyebrows were badly singed. Her hands were badly blistered.

Suspicion fell on her because she had no phone. No one can credibly call for help without a phone. To make things worse, three videos showed her throwing a piece of paper into the fire, feeding its rage. And she did herself no favours by holding a black cat in her arms. The evidence was strong. Police placed her under arrest.

Barry regretted not being there to break the story. He also worried that he would be implicated. He turned his phone over to the police.

"I took this video at about 1 p.m."

"Fourteen hours before the incident?" the detective said. "No relevance, but thanks for coming forward. They were just some yahoos looking for a burger in the wrong place. We had a chat with them on the Fireway. They're heading east."

"How could you know about them?"

"Not your problem. Now, why are you making videos of strangers?"

"I'm an apprentice journalist."

"You're an apprentice nuisance if you invade people's privacy. Don't take rights for granted. Watch your step, son."

Barry decided to suspend his journalistic persona for a time. He sought shelter under the wings of Jonah Flambo. Flambo's secretary rebuffed him. Flambo was busy linking the arson and suspicious death to dronecult. He happened to like dronecult, but the story came first. So he labelled Izzy a dronecult phony, a poser, a wannabe. Had Richie Spukwell spurned her sexual overtures? His readers would make that decision.

Then Flambo found out that Izzy was the daughter of Noah Burnet, the famous water scientist. All hell broke loose. He devised a single, "omnibus" headline to handle this troublesome family: "Edmonton's *Real* Environmental Hazard." He discovered that Izzy and Noah had minimum critical mass for an eco-terrorist cell: two. Noah had the technical know-how; Izzy was an impressionable youth raised by self-centered workaholics. She was predisposed to crime. He called for Izzy to be shipped to Prison Island without charges. What were charges but more government red tape? Listen up, Parliament. Canada needed discretionary shipping powers, and it needed them now. Delays weren't good enough for the Canadian people. As for Noah, he had spent much of his career *outside* Canada. He was a sham Canadian! Shame on the university for not revoking his tenure. Flambo urged anyone with information on Noah's parenting habits or miscellaneous hobbies to come forward. No one did.

Izzy's grade one spruce tree had grown to a height of two feet through eighteen harsh winters. Someone torched it with gasoline.

* * *

Noah and Simeon hired Delvis Blo, a top criminal lawyer in Edmonton, to help Izzy. Blo offered to sue Flambo's ass *pro bono* for assigning "eco-terrorist family values" to the Dryden-Burnets. *Footman* editors, relying on sound legal advice, damped down Flambo's firestorm of prose.

Flambo countered, hiring Dr. Blaine Wormug, his go-to expert psychological profile witness. Wormug confirmed, on condition that his name come first in the headline, that Izzy was an anti-social loner ripe for eco-radicalization.

At trial, Blo attacked the prosecution's circumstantial evidence. The fire could not have been started from close range given the huge fireball. Izzy would not have survived. And she could not have started the fire from a distance without a device. She carried a cat, not a phone. Prosecutors agreed. She must have used an app before throwing her phone into the flames to destroy evidence. No go said Blo: Simeon and Noah found her phone at home. It was far too primitive to support a laser app. In fact, it was really nothing more than a phone. Prosecutors found that hard to believe.

Motive? Prosecutors played the Flambo card, portraying Izzy as a woman scorned. She was a radical rights vegan placing a curse on *Richmond's End.* Why else the black cat? Perhaps the "poem" she threw into the flames was really an ideological training manual.

Judge Esther Timberbinch shook her head in disbelief. She dismissed all charges.

Izzy enrolled at the University of Alberta, but was seldom seen on the north campus by her second year. The Registrar required her to withdraw for low grades. She returned through the Fresh Start Program and took courses in creative writing and human ecology. These courses let her study and work downtown. She donated her e-phone to Edmonton's Food Bank when journalists, including Barry, kept asking her for grillings and sit-downs. Barry boasted on his blog that he was all over the *Drone I.V.* cold case. Izzy pushed Barry into a cedar bush when he followed her down a street asking to write her unauthorized autobiography. She wanted to be on Church Street where there were better things to do than be notorious.

* * *

Four years later, Izzy's journey to Prison Island began. It was an April afternoon on campus. Noah was giving a seminar to twelve graduate students in qualitative eco-hydrology. Simeon was in the lab, sweeping the floor, working the grime out of tile seams with a gentle, non-abrasive tool he had invented, and flossing the cupboard handles with strands of old sheets soaked in water and vinegar, a reliable green cleanser. He sang *Loch Lomond* throughout the morning. Its two roads made him think of his dear Izzy. Noah was giving a paper at Stirling University in June. They were planning a short vacation after the paper. After work, they planned a visit to the bank to purchase some Scottish pounds for the conference and some English Johnsons for a short side trip into the Lake District.

At three, a man wearing a catering uniform walked into

the lab. The name on the badge was "J. Venner."

"Can I help you, friend?" Simeon asked. He was sweeping the floor. Bach's *Goldberg Variations* played quietly from a laptop beside a vase of chrysanthemums.

"Are you Dr. Burnet?" the man asked.

Simeon felt uneasy. He knew this man's type.

"Yes, I'm Noah Burnet," he replied. "May I help?"

The man studied an image on his e-phone. "You're sure?"

"I'm sure."

"OK, well, creation or evolution?"

"What?" Simeon noticed a button on Venner's lapel. It showed Adam and Eve balancing like perfect figure skaters on the back of a stegosaurus.

"Creation or evolution?"

"Why do you ask, seeing that both are imagination?"

"Just answer yes or no."

Simeon saw the gun in the man's back pocket. "Your question brings to mind Blake's couplet. Let's explore it:

Two-horned reasoning, cloven fiction

In doubt, which is self-contradiction

"No bafflegab. Are you for it or against it?"

Simeon moved towards the alarm under Noah's desk.

He tried to think of a more mesmerizing poem. Somehow he could only think of prose.

"The world of imagination is the world of eternity. It is the divine bosom into which we shall all go after the death of the vegetated body. This world of imagination is infinite and eternal, whereas the world of generation is finite and temporal."

"Don't get technical with me," Venner scolded him, consulting some yellow flash cards in his shirt pocket. "One more time: creation or evolution?"

"Take care, son. The letter kills." Simeon reached for the alarm button. Venner shot him through the heart.

* * *

Izzy's life was a hurricane of pain from that moment. The university locked down. Flashing lights. Yellow tape. Police questions. A memorial service in Convocation Hall. Standing room only. "Simeon changed my life!" Reverend Phlap shouted from the back row. Newspaper headlines screamed: CASE OF MISTAKEN IDENTITY. At his hearing, Venner called out, "warming a blasphemy warming scientists will perish in the lake of fire stand aside for the front row seat of judgment" The judge nodded to her bailiff. The bailiff forced Venner back to his cell with a tranquilizer gun pointed at his ass. Julius MacPherson took copious notes in the front row.

Noah had a massive stroke. He fell into a coma. His doctor told Izzy that Noah might lose his speech, his sight and his mobility – if he woke up. The University had a strong support system. They assured her that Noah would receive the best care possible for what was now a long-term disability. Destiny and Jasmine offered to look after Noah at home. They loved cats. They could take turns in shifts. Izzy accepted gratefully. She could not cope.

She was far behind schedule with her writing project on homeless animals. She was drawing from her course on urban space to write a long poem called *Random Walk*. All she had so was a short induction when Simeon died.

Random Walk by Charissa Dryden-Burnet

In the garden   the red earth

Named creatures   linked steps linked acts

Then bloomed the homeless desert.

Now the rising of nouns

Streets   numberless

Alleys spread like roots

Now cats walk like human thoughts

Confused   distinct

Their paws light on banished verbs

Their eyes the grammar of space

Decisions   directions

Readings of singular worlds

Her supervisor was a distinguished poet. She liked it, but thought it needed a better balance of imagery and theory, and many many more pages. She advised Izzy to take a compassionate leave. Izzy agreed. She worried she might never return. She was mourning her own poetry.

The university flew its flag at half-mast for Simeon.

* * *

Izzy spent her afternoons at Noah's bedside at the U of A hospital. His doctor was doubtful Noah would ever awake. Jasmine and Destiny kept their promise, staying with Noah in four-hour shifts. They changed shifts at suppertime. Izzy bought them supper in the food court to thank them on their seventh day.

"I'm sorry you aren't getting paid for this," Izzy told them. "If he could be at home, I could find a way to pay you through the insurance. But I can't pay you for being here."

"No vorries," Destiny said. "Ve are fine. Ve love Otis and ve love you. Ve have more than you might expect."

"Isn't this too much for you? You have Reverend Phlap to look after."

"We have experience," Jasmine said. "And he's generous. His rehab's gone well. He's healthier than he looks."

"But he doesn't have a job."

"No – he has nest egg," said Destiny. "OK – I'm lie. His church helped first. For a time insurance. My mother also left me some money, so no vorries. Phlap blessed us and ve like his good energy. He von't always need us. He hopes to take us on a big cruise."

"What about you two?"

"Ve see each other in the morning – maybe a nice long cigarette outside and a talk, maybe. Or exchange brief affections. Then ve go to separate shifts. The heart grows fonder. Maybe solitude is sometimes good company. Ve fine."

The next day, Phlap learned the Cathedral of Normalcy was investigating his financial affairs, specifically his nursing care arrangements. He wrote a letter to the *Mercury* reminding readers that he had been in a coma. His nurses were accredited in their countries of origin. He called the investigation a witchhunt provoked by his new values and convictions. He chartered a helicopter and escorted Jasmine and Destiny across the border into the Natural Republic of Mondakosota. The trio left a note:

> Precious Izzy!
>
> Jasmine, Destiny and I must take flight to our southern neighbours. We must bring our message of hope to the benighted corners of those deeply damaged entities. Forgive us. I pray daily that our paths will cross again soon!
>
> Your servant Augustus Phlap
>
> Jasmine – Hugs for Nympho! xox
> Destiny – Pretty Fish! Love you! xox

* * *

Noah was stable but unresponsive. Izzy thought he could hear her when she read to him or reminisced. She didn't want to be alone in the Crescentdale bungalow. She wished that Jasmine and Destiny had stayed and lived with her. Perhaps even Phlap. She couldn't persuade Jesse to move in. He asked her to come downtown. So she asked the manager of *True Dough* to feed her fish, and gave him her house key. She took Nympho with her.

She met Jesse on Church Street that night. They slept in the basement of St. Anne's. Gidding had converted it into a come-in-from-the-cold shelter. In the mornings, they walked through the neighbourhood. She bought day-old cinnamon rolls for Johnny and Madge. Madge liked to break her roll into pieces and share them out like cards. Johnny dunked his in his church coffee until his bun became a floating wreck. Nympho roamed the streets for five nights, and returned happy and refreshed each morning.

On the sixth morning, Nympho did not return. Izzy and Jesse patrolled the neighbourhood calling "Nympho! Nympho!" A young police officer warned them about public solicitation. Jesse explained the name. He tried calling Nympho in Hebrew, Greek and Mandarin to be discreet. A woman in sunglasses with a briefcase told Jesse to get a job. Jesse told her to move along in Italian, and continued to call the cat.

Izzy and Jesse asked Reverend Gidding to photocopy some pictures of Nympho. They passed them out to Chinese Pentecostals, Croatian Catholics, Jews, Muslims, Buddhists and every other group or building they passed. They tried the coffee shops and shelters and temples and missions and Indigenous friendship centres. They roamed around City Hall before reaching the NHL arena, a world-class eating-shopping-entertainment-business-hockey-sports-office complex. Jesse felt the spirits of sunlit walkers circling the city. He paused to bow his head and whisper words at the luminous Iron Foot mosaic.

"What did you whisper?" Izzy asked.

"Missing names, missing people," Jesse answered.

They walked to the entrance of a vast glass casino four blocks north of the arena. It was one of three large casinos in the inner city. The giant word CASINO covered a wall that faced Church Street. A sign on the door read: "One of Marvelton's Top Five Must-do's in Edmonton!" Inside, a security man in a royal blue golf shirt held out his hand like a traffic cop, ordering them to halt. Jesse looked the man in the eye. The man's arm dropped like a slack yo-yo.

The interior was a tsunami of high-energy noise and spinning lights. Patrons sat in deep funks counting their losses. Some phoned home to say they would be late. A bright blue-green dot orbited the vast room like an atom in a particle accelerator. A casino orderly approached Jesse. "This is an entertainment facility, sir. Could you be in the wrong place?" Jesse looked him in the eye. The orderly's microphone headset fell to the ground. The orderly stepped aside.

Unable to find Nympho in the casino, they ventured east as far as the Riverdale Golf Course, where they walked the edges of the fairways for an hour. They feared a coyote might have caught Nympho. Jesse fixed his eye on a golfer searching for a lost ball in the forest. The golfer removed his tweed hat, wrung it in his hands and apologized for his slow play.

"Seen a ball?"

"Lots. Seen a cat?"

"No sir. Squirrels aplenty." The golfer gave up the search and tossed a new ball onto the fairway.

"Local drunks?" his mates asked.

"Lost cat."

Izzy panicked. She needed Nympho. How could she write a thesis on homeless pets and then lose Nympho downtown? She felt empty and wasted. She felt like a fraud.

Then she heard a news report on the radio. Canada's Minister of State for Fish announced that an as yet unnamed genetically modified fish species had survived for four months in a northern Alberta tailings pond. Fish factor producers could work hand in hand with genetic modification factor producers to maintain a multi-factored natural environment. This was the just the kind of research Canada needed.

Now Izzy got angry. Very angry.

She remembered: before the shooting, Noah was working on a small northern lake. Tailings ponds were obvious by-products of resource extraction. But what was happening to lakes? Drinking water could be slowly contaminated. But Noah also believed northern lakes might become tinderboxes. The federal government forbade him to perform experiments to test his claims. So he used mind experiments. He worked out flammability probabilities mathematically with data on seasons and microclimates and emission densities and distances. He used one particular lake as his model because of its area, volume and low probability of contamination: Olam Lake. Worried the lake was flammable, he made a power point presentation and spoke out in church halls, park gazebos, food courts and school gyms across northern Alberta. Flambo dubbed him the "lord of false alarmist ideology."

Police discovered that Venner had bookmarked Noah's speeches on his e-phone prior to the shooting. A map in his truck showed red crayon arrows joining each location.

* * *

Three mornings later, Nympho was still missing. Izzy walked for an hour all the way back to Crescentdale and got into Simeon's car. She drove around, wondering if Nympho had found her way back to the neighbourhood. Then she went to the house and packed some things. She drove to the Whitemud freeway, and turned north on the Henday. She stopped at *Downtown Discount Hardware* to buy a lock and a chain. Then she drove three hundred and one kilometres north.

She used the car's GPS to reach Olam Lake. She found it at the end of a long gravel road. She surveyed the scene through the windshield. The area looked deserted. Two giant trucks sat empty and idle. The lake looked fine, except for patches of gray foam on the shoreline. The water was clear; lake seemed another sky. There were no trees close to its shore. The wilderness distanced itself, leaving a stone landscape to frame the water. She was no expert. This all could be normal she thought.

She parked the car. She put her knapsack on over her

pale purple hiking shirt and a baseball hat to protect her hair. She had enough trail mix and water to last two days. Two tiny surveillance drones buzzed overhead. She did not have much time. She walked down a straight gravel path near the shore to an iron fence. A sign read NO FISHING. Someone had painted a line through the ING. She pulled the lock and chain out of her knapsack. She chained herself to the fence. She threw the key far out into the lake.

A light wind was blowing out across the lake. This was the direction she needed. She cut six short lines in a piece of paper with scissors. Then she wrapped a rock the size of her fist in the paper. She took a plastic lighter and set fire to the paper, giving the fire time to take hold. She threw the bundle as far out into the lake as she could. Time slowed down. Her anger started to drain away. She hoped nothing would happen. She wanted the lake to be healthy.

The rock fell away, releasing the burning paper. The wind wafted the paper out over the water. It hovered briefly before settling on the surface of the lake. In an instant, the lake burst into a fireball. It seared her shirt, scorched her hair and blasted her eyebrows. She covered her eyes with her forearm. Her chain grew hotter. Eventually, the heat subsided. The wind carried the smoke away.

She lay down by the fence and closed her eyes. A trucker saw the fireball from a distant highway. He called for help, and filmed the scene. A half-hour later, police and firefighters arrived in cars, trucks and helicopters.

* * *

The police charged her with vandalism, car theft, public mischief, public nuisance, public indecency, endangering property, arson of a freshwater resource, arson of a public recreation space, trespassing, arson of fish and wildlife and willful disruption of the economy. The last charge was by far the most serious: it was known as eco-terrorism. Under a statute passed by the federal government in 2030, "any deliberate attempt, successful or not, to disrupt or slow down the economic wellbeing of Canada, urban or rural, natural or artificial, indoors or outdoors, by any means, violent or non-violent, charitable or profitable, benign or non-innocuous, shall hereafter constitute an act of economic terrorism." Eco-terrorism was short for economic terrorism. Arrests focused on environmental activists and scientists, but often netted buskers, poets, union leaders, folksingers, academics, dieticians, architects, social workers and satirists.

* * *

Marcel Wikney, a Professor of Law who admired Noah, offered *pro bono* counsel to Izzy. He had experience with the malicious disruption statute. And his teaching area was environmental law. Izzy accepted his help.

On the morning of her trial, *The Infiltranslationers* protested on the court steps. They chanted with fists clenched:

Turn away no more!

Why wilt thou turn away!

The starry floor! the watery shore!

Is given thee till break of day!

Police huddled near the protesters. The poem did not seem to merit charges – yet. Barry recorded the scene from close range, ensuring he captured all the voices.

Throughout the trial, Jonah Flambo dedicated *Sincerely, Jonah Flambo* and *Jonah Flambo's Tomorrow* to outing Izzy. Police ascertained that Izzy lit the fire with a cheap plastic lighter. So! Izzy was a consumer of fossil fuels. To speak plainly, she was an anti-social loner and a shameless fossil fuel hypocrite. He applauded the mandatory minimum sentence Izzy faced for her crimes. Then he complained that it was too soft.

Commenters agreed:

Torchbird75: thanks for telling it like it is, Jonah boy.

Bananal452: Thanks, Jonah. Yeah, you always know to tell them to stick their political correctness. Yeah!

Petro66solomon: death penalty, that's what's needed for sabotageurs. Yup. It was good enough in the wars and good enough for the Europes. So it's good enough for now!

Veganthisdopehead12: @ Bananal452: WHO TAUGHT YOU TO READ?

Wikney fought hard against six local prosecutors advised by eighteen officials and two federal cabinet ministers. Desmond Runtness, a former Governor General, also joined the prosecution team. Two senior staffers from the Prime Minister's Office quarterbacked the prosecution: Wayne Sansdeak, the PM's Senior Minion Control Manager, and the ubiquitous Hester Roo.

Wikney established the truth of Noah's concerns about the lake. The lake was at risk for fire. How would Izzy know that? Through science: her father's science.

Bunsen Strumgrind, the lead prosecutor countered, reading from a note passed to him by Wayne Sansdeak: "Your honour, her father's so-called water science was just his way of disrespecting hard-working Canadians who fill up our tanks and fire up our coolers while sitting around their ordinary kitchen tables. When did Dr. Burnet ever meet a payroll, grow the middle class or talk to ordinary Canadians?"

Wikney objected: "This is a court of law, your Honour, not an election campaign."

Strumgrind withdrew the remark and handed the note back to Sansdeak, much to the displeasure of Hester Roo. Still, he continued dutifully: "If a public sign measuring the seasonal potential for a forest fire indicated low risk, would a person be less culpable for throwing a match into the forest? The defendant knew the risk was high, and still she acted with intent."

Sansdeak handed him a note: "make that criminal malice."

"But how did she know the risk was high?" Marcel asked Strumgrind. "Not through the company's publications. Her source was the best science. Her action merely confirmed Dr. Burnet's fears. Her crime was an experiment, and therefore an act of free speech."

"Nothing doing," said Strumgrind, watching Roo twist a rope around her water glass. "Dr. Burnet had no authority to conduct research on Olam Lake, whether *in loco* or *in cogitationis*. As your Honour knows, the Helmfloss Government banned fresh water research in 2025, except by federal license or corporate patronage. A thought experiment from a distance is not science. It's conspiracy."

Marcel suggested that Izzy was under duress from the death of a parent. Izzy forbade him to use words like insanity or incapacity.

"Many people lose parents without turning to eco-terrorism," Strumgrind warned. "What's the matter with young people these days? The defendant had a normal middle-class upbringing with many advantages. When did she decide to go wild? More importantly – why? Is a larger conspiracy forming around her? Who are those protesters chanting outside? Her cell?"

The judge was a former Retentivist candidate named Wusstershire Jeffreys. He pronounced his first name "Wustza." He caught Prime Minister Helmfloss's eye when he argued Canada's need for more island prisons on a breakfast talk show. Helmfloss invited Jeffreys to call him "Jay." Jeffreys did not correct the PM when he called him "West." Jeffreys ordered the police to investigate Dr. Noah Burnet under federal statutes that regulated freshwater research by federal license and or corporate patronage. Strumgrind informed his honour that Dr. Burnet was in a coma, and might not recover. His honour told Strumgrind not to waste the court's time.

Jeffreys gave his charge to the jury. They deliberated for an hour and forty minutes before finding Izzy guilty of all charges.

Jesse, Johnny Bizck and Madge Three rose to their feet in the back row. They "begged leave" of Judge Jeffreys to send them to jail with Izzy. The judge told them to sit "the hellcrap" down. Did they want to push the limits of his patience? He didn't recommend it. Madge lit a match and dropped it into the water jug on the judge's bench. She was disappointed when it fizzled out. Jeffreys' face turned tomato red.

"Alright then!" Jeffreys screamed at the sight of the floating match. "You'll bunk together tonight. Oh yes! The sentence is one night in jail for Ms. Madge Three. The sentence is twelve years mandatory minimum for Charissa Dryden-Burnet for assorted malicious disruptions. Remove the prisoners. And remember – stick them all together tonight like I told you. Enjoy your last embrace, conspiracy birds. And think about this – if I could strip your citizenship I would! Court adjourned!"

The courtroom hushed as Jeffreys' cheeks and forehead turned violet. He suffered a ruptured blood vessel behind his left eye when he rose from his seat. He collapsed. Police and paramedics bypassed Mercy Hospital and rushed him to the U of A where he recovered for three weeks. Noah lay comatose in the bed beside him.

* * *

Izzy and Madge spent the night in a cell in the Edmonton Special Custody Facility. Madge shivered with fear. Slamming doors and angry voices muffled by her partial deafness upset her. Izzy held her and rocked her. She stroked her hair, and kissed her damaged ear. She rubbed the tops of Madge's slippers with her feet. This gave Izzy the sensation of having her head banged on the floor, a dull screwdriver pushing her eardrum and tearing her ovaries, and unholy terror. Madge felt no more anxiety. She smiled quietly and fell into a deep sleep.

The next morning, Jesse and Johnny came to get Madge and say goodbye to Izzy. Reverend Gidding came with them, dressed in his white robe. They met in a small holding room with one guard. The group huddled together to avoid being heard. Jesse and Izzy intertwined their fingers.

"I understand there is something you'd like to say to each other," Gidding said to Jesse and Izzy.

Jesse fell to his knees and asked Izzy to join him in holy union. They had no license. Izzy fell to her knees.

"I'll wait for your return if it takes forever," Jesse said.

"Return?" the guard chortled.

"And I'll search for you forever," Izzy said.

Gidding placed a hand on each of their heads and pronounced a benediction.

"Many have married after ensuring their own security, and protecting their interests with legal firewalls and pre-nup warrants and self-immunizations in manifold ways," Gidding said. "But you, out of your poverty, have given each other everything you have. The Lord bless you and keep you. The Lord make his face to shine upon you, and be gracious to you. The Lord lift up his countenance upon you, and give you peace."

Izzy stood on the tips of Jesse's boots. She braced for trauma. Instead, she felt strength come into her feet and rise through her body. She saw shooting stars flaming in a dark sky over a long lake with a sunset smiling on a far horizon. Two eagles sat in contentment on a pine bough. So this was marriage. She would find her way back to this place.

Samson Gleau stepped forward and pulled a present out of his jacket. Nympho!

"She came back," he said. "And she says good morning!"

Izzy wept and rubbed Nympho's head and ears between her hands. The guard pried Nympho away. Two guards took Izzy in a van to the women's facility. As she entered the van, she noticed Barry huddling in the shadows of the parking ramp, live-streaming to Jonah Flambo.

Lucius Spukwell was also watching, hidden behind the dark tinted windows of a stretch limousine across the street. Lady Spukwell sat across from him, weeping for Izzy and Simeon and Noah. Lucius found her blend of emotion and dishonesty hard to process. He told the driver to return to Geogasm.

Chapter Ten

BOY WONDER OF CANADA

Geogasm, 2042

As Izzy began her life on Prison Island, Lucius began his lightning rise to power. He organized the second annual *Geogasm Conference.* The theme: *Forging a New Seventeenth Century for Canada.* Lucius decided that there would be just one speaker: Lucius Spukwell. He offered a fifteen-minute lecture: "Renewing Democracy: Propurgation as Ultimate Reform."

Reporters were barred from Lucius's speech to delegates. When he took to the podium, he was already the nominee for the new riding of Central Geogasm representing the western-based Normal Solid Retentivist Party. And he was just twenty-two years old. Party members turned out in force to hear him speak. Lucius dazzled delegates by appealing to their frustrations. Their list of grievances was long. Lucius chose to focus on one.

For many decades, decent Retentivists advocated petitions to recall underperforming, wasteful or off-message members of Parliament. Recall never seemed to materialize. Lucius asked a simple question: when, if ever, did real transparency happen in Ottawa? There was only one such occasion: when Parliament was not in session, and the house stood empty. He urged delegates to consolidate their hopes, fears, grudges and grievances in one bold device: propurgation. In theory, recall was rare, selective and inefficient. Propurgation would be extremely rare but very inclusive and highly efficient. Precedents? Propurgation had plenty, notably in seventeenth-century England, so no worries there. It took only a few choice words such as "you have sat here too long. Leave now." As an oral tradition, propurgation required less red tape than costly elections or unpopular prorogations. No expensive paper trail would be needed. Above all, it would consolidate the party's aspirations – past, present and future – in a single event at the centre of democracy. The propurged would not be ejected. They would be asked to stand up for democracy and selflessly walk out for Canada.

During the question period, a delegate asked: "If we move to purge as you've described it, will we need to get rid of the word 'Retentivist' in our party name?"

"Not purge, friend. Propurgation. Join with me in saying pro—pur—ga—tion. Propurgation. It's much easier to pronounce than prorogation. As for retentivism, I would no more rename the party than I would rename my own mother. Propurgative retentivism is no more of a paradox than progressive conservatism once was. Don't you feel nostalgic? Are you not now assured? But remember, this is between us for the time being."

And so Lucius launched his campaign for the riding of Central Geogasm. He earned a *Macleans* cover photo as a young up and comer to watch. The photo presented Lucius as a hard working, self-knowing youth in shirtsleeves standing beside a solid oak office door with GIPSMEFACS engraved in gold letters. The cover caption asked: *Is this the Boy Wonder of Canada?*

* * *

The Normal Solid Retentivist Party had a brief but proud history. It broke from the Stable Retentivist Party, a radical western sect of the eastern Progressive Retentionists who had bolted from the Good Old Retentionist Party, uniting the splinters into the Solid Retentivist Party, which banned the word "progressive" forever. In the year before Lucius's first election, the Solid Retentivist Party split over whether to build an oil pipeline under the Bow River in Calgary or under the North Saskatchewan River in Edmonton. The newly formed Normal Solid Retentivist Party championed Calgary, while the newly formed Careful Solid Retentivist Party preferred Edmonton. The Floral Solid Retentivist Party, an offshoot of the Normals, lobbied for the Milk River in the far south. Lucius ignored the Florals and shunned Edmonton, carrying the banner of the NSRP in Geogasm.

The NSRP held its annual policy convention in Phoenix, Arizona, a warm getaway from the Canadian winter, and generally inaccessible to meddlesome protesters. The mythical Arabian Phoenix, reborn every five hundred years from its own ashes, appealed to delegates as a symbol unifying sensible politics, right ideas and sound fiscal management. Nors Nimbull, the first NSRP leader, scrambled the leavings of former party names to create a clumsy motto for the new party: "Solid Tenets; Solid Tents!"

"Nimbull is a slithering piece of shit," opined Feenie in the living room of Geogasm manor. Lady Spukwell's face melted into grief at this sign of conflict. Lucius looked at his watch impassively, determined to impose closure on whatever debate Feenie had in mind. "Best case scenario: you win Geogasm in the general election and Nimbull loses his seat.

Consequence: leadership convention. You will be the youngest leader in history: the boy wonder of Canada!"

Lucius nodded his assent, but wondered why he was still putting a roof over this clodpole's head. Feenie was on probation in Lucius's mind.

"How exactly does he lose his seat?" Lucius asked.

"Well, I'm working on that. But you have to admit, the result appeals."

Lucius knew it was pointless to ask politicians *how* they might achieve something. He was already planning to make that weakness into a strength.

While Feenie sketched out some unfeasible mischiefs, Lucius reached for his e-phone and called *Footman* TV, asking to speak to the public affairs producer.

"Martin Smoar, public affairs speaking." Smoar pronounced Martin in the French manner.

"Mr. Smoar, this is Lucius Spukwell. I have a proposal for you. I'd be happy to do an exclusive interview with *Footman* News. I have one condition: the interviewer will be Barry Basewik-Quick."

"Who?" Smoar asked.

"Base Quick."

"Oh, him. Sure, why not."

"Base" made sense. Smoar was annoyed by the *Macleans* scoop, but was sceptical of Lucius's youth and lack of policies. He might have been wise to start with municipal politics. He was too aloof for provincial politics. And federal voting patterns in Alberta held steady for decades. Lucius would never make cabinet. He could be a one-week boy wonder. So Base could go bury himself with Spukwell.

Smoar had no idea of the vast stores of financial gunpowder at Lucius's disposal. *Sex is all there is* was steadily converting elevator rides into political napalm.

* * *

Jonah Flambo was miffed by the choice of Barry. Had he not given his "Fire Times Four" speech to *GIPSMEFACS*? His secretary confirmed it. Flambo spent four nights in hospital after that speech, she reminded him. His doctor warned him that his blood pressure was high. What would happen if he found a subject worthy of such passion? He could easily have a heart attack or stroke. He had to quiet his mind and slow down.

The doctor's warning caused Flambo to ruminate on how he would be remembered after his death. A memorial must celebrate his life. He phoned Martin Smoar to pitch a one-hour documentary on his life and times.

"Good to hear from you, Jonah."

"Look, Mart-tah," Flambo said, featuring his poor pronunciation skills. "I may be dying. I want to get out in front of this as regards broadcast tributes."

"Are you sure you're dying? You sound OK, Jonah."

"I want to call my memorial documentary, 'Bent but not Broken.'"

"Bent? You'd be dead, Jonah."

"OK –'The Lion in Winter.'"

"The movie on classic films this week? Plagiarism."

"'Demonize This.'"

"Blunt, crisp, provocative, but a tad ambiguous. Let's not decide on a title now."

"Fine. Let's talk time. I want a Tuesday night from 8 to 10 p.m. Tuesdays are classy in the TV schedule. I won't have it buried on Saturday night. This will be a two-hour retrospective of my life and times."

"We can't afford two hours. A half-hour could work."

"If it's half an hour, it has to be commercial free."

"There will be commercials, Jonah. That means twenty-two minutes of memorial. We could try to make sure the commercials are for cars or trucks. But why make your memorial a national issue? Why don't you sound out local news in Edmonton?"

"We'll talk later. I have an international call coming in."

There was no such call. Flambo felt betrayed, but also strangely invigorated. He summoned Barry and issued a directive: grill Spukwell on eco-terrorism.

* * *

Barry drove to Geogasm using GPS to find the place. He noticed something odd about the female GPS voice giving directions. It pronounced the "s" in Geogasm as an s, not a z. Ned Feenie greeted him warmly on the front porch. Barry was surprised by Feenie's embrace. This was Feenie's clumsy way of frisking him for firearms.

Feenie led Barry to a darkened living room lit dimly by a gas fireplace and a small reading lamp. Barry set his primary e-phone to video mode and screwed it onto a one-metre tripod across from the red leather armchair Lucius would occupy. He set his secondary e-phone to audio-record and activated the facial analysis app. He set his e-lapel pin to Lipstick to reconstruct the interview in subtitles in case of technical failure. He sat in the black metal folding chair Feenie offered him, and waited for Lucius. He hadn't spoken to Lucius since that fateful day and night in Crescentdale. He expected a tense greeting. He regretted quarrelling with Lucius hours before his father passed away.

"Barry Basewik-Quick!" Lucius boomed, entering with zest. He shook Barry's hand up and down three times.

"Hello Lucius, well."

"A while since we've spoken – yes! But you were at our inaugural *GIPSMEFACS* conference, I recall. Sorry we didn't find time for a sit down there."

"Yes, well."

"I'll tell you what. Let's do the interview, and catch up afterwards. Perhaps we'll even have a quick game of Canadian Monopoly for old times!"

"Sounds good to me."

Barry warmed to Lucius. The past suddenly seemed far away, and the awful pall of Richie's death lifted. They settled into their chairs. Lucius folded his legs and touched his fingertips together in readiness. Barry hunched over his electric notepad, scrolling to his first question. He smiled and nodded at Lucius. The interview began.

"Mr. Spukwell, thank you for taking time to sit down with *Footman* news. Let's get right down to it. As you recall, Jonah Flambo gave a passionate speech called 'Fire Times Four' at 'The Fourth Way,' the inaugural conference of the *GIPSMEFACS* Institute. I have two questions from that event. Did you ever witness such passion in a speaker before? In how many ways did Mr. Flambo inspire you? And one brief follow up – what is your policy on eco-terrorism?"

Lucius nodded thoughtfully for several seconds. He rose from his chair, twisted Barry's primary e-phone off of its tripod, and threw it into the fire. He extended his left arm to block Barry from rescuing his phone, then guided him firmly back to his chair. He took Barry's secondary phone and dropped it into a mason jar on the mantle. There were twelve hornets in the jar. As the hornets swarmed the phone, Lucius pulled a Teflon balaclava over his own head. Then he tossed the jar into the fire. The glass shattered. The hornets swarmed Barry's face, hammering it like a keyboard. Barry pressed his head into some sofa cushions.

"You don't seem to understand, Barry. You're here to be interviewed by me," Lucius explained.

"AARRGGHH!" Barry screamed.

"There now, Barry," Lucius said, pulling a second balaclava roughly over Barry's head. "Be a man. Let's get you fixed up in the kitchen. I believe we keep first aid paraphernalia there."

Lucius helped Barry hobble to the kitchen where Ned Feenie had already prepared a poultice.

"I find ice cold margarine mixed with lemon rind and egg white works best," Feenie explained. "I keep a pot of margarine and rind in the freezer at all times." Lucius whipped the balaclava off of Barry, and removed his own. Feenie plastered cold margarine on Barry's face.

Feenie settled Barry on a wooden chair at the table. Lucius removed an overhead lampshade, leaving a single fluorescent bulb suspended above Barry's head.

"I apologize for this inconvenience," Lucius conceded, "but there's one advantage in our current situation. My questions require a simple yes or no. Blink once for yes, and twice for no, please."

Barry blinked once.

"Have you enjoyed working for Jonah Flambo?"

Barry blinked no.

"Would you consider a change?"

Barry blinked yes.

"Would working for a young up and comer with serious plans to change Canada interest you?"

Barry blinked no.

"We have Paprika. Should Ned change your poultice?"

Barry blinked no.

Lucius paused. "Will Flambo search for you if he doesn't hear from you in, say, the next four or five days?"

Barry blinked no.

"Would you like to make more money than you're making now?"

Yes, Barry blinked.

"Barry, I need someone to steer public opinion for my movement. I need someone to tweak the message, and dampen flak. Someone with a low profile. A complete unknown. Someone who can't even keep his own name straight. You've been doing this for as long as I've known you. It's much like blogging, isn't it? You'll have your own, shall we say, studio. You can slide knobs up for agreement, and down for transparency, or whatever it is you do. I'll raise your salary and benefits by 50%, and give you a title with dignity: Senior Media Liaison."

Lucius swirled a second jar of hornets, perhaps thirty or more, as he would swirl glass of fine red wine. He caressed the sides of the jar and watched the insects dance against the glow of the light bulb.

“These mason jars are classics, Barry. Such workmanship. They’re like finely cut diamonds. I value the craft. Your answer?”

Barry blinked yes.

“Good. And is this your dream job, Barry?”

Barry blinked yes.

“Good. Very good. One last question, and then Mr. Feenie will take you to the contracts. It’s an important question, so take your time. Have I ever been to The Hague?”

Lucius placed the mason jar beside Barry’s ear.

Barry blinked yes.

Lucius beamed. “Welcome to the movement!

Chapter Eleven

ANNUS MIRABILIS

Ottawa, January, 2047

Lucius won re-election by a wide margin in the general election of 2046. He garnered 71% of the vote, which, though impressive, was still short of the record for an Alberta riding. His seat in the house was secure, his star in the party on the rise. And he was pleased to see that Card Dilbey lost a close race in Edmonton Crescentdale, running as a Green.

Feenie chose this moment to introduce Lucius to his circle of influence in Ottawa. There was only one person in his circle: Cardstone Lordso, amateur investor, analyst, pundit, raconteur, connoisseur, explorer, yachtsman, gourmet, hunter, pugilist, fisherman, rugbyist, chess enthusiast, culinary strategist, speed skater and life coach. Above all, he was a professional political consultant. He named his political consulting firm *4NP Inc.* 4NP stood for the four narratives of power.

Lordso grew up on a small dairy farm near Athens, Ontario. His father worked long days to pay their bills and get his milk to market. An avid auto-didact, young Lordso studied Greco-Roman culture intensely in early teens. His father tried to persuade him that Athens was a name from the past, and the cows needed milking and feeding. So Lordso set fire to his father's equipment shed and set out for Sparta, Ontario. At first, he set his sights on Rome, New York, but he had no passport. He chose Sparta in southwestern Ontario because he found the name worthy of his goals. He got as far as Kingston, where he became assistant general manager to a local landlord. The job involved fixing disagreements with stubborn tenants. The landlord took a shine to Lordso, and left him two properties in his will. The properties grew in value, providing his first million.

During the Kingston years, he changed his given name from Royce, his father's name, to Cardstone. He based the name on Stonecard, his maternal grandmother's maiden name. He liked his last name perfectly well. It was rare, though he sometimes wondered if it had evolved out of Lodestone or l'oiseau or some other plausible original. He won the Retentivist nomination for Parliament for Kingston-and-the-Islands after accumulating his first twenty million. He switched his hometown from Athens to Kingston in his campaign leaflets. He preferred the modern urban royalism evoked by Kingston to the antique air of Athens.

When election day came, he lost badly.

Three years later, with some forty million in hand, he was miffed when Manchester Helmfloss passed him over for Governor General. Irritated, Lordso ran as an Independent Retentivist in the next election. His campaign slogan was simple and direct: "All of My Ideas; None of my Money." The slogan failed to resonate with voters. He lost again. He ran again four years later, under the slogan: "More of My Ideas; Even Less of My Money." He lost again, failing to win enough votes to salvage his campaign deposit.

Disillusioned with the masses and their mulish resistance to common sense ideas, Lordso decided to change the country by naming himself its unofficial political consultant. He launched a massive online blog campaign in support of Arsenal Helmfloss to succeed his father, the late Prime Minister Manchester Helmfloss. Arsenal did not just lose; his twin brother Juventus humiliated him, winning 95% of the vote. Lordso was growing tired of voters.

Known to hold a fortune, he served briefly as a B-Rex on *Businessaurus Rexes*. He was asked to leave after three episodes. He called every pitch a "crude excrescence," making the show too predictable. Likewise, he was excused from *Panels on Politics* for continually saying, "let me pick up on your last excrescence" to his co-panellists. Lordso sued, claiming he was a victim of political correctness. The show's producers said they were open to synonyms, and gave him a thesaurus. Lordso dropped his lawsuit.

Dropped from the A-list of political consultants, he continued consulting for capital region businesses and local politicians. He worked from *Cardson Abbey,* his white brick mansion on Colonel By Drive. He still hoped for a major avenue to influence. His most recent achievement was a series of pay-per-view podcasts advising candidates for the positions of head boy or head girl in Ottawa high schools. The winning candidate at Lenester High School declined to mention Lordso in his victory speech at his parents' Constance Bay cabin, though he paid his bill on time. This was Lordso's low point.

A Kingston municipal runner-up in speed skating at twenty, he was now of greater girth, and impeccably dressed. The second-place finish continued to gnaw. So he streaked his gray hair with orange dye to suggest fiery speed. He combed his hair straight back to suggest a stiff breeze. He left his eyebrows, ear, nose and chest hairs a distinguished white. He teased the eyebrows upwards to suggest wisdom. He kept a manservant named Blondeau, and a companion animal, his darling Rotcocker Mackenzie. He put instructions in his will, addressed to "at the peril of whom it may concern," to rename Colonel By Drive in his honour after he passed away: *Le Champs d'Lordso.*

* * *

Feenie rang the doorbell, which blared the first nine notes from the theme of *Downton Abbey*, a popular television series of the early 21st century. Blondeau greeted Feenie and Lucius at the door. He led them to the solarium. Lordso was assessing the terrain of his latest historical re-enactment. A large plywood table some eight by ten feet occupied the middle of the room. Plastic figures of chariots, men and buildings lay in the margins of the board ready to be deployed onto the plaster landscape. Most hobbyists painted brigades of soldiers and positioned them as they were during important battles. Not so Lordso. He preferred plots and stratagems. Today's board showed Caesar walking abroad on the Ides of March. His toga was painted light beige and scarlet. Fourteen miscellaneous figures represented the mob. The assassins waited in the Theatre of Pompey. Using a long graphite croupier stick – a gift from the President of Nevada – Lordso advanced Caesar inch by inch towards his fate. He paused, deigning to notice his guests.

"Well met, Feenie," he intoned. "And this is young Spukwell. I recognize you from your pictures in the mainstream press." He extended his hand to Lucius, wasting no more breath on Feenie. Lucius shook hands and tried to smile.

"Don't discomfort yourself," Lordso said. "My smile too is seldom used and out of practice. Do you study history? It's not our friend, you know."

Lucius felt a slight pain in his abdomen.

"I ask because I thought of re-enacting *Gladiator* in your honour. But the history seemed dodgy to me; moreover, I disliked the ending. The divine emperor deserved better. He was a fool to challenge a mortal to combat. Let us strive to do better! Here we see the assassination of Caesar. History in its purest form is history to be improved on, not imitated. Write that down if you wish."

"Why pure?" Lucius asked.

Lordso frowned. "Your question is ugly, even inelegant, and certainly naive. In short, you've come at the right time to seek my help. Refreshments please, Blondeau. Black coffee. Put away the corkscrew. This young man's inelegant question has cost him a glass of *Cote Dur* 2022."

Lordso identified Brutus, Cassius and Casca, a necessary service since the figures were indistinguishable. The statue of Pompey, where Caesar would fall, was also indistinguishable. He raked Caesar, distinguished only by a small red sticker on his back, carefully towards the Theatre of Pompey, then pushed him through its gates. Lordso strode to the far side of the table, planted the croupier stick behind the crowd of assassins, then bulldozed them to their destiny. Some fell but still advanced head first in the prone position. Eventually, they overwhelmed Caesar with the sheer force of the croupier. Caesar was stubborn: the mobile mash of conspirators kept him on his feet, even raising him up above the fray. Lordso tried lessening the pressure, and finally, Caesar fell. Lordso picked him up by his tiny hand and squirted a species of red sauce on his body, as if he might consume the *hors d'oeuvre* rather than placing it at Pompey's feet.

"Well, gentlemen? What lessons here?"

The exercise reminded Lucius of ice hockey. He said nothing. Blondeau approached Lordso and whispered a message in his ear. Lordso whispered his response, and Blondeau took out his e-phone.

"Blondeau informs me that the neighbours are pairing Malbec with grilled salmon yet again. That is twice this month. Some day we'll crack down on these gross cultural habits. Trust me, we will! Now, what lessons please?"

"I recall you once staged Pharsalus and Armageddon on this very table," Feenie remarked.

Lordso bared his teeth. "We are not here to revisit the gross obviousness of war. Lucius?"

"Well, you seem to be a connoisseur of conspiracy. Is that the agenda?"

Lordso's eyes twinkled. "I think you and I differ on semantics. Consider: I have brought the assassination of Caesar to life before your eyes. We breathed the same air as Caesar just now! Was Caesar's assassination a conspiracy? No. I prefer to call it proactive change management. Conspiracy is about minding your enemies. Change management is about managing change!"

"Caesar was definitely relatable" Feenie said.

"No one is asking you to walk in Caesar's shoes, Lucius," Lordso seethed. "Caesar became a corpse for one reason: his list of enemies was woefully incomplete. If you must empathize, then empathize with change. If not, Blondeau will turf you out – oh, trust me he will!"

"So what next? Do we love Caesar more, or Canada less?" Lucius asked.

"Ha! We get rid of the frame of reference that makes your question coherent. We get rid of the constitution."

Feenie drove his index fingers into his ears to check for

debris. He was not sure he was hearing this correctly.

"Why spend time and energy getting rid of it?" Lucius asked. "Why not simply ignore it?"

"You and I are men of ambition, Lucius. We live and breathe fundamental change. Think legacy!"

"Abolition is not a viable word," Lucius declared.

"Then don't use it," Lordso advised. "I think defunctize would be more elegant and palatable. It would give people pause."

Lordso strode across the room and stood beside an autographed photograph of Prime Minister Manchester Helmfloss.

"Marvel not that I knew him," Lordso began. "Jay had fine qualities. A keen sense of injury, for example. He tried to ignore the constitution, I grant you, but he failed, and squandered the issue on mere electioneering. Even there, he lacked originality. Why didn't he heed me? Why did he shut me out? Few professionals forget the day Ambrose Orlu, a churlish outsider, became his campaign muse. And prorogation? Baby steps."

"Incredible! That's just what I told Lucius," beamed Feenie.

Lordso nodded to Blondeau, who quickly locked his powerful index finger and opposable thumb on Feenie's shoulder. Lordso and Lucius watched beads of sweat convene on Feenie's brow.

Lordso pointed to another gem.

"And there mounted on the credenza port-dais is the periwig I received from the hand of Arson Digits himself. He wore it throughout his first presidential campaign along with his trademark white hose to inflame patriotism. Oh yes! And let me share a secret about this wig in honour of our growing intimacy. Twenty percent of the hair came from Arson's twin brother Carson, felled by a poorly struck range ball. And he was barely twenty. Or so it was given out. The truth is often murkier in such instances. Well, let's not sit on our laurels, Lucius. Consult with me and your star will rise higher than either of these giants."

Lordso nodded at Blondeau, who promptly sprayed the periwig with a deodorizer called "rain forest mint."

"Next steps?" Lucius asked.

"First you sign with me. Then we set a deadline for your takeover of the party. Nors Nimbull will never be Prime Minister of Canada. Shall we be rid of him? Yes. Not by literal assassination, by any means. Leave that to our underperforming colleague Caesar."

Lordso paused to gather more thoughts.

"Let me use an analogy. Organizations are like human bodies. Tedious leaders like to speak of the 'heart' of an organization. They even speak of individuals as the brains of an operation. We've all heard of the conscience of Parliament, or the soul of a nation, or the hearts and minds of the people. Sentimental twaddle. I'll tell you what matters. Like countries, political organizations must move their bowels regularly – and robustly. Oh, I dare say we can manage the evacuation of Nimbull. This is where your minion Basewik comes in. Oh yes! – I know all about that excrescence!"

Lucius was surprised. How could Lordso know Barry?

Do you marvel that I know? Blondeau interviewed your manservant. Yes, both are manservants, but Blondeau is also a citizen activist in my employ. A true captain of the consulting movement. What's more, Blondeau has a charisma your man could never aspire to. Can he even spell? Never mind how I know things. Focus. I'm going to tell you the truth that concerns you most, and I'll tell you once only. If you want to be normal, Lucius, you must first make Canada normal."

"I see," Lucius said. "May I ask what kinds of normal you expect from this arrangement?"

"First," said Lordso, his eyes twinkling. "My long overdue Governor-Generalhood, at the appropriate time, of course. In the short term, I'd like to participate more in our national information conversation. I wish to return to *Panels on Politics* and *Businessaurus Rexes* with full and complete immunity from removal. After all, shouldn't political consultants and the media work more closely and cooperatively? Must we have these messy fallings out and even ugly dismissals on live television? Might information become a more unifying force in our national politics? Might fans point in just one direction when shit hits for a change? Couldn't I be of some help with that?"

Lucius kept his own counsel as Lordso's freight train of rhetorical questions rolled along. Still, he found Lordso's confidence stimulating.

"What will you miss most about the past?" Lucius asked.

"Persuading editors to endorse a candidate. That's influence! I recall the Helmfloss train of endorsements of 2024, a massive caravan rolling out from coast to coast to coast. Ensconced at Cardson, I forwarded my hologram – known affectionately to my minions as "the General" – in mass e-mails to din sound principles into beleaguered editorialists in Toronto. Importunity works sometimes. I paid a reputable dronecult songster handsomely to compose a major anthem: *The Canadian Endorsement Cavalcade.* Epic! It combined the right blend of energy with some vague nostalgia for 1967. The song should have drawn the youth of Canada to our side. It failed, and badly. Inexcusable! The songwriter issued a public apology. Satisfying! Jay won, then died. Juventus took the helm, regrettably. Arsenal would have been the better risk. He would never have lost a general election under my counsel, had he only won the leadership. Retentivism stalled. Ha! Now T-Solar is back with Magnus Suisse in charge. I liked Jay personally, but he was only a pioneer. Those were good days, to be sure, but I see a brighter future for renewal. As I look back on my career, I question the vicissitudes of politics. Must we have winners and losers again and again and again? Hasn't losing been done and done and done? Can a population endure such extremes? Can we not get ourselves off this tragic wheel called history?"

Lucius pretended to mull Lordso's bloated oration. Electoral reform was dangerous territory, he believed. He made a suggestion: "I think an Office of Media Freedom might be a good first step."

The two men locked eyes on each other and began to laugh heartily. They laughed for two minutes without interruption. And never once in that time did either man form a smile.

Lucius agreed to make Lordso his "Senior Director of Operations." Feenie was relegated to "Special Advisor," a title that stank of political carrion. Feenie aggravated his own marginalization by asking Lordso if he planned to leave anything to Lucius when he died.

"Die?" Lordso snarled as Blondeau gathered Feenie into a headlock.

* * *

So began the *annus mirabilis* of Lucius Spukwell.

Lordso renamed the solarium the Solar War Room in honour of his new client. He made a chart of operations complete with goals, illustrations, genres and roles. Genre was the centrepiece of Lordso's mind. On the afternoon of January 6, Lordso re-enacted the downfall of Richard II for Lucius. With the table set, Lordso shoved King Richard towards his rival, Henry Bolingbroke, who leaned against a two-dimensional replica of Flint Castle. He lifted the crown off Richard's head with a kabob skewer. He placed it on the head of Bolingbroke, now Henry IV, after three tries. He pushed Richard off the table with his croupier stick.

Satisfied the lessons were self-evident, Lordso put down his croupier stick and walked to his massive bookshelf. He chose a volume.

"Read this, Lucius," said Lordso, signing the title page. "This is mine: *The Genres of Influence.* Master it! It's your guide to the four narratives of power."

Lucius studied the inscription: "Lucius: magnus normalis."

* * *

Lordso described his book as a "legitimization" of a doctoral dissertation called "Seasons in Shakespearean Comedy." A Ph.D. student at the University of Toronto wrote it in 1978 under the supervision of Northrop Frye, Canada's greatest literary critic. Unable to find permanent work in academia and in need of cash, the student sold the dissertation to Lordso in 2005. Lordso revised it beyond recognition. Always one to warm to conspiracy theories, he deleted the names of Northrop Frye and William Shakespeare throughout the manuscript, taking particular pleasure in deleting Shakespeare, whom he considered too provincial to have written plays. Only a tier one blue-blooded aristocrat – properly nourished, patently superior, sufficiently idle and awash in manservants – deserved to own such genius. It had to have been an Upchalk man, not some rural crow. Nothing good could come out of a small provincial town in Lordso's view. He sometimes wondered if Leonard Cohen wrote all of Frye's books. He was certain Hitler acted alone when he killed JFK. He had yet to find satisfying ways to stage these conspiracies on his table.

He deleted words like myth, metaphor and imagery, converting myths into biographies, metaphors into facts and images into descriptions. The one word he fully embraced was narrative. The plays became historical documentaries with Lordso as sovereign narrator. He called it a "manifesto for political renewal." Disappointed by low sales – which his literary agent blamed on his choice of pen name (Signor Macho) – Lordso decided to take history into his own hands. He batted aside a lawsuit from the Frye estate, which claimed Lordso grossly misrepresented literary criticism as a whole and all of Frye's ideas and those of his student and Shakespeare. Lordso scraped up three academic witnesses who swore that Lordso's approach to Frye was fresh and unusual. The case caught the attention of Arson Digits, a rising political star in the United States. Digits requested a signed copy.

The book went out of print after a run of four hundred copies. He chose not to mount his book on his web blog. He preferred a rare book to spark rumours and attract clients. He sold the original dissertation to a retired financial analyst in Scarborough. She revised it into a cure for global warming: the colonization of Mars. She called it, *Let's Be Reasonable: Mars is Seasonable.* The *Scarborough Foundation for Rational Space Colonization,* where she served as president and treasurer, published her revision as an e-book. Sales were sluggish. Hits were low.

Ten years later, a version of her book, reduced to a thirty-page e-pamphlet, became a top seller in England for several days. The new title was *Lightly Seasoned with Supremes of Reason.* Royal Starking provided a two hundred-page foreword, abundant in references to *The Awful Building,* his long-promised work-in-progress. Buyers misconstrued it as a diet book. Demands for refunds were brisk.

* * *

Lucius studied the volume carefully. The epigraph was a verse of Lordso's making:

My Canada I see for thee

A crown, yea absolute

Thy charts, graphs, stats blush maidenly

Thy foot in honour's boot

A marginal note in Lordso's hand read: "make this national anthem @ right time."

Lucius was surprised to find so many graphs and diagrams in its pages. He expected more narrative and anecdote and more history from a raconteur. Still, the diagrams pushed Lordso's thesis. He used trigonometric sections to demonstrate the downfalls of various regimes. He argued for a permanent fix to the tragic cycles of history. He wrote equations for the cycles:

$$C = \Delta \text{ vice1vice2} / \sum (\text{virtue-1})$$

C stood for change. Δ indicated the disparity between any two of seven numbered vices, as in "George was a class 9 embezzler, but only a class 2 glutton. Therefore, Δ v = 7." The denominator ran a series of seven virtues, each of declining value. Chapters ended with problem sets for review.

$$C = (\Delta \text{ vice1vice2}) \text{ x2} / \sum (\text{virtue-1})$$

Let v1 = pride and v2 = greed.

Let virtue= constancy

Thus: (7 x 2) x 2 / 5-1 = 7

Let 7 be the amplitude for a manageable wave narrative of change.

He "recontextualized" and "de-secularized" change management to make it an ancient virtue on par with temperance, wisdom and fortitude. According to one footnote Lordso believed that Aristotle's lost treatise on change management would be found someday. Lucius found this section rather forced, but he engaged politely with Lordso in order to see where it all might lead.

Lordso told Lucius to lay the groundwork for the four narratives by tilting the playing field away from Nors Nimbull. He refused to see the playing field as a metaphor, and suggested a tilt of 85 degrees. This tilt required thousands of personal newsletters, signed anonymous, and sent to select party members. The task fell to Barry. He assured party members that Lucius empathized with their views, that they were intimates of a rising star, that their privacy was guaranteed. Change was coming, and with it, more empathy, more intimacy and more prosperity for Canadians. Barry sent this message in a mass e-mail to all New Solid Retentivist Party members.

In a second mass mailing, Lucius said he was outraged to learn of the e-mails. He deplored the internal rebellion against Nors Nimbull, a good and decent leader, a family man and a close personal friend. Lucius implored members *not* to leak samples of the newsletters to a trusted journalist – Base Quick. This flushed members who loathed Lucius out of their holes, as they began leaking information to Barry. Some leaked newsletters to the *Ottawa Resident*, Ottawa's newest newspaper. Lucius expected as much. He denounced the *Resident* as a bastion of the elite media. A miscommunication almost caused Lucius to denounce the story one day before publication. Heads rolled.

Lucius made the denunciation the unofficial start of his campaign to replace Nors Nimbull. Party comes before friendship, he proclaimed. Such are the sacrifices of public life.

A federal election was scheduled for the fall. There was no time to waste. Lucius opened his massive war chest of elevator music money. His face appeared on digital billboards on highways, in airports and on the boards at NHL games throughout North America. When players dropped their gloves and tore off each other's sweaters like wild animals, Lucius looked knowingly at viewers through kind eyes pasted to the penalty box. He purchased full-page ads in *USA Now* listing Canada's many faults. Meanwhile, Barry "in-sourced" evidence tracing the rebellious newsletters to the office of the leader, Nors Nimbull. Barry leaked this to Jonah Flambo, who was at a loss to explain it. He found the leak professionally flattering, and took it as a mandate to out Nimbull. He wrote three thundering editorials denouncing Nimbull's "culture of entitlement."

Party members voted for a leadership review.

* * *

When Lucius and Lordso next met on March 21, Lordso had already organized Lucius's rise to power into a strategic flow chart. Each of the four seasons had four sub-categories. Lordso called it: "Operation 4x4."

Step One: Spring 2047

Base Genre: comedy

Change Narrative: The Gunpowder Plot of 1605

Political Wave: Lucius Spukwell reforms the party

Lordso placed some firecrackers inside a gray, cardboard

structure on the re-enactment table. He doused the lights and lit a candle. A bald eagle with a letter in its mouth descended into Westminster on the end of the croupier stick. The letter exposed Guy Fawkes and his confederates. Lordso turned the lights back on, and placed Fawkes, who strongly resembled Caesar, under a small toy horse. He bulldozed him through the streets to Tyburn, where Blondeau, wearing a black mask, dispatched the hapless figurine with hedge clippers.

Action: With Nors Nimbull out of the race, Lucius turned Barry's attention to the sitting prime minister, Magnus Suisse. Barry produced a three-minute mini-documentary for social media. The sound track was a pastiche of small fragments taken from thirty-seven of Suisse's speeches.

> ". . . total job killer . . . let no one be mistaken . . . yes, there are problems . . . the future is coming . . . stating the obvious . . . taxes well spent . . . I have no favourite hockey team . . . but I digress . . . yes, I think about retirement, but first . . . more time with my family, but first . . . too many jobs . . . "

Visually, the mini-doc showed an animated Olam Lake on fire. Pictures of Izzy flashed across the screen. A close-up photograph of fishing pelicans lifted from an episode of *Earth Still Alive!* carried the caption: "Olam Lake before the eco-terrorist." A grainy photo of some blasted trees and cratered mud taken at Passchendaele in 1917 carried the caption: "Olam Lake after the eco-terrorist attack." Barry used footage of Izzy's transfer from the courthouse to Prison Island to end the doc.

Lucius studied frames of Izzy in the police van. He magnified the figures by sweeping his fingers across the screen.

"Were these her homeless friends?" Lucius asked.

"Some might be," Barry answered. "Some are protesters. Some could be both."

"And journalists?"

"Possibly."

Barry wondered if Lucius would burn the video. Lucius found Barry's imprecise answers disturbing.

"How does this end?" Lucius fumed.

"With a slogan. I have three. Varying the final slogan from place to place should prevent viewer boredom." Barry pressed a button. The narrator, known for his for deep-voiced, testosterone-soaked truck commercials, intoned the three final slogans.

Suisse's mind – on everything – except eco-terrorism!

Choose Spukwell!

Choose Peace of Mind – not Suisse of Mind.

Choose Spukwell!

Suisse's speeches: NOT part of a good breakfast.

Choose Spukwell!

"Are you working against me?" Lucius asked.

"I don't understand," said Barry, quickly pressing his hands under his armpits.

Lucius jotted some notes. He bent over the paper and shielded it from Barry's view with his left hand. "This is the final slogan," he announced:

Make Yourself at Home – with Spukwell.

"A tad domestic," Barry said. "But if you want to forgo

attack slogans, why not make a grand gesture? You could close Prison Island. How does 'Lucius the Merciful' sound?"

"Why are you whispering?" Lucius demanded.

"Was I?"

Lucius gave Barry a cold look.

"I'm not paying you to advise me."

* * *

The mini-doc went viral, thanks in part to Barry's use of the *HAG X-1* Hit Generator and Anthemizer app. Lucius won the leadership at a Canada Day convention held in Niagara Falls. Delegates were impressed that he criticized Suisse more than the other candidates. It showed a man on the high road. It showed a man thinking three moves ahead in the chess game of politics. As they stood for "O Canada," the animated cartoon of Olam Lake on fire blazed on the many screens in the convention hall. It reminded delegates of their archetypal enemy: Izzy Dryden-Burnet.

In his victory speech, Lucius presented a surprise motion. He wanted a new name for his party. Delegates expected him to propose *Propurgative Retentivist Party of Canada.* Lucius surprised them. When his motion passed, the *Normal Solid Retentivist Party* formally abolished itself, rising from its ashes as *The Fireball Party* of Canada.

* * *

Step Two: Summer 2047

Base Genre: Romance

Change Narrative: St. George and the Dragon

Political Wave: Lucius Spukwell slays the national debt

The re-enactment featured a desolate landscape made up of dead trees and dry grass. A dragon, consisting of a long beige dildo attached to a garden hose, roamed the landscape, crushing any signs of new vegetation or unexpected growth (Blondeau animated the dragon by sending a small whiplash through the garden hose).

In the sky above, a white drone missile with red crosses on each of its five wings halted in mid-air, a feat achieved because it dangled from Lordso's stick like a puppet. The drone paused and sniffed until it detected the dragon. From a small, cardboard console on the edge of the table, St. George, in full armour, piloted the drone with dials and knobs. The drone crashed into the dragon not once, but seven times, ending its insatiable rampage.

Action: Using a surrogate, Lordso arranged for Lucius to appear on *Businessaurus Rexes.* Celebrating the show's fortieth season, this episode would feature celebrities playing for the charity of their choice. Lordso bought advertising time, and ordered Barry to abridge the mini-doc for commercial use.

Businessaurus Rexes was now a mainstay of Canadian public affairs broadcasting following severe government cuts to the CBC's investigative news units. Time was short for four celebrities to make pitches. First up: a rock star who tried his pitch on Lucius in the makeup room. Lucius feigned interest. His charity: *Home Bass,* a convalescent home for aging rock stars. His proposal: convert his hits into elevator music. Proceeds would go to prevent elder abuse. It was Johnny Knotwad, now in his fifth solo career. Lucius shut Knotwad's babble out as he rehearsed his own pitch. Knotwad returned from his pitch a broken man. The B-Rex who dressed Barry down on defecation told Knotwad that elevator music was an over-saturated market. Current providers held long term contracts. Leaving his throne, the B-Rex spread his arms and advanced in exultation over Knotwad. He offered to drag him from the stage if someone could lend him surgical gloves.

Two other celebrities waited ahead of Lucius. The first, Canada's only certified iron chef, pitched a cookbook of Indigenous recipes with proceeds going to Indigenous Friendship Centres across the country. All four B-Rexes wanted to invest, which gave rise to a shoving match. The chef left in disgust.

The second, a well-known painter, presented the *TATTS* program: taking art to the streets. This meant providing art supplies to kids in inner cities, who could form art collectives. Vandalism would go down. Happiness would go up. Three B-Rexes balked. One invested, promising to show the art in willing inner city fast food franchises.

Lucius now stood before the B-Rexes.

"Welcome, Mr. Spukwell," the host said. "What's your charity?"

"My charity is Canada."

The B-Rexes looked at each other.

"Did you say Canada?"

"I did."

There was silence for five seconds.

"You do realize that you'll have to go on," one B-Rex observed.

"Well, I'm not one to ad lib, but Canada is on welfare, and taxation is the root cause. You could call my pitch the TTTTS program: "Taking Taxation To The Shithouse." I call it "T4" for short. The Canadian people may suggest other names when it becomes a broad, unstoppable movement. At present, Canada is both giver and receiver of its own charity, or welfare as I call it. Since the underlying cause is taxation, I will eliminate the perfidy of taxation, or slay the dragon if you will, or dragonicity for any elites watching." Lucius allowed himself a rare smile at this last quip. It hurt.

"Long have I waited for a message such as yours," one B-Rex averred.

"Did I hear you correctly?" asked a second B-Rex. "The shithouse? Voiding is a moment of intimacy for our species."

"Shut up!" the other B-Rexes screamed.

"And just how would you slay the national debt without taxes?" asked a third B-Rex.

"Look closely. See T4->S on my lapel pin."

The B-Rexes watched in silent admiration. None dared taunt him. Lucius had a disturbing charisma, born of a vegetable oil fireball in a south Edmonton traffic circle. Few liked him. No one challenged him. He neither needed nor wanted their affection. He was speaking over their heads directly to the Canadian people. He knew this clip, suitably edited, would go viral. Barry would see to that.

"So what are we buying here?" asked another B-Rex.

"You'll know when I tell you. And that will be soon." Lucius turned and walked out of the studio, leaving the B-Rexes relieved but wanting more.

* * *

Chaos was mounting throughout North America. The United States concluded its momentous implosion and was now cooling into various amalgamations of state-republics old and new. The last act of Congress was to rename the U.S.A. the Natural Republics of America. The act abolished the presidency, something congress often attempted by isolation, and now took pleasure in doing by a vote. Inflation in the new country was out of control. Property was worthless. Canada was vulnerable.

The writ dropped for a snap election in Canada. The Fireball Party produced bumper stickers and banners capitalizing on the special episode of *Businessaurus Rexes*:

Watch Him!

I <3 TTTTS

Charity begins where welfare ends: in the shithouse!

T4->S

TZZZZZT

Leaders of other parties demanded that Lucius explain how he would manage the national debt, let alone slay it. They countered with slogans of their own:

Spukwell: Economic Disrupter!

Spukwell: The Real Econ-Terrorist!

Spukwell: TCSR: Taking Canada to Skid Road!

LS->PS (Political Shitstorm)

In a televised debate, Lucius asked his opponents for patience. What had become of civility in our political discourse, he wanted to know. He would reveal his plan on election eve. He turned to the camera and smiled, "Watch me." The smile, formerly tenuous and atrophied, was starting to show promise.

Barry wrote a quick blog celebrating the smile:

"Lucius Spukwell is ready to sacrifice for his country, but his smile tells us more. It is a hint of depth, a note of complexity, a revelation of integrity, an equilibrium of head and heart, a sign of leaderly heft in a candidate many Canadians now embrace."

On election eve, Lucius faced the cameras on a *Footman* podcast ordered up by Cardstone Lordso. He leveraged the *Mercury* newsgroup into live-streaming the event as well.

Lordso instructed Lucius to forget about the House of Commons. Why speak to your critics? It was time for an imperial prime ministry in Canada.

Lucius stood on the lawn of Geogasm in front of seventeen microphones. Sixteen were placebos. Only one microphone worked. Three rows of retired police officers stood at attention behind Lucius. A phalanx of six corporate magnates representing the world's continents made a fan beside the officers. A simple message adorned Lucius's podium: T4: A New Normal For Canadians.

Lordso stayed out of sight, unwilling to compromise Lucius's popularity. Lucius announced an agreement in principle to allow global corporations to sponsor Canadian towns and cities. Hefty sponsorship fees would make taxation redundant. Sponsorship might even extend to whole provinces in the future, Lucius imagined. Perhaps even the entire country. But make no mistake: Canada as a whole was not for sale, and never would be as long as he governed. Full details on how this vow might work could wait until Canadians cast their ballots. The *Mercury* news teams had little time to parse this announcement. Voters were breaking to Spukwell. Twenty-four hours later, Lucius won his first and last majority government.

* * *

Step Three: Fall 2047

Base Genre: Tragedy

Change Narrative: Pride's Purge

Political Wave: Lucius becomes Lord Protector

Lordso placed a long cardboard box on his table. He placed a narrow cereal box on top. He meant to evoke the centre block of the Parliament Buildings in Ottawa. On Lordso's command, Blondeau cut Parliament Buildings in Ottawa. On Lordso's command, Blondeau cut open the Parliamentary structure with a Swiss Army Knife, exposing some 420 plastic figures inside. Some wore black. Many wore togas. Lordso placed the business end of his croupier stick firmly against the first row of figures. He pushed, and kept pushing until all 420 figures were on the move like floating timbers in a Tsunami. There seemed to be no exit. No matter. Lordso crushed them against the north wall, and then doubled his force until the entire house of Parliament began to move. He pushed the figures, the building, the entire lot, over the edge of the table and into a mini-dumpster. When Parliament settled in the bin, Lordso rammed it further down with his croupier stick. Then the lid fell shut.

Action: Lucius rolled democratic reforms designed to simplify government in the public mind. A streamlined cabinet would consist of three "super ministries" named for the three "assurances" in the insurrectionist newsletter that canned Nors Nimbull: a Ministry of Prosperity, a Ministry of Intimacy, and a Ministry of Empathy. Two junior ministries would provide the ballast of Canadian values: a Ministry of Memory and a Ministry of Tradition. Smaller government meant prosperity. A single ruler dedicated to his country would galvanize public intimacy. The empathy deficit, woefully obvious around the world, would shrink. Lucius assured members of Parliament they could caucus with the ministry of their choice. He valued their views.

The plan took the shape of a giant pyramid. The four seasons of power formed the base. The PIE super ministries of intimacy and empathy followed. Prosperity formed the pinnacle.

Barry produced a twenty-two minute "macro-documentary": *Son of the West; Son of The Hague: An Intimate Portrait of Lucius Spukwell.*

Opening montage: the sun rising over vast ranchlands in southern Alberta. The camera follows a highway at lightning speed, then stops abruptly at the front steps of *Geogasm.* A testosterone-soaked voice borrowed from a truck commercial intones: "Lucius Spukwell: son of the prairie."

Second montage: clouds scud and rack at tremendous speed over London, Lisbon, Jerusalem and Tokyo. The camera races over the churning Atlantic waves, then stops abruptly at the front steps of the International Court of Justice in The Hague. The narrator intones: "Lucius Spukwell: son of justice; son of the globe." Lucius appears in black and white photographs to suggest vintage history coming to life. The camera slowly pans up and down the still photographs. The narrator intones: "Lucius had a very normal childhood – until tragedy struck." A deep bell tolls while a solo accordionist plays Klezmerish notes ever faster up three octaves to a final, crashing C minor.

Malcolm Cuthbert Q.C. testifies to Lucius' courage in the face of tragedy: "The day his father, Richard M. Spukwell, was gunned down by a madman at The Hague, where he was defending Canada's interests, is difficult to talk about. But yes, that was a defining moment for Lucius. From that moment forward, empathy for his mother was his watchword. For the truth of my claims, please apply to Cardstone Lordso, an old family friend. His mother is not to be disturbed."

The narrator intones: "Could it be that Lucius was no stranger to tragedy? In fact, he was seasoned in tragic fires well before the main tragedy that shaped his life."

Barry appears: "Yes, I'd say Alvin Boneslaw was an intimate mentor for Lucius. And to see him die like that, writhing in a sheet of flame. Was he knocked unconscious quickly to spare him the pain? Or did he have time to gun himself down before the flames spread? It's too hard to say."

Charlotte Georgio, a member of the support staff at Crescentdale School, appears, reading Barry's flash cards somewhat stiffly: "Simeon Dryden infused empathic poems into Lucius. His favourite poem by Simeon was this one: 'Lucius is supreme in reason / Lower taxes is the reason.' Very moving. Lucius was helping Dr. Noah solve the problems of water and energy that his own daughter turned violently against. Lucius alone stayed true. Oh, the humanity!"

Images follow of Lucius working well into the night at *GIPSMEFACS*. The camera zooms into Lucius's steady eyes. Images of his Canada move through his corneas and irises like dolphins tearing the sea. Here is a champion bull rider overpowering the bull of debt; there a swat team ripping a Teflon balaclava from the face of a terrorist for a group of frightened grade ones; here the Peace Tower releasing fireballs from its pointed pinnacle; there, a judge throwing a heavy book at a prisoner's head. Barry intones the final message: "Lucius Spukwell: come friends, and know him well."

Lordso deployed the *Intimate Portrait* in multiplex cinemas, pay-for-view television and all social media outlets. On the eve of the referendum, Lucius promised the measure would be temporary, lasting only as long as it took Canada to weather the crisis in America. On referendum night, he claimed victory with a popular vote of 33.1%.

The next morning, December 20, 2047, he expelled a rump of opposition MP's from the House of Commons. It was exactly 1:15 p.m.

"By the stars in their courses you have sat here long enough!" some witnesses thought they heard when Lucius thundered at them. Others thought they heard, "In the bowels of reason you have sat here long enough!" Some thought he straddled the mace. Others thought he kissed its top.

And so the legend grew.

A rump of MPs sat for three more months, before yielding to the pressure of hunger. As they shuffled out, emaciated and haggard and under armed guard, Lucius condemned them as negative thinkers and professional obstructionists. He drafted them into a pilot project for his first major program: *The Homeless Education Mission (THEM).* The ministers of intimacy and empathy fought bitterly and publicly over which ministry should manage the *THEM* program. Lucius expelled both of them from his cabinet.

* * *

Step Four: Winter 2047-48

Base Genre: satire

Change Narrative: the fall of Troy

Political Wave: Lucius Spukwell renews the government

Lordso dragged a Trojan Horse through the paper walls of Troy, which flattened obligingly until the horse was through. It was the same horse that dragged Guy Fawkes to Tyburn. Lordso opened a box of toy soldiers, sprinkling Greek soldiers through the city. He gently stirred them into the streets with his stick, then bludgeoned down the towers. Blondeau crashed a tiny hand-held drone into the royal palace. He lit the crumpled cover of a comic book –*The Fall of Troy* – and set fire to the flattened walls. He stood at the ready with a fire extinguisher. Lordso spat a dash of rare Chablis on the blaze to control the fire's growth.

In his first ninety days as Lord Protector, Lucius changed Canadian political structures. He made the Lord Protector's Office a branch of government. His office staff replaced the dissolved legislature. He replaced the Supreme Court with the People's Court of Conscience, where ordinary, decent, non-elite citizens would finally have a say. He terminated environmental research grants. He gave corporations that sponsored names for cities control over grants to colleges and universities. Awards would go to the very best proposals. He established the "Lord Protector's War on the Arts," a regulatory commission managed by the *Office of Media Freedom.* The commission would make Canadian artistic expression more streamlined and efficient. He established the Lady Cassandra entrance scholarship program in fiscal common sense for grades one to three. He set aside .0000001% of Canada's GDP annually for the "Noah Fund" for green energy research. Funds would come on stream if and when Canada's oil and gas resources ran out. He razed archives to create open, healthy spaces for children to play in. Naturally, Lucius was disappointed that taxes had to continue indefinitely, often at pre-purge levels.

As he expected, the people gave him a grace period. They seemed to understand his good intentions and his lonely plight. He could no longer say before the next election, but someday, he promised, they would all take taxes to the shithouse together. He thanked his supporters for not taking his promises too literally. He ordered audits of groups concerned about the pace of social change, and gave the temporary *Bureau of Common Sense Taxation* sweeping powers of surveillance, investigation and role termination. As a final touch, Lucius added the "Monopoly clause": he ordered that a federal prison be built in any town or city that submitted an application, provided said town or city agree to global corporate renaming. Municipal councils could ask the Lord Protector's Office to include the costs of a prison when the LPO negotiated renaming rights with global corporations. Bids would be ranked by merit. Lastly, the bill mandated a national essay competition for pupils in Grades 4-8. Essays would explain why Bill LP-1 creates jobs and economic benefits. First Prize would be called the "Sovereign Interpreter's Medal."

To soften the impact of these changes, he placed them in a single bill – Bill LP1. Bill LP1 was a "rolling" ten-year bill. All changes to government, culture, law and society would enter and exit from this single bill. It would cover everything from changes to the names of streets, towns and cities to mandatory sentences for eco-terrorists. It contained everything from changes to Canada's food guide to curtailing investigative journalism. A *Ministry of Transparency,* designed to promote the bill, lurked deep in the bill's entrails. The Bill was flexible. It could expand and contract to meet the needs of Canadian society year by year. In addition to ingesting and secreting legislation, and expectorating and defecating inefficiencies, it promised to reduce waste. This was the only bill Canada would ever need.

Lucius felt like a caring father to his people. One night, he opened the bedroom windows in his yet to be renamed residence. He wanted to hear the cars in the distance. He found it hard to sleep. He turned on his e-phone and replayed Barry's micro-doc, but without sound. He froze the video on Izzy's animated face. He remembered her looking at him from across the traffic circle during the fall of *Richmond's End.*

He looked up a poem on the Internet. He scrolled through it while Izzy entered the cartoon police van in the video.

Pale through pathless ways

The fancied image strays,

Famished, weeping, weak,

With hollow piteous shriek.

Rising from unrest,

The trembling woman pressed

With feet of weary woe;

She could no further go.

Just then, a message popped up on his screen. It was from Lordso:

> Excellency: I am organizing a major conference and celebration in association with *GIPSEMEFACS* for the autumnal season. The conference title: *A Likely Story: Narrative Approaches to Post-Bias Democracy.* I will be chairing a closed-door round table on the changing pulse of political consultation: "Whither Narrative in Post-Change Canada?" May I count on you to favour us with a keynote speech?

Lucius pressed reply: Yes. It would be my delight.

Chapter Twelve

THE MESSENGER

Ottawa and Edmonton, July-December, 2049

One summer night, Barry had a troubling dream. He and Lucius and Izzy were teens again. They were at Izzy's house in Crescentdale. Izzy watched the fish swim in her aquarium while Barry and Lucius quarrelled over which board game to play. Lucius prevailed. He chose *Monopoly: The Canadian Edition.*

They picked out tokens. Izzy picked a fish. Lucius took the fish away and gave her a lighter. Barry picked a lap-pad. Lucius took it away and gave him a mason jar. Lucius selected his token without challenge: a Peace Tower.

The properties differed from the real Canadian *Monopoly.* The first square past *Go* was the Natural Republic of Florida, valued at sixty dollars. The last square before *Go* was the

People's Republic of China, valued at one trillion dollars. Between these squares was a host of Canadian streets.

Izzy rolled first. She landed on 96th Street in Edmonton. She bought it, and placed a church on it. On her next turn, she rolled zero, landing on 96th street again. She bought it, and placed a theatre on it. She rolled again, and landed on Go to Jail. She went to Jail. There were no get-out-of jail-free cards and no rules for getting out of jail. Izzy stayed in jail forever.

Lucius kept rolling doubles. He took forty consecutive moves. He bought Calgary, Edmonton, Ottawa and Regina. He placed National Portrait Galleries in all four cities. He bought China, and placed a National Portrait Gallery there too. He purchased The Hague, which was a small section of Edmonton inside Crescentdale. He bought it, and put a law firm there.

Barry questioned Lucius's right to consecutive moves. With each question, parts of Barry's hands crumbled into dust. Lacking hands, he managed to pick up the dice between his forearms. His arms fell off at the elbows under the weight of the dice. Barry watched his body turn into a growing pile of dust. Soon, only his mouth remained. He tried to pick up the dice with his teeth. His teeth and tongue fell out. Barry awoke in a sweat, clutching his arms and throat.

In that moment, he made a decision.

Barry didn't go to work that morning. He stayed home and worked feverishly on his old laptop. He wrote his first blog in opposition to the Spukwell regime. He invented pseudonyms, such as dissentingvoice1, dissentingvoice2 and dissentingvoice3. He felt lighter and freer each time he created a new dissenter. He worked hard all day.

At 3 p.m., two fixers from the Fireball Party breached the door of his apartment with crowbars. Fixer 1 slammed the laptop down on Barry's fingers. Fixer 2 opened his trench coat to reveal a mason jar. Barry had a choice: he could continue his campaign of slander and face charges, or he could quietly accept the position of foyer commissionaire at the Ministry of Intimacy. Fixer 1 pressed down on the laptop. Barry chose the foyer.

Barry tried to be positive. He could still write in secret. But Lucius had already declared him a cyber-outlaw, and announced his new job as a compassionate secondment through the *THEM* program. The government could trace any secretive blog in minutes. He would have to avoid technology. He made a list of alternative methods – letters, speeches, live theatre, busking. He would have to adapt.

* * *

One Thursday evening, Barry went to Ottawa Valley Pharmaceuticals, Stationery and Hot Yoga Football Place Stadium. The Ottawa *Elgin Bureaus* (Elbows to their fans) were playing the Quebec City *Courriels d'Urgence* (Coodoos to their fans) to decide first place the upstart, four-team TCSFL (Trans-Confederation Semi-Amateur Football League). Lordso owned both teams. He paced the Ottawa sidelines with Lucius for the hometown fans. He knew Ottawans disliked the team's name – and him. Lordso happened to despise the fans, with their wrinkled parkas, unremarkable thermoses and disturbing horns. Worst of all, he could not control the team nicknames they coined. Unjust! He reminded himself that he purchased the team so Lucius could acquire a rye-scented touch of humanity. Strategic! He supposed the fans were pleased. He supposed the league would fold.

Watching from the end zone, Barry was disgusted. He hit upon a new strategy to attack Lucius: comedy. Comedians were the vanguard of criticism in times past. Why not now? He left the game and took a bus to the Bytown Comedy Chute off Rideau Street. He signed up for their next open mic night. He wouldn't need jokes. He need only tell the truth.

* * *

Barry's open mic night coincided with a special performance by a rising comedy star from Chicago: Sam-D Vapsage. *Saturday Night Now* invited him to host. *Time* magazine placed him on its cover. His comic stylings mined the subject of oral sex, leaving audiences in tears. The *Time* cover photo featured a shrugging, hammy, "who me?" Sam-D. The caption read: "Is this the future of standup comedy?"

Open mic always followed the performances of professional comics. So Barry sat near the stage to watch Sam-D. A special guest comic, Norbet Freeman warmed the crowd up. He stood at the microphone and held up a box of pills.

"Do you suffer from eco-terrorism?" he asked. Patrons shifted their feet, shook their heads, and shrugged their shoulders. "Then I recommend Ecoterronix," Norbert continued. "Ecoterronix helps me control those uncomfortable urges. Side effects include apathy, loss of memory." A security guard gripped Norbert's forearm and led him away for questioning.

The crowd chanted: "We want Sam-D we want Sam-D."

Sam-D bounded onto the stage.

"Good evening gentles and ladies. Hey, is there some part of special guest that guy can't understand?"

The crowd laughed pleasantly.

"Mix politics and comedy? Is he crazy? Bad news, people! Altogether too rude. No such unprofessionalism shall I condone. We're not here to solve the world's problems, folks, since most of those really ARE rocket science. Hah!"

Sam-D launched into his routine. He told the same comedic story he had been telling audiences around the world for fourteen months.

"So how did I get into this line of work, folks? So here's

how. So this lady lived in the building across the street from me. Did I say in Chicago? I loved at first sight."

"Lust!" screamed a front-row wit.

"Bug off! I mean it. I say to you I loved. To resume, I thought, I must express myself. Show my inner feel. How? Easy. Can you say how people?"

"Oral sex!" the crowd roared.

"You're nailin' it, people! If I profess my inclination, could she avoid? On the other hand, conversely so to speak, we've never met nor spoke. So what do I do? I decide to stage it for her, like a dramatic telegram. What they called a *tableau vivant* tens of thousands of years ago. You know – I act it. Performance art. People! Do I need to draw you a diagram? Where do I so do?"

"Her car!" the crowd roared.

"You're nailin' it! On her car. So one night she parks like she does so every night and goes into her building, like so. Did I say in Chicago? I come out of my building, so as to be demonstrative. I choose an automotive surrogate. So obvious, yet so tasteful. I lie down on the road – on my back people! – with my head under the bumper. I place my face carefully on the back bumper, pantomiming my feelings and goals. I wait for her to add two and two. Hey, people – it's not rocket science! Duh, hello? What happened?"

"Dry ice!" the crowd enthused.

"You're nailin' it! Dry ice, people! Chicago's leading import is dry ice, even more than guns." Sam-D paused for two minutes until the laughter died down. "People – that was no succulent bumper!" There was another long laugh pause. "She doesn't come out. I'm thinking, what? Can't she see me? Oh-oh – could it be her apartment is on the far side of the building? Did I misinterpret something? So I'm there until morning – ten hours worth later – and finally – finally! – she comes out. I'm thinking – finally! – and well worth my terrible ordeal. So what happens?"

"She drives away!" the audience screamed.

"You're nailin' it, people! She scrapes off her windshield. The car is warming up. Exhaust in my face. I flail my arms, kick my shoes. Nothing! She gets in and speeds off. Taking half my tongue with her – that's all! Only half! Hah!"

This story was true in every detail. The tongue injury affected Sam-D's delivery. He pronounced his d's as t's. This endeared him to audiences. They found him hilariously disturbing and oh – so human! Secretly, he was terrified about finding new material. This was his only routine. He had nothing in store for the future. He was not very good at making stuff up. Fortunately, his agent was negotiating a reality Network TV show based on Sam's day-to-day life: *Sam-D in Real Time.* The pressure was off.

* * *

The Ottawa audience gave Sam-D two standing ovations. In tribute to Sam-D, three men lay on their backs and gnawed on the legs of chairs to impress their dates. One man cracked a front tooth when his life partner stood up to leave in disgust. A father dragged his young son to safety. Braces cost money. The rest of the audience purchased drinks and settled in for the open mic segment.

Barry was up first. He asked the emcee to introduce him as "Billy, the Hook and Ladder Comic." The emcee agreed, irritated that he had to scribble instructions on his hand.

"And now, Ladies and Gentleman, please give a Bytown Comedy Chute welcome to Billy, the Hook and Ladder Comic."

"Yeah, whatever," said an elderly man at the bar.

"Good evening Ladies and Gentlemen!" Barry intoned at the microphone.

"Yeah what?" said a young man in the front row.

"Folks, as you just learned, I'm the hook and ladder comic. Why? Because I'm here to put out a fire. A national fire! You're stuck in a burning building and I'm going to get you out!"

He paused, waiting for laughter. None came.

"Friends! There's a fire raging. It's not an actual fire, the kind that consumes forests and homes every year. It's a metaphor."

He paused, waiting for laughter. None came.

"Speaking of which, did you know that literal fires are actually part of nature's plan? They help forests produce new growth. There's only one problem. We're in the way!"

Silence.

"It's like scientists tell us: we couldn't live without bugs and insects, but they sure can live without us! Does the government get that? Nope!"

"It's Lord Protector, asshole!" shouted a burly man at the bar.

"OK. I'm no scientist. Friends, the fire in our country is political. I call it 'fire times one.' Take Lucius Spukwell, for example. What's with him anyways?"

"Trim your eyebrows, jerk," shouted an elderly woman at the back. The crowd laughed. Fixer 1 and Fixer 2 entered the club and sat down beside her. They smiled and nodded at Barry. A delicate menace sparkled in their eyes. One produced an old laptop computer from his coat and waved it over his head. Barry's heart raced. It was his laptop.

Barry took a breath, then resumed.

"Good question. What's with him anyways? 'Lord Protector'? What kind of shit is that? Bullshit? Dogshit? Does he think politics is an STD?"

A faint ripple of laughter spread through the room.

"I mean, seriously – Protector? That sounds like a condom."

The laughter swelled.

"I mean, why the condom? Is he practicing safe dictatorship?"

That was enough for the fixers. They asked the security guard to stand aside. This was an internal Fireball Party matter. They moved from table to table whispering in people's ears. Some patrons shook their heads and frowned at Barry. Others grabbed their coats and fled.

Barry took courage from the slight laughter. He had touched a nerve. But he would need to ad lib. He probed sex further.

"Lord Protector? How arrogant is that?"

Silence.

"How arrogant is that shit?"

Some giggling? No. A man was telling his wife a joke.

When Spukwell goes to couples counselling, it's just him and a bathroom mirror. Hear me, people?"

Some laughter.

"I mean – picture it. How hard can it be to give yourself couples counselling when it's just you and the mirror?"

"We heard you the first time, jerk."

"Gee – do you think they ever have fights?"

Boos.

"And then make up?"

Laughs.

"There's one advantage – at least they pee in sync. How compatible is that? As long as you miss the mirror! And leave the toilet seat up!"

"Fuck you, Billy!" shouted a man near the front, "What did Spukwell ever do to you?"

"Yeah. You're just a hater!" screamed another man, "Get the hell off the stage!"

"Give this bastardly fuckwad of a phony the hook!" screamed the elderly woman at the back.

Audience members began chanting, "Get off the stage! Jerk-Jerk-Jerk-Jerk-Jerk-Jerk-Jerk-Jerk-Jerk-Jerk-Jerk-Jerk-Jerk-Jerk."

"People! Hear me! There's a fire raging in Canada. It's the fire of personal rule. Wake up!"

The fixers mounted the stage and seized the microphone.

"Folks," Fixer 1 said, "we feel your pain, and we're here to help."

Fixer 2 held up Barry's laptop. "Folks, I don't want to say this comic's sex life is lousy – but we just found this device at his table. Care for a demonstration?"

The audience roared.

"Great! First, let's get rid of the racy screen saver! Oh, and by the way, this comic is Basewik Quick, just so you know. That must explain all the commissionaire porn on his hard drive!"

Audience members rose to their feet.

Fixer 1 held Barry in a full nelson. Fixer 2 manipulated the lid of Barry's laptop like the jaws of a small animal. The laptop nipped and snapped at Barry.

"Is oral sex the future now? Is it people?" Fixer 1 yelled to the audience. The crowd roared. The fixers shoved Barry towards the wings, then linked arms and took bows to a standing ovation.

Barry crawled off the stage. He lay in a fetal position near the exit. The general manager bent over to show Barry the waiver he had signed, releasing the Bytown Comedy Chute from liability for injuries, loss, theft or damage to reputation. He put a Tylenol in Barry's palm, grudgingly adding a second.

"Now get the hell out," he told him.

* * *

Ottawa was no longer safe for Barry.

He flew back to Edmonton. His plan: to write a play about Lucius Spukwell. He rented a small, walk up apartment in Crescentdale across from the elementary school. His parents, Severus and Talia, were still alive, but not in Crescentdale. They moved to Fort McMurray. Tal's Trolley provided safe shuttle services driving individuals locally from work, hotels, oil fields, hockey games, bars and parties to and from their parked cars and pickup trucks. Business picked up. Their stress went down. A few "heil forkwads" helped them unwind, Barry recalled. It was ages since he heard their voices.

Barry set to work. He lived off his savings. He took mid-afternoon walks for exercise and fresh air. He liked to visit the bakery beside the *Happy Village*. It was no longer *True Dough*. It was now called *Winstanley's Bakery*. It was a minimalist bakery, offering wholesome baked goods and twenty-two different kinds of coffee. It gave out a whole grain loaf of bread per week and all baked goods more than two days old to unwaged people. Barry did not consider himself unwaged just yet. He was working hard on a project. He drank *Winstanley's* coffee to keep up his feverish pace. He liked an extra strong café noiro.

One afternoon, he saw Caleb Timson sitting alone at a window table in *Winstanley's*. Timson wound his pocket watch while reading the *Edmonton Mercury* in paper form. Barry approached his table.

"Have we met?" Timson asked.

"No. I just wanted to say I admire your work." Barry noticed *The Economist* and *The National Geographic* on the table as well.

"Well, thank you, sir!" Timson beamed, putting forth his hand for a shake.

"And that pocket watch is, well, amazing."

"Thank you again. It's an antique. It was made in Holland in 1926 by a master, Boaz Bakker. Imagine the precision of a highly trained craftsman. I think of that when I set my watch. My father bought it in The Hague in 2016. He was teaching ESL to Syrian refugees. I treasure it. A cliché of praise springs to mind, but like Orwell I disdain prefabricated speech. Are you a student? I do hope Orwell is still being taught."

Barry shrugged.

Timson handed his watch to Barry. Barry saw his own reflection surrounded by trim Roman numerals in the antique glass. An ornate minute hand bisected his eyes. He handed the watch back.

“Are you working on a story?” Barry asked.

“I have two projects, one actual and the other on hold. First, I’m writing my memoirs. And I plan to self-publish this time. Second, I want to research the Dryden-Burnet case. I wanted to look into it at work, but Cardstone Lordso kept pressuring me with hologram e-mails. His servant badgered me from Ottawa with threats. I asked the poor devil if he had a name. He said, ‘can you not see, seeing that I am Manservant?’ Troubling. Very troubling. In any case, I went solo when they kept harassing me.”

Barry shuddered.

“I may yet look into that poor woman’s case on my own, but there’s no contacting prisoners. Lordso is the *eminence grise* behind Spukwell, that I know. What’s happened to our politics? Milton said it best: ‘Certainly then that people must needs be mad or strangely infatuated that build the chief hope of their common happiness or safety on a single person.’ But pardon me: would you like to sit down?”

“No, thank you sir. I should get back to work.”

Barry smiled, stifled a tear and turned away. He returned to his apartment with a black coffee and a spelt raisin scone.

* * *

Two weeks later, Barry finished his project: a one-act play called *Warning Stall.*

Warning Stall by Barry Basewik-Quick

A play in one act.

Time: the present.

Setting: a public washroom, somewhere in Edmonton. One urinal. One closed stall. One sink. One mirror. One fluorescent light above, with deceased insects on the shade. The stall sits on a large *Monopoly* square: "Public Washroom $1000."

Dramatis Personae: Stall Man, Man 1, Man 2, Man 3, Woman, Man 4.

Scene one.

The lights come up. The audience sees two beige bathroom stalls. One stall shows the word "death" spray-painted in black on its door. The second stall shows the word "taxes," also in black paint. A cardboard sign affixed to the "death" door reads: OUT OF ORDER. PLEASE USE OTHER STALL. Inside the "taxes" stall, Stall Man's pants are pulled down to his shoes as he sits on the toilet. The stall door is closed and bolted, blocking the view of the audience except for the man's feet.

The man sighs. He pulls some toilet paper from the roll and blows his nose. He yawns. Man 1 enters, hurriedly. He straightens his tie and washes his hands and face. He finds there are no paper towels.

Man 1: Can you give me some toilet
paper, man? I need to dry my hands.

Stall Man: Sigh.

Man 1: Man? Are you stuck in there or
something?

Stall Man: Yawn.

Man 1 kicks the door: selfish bastard! (exits)

Scene 2: Man 2 enters washroom. Pees.

Stall Man: Birth!

Man 2: Excuse me?

Stall Man: Birth!

Man 2 whispers: idiot. (exits)

Scene 3: Man 3 and Woman enter. Man pees. Woman checks her phone, waits. Man's penis gets stuck in his zipper. He cries with pain. Woman talks on phone with finger in hear ear.

Stall Man: Hey! I'm using this washroom!

Man 3 (still in pain): What?

Stall Man: Get out of here. Do you expect me to come out while you're still in here? I can outlast you. Don't think you can lay siege in here.

Man 3: You're crazy. (exits with woman)

Stall Man: Don't tempt me. I've memorized your shoes. I'll find you!

Scene 4 Man 4 enters. Combs his hair in the mirror. Comb gets stuck in a hair mat.

Stall Man: I'm old now. I made mistakes. I have regrets. But you can't break me!

Man 4 begins kicking in the door.

Stall Man: the door's stuck! Ha! You can't win!

Man 4 kicks door furiously, then exits.

Stall Man: the people defy you!

Barry applied for a spot in the *Fringe Festival.* They allowed him a spot, but told him to find his own venue.

Barry began with casting. He would play the man in the stall. He hired Juan Ramero, the dishwasher from *Winstanley's*, to play the various men who enter the washroom. Juan understood his pay would depend on ticket sales. Good acting would help. Barry worked *pro bono.* He couldn't afford a third actor for the role of Woman, so he adjusted the script. As Man 3, Juan would tell Woman that he would be back in a few minutes. He couldn't afford props, so he searched for a real washroom. He found one in a building scheduled for demolition near City Hall. The stalls were bolted to the floor, so he wrote "Public Washroom $1000 (like in Monopoly)" in chalk on the floor.

Twenty-three people came to the premiere. Two were looking for a place to pee. Moira Chrome, the reviewer from the *Edmonton Mercury,* took copious notes during each scene. She saw existential themes. She sensed some Beckett in the long sighs emanating from the stall. It was no urbane laugh-fest, but this play was worth a look, she thought.

In the final scene, Barry pulled up his pants, emerged from the stall, and began a fifteen-minute tirade against Lucius Spukwell.

"Listen people! We're all stalled with this bastard of a Protector in charge! We've got to protect ourselves. And Canada!"

A man shouted from the audience. "C'mon – you're just a hater. What did Spukwell ever do to you?"

Another joined in: "Yeah, hater. He creates jobs – probably even yours."

Another: "You won't be dissing Spukwell when taxes are abolished, right?"

Another: "Regarding taxes, your play's set in a shithouse, right? That's plagiarism – of Spukwell no less. He takes taxes to the shithouse, not you!"

"That's right!" shouted a woman. "Don't you even have a plagiarism app, jackass?"

The audience began to chant: "Plagiarist! Plagiarist! Plagiarist!"

Two burly men offered Barry a shoving contest. Moira Chrome folded her notes and walked out. The rest of the audience fell silent and drifted away into the night.

* * *

Barry sold his sofa and gave half the money to Juan, whose services he could no longer afford. He staged the show two more times, performing all of the parts himself. This made scene changes risky. He turned off the lights, and placed an old pair of boots in front of the toilet to create the illusion that he was still in the stall. With the lights still off, he quickly assumed the position of the men entering the washroom. This worked in rehearsal, and came oh! so close in performance. He tripped over his pants in the final scene change. A sharp pain buckled his left knee and strained his right ankle. Time to ad lib. He ranted about Lucius while lying on his back in the dark. He could hear the audience leaving. A member of the audience found the light switch using a plastic lighter. He helped Barry to his feet, but wanted a refund.

It was time to close the show.

* * *

Alone and unemployed, Barry accepted a bun ration from *Winstanley's*. He began to drive aimlessly around

Edmonton. He drove past his parents' old house, where strange children now played in the living room. He felt the waves of long gone heil forkwads emanating from the walls.

He parked in front of Izzy's old house. Strangers lived there too. It was dark, though a light went on and off for a moment through the kitchen door. Someone was putting away dishes.

He passed through the traffic circle. The old McDonald's, destroyed in the fireball that consumed Lucius's father, was gone. In its place was an empty gastropub with wooden shutters and a sorry looking patio. A sign occupied the front window: "For Lease – Office / Retail / Restaurant Space."

He wandered into other parts of the city, finding corners he had never seen. He broadened his drives to the outer ring road, where he could cruise at speed. He listened to talk radio shows on 24-hour news channels on these drives. There were plenty to choose from. Barry set his dial to *Canada on the Level,* hosted by Al "the Cobra" Woozner.

"So, Edmonton, our topic tonight is: whatever happened to Jonah Flambo? We haven't heard from him for some time. I mean, what the hell? Anybody know what's up? Give us a call or a facelink. Caller one, go ahead!"

"Yeah, Al, I heard he was on a coma respirator after that girl was charged with eco-terrorism years ago. Could that be right?"

"It could well be, caller one. He was warned to take it easy. But he was brave. And in the unlikely event that viewers know not of whom you refer to: you refer of course to the notorious Izzy Dryden-Burnet, who is now incarcerated on Prison Island duly and rightly."

"Yeah – I bet the bleeding hearts will start calling right now to bleed their hearts on your show, Cobra."

"Bring it! I like nothing more than to joust with saps. Thanks for the call! Caller two – you're on the air."

"Yeah, Al, didn't anyone just think of shooting that girl, or woman, you know, when she was chained or ex-caping? It's legal and a lot cheaper. We pay too much taxes already for prisons. A bullet costs dick."

"I can't condone vigilantization, caller – but that's just between you, me and the lamp post! On the other hand, if you want to talk about reinstating capital punishment for especially unique cases – like her only – bring it! I've got all night to agree. Caller three – you're on the air."

"Yeah, that was a hell of a case, Cobra. I still can't figure out how she did it. Torching an actual lake. Surviving and all. That must have taken some brains. I'd even say guts."

"The word you're looking for is criminal mind, caller. Good night! Caller four, you're on the air."

"Good evening. I'm just calling to say that the conversation is getting off topic. Aren't we supposed to be discussing Jonah Flambo?"

Barry shuddered. He recognized Flambo's voice.

"True caller. But hell, it's a free country, especially with the new guy in Ottawa."

"Fair enough, but could we get back to Jonah Flambo? I have an idea. How about a commercial-free retrospective radio documentary of his entire career. You know – a prime-time special to investigate this topic in depth. You could highlight Flambo's ideas, his achievements, his legacies. I mean, this man had serious ideas. He was a visionary."

"Sure fine, but the only thing I vision without commercials is an economy ground to a halt. What are you – a freaking socialist? Thanks for the call! Caller five, go ahead please!"

"Yeah, I'd give her lots of free time in the prison yard. Those other prisoners would take good care of her. Do you kind of get what I'm meaning? Eh, Cobra? Eh? Oooh yeeaah."

"No, but you're turning me on, Lady! Thanks for the call. Go ahead line 6."

"Look – I can tell you exactly what happened to Jonah Flambo. He got canned because his editor found out he was doctoring his comment sections. I know. I used to be his special assistant."

"Do you have tangible proof, caller?"

"What? You want a video? He made me use pseudonyms. I wasn't the first. Most of his assistants are out of work. Ask them."

Barry turned off the radio.

* * *

As the midsummer sun faded, he cruised along the Whitemud Freeway, flowing with traffic, exiting in the city's southeast corner. Another half hour brought him into farmland and range roads. He turned on a whim onto on a dark, lonely, spruce-lined road. He drove slowly past the warm, flickering lights of acreage homes and small farms. Some pickup trucks passed him at high speed. They knew the road, and were going home.

He watched the full moon above the trees to his left. White clouds clustered around it, creating the image of an eye with cloudy eyelids. He stopped on the shoulder and watched the moon rise. It seemed like a kindness peering down from above. The screaming cacophony of spins and tweaks, deceptions and inceptions, indignations and fixations, talking points and stalking points, demagoguery and skulduggery that made up his career in journalism and politics stopped for a moment. The moon was silent.

What if he could be the moon, he thought, patiently surveying green fields and highways, city streets and restless tides? He took a picture of the moon with his e-phone. He felt the warm June wind in the treetops. He saw the deep blue of the midsummer night surround the bright celestial stone. Then, when he looked at the moon on the e-phone, he saw the face of Lucius. The silence imploded. His mind erupted.

He drove on.

Ten minutes later, he saw neon lights: "Mitch's Gas, Snacks and Range." Barry pulled in. He entered the store. The cashier was a tall elderly man in a gray sweater. Barry told him he was just browsing. He saw some rifles, bullhorns and umbrellas crammed into a clearance bin. Most were in the $1500 range. Two *Ogresso Gamemaster* rifles were marked down to $700. There were four *Ogresso Rapiers.* These umbrellas concealed sharp metal prods in their points and taser cannons in their handles. $165 each.

"Those are damn good prices," the cashier observed from the counter.

Barry saw two *Ogresso Messengers.* These were X-10s furnished with laser pointers, digital projectors and voice substitution apps. A speaker could use the voice of almost any celebrity. The *Messengers* had "Property of Prison Island" stencilled on their sides. $160 each.

"Those are good for herding, or crowd control, or getting the ref's attention at your kid's soccer game," the cashier mentioned. "But they're illegal at Esks games. Too loud. Seven is ample. Ten is painful. Eleven will shatter glass and puncture eardrums from twenty metres."

Barry nervously picked out a bag of potato chips, some wine gums and a diet cola.

"Nothing else?" the cashier asked. "Rifle, rapier, bullhorn? Like I said, those are damn good prices."

"OK, sure," Barry said, pointing at the clearance bin. "I'll take one of those."

Part Three

Prologue 3

Ottawa, July 1, 2050

Deep in Sussex Drive, the protectoral entourage was behind schedule. They were just emerging from *Geogasm Hall.* Once known as *24 Sussex Drive, Geogasm Hall* now bore a name close to the Lord Protector's heart. A simple address was boring. The Natural Republics made the White House a redundant museum honouring the lapsed congress. Canada needed to name its most famous house. Lucius Spukwell obliged.

Geogasm was the name of Lucius Spukwell's ancestral home in Henrymart, Alberta. Henrymart was a town of six hundred and fourteen people halfway between Edmonton and Calgary. Geogasm belonged to his great uncle George Feenie.

George claimed to have lost the estate through the treachery of the "central banks." Showing remarkable resilience, George never moved out, and lived quietly at Geogasm for the rest of his life. George created the name Geogasm as an amalgamation of "George," his given name, and "gas money," his source of income. His business was fracking, but he could not coin a name he liked from those syllables. He tried "Geoking" on a focus group, but they insolently pronounced it "joking." "Frackfee" was also a dud. So he chose Geogasm without the nuisance of a focus group. He asked people to pronounce the "s" in Geogasm as an s, not a z, in a full-page ad in the *Globe and Mail*. People did not oblige.

When he died in 2015, he left the house to his young son, Ned Feenie, Lucius's uncle. George left no money in his will, though he did leave a forty-minute DVD ranting against socialism to a cable network. With the exception of Ned, people admired George for riding out the economic cycles without saving a dime. He was a free spirit to the end.

George's will stipulated that the name of the house must never change. It even cited possible names, like *Feenston Abbey, Geofen* and *Nedgasm*, in order to ban them. He left instructions to burn *Geogasm* to the ground if progressive social democracy ever came to Alberta. It did, but some partisan journalists insisted it did so by some cosmic accident. Ned used their argument to ignore George's will. Ned had no children, but remained supportive of his sister and her son. Lucius was born and raised in Edmonton, but he chose Geogasm as his ancestral home when he entered politics. Lucius cherished his first campaign slogan: "Conserve Geogasm!" Focus groups liked the tone.

* * *

A cordon of security personnel insulated the Lord Protector as he emerged from his front door. He walked slowly to the protectoral landau. Its gold fixtures and ebony finish glistened in the noon sunlight. Six inmates from the Bytown

Correctional Facility, conscripts in the *THEM* program for social offenders, were yoked into position. *THEM* stood for *The Homeless Education Mission.* They had the honour of pulling the landau on this occasion. The program was part of Lucius's policy on homelessness. Most offenders were seniors over 67, a growing and troublesome segment of the population. The *THEM* logo, embroidered in a phosphorescent red Lucida font on each torso, ensured easy identification of escapees for officers in close pursuit or for marksmen. Their orange jump suits contrasted with the blue sky. Lucius expected the contrast to remind spectators of Canada's successful break from parliamentary government.

Lucius cherished the memory of propurgation. He liked to replay the event in his mind with different scripts and timelines. Today, he felt in the mood for a crisp, hybrid version: "Your sitting here is no longer tenable," Spukwell thundered in his head at MP's at the moment of propurgation. "Tarry here no longer! Get out!"

He held the results of a recent referendum in his hands. He was anxious to see its contents, but that could wait for his arrival on the former Parliament Hill. The question put to the people was simple. It used word cloud technology to ease reading:

Do you, a citizen of Canada, authorize Lord

PROTECTOR

to make permanent the abolition of the

Canadian Senate

and permanent the hiatus of the Parliament of Canada in

accordance

with the **results** of the provisional

referendum of

December 17, 2049 and the favourable headlines of
December 18,

in other words, "**sovereignty**"

and

Do you further authorize Lord

PROTECTOR Spukwell to associate with the

former speakers of the Senate and the **Commons** to
formalize

the instruments of permanence,

in other words,

"**association**."

Yes or No / Oui ou Non

Lucius had no doubts about the outcome.

The landau gave Lucius a sense of privacy. He enjoyed a special solitude on its velvet cushions that he felt nowhere else, not even at his official residence, where he lived alone with his black cats, Loki and Rico. The Landau reminded him of his childhood home in south Edmonton. He learned to screen out background noise in that home, where he often felt vulnerable. As a man, he applied that skill amid throngs of people. He didn't feel their eyes. He liked to film crowds randomly with his e-phone. He would play the video at home by himself, scanning for enemies or signs of sedition.

The crowd was under electronic surveillance. Lord Protector Spukwell was not. He used the Internet in a special "black zone" designed for him. Lucius looked forward to privacy between public duties. Later in the day, during a break in the festivities, he might scan the Internet, time permitting. He liked to check up on fugitives from justice, defeated adversaries and fired staff members. He sometimes veered compulsively towards three search terms: "homeless people porn," "fast food porn," and "porn road managers." His texting speed was too fast to be detected thanks to childhood accordion lessons. Today, he planned to watch a short documentary from his campaign days. It showed him being tough on eco-terrorists. He placed his hand over his face when it appeared on screen. No satellite passing overhead could gather evidence of narcissism. He selected the documentary on his phone, and watched it without sound. Lowering his eyes to the screen might even suggest humility, he supposed.

The landau lurched forward. The yoked men settled into a severe rhythm.

One minute into his campaign video, a reminder flashed across his phone screen. The Protectoral Gala! He mused on the gala. He would attend this night in the company of Danielle Laidlaw, Canada's foremost operatic soprano. His rare dates with accomplished women swelled the nation's rumour bladder. Had Lucius found love? Was he working too hard to have a life? And when would he make that long expected state visit and personal pilgrimage to The Hague? Lucius let the bladder fill to just the right amount of tension – not quite an emergency, but not quite comfortable either – then relieved it through the web site of the *Ministry of Intimacy*. Of course, the gala could imply recreation with Ms. Laidlaw, putting just a little more pressure on the rumour bladder. But the final message was always the same: Lucius was married to his job.

He switched his e-phone to mirror. He observed the streak of gray he had deliberately placed in his sandy blond hair, parted to the left above his dark brown eyes. It confirmed that he was working far too hard. He made a mental note to start rumours of a love life. He texted a coded reminder to himself: "srtsxrmrwldlwpstgla." When the message came through he deleted it. Then he clicked open an article on the *Edmonton Mercury* news site: "Fifth earth-like planet confirmed in distant galaxy." He practiced his speed-reading skills on this piece.

One of the prisoners was younger than the others, though his tired eyes and greasy hair testified to a life of struggle. He peered menacingly back at Lucius. Salt and pepper whiskers garnished his fiery glare. A large number 41 was stencilled on the back of his jump suit in a times font. Lucius was certain he'd met this man. Where? Edmonton? Possibly. Had be met him in the flesh? Perhaps. In porn? No. There were no lively eyes or memorable faces in porn. There were feet, mostly upside down or sideways. He looked at 41's feet. He wore plain *THEM* thongs. Their floppy sound could irritate on state occasions, but they discouraged escape.

41 lacked the mannerisms Lucius would have expected from a homeless person. The others, all seniors, slumped under their burdens. Not 41. His bearing was resolute. Well then, did he see him in an electronic newspaper? Had he scanned him in a crowd of protesters? He hated going blank, but tried not to force the recollection. If he relaxed, 41's name would come back to him.

Lucius made public speeches in his role as Sovereign Interpreter of Canada. Invoking this title let citizens know that history was about to change. He opened the notes for today's speech. Canada had moved through the transition from Parliament to Protectorate, normalizing relations foreign and domestic, and enshrining new policies guaranteeing long-term prosperity, intimacy and empathy. The United States had discarded its federal government and imploded into separate natural republics. Other G80 nations were in acute rather than terminal crises. Canada alone remained stable.

Today would be another renaming day for Canada! One year earlier, he had announced the renaming of three major cities: Ottawa became Ottawa Global Pharmacy Chains Place; Toronto, became Toronto Colossus Sensible Bank and Entertainment Chains Place; Montreal, became Montreal-Brazealco Place, leased to Mona Angela FitzBrazeal, the highest earning player in women's tennis history; Winnipeg became Winnipeg Ogden and Norble Corporate Injury Lawyers and Pharmaceuticals Incorporated Place (Winnipeg*ONCILP* for short, with a soft "c"); Vancouver, became Vancouver IT Global Security Solutions Theme Park Place. These corporations, all global giants, had paid fifteen billion dollars each for "naming rights" to these cities for a period of ten years. Lucius borrowed the idea from major league hockey: team owners sold naming rights to corporations on a five to ten-year lease. Why not cities? Some called his decision a corporate sell off. They made Lucius puke. And the *Salon Epicentric,* a new splinter party in Quebec, was howling mad at the non-refundable name for Quebec City: *Place Croisieres Pacifique d'Aventure Quebec.* Whiners. He was slaying the debt *and* lowering taxes. This was nation building.

Sirens howled in the air above. A squadron of three unmanned jet bombers was forming up for its fly past. Their mission: to spell the letters "R&L" in a heart made of royal purple smoke. People wondered if the "R" stood for renewal or reform. And the L must mean Lucius, surely. Lucius alone held the secret of interpretation.

He switched his cell pod app to zoom lens camera mode. He trained it on number 41, hoping he would turn his face backwards again so that he could analyze it at home. No luck.

Lucius nodded to his Senior Protectoral Security Commander, who ordered the prisoners to pull harder. The jump-suited men pushed harder on their yokes. Together, they heaved the landau forward towards Wellington Street, under orders to reach to "martial speed" in the next two minutes.

Reclining alone in the back, Lucius wondered about the whereabouts of another notorious criminal on the loose. Charissa Dryden-Burnet, known to police as "Izzy," had escaped from Prison Island with the ex-commandant and two notorious women. She might have drowned. She might be in Florida. She might be on the move. Could she reach Canada, Lucius wondered.

Sussex Drive reminded Lucius of Izzy. They went to the same public school and high school in Edmonton. They were in the same grade. They played Canadian *Monopoly* from time to time with Barry Basewik-Quick. Lucius always aimed to buy Sussex Drive early in the game. He could even get angry if someone bought it first, or someone touched his token. He strained Izzy's middle finger once after she mistakenly moved Lucius's shoe token.

Barry tried to interest Izzy and Lucius in a video game called *Strikedown.* Players guided precision drone strikes on cities in the Middle East. The exploding buildings resembled over-toasted marshmallows. Izzy cried whenever a drone hit a building. She said it looked like drops of fire falling on a silent northern lake. She loathed the game. Barry thought Izzy was crazy.

Should he play a short game of *Strikedown?* He hadn't played for years. He would have to upload the game. And some rogue journalist could photograph his screen from an office window. No, this was no time for *Strikedown.*

These gaming memories turned Lucius's mind to street names. He had recently renamed Ottawa's Kent Street. It was now called Knotwad Lane. And Colonel By Drive would eventually become Le Champs d'Lordso. He supposed it was time to think of a new name for Sussex Drive. He typed in a few ideas on his e-phone: 109th Street; Lady Cassandra Walk; Rue Nouvelles Politique. He was leaning towards "Calgary Trail."

Lucius slipped off his shoes and rubbed his socks on the floor of the landau. He tried to gain enough static electricity to spark his index finger on the door of the landau. No luck. He returned to his notes for his speech on Parliament Hill. Rumours swirled around the possible announcement. Some thought he would rename the flame on the former Parliament Hill. Some wondered if Lucius would rename Ontario "Lordsovia," a change endorsed by *Footman* news pundits. Some extremists anticipated the renaming of Canada in a suitable global matrix.

Yes, it would be a renaming ceremony – and a momentous one – but not the ones expected. First, he would announce the results of the referendum on sovereignty. With sovereignty affirmed, he would initiate a new age of Canadian normalcy. He would add to the titles of Lord Protector and Sovereign Interpreter in studied humility by dropping his surname. Henceforth he would be called, "Lucius Maximus."

Chapter Thirteen

A NORMAL CHILDHOOD

Prison Island, May 2050

Izzy and Ruth began another day on Prison Island. Izzy sensed a difference that morning. Otis paced the floor, as restless as a starving hamster. This was more than a lack of endorphins. He had a letter in his hand.

"This is from Global Pharmacy Chains Place – oh shit – just Ottawa! The government's changed."

Izzy didn't care. Did it matter which party was in power? The Solid Retentivists held power when she was arrested. T-Solar sometimes won. Splinter parties like the Accountability Party, the Transparency Party, the Whistleblower Party, the Croque-Salon and the Progressive Fish and Foresters won a few seats in their regions. The heat was sweltering, and the keys on the Sutton X1 were stiff and noisy. She had a mild headache.

"So?" said Izzy.

"You don't understand," Otis snapped. "The system of government has changed. The Fireballs abolished Parliament. Spukwell is now Lord Protector of Canada."

Izzy felt a sharp migraine flood into her head.

"The what?"

"Fireball Party. I'm breaking black zone protocol telling you this."

"How can he change the system? It isn't legal."

"There is no legal. According to this letter, Spukwell turned a few 360's with the Mace, then spun it like a top, rode it like a hobbyhorse, then he told Parliament to get the hell out. Or something like that. Here's a transcript: 'Long, too long and too too long have you sat here, ladies and gentlemen. I prithee in the bowels of reason, evacuate this chamber now.'" And they did! Some MPs sat in protest, but he starved them out.

"Well, life goes on here," Ruth remarked.

"Brace yourself, women. Your sentences no longer mean anything. You're in indefinite detention at Spukwell's pleasure. He's planning multiple life sentences for eco-terrorism. You can't appeal. The G-80 registered solidarity with a minor protest fly past of, quote, 'twelve Russian Suckclass bombers on loan from North Korea.' We let them fly over Tofino, apparently."

"I've got three years to go here. What's indefinite detention?" Ruth asked.

"Life," Izzy muttered.

"It gets worse," Otis wailed. "They found out about our camp anthem. It was supposed to be for sleep deprivation, not dancing. I'm being charged with misappropriation of lyrics and wasting tax dollars. I'm relieved of command. A Shuttle Boat is coming to arrest me. I'm to stand trial in Ottawa – outdoors!" He pulled a photograph of Fitzputman Otis out of his drawer and burst into tears.

Ruth tried to comfort him. "If it's any consolation, I had a so-so lawyer. Not great, barely OK. I can give you his name."

"There's more. They've revoked my citizenship. And yours too!"

This hit Izzy like a slap on the face. She felt separated from Noah and Simeon and Jesse.

"What about the other prisoners?"

"It's just you so far, Izzy."

"What now?" Ruth asked calmly.

"We leave," said Izzy.

"Leave?"

"Yes, leave. Migrate. Exit. Prorogue. Get the hell out. I'm pretty sure the mainland is maybe ninety kilometres west. We can row that old scow into open water and take our chances with the currents. If you come with me."

"*Us*?" yelled Ruth.

"Yes us. And Sadma too, I hope. Don't be afraid. It's time to leave this hole."

"Not on my watch!" Otis barked. "That's treason!"

"Your watch is over, sir."

Otis's face turned crimson. He rubbed his forehead with

his palms.

"The migration vehicle will need a captain," Izzy said, reforming her tone. "You could make this an order, Otis sir – an *executive* order?"

Otis smiled through his sheet of tears. "Yes. Yes! Print it for my signature!"

"I recommend against a paper trail, sir," Izzy suggested. "Let's make this a covert operation?"

"A black op? Excellent! Let's do this!" Otis agreed.

Sadma walked in, letting off a big yawn. Izzy told her the situation.

"Sorry to hear that," she said. "I'm not a big expert on Canada. Never have been. But I know this is bad news for you guys. My sympathies. I get how you feel. I felt bad when the U.S.A. crashed itself into the rocks. Not surprised, but bad."

"Canada isn't crashing," Izzy said. "It's purging."

"That's not the word they're using," Otis said. "It's propurged."

"All the same, I like the plan," Sadma said. "Exitus 1:1: "get me on the water tonight, girl!"

"We don't say I," Otis said cautiously. "It's us now. Isn't it, Izzy? With me in charge?"

"Well said, sir," Izzy assured Otis. "But I advise no further Chablis until we're far away from here."

* * *

Otis took well to meaningful work. He ordered four guards to winch and anchor the scow fifty metres up the shore. He told them the scow might invite an escape attempt, even though it had been stuck in one spot for twenty years. Twenty years ago the spot was dry land. Now it was waist deep. Prison Island was shrinking.

Before dawn, he sawed through the gas main that fed the wall of fire. The main ran underneath the *Stuart Otis Communications Centre*. He wrapped metallic tape over severed ends of the pipes. He sealed the end leading to the wall of fire. He poked a pinhole in the end that supplied the gas. A slow leak filled the SOCC. After roll call, he ordered three guards to stand ten metres from the wall of fire. The wall ignited, consuming the fuel remaining in the jets in two minutes. He ordered the guards to step back.

"Test successful!" he beamed. "No-one will be escaping from this island tonight!"

The guards shrugged lazily, lit brown cigarillos, and returned to their towers.

When night fell, Izzy, Sadma, and Otis followed the anchor line to the scow. Sadma had a sack of water bottles, wine gums and trail mix from Otis's personal stash strapped to her waist. They looked back at the dim lights. One of the guards lit her hash pipe near the SOCC. The shed exploded in a vortex of fire, knocking her ass-backwards. Three guards ran and helped her to her feet. They supposed that Otis was now a swatch of melted bone, teeth and ash, along with his female assistants. They held a quick roll call to confirm the number of the living. Then they and the remaining prisoners searched for Chablis.

* * *

The escapees pushed the scow out into open water. They rowed for two days. They took turns sheltering from the heavy sun with a canvas mat. They shared a wine gum, a cashew and a sip of water every three to four hours. Otis was delirious after eight hours. His dress whites were muddied from the escape. His epaulettes and braids still gleamed. The women kept rowing.

At noon on the third day, a G-80 destroyer leased to the Natural Republic of Delsylvania hailed them from five hundred metres.

"Stop your ship. Stop your ship."

Izzy and Ruth raised their oars. The scow began to drift.

"Raise your hands or we'll fire. Raise your hands or we'll fire."

The women raised their hands high above their heads.

"Fire one."

A lethal foam line exited the bow of the destroyer. Sadma saw the torpedo heading straight for them.

"Stay calm. We're too small a target. It'll miss. It has to miss. Take it cool."

Otis screamed and jumped over the side. The torpedo whirred past the scow, barely missing him. He sighed with relief. Suddenly, two shark fins were orbiting his flailing body. His chevrons and epaulettes weighed him down as he tried to swim back to the scow. Sadma reached out to him with an oar, but he disappeared below the surface. He resurfaced in a mass of fingers, epaulettes and feces. The sharks snapped happily at buttons and bits.

Izzy and Sadma watched in horror. Ruth threw up violently over the side. Suddenly, another engine whirred from the west. A rusty green PT boat slammed into the surging waves at high speed. A bearded gunner on the bow, wearing orange plaid shorts and a white, pizza-stained tank top, fired a mounted machine gun wildly at the destroyer.

"These are international waters. These are international

waters," the destroyer announced.

The gunner buckled on his safety harness and flipped two middle fingers at the ship. Then he feigned the thrusts of intercourse with his hands behind his back. Then he raised his hands and extended his two middle fingers to the sun and moon. Then he pulled down his UV filter sunglasses and resumed spraying the ship with bullets.

Two others on the PT boat pulled a brown tarp off of a metallic device roughly two metres in length. It looked like an aluminum locust. It burst into flight, clipping the jaw of one of the crewmen on its way up. The destroyer began to execute a tight 180-degree turn. The locust raced towards it, skimming the waves. It soared above the destroyer, then slammed down into the rear deck, exploding. Sailors beat back the spreading flames with hoses and foam as the ship hastened away.

The PT boat turned tightly and roared towards the scow. The women held hands. They looked into each other's eyes. A crewman on the PT boat launched a grappling hook towards the scow from a bazooka on his shoulder. The hook clutched the stern rail. The scow gave a thundering jolt that sent the women flying backwards. Sadma suffered a cut on the back of her head. The PT boat began towing the scow at top speed. Izzy discerned their direction: northwest.

* * *

Izzy and Sadma shared the last wine gum. Ruth was seasick from the banging of the hull. All three slept for an hour, despite the droning noise and intense sunlight. Izzy awoke. She felt the PT boat cut to half speed. She saw a lone dolphin jump in the wake. She saw dim lights in the distance and small buildings against a setting sun on a sandy shoreline.

"Are we back on Prison Island?" Ruth asked.

"No," Izzy said. "We're pointed west. This could be Florida."

The PT boat dropped anchor on a sand bar. The gunner ordered the women to place their hands on their heads and walk to shore. He led them to a campfire near a large, wooden hangar. An elderly man wearing a yellow bandana and floppy red shoes was roasting baby mackerel and marshmallows. A young girl, perhaps fourteen years old, sat in the sand beside him. Behind them was a tall wooden water tower. On its side was: BOO VALLEY FOUNDED 2047. Five white huts stood in a semi-circle behind the water tower. When the crew arrived the introductions began.

"Daddy," said the PT helmsman. "We caught' em thirty miles out about to tangle with a rogue destroyer. We droned the destroyer's ass and it sure took off. That navy's got dick for weapons. And we brung these women back. Fresh kill!"

"Welcome to the Natural Republic of Florida!" the old man grinned. Then his face turned sour and ugly. "And just so you know, you're all under arrest."

"For what?" Sadma demanded.

"That's for later," he replied. "Right now, we're gonna process you. Give us your names and places of business."

"We're escapees from Prison Island. And we're not going back," Sadma said.

"Oh, you're not goin' back alright! You're our prisoners now. So, let's make it nice and polite and meet my family. Just so you know, I'm Gopallcaps Boo the second, local governor, but folks call me Jack. Jack sets me apart from my dad, the late Gopallcaps Boo senior, bless him and his fine memories. This is my daughter, Normal Boo. These here men of the boat that towed you are my boys: Deke, Dade and Desi."

The women nodded grimly and spoke their names. Desi Boo looked nothing like the others. They had fiery red hair and green eyes that bubbled like foam on the surface of their faces. Desi had curly, raven-coloured hair and dark, lowering eyes set deep in his forehead. His black, lasagna-stained t-shirt read, "God Bless N.R.F." His eyes reminded Izzy of the guard towers on Prison Island. All three boys bore automatic rifles on their backs.

Normal looked more like Desi that her other brothers. She had dark shoulder length hair, suntanned skin and deep brown eyes. She did not share Desi's sullen expression. She seemed curious.

"OK, no more formalities," said Jack Boo, after he scribbled down the women's names on his hand. "An' you boys can get the brides for brothers look off your goddam faces. This is business. Get 'em washed, get 'em fed, get 'em ready to stand trial."

"On what charge?" Izzy demanded.

"Relax. We'll get you some charges. And plenty! Let's all take this one step at a time."

He rose and left the hut.

* * *

Deke and Dade led the women to a hut. There was a broken shower stall with an empty bucket and sponge on a rough wood floor. A light bulb covered with dead flies hurt their eyes as they showered quickly in cold seawater. An old pizza box was growing mould on the floor. A yellow dog with a sand dry nose breathed heavily in the corner. Izzy stroked its side and looked at her image in its open eye. She could see she was changed by time. This dog was ill.

Normal brought them towels. She wanted to talk. She had never seen such a brave new world of women.

"How old are you, Normal?" Izzy asked her, as she towelled her hair.

"Fourteen, maybe fifteen, I guess. Maybe even sixteen. Or twelve."

"Do you go to school?"

"Nope – I went straight into the economy."

"What is this place?"

"Boo Valley, Florida. We named it that after other folks pulled out. I can't recall the old name. We're the only people now for about a hundred miles. Maybe two."

"But 'folks' call him Jack," Ruth said.

"Can you tell us what'll happen here today?" Izzy continued.

"Oh. You'll all stand trial. Then you'll get executed."

Ruth and Sadma stared. Izzy wasn't surprised.

"Ok, thanks Normal – why?"

"It's the economy. Wouldn't be any jobs otherwise. Tourists don't come here, even though history started right here in Florida. Everyone knows this is the birthplace of the real America."

"How often does this happen here?"

"It's not steady, but it's enough to keep us going. People wander in, or get washed up, or miss a boat, or my brothers snag them like they did you. It can be boom and bust like most economies. We had two executions last month. We average about two. There's two brothers waiting two huts over, but dad's saving them up for something big. He wants lots of pay-per-views."

"What kind of justice is this?" Ruth wailed.

"It's not for justice," Normal answered. "Like dad says:

it's the economy. The economy flopped when we became the Natural Republic of Florida. We tried to start different things of an independent nature. Enterprenoorship. But nature is pretty messed up here. Most of south Florida got washed away. Not much wildlife here in the north. You get the feeling you can't enterprenoor without nature. That was a shock, and lots of folks left. So, in the end, the only economy we can do regular is reality TV. Otherwise, we'd starve. So, your trial and everything else will be on TV. You'll like that, maybe?"

Ruth's knees buckled. Izzy grabbed her arm and held her steady. Sadma shook her head at Normal Boo, narrowing her eyes in contempt, feeling she was looking at the Nobel Prize for stupid.

"I feel bad for you," Normal said. "My brothers once asked to go on strike. There's been no pay raise ever. But dad said the Network would terminate him if he tried it. No holidays, dentists or nothing."

"You poor thing," Ruth barked.

Normal picked up her bucket and sponge and left the hut. Dade Boo, who daydreamed about Ruth through the conversation, locked the women inside.

* * *

Izzy remembered the second time she put on Ruth's shoes by mistake on Prison Island. Her body flattened instantly. She swam like a fish wiggling from side to side through a dense red gel that ran through an intravenous line into the arm of a hooded man. She swam harder and faster in terror. An automated bank teller spat her out in the form of a white receipt. Giant blue hands tore her up and passed the pieces around, then stuffed her back into the intravenous line again and again and again. There was no bottle at the top of the line. The line was a miniature camera, with a glass tip and a lithium battery. Revealed, the line became a ferocious worm burrowing into her skin, covering the wound behind it and circling her lungs and kidneys.

"Ruth," Izzy whispered. "What troubles you? The TV?"

"Yes, it is! Just please – don't let them film me. Don't let them put me on a screen!"

"Well, I haven't seen a camera yet," Sadma proclaimed. "And I'm sure as hell not planning to die here in Stupidville either,"

Izzy slid her toes under Ruth's feet. A fly hovering before her face morphed into a dazzling blue light. Izzy pulled her feet away from Ruth. She breathed and recovered slowly from her ordeal. She narrowed her eyes like a lioness watching her cubs, and looked scornfully towards the door as she held Ruth in her arms and stroked her hair. Sadma sat down and circled her large graceful arms around Izzy and Ruth.

* * *

Four hours later, at two o'clock in the morning, Izzy, Ruth and Sadma were arraigned before Jack Boo. Court convened in an aluminum shed. Jack took his seat at an old fashioned TV dinner table. A frayed picture of former President Arson Digits was taped to the wall. The word "America" appeared in a caption. The rest of the caption was torn away.

A pencil and paper sat gathering dust in the middle of the table. At Jack's right hand was a tumbler with the Little Mermaid on it, and a half-empty bottle of Beak Brothers Bourbon.

"Silence in court," Jack cried, banging his tumbler on the table. "There's only one thing women go to Prison Island for," he began, pouring some bourbon. "And that's economic terrorism. Eco-terrorism for short in Canada, so named, let the record state. You think I don't know Canada law? Ha! Well I do. Fucking-A. You all did something to bugger your economy. Am I getting warm? Blocked a highway? Messed with the environment? Therefore, in accordance with my memorandum of understanding that I'm firing off to Commandant Otis tomorrow – boy, he'll be ticked, but finders keepers – and by the powers bequeathed by Gopallcaps Boo senior and the N.R. of Florida – meaning me – you all three stand convicted of the aforeto said eco-terrorism on other-than-your-own-sovereign-territory or soil. In other words mine. Sentence is death by choice of means. Here, you can choose one out of two ways. We can lethal inject you in prime time, or we can mini-drone you in a one-hour special. Date or special holiday to be announced. Check your local times and listings."

"What? No trial? No witnesses?

"Oh, you brung a witness? I didn't think so."

"Tell us about mini-drone," Sadma muttered.

"Well it's not rocket science!" Jack Boo laughed. Deke and Dade broke into hearty, phlegm-coated laughter. Desi glowered at his brothers. Normal looked sad.

"You saw that drone on our PT boat?" Jack bleated. "Well, we'll give you a microchip to home in a drone on you. Not as big as that one as bit the ass off that destroyer, but a real nice one for sure. That was a fixed wing pursuit. Yours'll be a compact stalker. Next, we set you loose. There's cameras hidden in the woods for miles, never mind how many, and aerial cameras if we need 'em. So we'll get a good decent feed we can edit down. When we please, and don't ask when, we send the mini-drone, addressed personal to your chip. Oh, it'll find you, and trust me, it'll surprise you. You get to die in a big season-ending finale."

"And just how long does it take before the mini-drone arrives"

"On average? Never mind. We need good footage, but

not as much as you think. You ladies had best mind your own goddam business and focus. Decision time. Miss Izzy?"

"Mini-drone," Izzy said, calmly.

"She's a gonna be mini-droned!" Jack Boo cackled. "Deke, you're gonna film at the starting line. Normal – you're gonna assistant executive produce! Miss Sadma?"

"What she said. Mini-drone."

"Ha! That'll work! Now, Miss Ruth, I hate to do this, honest honey, but you don't get a choice. We need to lethal inject you to balance the TV schedule. Mini-droning takes a lot more time and money. Lethal injects pay the bills steady and tide us over each month. They sort of sponsor the dronings. Sorry, but you can see how it is."

Ruth fainted into Izzy's arms.

"When?" Sadma asked.

"Lunch time tomorrow she'll have already been on the business end of a lethal inject. You other two'll be put on the road after so's the mini-drone can start the hunt. Deke and me'll point you north. Night all!"

Deke pinched Ruth's cheek and shook her. Dade threw a cup of seawater in her face. When she revived, the boys marched the women back to their cell. Normal Boo followed along.

All the way back, Sadma muttered over and over: "I'm not dying in Stupidville. I'm not dying in Stupidville. I'm not dying in Stupidville. I'm not."

Chapter Fourteen

THE DIAMOND LADDER

Sadma's Inspiration

Izzy, Sadma and Ruth were exhausted. They huddled together in their cell. Izzy rocked Ruth gently to sleep. Sadma sang a song in a low voice: "I want to cross over into camp ground." Time was short, but sleep was a healer. Sadma and Izzy lay down side by side. Ruth breathed gently in her sleep. Izzy listened to Sadma's breathing change from waking to sleeping. Knowing she was the last to fall asleep helped her to sleep.

Izzy had a nightmare. The Boo family adopted her. They liked the sound of Izzy Boo. If she joined the family, they would cure her papoutsiosis. She could take it easy. She wouldn't have to participate in executions. Normal Boo needed a female mentor, a peculiar friend, maybe even a big sister. Jack Boo cooed possibilities as he removed her shoes. He poured warm lavender water and let her gently move her tired feet through a delicious lavender and seawater brine.

"There's only one cure," Jack Boo assured her. "This here is it."

"No executions?"

"None! The execution room used to be a hot dog stand. Now it shall be again. See, I'm not so bad. And no more being infiltrated in your soul. Look, the critters are taking away all that empathy and pain from you right now. Score!"

Izzy lifted her feet out of the seawater. Hundreds of bright orange worms were feeding on the soles of her feet. With each bite she became forgetful, vacant, alone. Her feet disappeared, then her ankles and shins, all erased by scavenging worms.

She woke with a cry.

She peered into the dark humid cell. Ruth snored lightly, her right palm turned outwards to block dreamy cameras. Normal Boo was in a deep sleep on some straw outside the cell. She was holding her *Jenna The Counter-Terrorist* doll in her arms. Izzy couldn't see Sadma. Sadma was gone. She saw a pair of shoes just outside the cell door. She pulled them through the bars and slipped them on.

They were Sadma's shoes.

* * *

Wearing Sadma's shoes raised Izzy up into the stars and set her down gently on a long front porch. Sadma was rocking gently in a rocking chair. She held a baby in her arms. Three older boys played a dancing game on the lawn. The ocean swayed lazily on the orange horizon. A pelican tipped and rolled over a low white cloud.

Izzy knelt by Sadma's rocker.

"So you found them," Sadma said to Izzy. "I hoped you would."

"Your shoes?"

"Yes. They made me leave them there for the next person they drag in on their boat. I put them close to you."

"I wasn't sure."

"Well, good guess girl."

"What happened?" Izzy asked.

"I died in Stupidville, contrary to my first intentions. Now I'm home with my family, with the grandchildren I thought I'd never see."

"Why?"

"Because those Florida dickheads don't know what they're doing. And Ruth had her share of trouble early on. She deserves her chance. She's a stronger walker than me. Better for her to go on. I was happy for both of you. Well, up to a point. I'm older, or I was older then, compared to you. Not so much now."

"You were only forty-three!"

"Well, now I'm six thousand. Take it slow, child. In my end was your beginning. And I've been waiting on you for ages."

Izzy looked down. She thought of Jesse. Sadma tossed a pebble on the green grass beyond the porch. The grass rippled outward like water and became transparent, revealing the Boo family down on the planet beneath their feet. The Boos seemed to have noticed the pebble. They looked around in stunned bewilderment.

"Don't mind them. Stunned is their default. They couldn't see squat with a telescope. They don't know what they're doing." Sadma reached her foot out into the rippling hole and kicked away a pure diamond ladder that joined Boo Valley to the green rippling grass. It fell near Jack Boo, but he couldn't hear it. After the ladder fell, the green grass covered over the Boo family like still waters.

"Don't worry. The ladder will be back soon enough. It always does. So I'll have to see those assholes again all too soon. There's second chances, not just for friends or loved ones, or for those we just respect. A second chance is a big event. Some die for a loved one, a friend or maybe even a good person we hardly know. But to die for assholes – that's out of my league sister. And yet it happens. Lord's done it, but I need to work those Boos out of my system. You know, make room. The miracle is that even while total assholes go killin' folks for vengeance and profit and whatsoever things are useless, the ladder comes back. Some folks find it. Those Boos might even find it, but not as long as reality TV is stuck up the natural republic of their butts. I tuned out their batshit and betook me to my dignity. Smell the sea, girl. Feel the breeze. Listen to the poems baking in the oven. Rest your feet. You're gonna need them."

"That was gracious, Sadma," Izzy said. Tears welled in her eyes.

"And knowing you's been a grace, dear child. So right back at you. I've been here six thousand years, a moment, a pulsation of my artery. The moment of grace is the one that dickhead boo of a devil can't find. It expands out, and there's no more boredom. Time's deep as deep river. That's concentric time, not the irksome time most folks keep. It's not the time those Boos make a living from, but as long as the Boos have a .01% chance of seeing what's in front of their faces, the ladder comes back. Do angels put it back? I'd say so. Angels have a real crap job in my view. Real crap! I'd rather clean a latrine. The ladder's a second chance. The diamond lines up more second chances than the universe can hold. So angels never get tired. I'm no angel."

"What makes the Boos so violent?"

"They were told violence solves problems. Told, and they never gave it another thought. That's the difference. Economic problems, social problems, political problems. Foreign countries. Told for many generations. Take Desi. He's smart as a whip, but no learning. That's why he glowers at folks. Those boys were told the constitution starts with stand your ground. Told but never once taught. They've had no education from anyone, no lifeline from anyone. My sons were studying the actual constitution for a history test the night I got arrested. Langston loved to learn history. They all did. Think on that. Ha!"

"Can I tell Ruth?"

Sadma shook her head.

"Ruth gets the plain version. Human folk can't bear too much reality. I did what I did and gladly. Plain down to earth'll do her for the time being. She needs her second chance. It's as it was and is and ever shall be. Hmmm."

Izzy took that as a no. She looked out over the lush grass. She felt the wind in her hair. She had grown to love Sadma's voice. She didn't know how much.

"Was it hard to leave?"

"Oh yeah. Most definitely. That old river has been a terror to lots of folks. And I was raging inside me against those stupid Boos, which is not the best way to go. But when I let you matter more than them, I could breathe again. And when I knew I was in the river and there was no turning back, I felt real easy inside. I could feel my feet in the cool bottom, and the bottom was made of footprints, and I felt seriously easy inside. I could feel my feet in the prints of so many others, slave and free, mostly slave, some free, who stood there for a father or a mother or a friend. I just love my sisters so much. I couldn't have done it for an idiot, least of all a bunch of batshit crazy idiots. The Lord could and does and will, but I'm not there yet."

Izzy knelt close to Sadma and rested her head in her lap. She became the baby that Sadma held. She melted in a sleep of tears. She slept a holy sleep for a period of 6000 years. And the pages of her sleep were filled with healing dreams.

When Izzy awoke, she was in her cell. Normal Boo was clutching her Jenna doll. Ruth was wheezing snoozily and whispering in her sleep.

* * *

Jack Boo arrived in the early light, cleaning his nails with his rusty army knife. Dade and Deke raked the bars of the cage with garden trowels, which they kept in holsters.

"Get up women!" Jack screamed.

Ruth and Izzy squinted into Jack's menacing face.

"I've got news," Jack dissertated. "Miss Sadma woke Normal last night while you two were sleeping. She told my girl she wanted to see me. She formally requested me to let her die instead of Ruth, and I said fine, permission granted, now let me get some goddam sleep. She said no, it had to be right then, right now. It's no skin off my front dick, but I could see her point. She said it had to happen before you woke up to spare you and her a lot of fuss. I agreed. I'm not so bad. I offered her fifty bucks to die nude, or just apologize for whatever she did to society, or ten bucks just to look straight at the camera once or twice, but she shouted no, and then said no more. Real anger issues, I'd say. Violent type? You betcha. Needs professional help. Special handling. Bad egg. I showed her my balance sheet still worked, in case she thought I gave a rat's damn. I even get some scores. I still got my two drones to one inject ratio. Score! The secret deal makes a neat little plot twist for viewer interest. Network'll like that. Score! We got to do our work in the cool night air instead of the hot noon sun. Score! And Ruth – you're heading for a mini-droning with Izzy. You get to live some more. That's a score for your side. So you should thank Miss Sadma next time you see her, which might be pretty soon. Ha! Now get your shoes on, ladies. It's time you hauled ass out of here."

Ruth gripped Jack's arms and tried to pull him through the bars. Dade and Deke pulled her off.

"Suits me, young lady," Jack said, rubbing his bruises. "That's going on TV too."

Ruth fell into Izzy's arms and wept. Normal held her Jenna doll tight and closed her eyes.

* * *

Out in the compound, Deke was polishing the drone with a can of heavy-duty bathroom cleanser. He cleaned up the drone's name painted on the fuselage: *Spirit of Real Guts I.* He pointed with pride to the words "anti-bacterial" on the label and grinned when Ruth and Izzy appeared. Dade and Desi were lashing the Bomponce brothers, Shaft and Fargo, to the arms of the drone. They lashed their heads with extra duct tape to prevent decapitation by the vertical propellers.

"And here's another plot twist. These boys'll bring us prequel ratings," Jack crowed. "We've been emaciatin' them on carrots and beans and bad water so's the mileage won't be too bad, and the drone won't stall. If the Network shows this part first, it'll give you ladies what Network folk call a pull in. Score!"

Shaft called out for water. Jack grumbled and nodded to

Desi, who gave him a sip from a plastic jug.

"You're not helpin' your cause by not cooperating," Jack warned Shaft, as he wet his lips on the jug.

Deke left the drone and took his position behind the camera. The camera rested on a small rail car that would follow a track for the first five miles. It was a converted roller coaster salvaged from the ruins of an old seaside resort. Deke would film the start of the journey. Jack would narrate, knowing full well The Network would replace him with a mellifluous voice-over. Normal got to say go.

Dade gave Ruth and Izzy each a plastic water bottle, a box of pink popcorn and a pair of gym socks. Then, Desi and Deke held Ruth and Izzy in full nelsons. Normal Boo swabbed their necks with alcohol. Using a box cutter, Jack cut them from behind at the base of their necks. He used tweezers to force drone-guiding microchips up into their necks. He cauterized the wounds with a small branding iron that burned an N into their flesh. Dade coughed from the smoke, then swabbed the blood with peroxide and sprayed the wounds with a clear, pungent lacquer to secure the chips and keep the women from picking at their wounds.

Their knees weakened with pain. Desi and Deke held the women upright, gripped their shoulders and aimed them forward.

"Desi's made you a nice stencil for your drone," Jack announced. "It's a Confederate flag with nice little white maple leaves on the bars instead of stars. That's a big score for you. It might just stretch our audience share over the border. Score!"

He stood in the road and pointed a bony finger.

"That's north," he said. "Now get your asses walking."

Chapter Fifteen

THE MIDDLE WINDOW

Palace Junction, May 2050

Izzy and Ruth walked north for four days. They slept in their canvas prison fatigues, which were too tough for flies to penetrate. They brushed flies off each other's hair. They walked in the early mornings, the late afternoons and the evenings. They rested in the midday heat.

They were both surprised to be still alive. They assumed the Boos would film their walk, then send the drone in for the kill. The sky was hot and quiet. Motors startled them at times. They came from unmanned barges in the nearby sea. There was no sign of a drone.

They decided to lie down by the side of the road. They pretended to sleep, but kept their ears open. Izzy heard shoes scraping the shoulder of the road. She opened her eyes. Normal Boo stared down at her.

"Thought you might be dead. You can see I'm glad you're not, right?"

"What are you doing here, Normal?" Izzy asked. "Do you know how dangerous this is?"

"You mean the drone? Nah – it's still early for that. They're lengthening your spot cause you're women. Most shows are men. Sure, I'll be in trouble if dad finds me here. Right now, he thinks I'm beachcombing for junk. I came to help."

"How can you help?"

"I know where stuff is. And I know they put a box of life support for you two to lengthen the show. Look there."

She pointed to an aluminum dumpster beside two small palm trees up the road. Inside they found three burlap knapsacks filled with water bottles, protein bars and hygiene products. Viewers expected and The Network demanded standards.

"Why are there three?" Izzy asked, warily.

"Should've just been two, I guess. The third must have been executive produced in case anyone survives droning maybe. It happens once in a while. When it does, we keep filming and call it *After the Final Droning.* Alligator got a survivor once. It's a popular special, 'specially round Thanksgiving."

"Has anyone ever gotten away?" Ruth asked.

"Dunno," Izzy replied. "But if they did, dad says there's always Plan B to get em."

"What's Plan B?" Izzy asked.

"Dunno. It's top secret. I'm pretty sure Deke, Dade or Desi don't even know. It's between dad and the Network. I'd have to make senior executive producer to know, and maybe not even then. Network calls it a teaser."

"Nice to see you have goals, bitch," Ruth said.

Izzy, Ruth and Normal sat on the shoulder of the road. Izzy opened one of the protein bars. She broke it into three pieces and passed two to Ruth and Normal. Then she took a sip from her canteen and passed it to Normal.

"Why are you passing stuff around?" Normal asked. "The packs are individualized."

Izzy held the canteen to Normal's lips. Normal finally took a sip. They each donned a pack and headed north.

* * *

They walked for two more days with no sign of a drone. Izzy turned closer to the ocean, missing the checkpoint for the next dumpster. Normal wondered if something was wrong. Izzy noticed her agitation.

"Well, Normal, you seem to know a lot about where things are. Did you run away to be with us? Or are you still working as a production assistant?"

"Assistant executive producer. I wanted to talk. I never met women. Dad sends them up the road too quickly."

"Then what are you worried about? You don't have a chip in your neck."

"I'm thinking about the next dumpster. I know they're not on the beach. How do we survive without dumpsters?"

"How do we survive with them? If we stay on course, we'll be droned. If we go off course, we'll still be droned thanks to the chips. I think we have a better chance off course. At least we can ruin your TV show."

Normal found this hard to process. She wasn't used to choices.

"Where exactly are you folks from?" she asked.

"Thanks for asking," Ruth said sarcastically. "Izzy's from Edmonton in western Canada and I'm from Anne's River down east. Your lunatic father never asked us."

"Well, he's on a schedule, It's a lot of pressure, you know. You'd understand if you were in his shoes."

"If I were in his shoes, I'd blow my head off," Ruth said.

Izzy led them onto a narrow beach. There were no cars, no aircraft and no boats on the horizon. The coastline widened to the east. Years of rising ocean levels had reduced Florida's long peninsular shape to a small sack. The smaller land mass sagged under the border of the Natural Republic of Lobagoca, an amalgamation of Louisiana, Alabama, Georgia and the Carolinas. The 'g' in Lobagoca was soft.

They saw hundreds of seagulls crowding, hovering, descending on a long blue barge. The barge was stuck in a sand bar. Its little motor continued to push forward, but the sand was too firm. The motor pushed away some dead fish that floated upside down. Izzy looked for human life on the barge. It was vacant.

"Is this your drone?" Ruth asked sarcastically.

"No ma'am. It's a garbage barge," Normal said. "She's unmanned and unnamed. You put your garbage on and point it out to sea or up the coast as a courtesy to other users. Eventually they sink or drift away. This one looks stuck."

"Geniuses," Ruth said.

“Well, dad says it's loads better than payin’ high taxes for a government nobody wants,” Normal insisted.

“What if we push it out and point it north?” Izzy asked.

“Touch it? It’s rancid!” Ruth cried.

“No one will look for us on the ocean,” Izzy observed.

“Drone would,” said Normal. “You’re chipped. You’re easy marks any place.”

“And will they broadcast a floating garbage can? I doubt it. This barge could buy us time,” Izzy said.

“Or would garbage make a nice plot twist, Normal?” Ruth asked.

“I say go back to the dumpster trail. I say trust dad. He planned it out,” said Normal.

“No thanks. We’ll ride the barge north as far as we can,” said Izzy. “It might be low on fuel. If the drone comes, we’ll swim in different directions to confuse it. The seagulls might screen us, or even hit the drone’s motor. One or two or all of us might survive.”

Normal frowned. “I don’t fancy being shark food.”

Izzy picked some broad leaves and palm bark and wrapped them on her hands for protection. She waded out and pushed some garbage to the front of the barge, making a clear perimeter around the outboard motor. An old syringe snapped against her tree bark mitten. She saw intravenous tubes stuck to cheese encrusted pizza boxes. A clump of wet brochures stuck to the deck: “Worry-free retirement? Executive homes in South Bedford Acres bring peace of mind. Call today!”

Ruth helped Izzy push the barge out of the sand bar. Normal hesitated. She looked at the sky and back to the shore. Then she climbed aboard.

* * *

Ruth found some deodorant in her pack. The canister promised dryness under pressure and a floral scent. She applied some under her nose, and then did the same for Izzy and Normal. It lowered the stench of garbage, with the aid of sea breezes. They turned the barge into a north headwind. Izzy told Ruth and Normal to sit at the front. The stench would be lower there.

"What about you?" Ruth asked.

"I'll be fine. I've smelled worse," Izzy said.

The motor drew fuel from three metal drums. Izzy knocked on the outsides. Two sounded hollow. The third sounded full. It was hard to know how far they might get with winds and weight.

"Just so you know," Normal said, "using this barge makes you hypocrites."

"Why?" Ruth asked, tempted to bury a syringe in Normal's nose.

"Cause you're eco-terrorists. You're the kind that complains about gas, but then you use it to get around."

"Who told you that?" Ruth asked.

"Dad told me."

"Is this what you wanted to chat about, Normal?" Izzy asked.

"I'm just trying to contribute."

"Drones need fuel. Are we the first women to get droned?"

"Nope. Dad got two last fall. I didn't get to talk to them

much, but the man they were with talked to me a lot at first. They got kicked off a cruise ship for upsetting passengers. It was an end times cruise – dancing, dining, kids activities and end times movies and end times prophetic lessons, all on a luxury ship. Minister Phlap, that was the man, and his two women friends, Jasmine and Destiny, booked the cruise to make trouble. They picked fights with passengers who said the Middle East would kick-start the end times, so the more wars the better. Phlap said no sir and no ma'am. Jesus is anti-war, pro-gay, scourge of lynchers, friend of reprobates. The passengers got pretty upset, but he wouldn't take those words back. So the captain set him and the women adrift in a rubber raft with just some salad tongs for oars. Dade and Desi bagged them on patrol. Dad didn't want to sentence Phlap because he was a man of the cloth. Family honour. He convicted the women, chipped them, and sent them up the road. They had big high heels and leather coats, one light blue, one a real nice red. Dad offered them running shoes. He's not so bad. But they said no, heels were fine. They asked me to lend them some soap and toothpaste, so I did. They both teared up when I gave them stuff. I loved their clothes. Then they smiled and put their arms around each other as they walked. I felt sad watching them walk away. I remember they stopped up the road. Jasmine leaned on Destiny to get a stone out of her shoe. That's when I cried. I hid it from dad though since he's got enough on his mind. They were so elegant. I wanted to get to know them, but dad processed them fast. My brothers were pissed about it. There's no dating in Boo Valley and no friends. Just the economy."

"What happened to Reverend Phlap?" Izzy asked.

"He sort of died inside when those women walked up the road. He wouldn't eat, wouldn't say much, wouldn't spread his message after they left. He talked about people he missed: some girl in Canada, some woman with a dog and a weird name, but mostly Jasmine and Destiny. His talking wasn't very organized. He was really down. Then one morning he started talking to me. He kept saying the same words over and over."

"Can you tell us?" Izzy asked.

"Sure. But remember, he was down in the dumps.

God hath forsaken me, and my friends are become a burden,

A weariness to me, and the human footstep is a terror to me

When shall all manner of thing be well?

That's what he said. I didn't get it. I told dad, and he got angry. He made me repeat the first part slow. He thought Phlap was daring to call us godforsaken. What does he mean, godforsaken, dad said. There's no such thing in the Bible, dad said. In God we Truss – that's all the Bible a Florida man needs, dad said. And as for friends, we weren't Phlap's friends. It's just business. One thing about dad, he's an organized talker. Then dad asked me to repeat the second part. He got really angry. He thought Phlap was calling us terrorists. So dad called Phlap a phony, and decided to lethal inject him, minister or not. But Phlap curled up and died that night. We figured his heart gave out. Dad cursed his luck and decided to inject him anyways. He said it wouldn't stain our honour since he was already dead. So dad and the boys dragged him to the table. But it didn't look real because he was dead. Dad put some apple jelly on Phlap's cheeks to make him look alive. The Network sniffed it out and said nothing doing. They like to see real facial movement and lots of body language. Authenticity they call it. So Dade, Deke and Desi drove Phlap out to sea and dumped him feet first tied to a rock."

Izzy bowed her head.

Ruth had a different view: "How stupid are you,

Normal? You talk like that's a normal story. Like buying an ice cream cone. Your father's a mass murderer you fucking dope."

Normal turned red. She held her hands over her stomach. Ruth turned away. Izzy kept steering the outboard motor, watching Normal to make sure she didn't jump over the side.

"Help me steer, Normal," Izzy said.

Normal put her hand on the tiller as the barge chugged slowly into the north wind. The seagulls weighed the pros and cons of feeding on cheesy cardboard, coagulated soda and old syringes in the teeth of a wind. Many began to leave.

"Tell me something special about yourself," Izzy said.

"I've got a special job this episode."

"Assistant executive producer. I knew that already."

"There's more to it," Normal said. Her face reddened. Izzy felt dread.

"Tell me, child."

"There's a camera in my shoe. I'm not just assistant executive producing. I'm the shoe-cam operator!"

Izzy looked at Normal's flappy shoes. Nothing looked unusual. Then she saw tiny black tube with a glass tip protruding from a crude hole near Normal's big toe. It looked like a frayed shoelace. Izzy decided not to tell Ruth, who was alone at the front of the barge. She thought Ruth might throw Normal overboard.

"Tell me how it works."

Normal cheered up. "It's called a Vipercam XL-7. I'm supposed to get extra footage for final editing. That's good. It means The Network's thinking of using you for Thanksgiving."

"Where does the sound go in?"

"There's no sound. Just video. This tape'll have a narrator. The Network makes its own sounds. They even do voice-overs for me and my family. The actress who does me sounds pretty grown up. Dad says she's sexy. The guy who does dad is called a bass baritone."

Izzy was relieved. The shoe-cam wasn't leaking their conversations.

"Normal, if we're going to talk – really talk – we have to have truth. I thank you for telling me this truth."

Normal beamed.

"And here's my truth for you. I don't like the shoe-cam. And Ruth won't like it either. When she was a few years older than you, some creepy people posted pictures of her friend. It made her angry, and she ended up in jail. If she knew you had a shoe-cam, she'd never like you again. And she doesn't have to be told it's there."

"Are you saying there's no reality TV in Canada? Can't be much of an economy."

"It's the camera, Normal. Can't you see that? Try to imagine being someone who can feel a camera without seeing it. What would that be like?"

"Well, I don't think Ruth likes me anyways," Normal said.

"Maybe it's the shoe-cam. Ruth can feel it. If we take it out of your shoe, we'll be better friends, maybe even good friends."

"But if there's no shoe-cam, dad'll only have the drone-cam. You can kiss the holiday special goodbye. Don't you have ambitions?"

"Ruth and I plan to stay alive. Are you with us?"

Normal frowned, then nodded.

Izzy pulled the black tube slowly through the hole in Normal's shoe. It uncoiled into a length of thirteen inches. The glass tip concealed a lithium battery and a thin digital card.

"Maybe we should try to catch a fish with it. We might get hungry," Izzy said. She tied the camera to the end of an old plastic coat hanger lying in some trash. Then, she lowered the tip of the camera into the whirring blades of the outboard motor, and cut off its head like a snake.

When Normal saw the decapitated tube, her eyes widened. Then her body relaxed. She was sorry to lose the title of assistant executive producer. Still, this felt good. She fell asleep with her head in Izzy's lap.

* * *

When Normal awoke, she asked about names.

"What's Izzy short for?" she asked.

"Charissa."

"What's it mean?"

"Grace."

"Why not just be Grace? It's a name."

Izzy shrugged.

"Why did your dad pick it?"

"Both my parents picked it. They loved words."

"What were their names?"

"Simeon and Noah."

"Are you sure about that?"

"Yes. Those are Bible names, Normal."

"Noah sure is. Preacher Phlap mentioned Noah's flood. He called it the power of words. I thought it was about weather."

Izzy wondered what Simeon and Noah would think if they could see her, floating on a garbage ark, bearing the refuse of a broken nation, with women who might not survive and never procreate.

"How did you get your name?" Izzy asked Normal

"From dad. We got everything from dad. I wish there was a short form for it. What do you think of 'Mal' for short?"

"I don't like Mal," Izzy said. "What about your last name?

"That's from the true history of my family. Here goes. About two summers ago, we had a real professor locked up in our jail. I liked his accent. Said he was a linguist from Turkey looking for the last Florida dialect. His name was Ateek. He actually wanted to meet folks like us for his research. He wanted to study our talk. Got tried and convicted instead. He asked me about our background. Dad said there's only one true language in Florida. Ateek said, nope, there's lots. Dad said he was one of those damn elites he warned us about. I talked to him in his cell. He thought we must be French-Cajun cause dad's grandpa was named Bo Doo. Bo's mom was Mo Doo. Might be 'Moan Dew,' the professor said. So he thought we came from old Louisiana, and maybe down from the north before that. He said Florida was rich in slave and Indian and Spanish and French words, even after it became a state in 1845. That's not what dad told me, so I doubted him. He laughed and cried and got angry and said we was playin' God, the day before his inject. He kept repeating, *media vita in morte sumus* over and over. I memorized it. I reported it to dad. Dad said he got the media part right. So how'd we get from Doo to Boo? Well, dad married my mom, Miss Mala Scula, before I was born. She naturally took Dad's name and became Mala Doo. She was crazy for guns. Dad says she dumped us a week after I was born and went off to terrorize most of North Florida. She was notorious. One time, she vigilanteed a security guard who shot a woman who wouldn't get out of her car, Turned out the woman was in labour. Mom kept it up, but eventually got gunned down by police. Did dad feel sorry for himself like he could've? Nope. He got back up and started to enterprenoor. He never asks for handouts. The Network asked if he'd like to parlay the prestige of mom's gundown into a reality TV show. Dad was tickled. He was used to being ignored, and tired of it. The Network gave him control so long as he did what they asked and met their production schedule. They only had two conditions. The whole family would have to work for dad. And we'd have to change our last name to Boo."

"Why?"

"Because all the news sites spelled her name 'Boo' when she was gunned down. Boo was wrong, but no one would admit it. So the opportunity depended on calling ourselves Boo. The Network wanted the gundown for context."

"But wasn't she already notorious? Her name must have been famous around here."

"She wasn't gunned down as the notorious Mala Doo. She was gunned down for stealing a diet cola. She ignored police when they told her to stop, and even gave them her finger, though the police never said which one. The body was hard to identify. They say her face looked like a run-over tomato. The Network talked about making her black, or maybe Islam. They reserved the right to change mom's race or religion, but decided the name change would do. So the new name stuck. The notorious Mala Doo said she was a freedom fighter for Florida's independence. But she went down in history for a cola. Dad was happy. He said he couldn't control mom anyways. Says he named me Normal because it combines Nora and Mala. He says Nora was his first true love before Mala was my mom. I think my name means that him and mom hated each other. I often wish I'd gotten her story from her. Dad said the name change was a score because Boo comes off the tongue easily. He was all for Boo."

"Do you have a middle name, Normal?" Izzy said.

"Doreen, cause it reminds Dad of drones. Oh, and that reminds me of one more thing history-wise. I had a twin brother. Dad lost him in a card game up the coast. I don't know his name. And Dad had a brother Jake. He got mini-droned from the get go, not for a crime, but 'cause the pilot drone went haywire, like it had a mind of its own. He was our mechanic. Drone blew up in his face. His pliers and wrenches got embedded in his chest. His head got burned past recognition. The Network didn't use him cause there was no before and after pictures – just after. Not much to go on, is it?"

"Was your mom a white woman, Normal?" Ruth asked.

"I expect so," said Normal. "Who knows? Like I said, The Network reserves rights to race. Nobody ever talks about her. Dad has bad blood for her."

Ruth whispered to Izzy: "Should we mention that Sadma's mom was shot running a stop sign?"

"Little steps," Izzy whispered back.

Ruth nodded.

"Have you ever met a Ruth before?" Izzy asked Normal.

"Not a one. Dad hates names like that. He wants Jezebels or Scarlets or Dhalias for the ratings. They lower viewer ambiguity. But they're scarce. You're lucky you got to keep your own names on air, unless The Network decides to change them. Since you're notorious, I expect they'll leave your names be."

"You told me your story, Normal. I have a story for you," Izzy said.

Izzy looked Ruth and Normal in the eye as she told them the story of Ruth and Naomi. Ruth the *chesed,* the loyal. Call me no longer Naomi, but Mara, bitter. Whither thou goest I will go. Ruth clave unto Naomi in the middle of a long, empty road in a deep time of loss and death and abandonment, in the fear of age and hope of youth. Ruth and Naomi walked and walked and walked. Ruth gleaned. Ruth uncovered the feet of Boaz, who was a good man, who treated his workers like princes. Ruth is in the tree of Jesse.

"Who's Jesse?" Normal asked. "And how come they didn't get droned on the road?" she asked.

"It was long ago," Izzy said. "And it's a family tree."

"And Boaz wasn't a stunned asshole like your dad," Ruth snapped.

"So there's no video of those women? You can't be sure they lived, but I'm glad they lived if you say so. Are there more woman-to-woman friends in the Bible?" Normal asked.

"Yes, if you know where to look," said Izzy.

"Hmm. Dad never read much, but he showed me the Book of Bambi on video once. I cried when those old AR-15s unloaded a crossfire on Bambi's mom. It seemed to take forever. The mom took five thousand rounds nobly. You must have seen it when you were kids. That must be the saddest thing in the Bible. Dad told me the Bible was written of, by and for the real men of Florida. Bambi's mom put God and country, which are pretty much the same thing, before family. Good on her, he told me."

"There are no AR-15s in the Bible," Izzy said. "Try to

remember the Book of Ruth. I'll tell the story again if you like."

"No need. Dad says the Network updates the Bible by wireless all the time. You have to stay current."

"Your dad's a total asshole of a serial killer," Ruth shouted. "And your brothers are ragingly inflamed viral assholes. Now get the hell away from the tiller, moron. I'm going to steer." She lifted Normal by the upper arms, and deliberately pinched them. Normal winced, and tears came, as she rubbed her arms.

"Try to stop hating," Izzy whispered to Ruth.

"Hate?" Ruth snarled. "Fine, sure, her dad's a murderer. And her brothers are murderers. But what the hell, they're her family. Her real family and her TV family! Hell, they could do a spinoff show. Each week they could induce a suicide. Set a world speed record. You've seen one execution you've seen them all, right?"

"She isn't a camera," Izzy whispered, "She's a child."

Ruth wept.

* * *

Dark clouds followed them up the coast. It looked like heavy rainfall to the south. Ruth steered the barge inside of three small islands lying off a wooded coastline. A ragged Confederate flag flew from a tall pine on the middle island. A clap of thunder and a bolt of lightning incinerated the flag.

Ruth thought the thunder might be a drone. She turned up the throttle. The engine gulped and ran out of gas. The barge coasted into a sand bar near the shore. Above some trees they saw a tall white steeple. The women walked towards it. A sand path on the beach widened into a gravel road. Then a paved, potholed, empty street arced to the right. Empty houses with peeling white paint and green shutters lined both sides of the street. The steeple was atop an old Episcopal church. The church was in disrepair. An old man sat in a rocking chair on the front porch. He wore wire spectacles, and a frayed red T-shirt with the words "Beaufort Volunteer Fire Department Softball Team."

"Hello," said Izzy. "Are you the minister?"

"Minister? No. I'm the curator. Welcome to the Museum of the Freed!"

He rocked slowly. He seemed to have nothing more to say.

"What's the Museum of the Freed?" Ruth asked.

"The reincarnation of the old Episcopal church, first built on the coast of South Carolina in 1786. The rectory was burned by northern troops in the Civil War. You're looking at the original church."

"Is this Beaufort?" Izzy asked.

"It's Bew-furt, not Bo-Fore." the man replied. "Canadian, eh?"

"Yes, Canadian."

'This is a shirt a fellow gave me a while back. He was taking his family inland away from the rising waters. You're not in Beaufort. You're in Palace Junction, sisters."

"Where's all the people?" Ruth asked.

"People moved inland at least eighty, ninety miles two years ago. They thought the ocean level would sweep us away by now, like most of south Florida, Savannah, the Sea Islands and points north. I've heard the coast is already gone past Civilityville But it stopped right here at our old church. Hasn't risen since."

* * *

The old man took them into the museum. There was no electricity. The museum was a little musty, but the dust held the sunlight in a broad shaft that revealed its dancing universes. The pews were intact. Hymnals and leaflets from the deep past lined the seats.

Normal looked at the middle window. She saw a deep pink and purple sunset lighting up the Atlantic Ocean. A black mother knelt beneath a broad green palm tree. She was reading a book to her child. In the far right corner, a warship sailed away into the distance.

Ruth looked at the middle window. A golden lion was leading a girl in a white dress through a dark forest. The stars rose above the tree tops, forming constellations never seen or named before.

Izzy looked at the middle window. A black pilgrim dragged a long diamond ladder behind him. He dragged it by a singed rope around his throat. Black Pilgrim looked patient, kind and understanding. For a moment, he raised his hands as if he was being arrested, or held at gunpoint. His stigmata appeared. He made eye contact with Izzy. Behind him a Roman centurion was taking a selfie with his e-phone pole. His red cape fluttered in the cold wind. Orange maggots slithered in bleached rib cages near his sandals. The dark sky shimmered with meteors and a crescent moon. A column of slaves walked north in the distant horizon. A slave with a baby in her arms looked back over her shoulder at Izzy. A tiny black dog followed at her heels.

"These windows can't be very old," Izzy said.

"Why? Do you see something new in them?" the old man said. "I see them pretty much as they were at their beginning. You see them as they are now. They're old as the first building, no doubt about it. But they started morphing for people when we became the Museum of the Freed. They anneal in glass your stories. They'll change for the next folks who come along, trust me. Look carefully, ladies. What you see is there special for you."

Izzy studied the diamond ladder in silence. "Do you know what I'm thinking?" she asked Ruth.

"Yes. What would Sadma see? I wonder if she would want to smash them."

"No. She could help us read them."

"I understand, Ladies," the old man said. "Lots of church windows are there to soothe people. Jesus looks sort of Swedish and all. Not here. Windows here disturb people. Seriously. I've seen people just break down and weep. Maybe we could learn a thing or two from you Canadians. We're proud people here, and kind and decent often. But we could just maybe pause and learn to say we're sorry for some things, like you do. Big things. Now its almost too late. Anyways, I'll share something with you. What I see is three beautiful women in the centre window. One black, one white, one Native American. The black and the native are holding up the white. She wears a double string of pearls and looks down. She's not sure what's going on. She's never been in the sun it seems. A little out of it. The black and the native are wise. They're making pretty serious eye contact with me. They know what's going on. Which things are an allegory I trust."

The church was once a station on the Underground Railroad. The old man showed them artefacts: a drinking gourd, a rusty compass, a pair of dungarees, and six pairs of shoes made for slaves who had run away barefoot.

"Are you saying these shoes have never been worn?" Izzy asked.

"Not that I know of," the old man said. "They were donated before the war. They sit here, waiting their turn."

"Can I try?" she asked.

"You sure can," the old man replied.

Izzy slipped on a pair. She braced herself for a flogging. Instead, she felt she had slipped into the golden shaft of the sun that glittered the room, and made the shoes golden.

Izzy wept.

Ruth embraced her. Normal clutched at her hip. The old man patted her on the back.

"There now," he said. "That's the good old way. Shoes for your journey; friends for your joy. Hallelujah."

* * *

The old man led them to the front of the church. In front of the wooden altar was a pile of chains, leg irons, handcuffs, blindfolds, duct tape, rifles, cattle prods, tasers, bullhorns, fire hoses, nooses, whips, syringes, napalm recipe books, slaving with chivalry manuals, waterboarding how-to manuals, droning how-to manuals and sleep deprivation how-to manuals. They were all piled up in front of a bare wooden altar. A crucified 2 lay on top of a book on ethical torture.

"Do we get guns?" Normal asked.

"This place is for leaving things behind, sister," the old man explained. "Is there anything you'd like to lay down here? I can see you're already travelling light."

Ruth saw an obsolete camcorder at the side of the pile. She picked it up and spiked it on the floor, then kicked it down the aisle out the door and smashed it against a tree.

"Ruth, it's a museum!" Izzy said.

"There, there," the old man said. "She's perfectly welcome. Thou art a Ruth indeed!" The camcorder instantly returned to its spot in the pile, much the worse for wear.

"What's your name?" Normal asked.

"Why ask, seeing I am Watchful? I've been minding things here for a long time before your time. Now daughters, is there anything you'd like to donate to our collection of artefacts?"

Izzy and Ruth shook their heads. They had nothing.

"Oh, I think there is!" He placed his right palm on the back of Ruth's neck and his left palm on the back of Izzy's neck. He waited until their temperatures matched, then began kneading their muscles gently.

"What the hell?" snapped Ruth.

"Sshhhh…" he said. "Patience." After two minutes of kneading, he closed his palms and held them in front of Izzy and Ruth. He opened them, revealing two blood soaked microchips. "Will you do the honours or will I?"

"You," said Izzy.

The old man tossed them over his shoulder onto the pile. Then he wiped their wounds with his handkerchief. The bleeding stopped.

"The people who put those in us are dangerous," said Ruth. "They mean to kill us."

"The Boo boys? I know about them and their chips," said the old man. "Tragic, aren't they? Well, they won't find you here. They've passed here lots of times, rocking and jocking their boat, but they never see or hear anything."

"How can they not see it?" Ruth asked.

"I'm guessing they're stuck in childhood, and not the good kind. The dream didn't include them. So they went backwards. With no ladder, they grabbed a lifeline, and a mean one. Now they're like the men of old, back when this church was built, who killed without eating, and broke up families with a roll of dice. More particularly, they're mal-educated. No mom. No teachers. No interpreters."

"You mean enterprenoors, don't you?" Normal said. She didn't like all this Boo bashing.

"No, daughter. I mean folks who can read the signs."

Normal turned red.

"Now then, don't you feel bad. I have a feeling you've got something ready to lay down too. What could it be?"

Normal puzzled for a moment. Then she stepped forward. "I do have something." She pulled the decapitated shoe cam out of her pocket and shook it.

"Whoa! That's a nasty one!" the old man said.

Normal held it up to the light. Then she wrapped it up in a black blindfold and threw it on the pile.

"There ya go!" said the old man. "Feel better, don't ya?"

The blindfold began to squirm and wriggle, as if the camera was alive again. Ruth and Normal clutched each other. The old man stomped the camera three times under his heel. It lay quiet and dead.

"I thought it was powerful," he said. "That'll do for it."

* * *

The old man led them to the upstairs pews where slaves were allowed to sit in church. The stained glass windows rose out of their frames, flew up to the pews and sat down and sang together. Black Pilgrim, alone with no rope now around his neck, gave each of the women a motherly embrace with his warm glass arms. So did the lion and the slave mothers. The old man led them downstairs and out the back door. Some bed sheets fastened to tree branches concealed a big white bathtub. Water was boiling over an open fire. He told them to help themselves to hot baths while he prepared the fire ceremony and supper.

Ruth and Izzy poured boiling water in the tub for Normal, and then fetched cold water from a hand pump to make the temperature right. After her bath, Normal fell asleep near the supper fire. Ruth and Izzy were tired from carrying water. The tub was big, so they agreed to bathe together. When they got into the tub, their dust turned the water deep gray. It was as if they were up to their necks in the road they had travelled. Ruth asked Izzy for help with her back. Izzy spelled Ruth's name on her back with the bar of soap. She told Ruth the letters would replace the thousand eyes that seemed to bear down on her, not now, but sooner or later.

"I think they're gone," Ruth said.

* * *

The old man returned with white robes, knowing they wouldn't want their prison clothes.

"Read your mind, didn't I? Time for the fire ceremony!"

They walked to the fire pit. A beautiful young woman was suddenly walking beside them. She was the same height as whomever she walked beside. Her skin and eyes were dark. Her hair was a bronze. Izzy smelled cedars and magnolias and mountains in her bronze hair.

"This is my great-great-great-granddaughter, friends," said the old man. "Her name is Aimee. It wouldn't be proper for me to do the whole ceremony with you. Aimee will assist for the lady parts."

They gathered around the fire pit. Aimee invited them to

throw their prison clothes into the fire. Izzy and Ruth were delighted. Their eyes smiled as the flames embraced the rags. Normal was unwilling to toss her jeans and t-shirt. Ruth helped her.

"Clothes are dear. They don't grow on trees. Your dad's hard- earned money. He never gave you one more thing than he decided you needed. Am I right? And yadayadayada was his reason. Well, shazaam!" With those words, Ruth took an end of Normal's clothes and helped her hurl them into the flames. Everyone laughed and clapped.

The old man gave three sets of new travelling clothes to Aimee and averted his eyes. Aimee gave them a choice of different coloured trousers and t-shirts and socks, and new underwear. Such were the perks of an empty town. They took off their white robes and dressed. They shared a supper of red beans and rice and carrot and celery soup with caramel popcorn for dessert. Aimee moved among her guests refilling their glasses with fresh lemonade.

* * *

The old man asked them where they were going. Away from Prison Island, and away from the Boo boys, away from a drone that might show soon, even if their microchips were gone.

"Away where?"

"North. Canada," Izzy whispered.

"Canada!" The old man chortled. "Sure, that's the far end of the railroad. Any place in particular?"

Izzy shrugged. "First the middle, then the west."

Ruth kept eating. Normal began to think about Canada.

"Any place dear to you? Do you have people?" the old

man asked.

"Edmonton," Izzy said.

"Izzy's my people now," Ruth said.

"Same for me," said Normal.

A white pelican that had been circling overhead landed near them. It watched them calmly. It didn't try to take food. It brushed its head gently against Izzy's foot, and sat down and purred like a cat.

"Oh my. I'm sorry for your loss," The old man said, bowing his head and closing his eyes. "One of your people, I believe."

Then Izzy understood that Noah died. She did not weep. She felt empty inside.

"Yes. My father was in a long coma. He never awoke as far as I know."

"North still calling you?"

"Yes. Still."

"The bird's a real gift. And what's worship if not honouring other folk's gifts?"

The old man beckoned to Aimee. She brought him his banjo, and sat down beside him.

"Aimee and I would like to sing to you, remembering Izzy especially tonight, and her loss. This is a tune for travellers. It's helped thousands." He tuned his strings, then began a soulful strum:

Follow the drinking gourd,

follow the drinking gourd

For the old man is a-waitin'

to carry you to freedom

Follow the drinking gourd

Ruth and Normal picked up the chorus, and sang it in harmony. Izzy somehow felt that Simeon and Noah were beside her. Her feet ached. She rested her forehead on her knee.

* * *

Izzy lay awake looking at the stars. Ruth and Normal slept on the front porch. Normal made a soft "bubabuba" sound when she exhaled. Ruth sometimes raised her hand slightly in her sleep, as if warning paparazzi. Izzy tried to remember Noah through a poem.

Hear the voice of the bard

That present, past, and future sees

Whose ears have heard

The Holy Word

That walked among the ancient trees.

Then Noah would chant the second verse:

Calling the lapsed soul

And weeping in the evening dew

She couldn't remember the rest. Trying too hard was no use. She hummed the gourd song. She saw a shooting star.

The old man made them a breakfast of peanut butter toast and boiled coffee. He gave them each a shoulder bag with a canteen and some dried fruit. Aimee kissed their feet. The old man kissed their foreheads and wished them peace.

Chapter Sixteen

TIME SQUARE

Old New York, June 2050

The women walked north for three hours. At noon, an engine startled them. It was behind them, grinding loudly, close and low to the ground. They turned and saw a slow-moving freight train pulled by an engine. It creaked and moaned around a bend beside the road. The engine pulled twelve cars and eight empty flatbeds. There were no people on the train.

"All aboard!" said Izzy.

"I dunno," said Normal. "It's not smart to keep breaking with the script, is it?"

"The script where we all get blown up by your not-so-bad dad?" Ruth asked.

They climbed on to the second-last flatbed.

The train rolled on, picking up speed and slowing down, as if it had a mind of its own. They slept most of the night. In the morning, they passed a rusting sign in a dense forest that read: "Now Entering The Natural Republic of King Arthur Reborn." Beyond the sign, a large bronze statue of an old bearded general on a horse lay on its side. Rotting ropes surrounded the old general's neck and chest. His bronze sword swarmed with spiders. The pedestal was overgrown with tangled brush.

A half hour later, the train passed through dense forest again. The women heard a banjo and a man singing:

Behold ye, how these crystal streams do glide

To comfort pilgrims by the highway-side

Ruth recalled Sadma's songs. She sang *Swing Low Sweet Chariot* for Sadma when the banjo man voice was behind them.

The train pushed along near the shore, and ploughed through seawater, and veered away from the coast as it headed north. They saw abandoned golf courses with dead fish on the greens. They saw an abandoned family shooting range where two old deer grazed around targets. When the daylight waned, they formed a small triangle using each other's tummies for warm pillows. They slept through the night again.

* * *

When they awoke the next morning, the train was at a standstill in the middle of Old New York. Izzy recognized the location from pictures. They were in Time Square. It was once called Times Square, and Old New York was once just New

York. The Network reduced the name to the singular Time Square after millions of New Yorkers migrated away from the rising ocean waters.

The clocks were stuck at 11:55. The square was deserted, except for hundreds of stray cats and dogs that slept in the shadows or roamed the pavement. These animals told Izzy that there was fresh water somewhere. The ocean pressed heavily against a giant dike some thirty metres high. It ran for the length of Manhattan island beyond the eastern side of the square. It leaned on crumbling buildings for extra support, and cast a massive shadow. Pressure made the dike moan and bend.

There were no people, but there were thousands of faces. Brilliant electrode screens featuring chattering heads faced off from all directions. Some heads delivered long continuous monologues. Some showed interviewers and interviewees staring and speaking from split screens. Some talked about nutrition. Some offered pills for memory loss. Some analyzed world news.

Izzy closed her eyes and heard the dense cacophony:

mythofclimatemythofclimateyoudenyyoudenyyoudenyec
onomystupidlowertaxeslowertaxeslowertaxesamendpatro
lamendpatrolamendpatrolsecuritytrumpssecuritytrumpss
ecutirtytrumpsreloadlockreloadlockreloadlockperfectpotr
oastperfectpotroastginkoginkoginkospeedoftheraptureesp
eedingupspeedoftherpaturespeedingup.

The volume was ear piercing.

* * *

A vast screen, higher and wider than all the others stood above a ring of crumbling signs that said Disney and Gucci and

Dodge and Coke. Suddenly it lit up. A giant white face appeared. All the other screens went dark and silent.

"Live from Old New York!" the giant face screamed. "And thanks for joining us. We know you have choices. Much appreciated. To whom do I have the pleasure of speaking?"

The face was pudgy. The eyes beady. The lips sweaty. The hair wispy. A thin, withered hand scratched its nose, secured the headphones on its ears and adjusted the microphone.

The women did not answer.

"Is silence yes?"

The women did not move.

"Silence. Yes, then," the giant face said. "Might you be Izzy, Ruth and Normal, two fugitives from justice and one under-contract employee of The Network? Silence? Yes, then."

"Are we arrested?" Normal asked the giant.

"She speaks. Arrested? Well, if you mean you aren't going anywhere, yes. Back in a moment after a word from our sponsors. Don't touch it."

The giant disappeared and the screen shifted to an advertisement for a Reality TV show.

Bright colours swirled around the screen like vomit circling a drain. Then the drain froze. A word splattered on the frozen drain like a rotten egg:

Dronestrike!

This week on *Dronestrike,* catch the action as we track down

A sequence of rapid, split-screen images swept across the screen, enticing viewers to tune in. The screen showed close-ups of pairs of feet clad in prison shoes trudging down a dirt road. It showed the bare backs of two blonde women in prison uniforms running hard and away from the camera. The screen showed women peeling off their prison uniforms, stepping out of them with tanned, shaved legs, and bringing their lips together as if just about to kiss. The screen flashed Sadma shaking her head then foaming at the mouth. The screen showed Izzy and Ruth searching through the aluminum dumpster looking for supplies. The screen showed the Bomponce brothers crucified on the wings of a mini-drone as it took flight. The screen showed an aerial view of the north Florida coast taken from a drone-cam scanning for humans. The screen showed alligators snapping at prey, and flamingos fleeing the sound of rifle shots. Then a woman narrator resumed, in a seductive voice:

"*Dronestrike: The Women of Prison Island.*

Don't miss the action!

11:30 EST."

Ruth looked around for a spade. She found a small rock

and hurled it at the screen. The screen was too far and too high. Izzy waited. When the giant returned, she raised her middle finger and shoved it towards the face.

"Murderer!" Izzy screamed.

"Murderer? But we're back live," said the giant. "And she speaks. And what a temper. You're none other than Izzy Dryden-Burnet, the notorious Canadian, daughter to a dead scientist, non-legal wife to a homeless person, neglecter of a black cat, inventor of a lake of fire. Speak. Or learn from your friend Ruth. She's no stranger to screens. Cast the first stone, Ruth? Are there cameras crawling all over you like bugs? Right now? Good. Well, that's our time for this evening. Hope to see you all back here tomorrow. Thanks for watching. Good night live from right here atop the one and only Truth Tower in the one true Old New York folks."

* * *

The screen went black. Izzy helped Ruth to the flatbed. As the sun went down they ate dried fruit and shared a bottle of water. Izzy took a walk around the perimeter of Time Square. She passed a luxury hotel, its doors blocked with iron bars. She passed a designer fashion store. Gold dresses curled in green mildew in the cracked window. She passed a store that offered free e-phones with every purchase of a hologram. Two mice scuttled over the floor.

She passed a deserted theatre ticket window. Torn posters advertised old Broadway shows: Sniper: The Musical, Fugitive: The Musical, Die Hard: The Musical, End Times: The Musical. She passed a restaurant, and heard a refrigerator humming. She went in. The refrigerator unlocked. She found five apple pies frozen like granite. She put them in her bag, along with a clump of paper towels. She passed a liquor store, its unlocked door banging gently in the breeze.

The shelves were empty and broken glass covered the

floor. A bottle of 2020 West Kelowna Pinot Noir with a gold medal around its spout lay on display on white satin in the window. The bottle was cracked at its base. The spilled wine was now a dry purple shroud. Izzy wondered when she would taste wine again. She found some bottled water behind the counter. She tossed three bottles in her bag and moved on. She came to a gun store with a shattered front window. The guns were all gone. An *Ogresso* crossbow was in the window. She lifted it from the display, along with its quiver of nine arrows, and carried it back to the flatbed. It felt heavy and alien. The shaft was rotting.

The electrode screens continued to dance and wail. No stars pierced the deafening light of the square. They fashioned earplugs from the paper towels and managed to fall asleep. When they slept, the giant screamed them awake.

"Sleeping still? Up up slugabeds! What has night to do with sleep? Your judgment sleeps not. Your crimes have murdered sleep. And for the folks at home, don't forget: Favius Nugent, First Consul of North Dakminwasas, will be our guest for the full hour next week, talking about the middleeasternmostintervention. And later next week, the Woman Clothed with the Sun will be our guest. Don't miss it!"

The screen went black. Izzy broke up one of the pies and fed it to three black dogs. She tried to sleep. The giant returned.

"Breaking news. This just in: drone sighting confirmed off the coast of King Arthur Reborn! Women armed and dangerous! I wouldn't want to be in your shoes! I've always been a strong advocate for sleep. It has my full support. You? Silence. Yes, then. Undivided attention!"

The screen went black. They slept fitfully. The giant returned.

"Do you ladies know what kind of trash you're walking

with? Meet Izzy!"

The screen played Barry's animated mini-documentary of the burning of Olam Lake. The video played fifty times at ten times its normal speed. The soundtrack was "I'm Walkin'" by Fats Domino at five times the normal speed.

Then silence returned for an hour.

"See how the morn in russet mantle clad! Was that a favourite of your forefathers, Izzy? I mean your parents, listed here as liking poems. Silence. Yes, then. Why hurry little river? The sea might come to you. Ha! Despair."

Izzy gave him her finger again.

"Was that a question? Question me not. I have a question for you. Wouldn't you rather make a quietus? Why run like a river in fear from I when you can command and captain your soul? Silence. Yes, then."

"What the hell?"

"Was that a question? Question me not. If you walk to the perimeter of the square and turn to your immediate left, you will find an old gun shop. It has everything you need to find peace. Knives, bullets, arrows, even ropes and poison under the counter. A crossbow if your tastes run in that direction. No spades, ladies, not with her skill, unless you want to dig your graves. Wouldn't that be lover-ly? I love a good Broadway tune. We can even arrange for you to drown yourself, Ms. Izzy. Those are fish that were your eyes. Appealing? Silence. Yes, then. You could say your goodbyes, embrace, share. You could even strip, like the Romans."

"Romans?" Ruth asked, incredulously.

"I think this guy's trying to executive produce your deaths," Normal said.

"Is this guy from The Network, Normal?" Izzy asked.

Normal shrugged. "Dunno. Never saw him. Never been out of Boo Valley. But I don't like this guy. Why should I?"

"Was that a question?" screamed the giant. "Question me not. Despair and die. Alternatively, if you won't die Roman, tie each other up. With luck, people will think you had a fetish mishap. Or is it mashup? No law against that. I'd vouch. I be Roman myself. There's four old Canadian flags over at the magazine store, if that helps. *Pro Patria Mori*. Well, I'm ready for sleep, and a big breakfast. Canadian bacon. Back soon."

A bright band at the top of the screen scrolled a headline: "Breaking news: bodies found droned in a dumpster near Palace Junction. Details at 12. Elsewhere in the news, women of Prison Island reported near border. Reports unconfirmed."

Then the screen went black and silent.

"What about the drone sighting," Izzy asked Normal. "Is that part true?"

"Dunno," Normal said. "I never got to assistant executive produce before. Your chips are gone since Palace Junction, but maybe this giant knows my dad. Maybe Time Square means dad's saving you for New Year's Eve. Maybe this is Plan B. Maybe dad's watching. I dunno."

Ruth remained calm. "It's we now, Normal."

* * *

Izzy studied the crossbow. It had holes and buttons. It seemed like a giant mousetrap. She tried shooting an arrow at the screen. The arrow flew listlessly for ten metres and bounced on the pavement. She handed it to Ruth. Ruth held it by its back end like a short-handled spade. She made three swift rotations like a hammer thrower. The crossbow spun through the air all the way to the base of the screen. It smashed into pieces doing no harm.

Izzy tried to think like Noah. Why did he send them to the gun shop? She had already found it herself. She had already found the crossbow. Why did he answer questions with questions? And why the same question?

They waited in silence. The sky grew clear and blue. The wind was light. The electrode screens seemed quieter by day. The sea breezes helped. Izzy even heard a faint gull cry in the distance.

The screen flashed on. A short film showed a drone skimming over the waves, leading schools of dolphins, soaring above pristine waterfalls and lakes, waggling its wings before climbing high to fly with a bald eagle.

The giant appeared.

"Drones are environmentally friendly ladies. Decision time. Drone approaching. Will you die like men?"

Izzy tried a scientific experiment.

"Could you repeat the question?"

"Was that a question? Question me not. Despair and die."

"Silence consents. Was that silence?"

"Was that a question? Question me not. Despair and die."

"Why silence?"

"Was that a question? Question me not. Despair and die."

"Book flog apples butter crack wheels?" she asked.

"Was that a question? Question me not. Time's a-wasting ladies. Despair and die."

"Stum blew quince withal non-story bland gum balm?"

"Was that a question? Question me not. Despair and die."

"Nymphos fish convicts glass temple bland true dough?"

"She speaks. Edmonton. Gateway to the North. The cat came back. And your dads? Never never never never never! Think on your blame, and despair."

Izzy formulated another question.

"North road chain fence Olam?"

"Think on your crimes, you impudent slut. So stretched out huge in length the arch-fiend Charissa lay chained on the burning lake."

Izzy tried another question.

"Blind sort ding brick tube fort wang?"

"Was that a question? Question me not. Despair and die."

"Why the silence?"

"Was that a question? Question me not. Despair and die, bitch."

"This thing isn't human," Izzy whispered. "It's an imitation."

"What does that mean?" Normal asked.

"Lots of connections, no real friends," Ruth said.

"Let's get out of here," Izzy said.

"I want one more chance with a rock – or a truck," Ruth said.

"You don't mess with The Network. Can we please just go?" Normal said.

Ruth put her hand on Normal's shoulder. "OK. Let's go."

They quietly walked out of the square. Izzy sang "Why the silence?" to the tune of "O Canada." The giant's speech accelerated: *"Was that a question? Question me not. Despair and die! Was that a question Question me not Despair and die Was that quest?menotpairdie!aquest?"*

When they reached the edge of the square, a giant column of fire sprang out of the pavement blocking their way.

"Now what?" Ruth asked.

"It's fake," Normal said. "The Network uses hologram fire. Greener economy and less cost, dad says."

"Oh great. We're daddy's little girl again!" Ruth said.

"It doesn't look fake, Normal," Izzy said. "It's blazing."

"It's fake. Dad never lies. I overheard him telling Desi. Watch." Normal walked through the fire like an open door. Ruth and Izzy were frightened, then amazed. Then they followed Normal's path and were not harmed.

"Good call," Ruth said to Normal, giving her a hug. "But if I find a short-handled spade, I'm going back. I can take that bastard down."

* * *

The giant kept babbling after the women were gone. He vomited the commercial for *Dronestrike* out of his mouth and ears and nostrils. Then he ingested the coarse digital puke, lapping up every syllable and letter with his purple tongue. He repeated his question. He secreted and ingested the digital puke every third time he asked his question. The loop deteriorated until his refrain was simply "questndie questndie" voiced into a bowl of blue light vomit, endlessly turning, accelerating around and around the drain mouth for as long as there was Time Square.

Chapter Seventeen

CROSSING THE RIVER

Morrisburg, Ottawa, June 30-July1, 2050

They slept in a park, then walked north for three hours at dawn. They stopped in a deserted playground in Harlem. Swings sat idle in the summer heat. Izzy pulled out a thawed apple pie. They sat on the swings and shared it, passing it along and scooping out pieces with bare hands. Ruth dabbed some filling on Normal's nose. Normal dabbed some filling on Ruth's kneecap, then took it back and licked it off her finger.

They walked north again, passing the Cathedral and Columbia, never seeing another human being. Two more hours brought them to the base of a hill overlooking the Hudson River. They began the climb, hoping to survey the landscape, spot some bridges, find a boat.

The top of the hill looked like a medieval village. A man on a stone turret looked down on them through binoculars. They hid quickly in a grove of trees.

"Hello down there!" the man shouted. Ruth looked around a tree trunk. He was waving at them to come up.

"Who are you?" Ruth shouted.

"Just a traveller, down from Canada," the man said.

"Are you alone?"

"100% totally and completely alone."

Weird, Izzy thought. A simple yes would do, Izzy. But the word Canada was a happy surprise. They walked out cautiously, climbed some stone stairs and emerged onto the top of the wall. Izzy nearly wept to see the Hudson flowing in the distance.

The traveller stood beside a short structure. It was covered with a rough brown cloak. Izzy and Ruth froze. Was it a gun on a tripod? A drone guidance system?

The man lowered his binoculars. "I'm Gomer Grayson."

"What's that under the blanket?" Normal asked.

Gomer removed the blanket. It was an antique telescope. There were oak panels and brass rings around the tube. It stood on a brass tripod. It cocked idly up towards the sky once the weight of the cloak was gone. Underneath the tripod was a clipboard holding papers. The papers showed with numbers, sketches and graphs in pencil and black ink. A plastic ballpoint pen lay on the paper. Izzy looked for wires and antennas. There were none.

"What's it for?" Ruth asked.

"I'm studying sea levels and river levels," Gomer replied.

"I'm a water scientist."

* * *

Gomer shared some dates and figs and salted cashews. He had four Macintosh apples that reminded Ruth and Izzy of home. He turned over his knapsack. A Canadian flag was sewn to the flap.

"My granddad sewed that flag on when he was nineteen. He loved to travel. Where are you people from?"

"I'm from Canada and so is Izzy," Ruth said. "Normal comes from Florida."

"Small world. Where in Canada?" asked Gomer.

"Anne's River. Izzy's from Edmonton."

"Way down east and way out west. Cool. I'm from Kingston, or Kingston Pan-Arctic Capital Investments Place for the next five years based on its corporate lease. Our last corporate sponsor was a Toronto-based terrorist solutions firm. Our new name's a little more cheerful, I find."

"What about Edmonton?" Izzy asked.

"Edmonton Trans-Pacific Consolidated Mall, Arena and Gateway Solutions Place. I may be mixing up the order. It's Edmonton for short."

"Fredericton?" asked Ruth.

"I heard the World Golf Association is taking that over. I forget the full name. How come you don't know the names?"

"We've been out of touch." Izzy said. She told Gomer their story.

"Are you kidding me? Noah Burnet is one of my biggest heroes. He had amazing, futuristic ideas, way ahead of his time."

"Futuristic's an odd word," Izzy said. "Do you read sci-ci?"

"I'm just an amateur scientist," Gomer said. "Believe it or not, this is my vacation. I like doing this work, even though it's depressing at times. My condolences on your dad's passing, by the way. He was in that coma for a very long time though, so perhaps it's for the best. I read he had no family at the end, but he sure had a big memorial service. And you're his daughter! For what it's worth, I applaud what you did. That story's faded a bit for Canadians, but not for anyone who cares about water. Still, would it have been better to put your dad ahead of your activism?"

"Piss off!" Izzy growled.

"Sorry. It's just that I've heard people in comas respond to family voices," Gomer replied nervously. "Of course, you did something brave. Look, he's the reason I'm here, fact-finding and surveying for posterity's sake. I'm doing this survey on my own dime, you know. That's why my equipment is primitive – just my old telescope and a pair of binoculars and my Nikon. Still, time-lapse photography is about as sophisticated as water science gets nowadays. People seem to think the planet's immortal. You and I know better. My photos have been in documentaries on climate change. That's the payoff for me."

"What kind of network would do science?" Normal asked.

"It's almost impossible to get science docs aired," Gomer admitted. "Even the film makers are amateurs. I keep records and hand them off. We need to witness to our times."

The telescope reminded Izzy of backyard fires in Crescentdale.

The white pelican alighted and began to pick crumbs from Ruth's shoelace nibs. It beat its wings. It seemed agitated.

"How long has that pelican been following us?" Normal asked.

"Since Palace Junction," said Izzy.

"Should we trust this guy?"

"That's a good question, Normal."

* * *

Normal looked through Gomer's telescope. From the height of the wall, she saw gulls sailing above a garbage barge, and the glassy surface of the ocean pressing against the dykes. Izzy and Ruth checked the sky for drones. Gomer told them that this was the last stop on his survey. Cape Cod and Nantucket to the north were gone. Long Island was disappearing. Old New York was holding up thanks to the dykes.

"I'm heading home to Kingston on the highway 81. I'd be happy to take you that far. It's about a seven-hour drive."

"How will we get across the border," Ruth asked. "We're fugitives."

"Yep, and notorious," said Normal.

"Let's just go north," Gomer said, confidently. "I owe Dr. Burnet. We'll figure it out when we get there."

They got into Gomer's Volkswagen van and set out for the border. As they moved west away from the coast, a few cars and people began to appear. They passed towns with enchanting names: Amsterdam, Utica, Rome. They shared another apple pie, spoon-feeding bites to Gomer with his library card.

"The Coalition is sure making a mess in Syria, don't you think?" Gomer opined, trying to stir up a conversation. Ruth and Izzy were silent. Normal had never heard a newscast.

"Forgive me," Gomer said. "I forgot you've been away."

"Who won the Stanley Cup last year?" Ruth asked.

"Oh, Mobile took it in eleven over Las Vegas. It's the S-FAC Cup, for now at least. Senate Foreign Affairs Committee Cup. Quebec City might get a franchise next year if they turn down Tulsa and Jackson."

Gomer turned north on Highway 81 at Syracuse. They passed Cicero and Watertown and came to the Saint Lawrence flood plain. The ends of the International Friendship Bridge were awash in shallow water. Cars could wade through the vast puddle and then cross over the high, giant, iron span that rose above the river. There was a new hydrofoil ferry, but it wouldn't return for another hour. The bridge was free. The ferry cost two hundred dollars.

This was the moment Izzy dreaded. She felt the loss of citizenship like the theft of a blanket from a homeless person.

"They took away our citizenship," Ruth told Gomer.

"Bastards. Typical government bullshit," Gomer said. "The water's pretty fast. We'll have to take the bridge. Let me see what I can do." He donned some hip waders in the confines of the car, got out, and sloshed his way to the border guards who sat in a tiny flat skiff with a 5 hp outboard motor and oars. They let Gomer push their boat inside their half-submerged aluminum office.

"So I guess this brings you two full circle," Normal said.

"If my father's still alive, he'll be in New Brunswick," Ruth said.

"Edmonton," Izzy said. "And don't worry, Normal. You can come with me if you don't want to go back."

Six minutes later, Gomer re-appeared. He was sweating from his slog through the water, but smiling with four tickets in his hand. He gave the women a thumbs-up.

"I explained that we all lost our identification in a flash flood in Old New York. For our purposes, you're all Natural Republicans, not Canadians. They're OK with my story, as long as I bring an empathy affidavit to the Bureau of Security in Ottawa within three days. No thanks. Bridge security isn't as tight as it was during the U.S.A. The natural republics can't afford borders let alone fences, not since President Digits denatured the country. Security's tighter on the ferry, so it's just as well I can't afford it. Ladies, you're going home!"

Gomer drove slowly across the bridge. The sign said "Bridge to Canada." The other side of the sign said "International Bilateral Glorification Bridge." Izzy and Ruth nodded off as the tires hummed over the iron surface. Izzy dreamed she was around the fire pit with Simeon and Noah and Lucius and Lady. Noah and Simeon drank from the same gold cup. Lucius didn't lie about The Hague. Lady was cheerful and chatty. She said she had taken a lover. She would not shut up.

* * *

Izzy awoke. They were heading down a broad highway. A sign said Highway 401. An electronic billboard advertised the Chrysler Farm Battlefield Park ten minutes ahead. The billboard showed Liberty holding a Canadian flag. Soldiers in blue and black business suits followed her, mowing down American soldiers with musket fire. Izzy recognized the painting. Simeon once showed her Delacroix's Liberty Leading the People in one of his art books. This billboard was a knockoff. She recognized the man in the top hat beside Liberty. It was Lucius.

Gomer passed the battlefield and pulled into a large parking lot. The sign said Upper Canada Village. A large LED sign over the main entrance read: "This month only: Homage to Geogasm: the Spukwell Homestead on National Pilgrimage." The homestead was now a mobile national historic site on tour.

"Why are we going east?" Izzy asked.

"Where's Kingston?" Ruth asked.

"Kingston is west," said Gomer. "Don't worry, I'm in no rush. Remember, you have to go northwest to reach Alberta. Straight west would mean Toronto, London, and then Detroit. You don't want that. These small towns are safer. This theme park's quiet and family friendly."

"Where are we going?" Normal asked anxiously.

"Edmonton," Izzy sighed. "How, I don't know."

Gomer went to the ticket window and spoke to the cashier. She gave Gomer a discount family pass. He waved the women to the entrance.

They walked around the grounds, looking at wooden cabins, rail fences, old tractors and an old white church with clear glass windows. An animator walked by them carrying a pitchfork. He led an ox that pulled a cart full of hay. A purple tattoo was visible on the back of his neck. It said *Drone I.V.* in dripping gothic letters.

The Spukwell homestead was in the centre of the park. A large tractor-trailer was parked beside it, ready to take the house to its next stop. The homestead was not Geogasm. It was a small log cabin. An antique Schwinn bicycle with streamers leaned against the side of the cabin. A sign on the roof read, *Make Yourself at Home, with Spukwell.*

Inside, they found a rustic stone fireplace with a braided

rug and two rocking chairs. An electric atomizer released the smell of fresh baked bread into the air. On a coffee table, a Zen water fountain splashed purified water onto some pebbles in a ceramic bowl. Some soccer medals and volunteer service certificates hung from pegs on the kitchen wall. An accordion sat in a corner.

On the mantle, photos showed Lucius's father working hard at The Hague. Izzy studied the photographs. One was the photo Noah had given Lucius. In this version, Lucius stood beside Noah on the steps of The Hague City Hall. Noah's face was replaced by a face she did not recognize. Another photo showed Lucius outside Crescentdale School, shaking hands with the principal, accepting a distinguished graduate award. Another showed him feeding fish in an aquarium at the Calgary Zoo while explaining fish life to some school children. Izzy looked past Lucius and peered into the aquarium. It warmed her heart.

* * *

They left the cabin and sat in the homestead garden. Izzy soaked up the vibrant greens and yellows. This was different from the parkland of Edmonton. There were stout red maples and vast weeping willows. Ruth told Normal that weeping willows grew in New Brunswick. Tall sunflowers overshadowed purple clematis. Three cornflowers grew beside a throng of white daisies. A row of globed peonies lined the edge of the cabin. In the western sky, the sun, in a summer fireball, set like blood beyond the swaying green walls of trees. Izzy closed her eyes and saw the high banks of the North Saskatchewan absorbing the same sunlight.

Normal seemed a happy child in this sunlight. Ruth seemed free and relaxed, with no worries about blue light or cameras. She handled some fronds of willow branches and knelt to smell some marigolds.

"How's your pain, Ruth?" Izzy asked.

Ruth hugged Izzy and kissed her neck.

"I want to go to Edmonton with you," she said. "Take me with you!" She rested her head on Izzy's shoulder and sighed contentedly.

Normal burst into tears.

"What's the matter, Normal?" Izzy asked.

"What's going to happen to me? How can I live up here?"

"Well, you didn't have any friends in Boo Valley. And no school. Do you miss your father and brothers?"

"It's not that."

"Hallelujah," said Ruth.

"What then?" Izzy asked.

"I can't live up here."

"Why not?" Ruth asked. "Lots of people moved up here when Arson Digits got elected."

"It's not that. It's the Network. I've never been cut off from the Network. It's scary"

"As in Time Square?" Ruth asked. "Or the bastards who invented *Dronestrike?* To hell with that."

Izzy gathered Normal and Ruth into her arms.

"We're your network now, Normal."

Izzy closed her eyes in peace. Then she realized Gomer was not with them. As the shadows lengthened and the sky darkened, a crowd of men appeared pointing high beam flashlights restlessly in all directions. Gomer was leading them.

"Hey Izzy!" Gomer said, reaching out to hug her. At that instant, twelve high beam flashlights converged on her face at once. A thirteenth man filmed the event with his e-phone. Ruth bent over in pain, then looked around for a spade. Normal scanned the crowd for her brothers. The men were all strangers. She flew into Izzy's arms.

"Thanks for bringing me!" she screamed.

Ruth stood up. She put her left arm around Normal. She picked up a rock with her right hand to throw at the camera. Izzy gently pushed Ruth's hand down. Then she slapped Gomer across the face.

Gomer turned red and grinned sheepishly. Blood dribbled from his mouth. Some blood came from his cut lip. Most came from his gingivitis.

"Move her," Gomer said curtly, dabbing the blood with his fingertips.

The men pushed Izzy to a police van. Ruth and Normal kicked two men in the shins. They wanted to be arrested too.

"Never mind them," Gomer said. "Just her."

"Too late," a uniformed man said. "They're all bunking tonight."

* * *

Ruth, Izzy and Normal spent the night in a vintage nineteenth-century slammer, restored right down to a wooden piss pot. The slammer was near the Chrysler farm battlefield. The guards confiscated Izzy's bag, and wolfed down the last apple pie. The sky turned a dark gray at dusk, and the night brought winds that roared through the nearby poplar groves. Izzy, Ruth and Normal slept fitfully in the cramped heritage jail.

* * *

The next morning, the guards herded the women into a van.

"Where's Gomer?" Normal asked.

"Heading back over the border on another mission," a guard answered. "And since you ask, he's a real hero, the kind this country needs more of. Look at you. I know all about your generation. You grew up spoiled, glued to a screen or a phone, never meeting a payroll, landing in jail. Gomer's keeping us safe, and you included."

Izzy, Ruth and Normal sat on a cold metal bench. A wire cage separated them from the driver and the guard. The van headed west on Highway 401 to Morrisburg Party Superior Party Goods and Catering Place, then turned north. Izzy tried to orient herself. What was north of Morrisburg?.

Ottawa.

Izzy rested her head on the wall. She smelled hay in the plotted fields, and felt wind in her hair through cracks in the window. Silver barn roofs flashed in the summer heat. Trees and shrubs near farmhouses seemed strange after the sands of Prison Island and the changing landscapes of her journey north. She wondered if she would find Jesse and Madge and Samson and Johnny and Reverend Gidding. She liked the weeping willows.

She looked through the cage to the windshield. At the side of the highway, children attached Canada Day balloons to a sign: Williamsburg Alternative Energy Control Place. Further down the highway, townspeople painted a sign: Winchester: 1-Stop Lo-cost Paint and Wallpaper Place, est. 2050. Izzy stripped down the names. Morrisburg, Williamsburg, Winchester. The names sounded like weathered barn boards and broad, leafy trees and old, split rail fences and summer pastures with thunderheads forming in the heat. She could love this landscape.

She remembered names from home: Camrose, Mundare, Lamont, Ponoka, Fort Saskatchewan, Athabasca, Wainwright, Vermilion, Edson. She closed her eyes and imagined the edge of a canola field on the highway to Jasper, a field blooming, vast and brilliant, green and yellow, reaching under the sun to the height of a late summer, gray-sky storm in the distance, then morphing to a million spruces spread at the feet of mountains, and a river churning gray milky waters through, carrying the weight of glaciers. Why hurry, little river? The verse came back to her:

And the faint and far-off line

Where the winds across the brine

For ever, ever roam

And never find a home

She remembered setting fire to Olam Lake. She wished she could see Olam Lake as it was a thousand years ago.

The van passed the steepled town of Vernon Home, Office and Mental Security Services Place. The road widened and picked up more traffic. Ottawa Suburbs appeared. The road dipped and rose and curved. Suddenly, the van sped up. It rocked awkwardly, racing to a dangerous speed. It crashed into the mouth of a ditch, flipped over once, then rested against a maple. The crash popped the back door of the van open like a crumpled beer can. The guard and driver wriggled out of the front seat and fled. Two guards providing escort in a lead car doubled back to the wreck. They picked up the driver and the guard, then hit the gas and sped south back to the Saint Lawrence.

* * *

Izzy, Ruth and Normal crawled out the back of the van. They examined each other for wounds or bruises. Normal's right ear was ringing. Ruth had a cut on her left ear, and a bruised forearm.

A dull motor churned in the sky. A rusty, filthy drone turned an awkward figure 8 at low altitude.

"That's why the security boys fled," Ruth remarked.

The drone's engines stopped. It nosed down towards a small building on the corner of a rapidly emptying intersection. Izzy saw the drive-thru lane. It was a burger franchise at one time. Its windows were painted black and orange. A sign in its tiny parking lot read: *National Research Council of Canada.*

The drone crashed half-heartedly into the empty parking lot. It did not have enough accuracy to hit the *National Research Council*, or enough self-respect to explode. Izzy was relieved.

"That's not one of dad's," Normal said. "Wrong colour, too old, and ours don't have this range. If it was one of dad's, you guys'd be dead, trust me."

"And no starving men strapped to the wings," Ruth added sarcastically.

"Maybe this is somebody's hobby drone. Or maybe it's one of yours," said Normal.

"Ours?" Ruth asked.

"Canada's. Your government's been short-changing your military, maybe?"

Izzy scanned the signs at the intersection. The highway was now Bank Street. The cross street was Walkley Road. What a name, she thought. She thought of Cresentdale, the village green, the bakery, the green onion cakes on Friday nights, soccer parents conjuring goals, dogs chasing tennis balls, her aquarium's footless travellers. And Nympho.

They looked at the upside down van. In their rush, the guard and driver had spilled their handguns onto the ground. The side of the van said: *Great Canadian Prison Solutions:* Customer Satisfaction at Low Cost is our Mandatory Minimum!

Normal picked up one of the guns.

"Normal, put that back," Ruth said.

"Nuh-uh," said Normal. "Dad told us, the one thing better than a bad guy with a gun is a good guy with a gun. That's a direct quote from the third amendment. It's even in the Bible. A saying wise and true."

"Izzy's father died from that goddam thing. And so did your mother," Ruth added. "I thought we agreed: no more Network and no more Dad says ever!"

"Mom especially loved her gun," said Normal. "Dad said so."

* * *

Izzy left the quarrel and walked to the intersection to look around. A large mall stood on the northwest corner. The smoking drone lay to the southwest. On the eastern side, large maples and cedars covered an old brick building. A tilted, fading sign read Great Canadian Shoe Factory. Izzy's instincts told her to go north. They couldn't turn back. They needed water and anonymity. She led Ruth and Normal along the margin of the highway. Cars passed from behind. Some honked in Canada Day spirit. No cars passed from the front. People were converging on Ottawa.

They crossed a bridge over the Rideau Canal. A sign read "Noah Bridge." Izzy though she was dreaming for an instant. The crowds thickened on Bank Street. They smelled barbecues and bistros and felt faint with hunger. Children licked soft white ice cream and chocolate sprinkles from waffle cones. Izzy led them away from the cooking, to the shelter of a quieter street. They walked east and then north again. O'Connor Street. Metcalfe Street. Pedestrians were streaming north.

The hot pavement made Normal's feet ache. She had no fear. She loved her women friends. They took no joy in the sufferings of others. Her dad said he worked hard for his family, and said he took no pleasure in it. But she remembered how his eyes twinkled when he passed sentences.

Walking was now second nature for Ruth. She wished she could carry Izzy and Normal all the way to wherever in her arms. But she knew she could not manage it, even with the weight they had lost.

Wellington Street.

The street was closed to traffic and packed with people. To their right stood the War Memorial, and the stark drama of a horse struggling forward in bronze mud with human companions. To their left was a statue of a young man running. He pushed a left foot forward. He pulled a right, prosthetic leg behind him.

"Who's that guy?" Normal asked.

"Terry Fox," Izzy whispered. She told his story briefly. The women touched the statue's feet. A tear from Ruth fell on the left foot. Izzy thought she could see Sadma's face in the dark tone of the statue.

The crowd cheered. A parade was coming, barely visible above the heads of the thronging crowd. Cheers ascended. Izzy gripped Terry Fox's left arm, pulling herself up to gain a better view. A loudspeaker announced the names of each dignitary as they appeared.

"Ladies and gentleman, please give a warm Ottawa

welcome to Cardstone Lordso!"

Lordso appeared in a scarlet robe with fur trim. He had purchased the wares of the old Supreme Court when it was abolished. He renamed the robes "The Legion of Honour of Colonel By Drive." He rode on a silver Segway. Ned Feenie, wearing a green tartan tam, pressed his hands securely on Lordso's buttocks to keep him in place and keep him moving forward. An honour guard of eight Elbow linebackers coxed by Blondeau marched in two columns of four on either side of the Segway. Behind them came the members of the Lord Protector's executive staff. They wore Bermuda shorts with Wellington boots and blue sweatshirts bearing the words, "I Love Lucius!" on their chests.

"Ladies and gentlemen, please welcome Lord Protector Lucius Spukwell!"

The landau came into full view, pulled by the yoked men in orange *THEM* jump suits. Lucius waved to the crowd with his right hand, and filmed the crowd with his left.

Izzy gasped. She jumped down from the statue and pushed through the crowd. She ran after the landau as fast as she could. Security men gave chase. She came abreast of the landau and Lucius. She ignored Lucius, and kept running. Lucius filmed her instinctively. Then he recognized her and gasped, and dropped his e-phone. Izzy kept running until she came to the men pulling the landau. She jumped on the back of one of the prisoners. It was 41. It was Jesse.

Four constables trained their pistols on the yoked men, ordering them to keep moving. The men stopped. Ruth and Normal weaved through the crowd and slowly made their way to Izzy. Lucius stood and bade the crowd be still. A hush fell over the celebration, save for a lone voice crying "thanks for the jobs!" The voice came from Spukwell's communications director.

Izzy tried to raise the yoke over Jesse's head. It was chained to his waist. He looked into her face with tired eyes, and smiled.

"Don't fire!" Lucius ordered. The constables lowered their guns.

A shot rang out.

The crowd gasped, looking towards Lucius. The sound sent frightened birds skyward in all directions.

A lone pelican circled down and landed beside Izzy.

Chapter Eighteen

THE STARRY FLOOR

Izzy's Inspiration

Izzy was suddenly able to remember more of the poem:

Calling the lapsed Soul

And weeping in the evening dew:

That might control,

The starry pole;

And fallen fallen light renew!

O Earth O Earth return!

Arise from out the dewy grass;

Night is worn,

And the morn

Rises from the slumberous mass.

But there was still another verse. It would come back to her. She tried to be patient.

She stood up, shaky from her long walk north, and felt the sand embrace her bare feet. She walked toward the shore, her long skirt flowing in the gentle wind. She looked up at the sky. The "stars that ushered evening rose," she whispered. The skies between mountains at the end of the long lake lit "a lovely mile." Constellations appeared. Shooting stars flamed in the atmosphere. Extinct plants and animals emerged from black holes in the cosmos. The earth sighed as its wounds closed. The air was made of cinnamon and sweet grass, cedar and aloes, forests and ice fields.

There was a fire pit by the shore. Simeon and Noah were playing memory games with poems. The fire glowed, illuminating their eyes. Farida's parents sat with them, sharing North African poems.

Reverend Phlap sat in the sand and smiled as Richie played a song on a harp. The song was for Lady Cassandra. Jasmine and Destiny slipped off their high heels and danced slowly in the warm sand, emparadised in each other's arms. The stars listened to their arms, and shivered with pleasure. Caroline Squirrel rested her head on a grass tuft, and watched the dance. She waited to request a song for Barton. Alvin Boneslaw stood nearby, working up the courage to dance. Stuart Otis wore no sunglasses. He swayed gently, inhaling the joy of the dance.

Sadma rocked on a wooden swing. She held Nympho

and Mavis in her arms. The two cats boxed gently with each other. Atiq the linguist was telling Kati-tie's birth mother the story of the English language. She had wet hair because she had been in the water. Her eyes widened in the starlight as she listened. Sadma was telling the Bomponce brothers stories that were never written down. She told them with skill and delight, taking time outs now and then to remind them that Jack Boo was and still is an ass-face singularity with no eye for the ladder, astro-physically or otherwise. The brothers were in for a long evening.

* * *

Abdielle emerged from a grove of palms. Her black dog was now a little puppy. He had no leash. She threw a red ball, letting him run along the shoreline. He overran the ball and had to pivot back to fetch it. Izzy saw the smile of the sun across the mountain shift. A narrow track of light bisected the lake, moving rapidly from the horizon straight towards her feet. Now she began to worry.

"What time is it?" Izzy asked Abdielle.

"The seventeenth century in their labyrinth of time. We are on the outside curve. Soon we will be in their eleventh century, nearer to the centre. One thousand ordinary years. This is Olam Lake."

Izzy looked out over the lake as far as she could see. It teemed with fish. The sky teemed with stars.

"What is the time?" she asked.

"That was your sixth time. This is the seventh. The lake is for the healing of those the nations rejected. The water will heal their burns. Many of the long wandered will pass here thanks to you."

A woman, perhaps thirty years old with a long rope of black hair, walked towards her. Her eyes were fire green. Her face changed according to each person she encountered. For Izzy, she bore the likeness and similitude of Aimee of Palace Junction. She called herself Starblanket. Izzy knew her as Madge Three as she was in the seventeenth century. They embraced, and cupped their hands playfully over each other's ears. Then Izzy followed Abdielle to the shore.

* * *

Izzy sensed some kind of ritual was going on. She looked out over the still waters. "I'm really tired," she said.

"I can imagine," Abdielle replied.

"And the child is safe?" Izzy asked.

"Yes," said Abdielle.

"Do I have to go back?" she asked, troubled.

"No," Abdielle whispered.

"I don't like reincarnation."

"We don't use that word anymore. Think of it as empathy."

"Empathy's a tragic wheel. I'd rather be a fish."

Abdielle shrugged. "It is there, but not here. The nations still follow their detestable Molochgods in pomp of warlike selfhood and religion hid in war."

Izzy looked at the shoreline. "I dreamed I was here with Jesse once," she said. She saw a fish jump close to shore. Clean drops of water sparkled like new worlds. "Where now?"

"Clashes of horrors. Chasms of sinking contradiction. Furnaces eating children. Lives grinding under chariot wheels."

She felt the urge to curse. She remembered the speechless strangers of the earth. The frozen man who spoke

Cree in Edmonton. To be owned in your language at the moment of death. This place had new planets and constellations. No names issued by silly slaves of the sword. Here the planets speak their own names in their own time. Sedna and Black Pilgrim shimmered above the lake. Jesse could name in every language as long as someone provoked him. She saw a star in the west and named it Jesse.

Then she worried. She felt a sudden revulsion for people. She closed her eyes in tight concentration. She opened her eyes slowly. She relaxed and smiled. Abdielle gave Izzy a drink of lake water in a golden cup. Then she knelt down and invited Izzy to sleep with her head in her lap. Izzy slept for a period of six thousand concentric years.

When she awoke, the rest of the poem came back.

Turn away no more:

Why wilt thou turn away

The starry floor

The watery shore

Is given thee till the break of day.

She looked around. In the distance, Noah cupped some water in his hands, splashed his face, and shook some drops from his hands. She looked below her feet. The sand rippled outwards like the pulsation of an artery, revealing a crystal window with a diamond ladder descending onto Wellington Street. Her heart sank as she watched Jesse weep over her body. Ruth touched his shaking shoulders. Izzy shed a tear that plummeted through the crystalline floor, sounding the depths of the lower world, landing gently on her body's face.

She thanked Abdielle, and kissed her on the forehead.

"Well then," she said. "I'll go down to see if morning breaks."

She stepped into the water, and set her feet in the long track of light.

"You don't have to go!" Abdielle cried out, after Izzy had walked out from the shore for 6000 years.

Izzy waved and splashed her hands on the surface and kept walking. She loved to feel her bare feet moving in the waters of Olam Lake.

Chapter Nineteen

THE END TIMES

Ottawa, July 1, 2050

Barry recoiled at the sound of the shot.

He pulled out his earplugs to be sure of what he heard. He looked through his binoculars. He quickly detached his e-phone from his *Ogresso Messenger* bullhorn, and hid both in a notch of stone on the side of the Peace Tower. The phone contained his speech denouncing Lucius. The sound would have carried as far as Walkley Road. He hoped no one would find the bullhorn.

He turned to the elevator. Security men emerged from its doors and sprinted towards him. They pinned him to the ground and manacled his hands. One man gripped Barry's eyebrows in his fists and closed his thighs on Barry's ears to keep him still.

Fixer 1 and Fixer 2 stepped onto the deck, wearing sunglasses and wide brim sun hats. Fixer 2's left cheek was bruised.

"I haven't done anything!"

"Really?" said Fixer 1. "Our friend might disagree." He gave a signal to the street below. A three-dimensional image of the man with the swollen eye appeared on the clock face. But now he did not have a swollen eye. Now he wore a dark shirt, and held a rifle in one hand and a newspaper in the other. He had a mindless smirk on his face that rippled and reflected through the deck's glass panels.

"A hologram!" Barry cried.

"Correction: an X-51 BJ Hologram. That's BJ for 'bring to justice.' It's the latest hi-tech judicial entrapment. Hold still till I get a picture of you two together. One's a lone gunman, two's a conspiracy."

"Gunman?" Barry cried.

"Wasn't that the plan?" said Fixer 1.

The two security men who had escorted him to the tower elevator appeared carrying metal detectors. They found the bullhorn and Barry's e-phone in five seconds.

"'Property of Prison Island,'" said Fixer 1, feeling the bullhorn's antiquated on-off switch. "This is primitive. You'd need at least one drone hologram to achieve your ends. But they cost money. I imagine you don't get a lot of donations."

"I bought that in Edmonton. It has a donut trigger. I planned to hit the landau with the laser app, melting its tires, stopping the parade. But it turns out it's just a laser pointer, the kind people use to give talks."

"You've got an X-10 here," said Fixer 2. "The X-12s can flatten tires. Hell, you can't even plan your own downfall right."

"I was going to make a speech at full volume. Eleven! Eleven will shatter the glass. Then - a big loud flood of reality right in the heart of Ottawa. No more bullshit! No more propurgation! Search me. I'm unarmed."

"Oh?" said Fixer 1. He placed some bullets in Barry's shirt and pants pockets while Fixer 2 snapped some pictures. He pulled Barry's belt out and dropped more bullets into his crotch. The overflowing bullets spilled out onto the observation deck.

"You're trying to frame me!" Barry cried, pointing at the hologram image.

"Of course. That's what holograms are for," said Fixer 1.

"But I talked to him!" Barry pleaded.

"You mean your co-conspirator? What's his name?" asked Fixer 2.

"It had an O. Oswald! It was a dream. I couldn't record it."

"You're lying," Fixer 1 declared. "Holograms can't talk. Insanity's no defence for sedition, Base. Drop the act."

"The next generation of BJ X-57s will be able to talk – and fly, and yes – someday even dream!" Fixer 2 said.

They pulled Barry to his feet and forced an *Orgresso Gamemaster* into his hands. They snapped pictures of Barry with the hologram.

"Guns blow away glass too, Base," said Fixer 1. "Mr. O might agree, but then, he's just a prop. He'll be more real when we paste your head onto his shoulders. Fun!"

Security man one wrapped the bullhorn in plastic and placed it in a black bag labeled "national memory." Security man two tossed Barry's e-phone into the same bag. The fixers placed the unwrapped rifle in a separate bag and tossed in some handfuls of bullets.

"Get your ass moving, Base," said Fixer 2. "I'm sure they can use a comedian on Prison Island."

* * *

Two hours earlier, while Barry was entering the old Parliament Buildings, the Fixers visited his motel room. They discovered a paper manuscript in his suitcase, and a file matching it on an old laptop on the bedside table. They scanned the opening pages. It was some kind of satirical novel aimed squarely at the Lord Protector.

"So this guy thinks Canada needs the services of a satirical elitist," Fixer 1 said. "This son of a bitch doesn't get the meaning of sovereign interpreter."

"True, but this part about hornets on page three sort of resonates with me," said Fixer 2. "You gotta feel for the guy."

Fixer 1 smacked Fixer 2 hard across the face with Barry's laptop. "Bag the evidence! Coordinate BJ entrapment protocol. Never mention this manuscript again."

* * *

Confusion filled Wellington Street after the shot rang out. Lucius sat in silence, staring at Izzy's body. He remembered a dream he had the night before. A dark-eyed woman cradling a small black dog appeared. She said: "The ruins of time build mansions in eternity." Meaning what? He already had a mansion. He remembered the enormous pile beneath the woman's feet in his dream. It was a pile of splintered rifles, smashed knives, shattered gas masks, broken chains, cracked lenses, molten handcuffs, swords, electrodes, i.v. lines, blindfolds and water hoses. What to make of it? He woke up, and typed it all into a world cloud app. Only five words appeared.

eternity time

ruins build

mansions

He looked east. The great bronze warhorse pushed forward with soldiers through the darkness in the arch. The fire above made cratered lakes; the wet mud turned to bronze.

He looked at Terry Fox. A t-shirt, shorts, running shoes, a hop and stride. The world turned on its axis beneath his feet, but he could not reach the sea. The look of the runner's scant clothing made Lucius's skin burn beneath his regalia. His skin tried to tell him his costume was a cypher. A nothing. An 0.

* * *

Lucius stepped down from the landau.

The crowd now stared in silence. Children too young to recognize a gunshot began to point at Lucius. One pointed at Lucius's feet. Lucius forgot to put his shoes back on. He was wearing odd socks, one blue and one orange. The child laughed. Their laughter grew wild and wilder, despite efforts of grownups to silence them. The white pelican that followed Izzy from the south flew above the children, its beating wings conducting their laughter like a symphony. It tried to land on Lucius's shoulder. Failing, it landed on his sock. The children laughed.

Lucius's e-phone buzzed. It was a text from his mother. Lady and her new lover, retired *dronecult* poet Joey Knotwad, were watching the parade over breakfast at *Winstanley's* following a night of intimate conversation and advanced sex. Joey saw Lucius as a threat to his new romance. Lady dismissed his feelings as childish tension. He believed her.

Lady's text read: "Lucius! This is your chains! Remember inner life. xox Lady." Your "chains" was an auto-correct of "chacne."

Lucius believed her.

* * *

Lucius felt ten thousand eyes bearing down on him. Feenie removed his hands from Lordso's buttocks. Lordso strained to stay upright, then crashed to the ground. Blondeau took off his belt, tied Lordso's feet like a steer and dragged him to the safety of the landau.

"Release the prisoners," Lucius ordered. Security men raised the yokes from the shoulders of the men pulling the landau.

Jesse went to Izzy. Lucius looked at Normal. Normal looked horrified.

"Where am I?" she sobbed.

Moments before, when Normal and Ruth reached Izzy, Jack Boo, pressed a button in his death chamber hut in Florida. The button was labelled Plan B. It sent a signal to a Network satellite. The satellite activated a microchip in Normal's brain. The Network put the chip in before she could walk or talk. When Jack pushed the button, her memories disappeared. She became nothing. She breathed in a void. Her muscles obeyed the microchip. She produced the gun she had taken from the crashed van. Normal shot Izzy.

* * *

Lucius pushed his way through the security detail. He looked at Jesse. He watched a vein pulse along his matted hairline. He looked at Normal. Her jugular vein was beating at an alarming rate. He looked at Izzy. She was still. He searched for life in her blank eye. He saw his own face in the mirror.

A nurse in the crowd took Izzy's pulse. She shook her head. Lucius rested his hands on his knees and breathed. He could not look Jesse in the eye. So Jesse made him look. He saw Izzy in Jesse's eye. He placed his hand on Jesse's arm. He felt his own pulse in the pressure of Jesse's skin.

He texted pardons for all the *THEM* men on his e-phone, and pressed send. He closed Prison Island, and pressed send. Then he pressed the autodestruct command on his e-phone, confirming it with his personal seventeen-digit code. He threw his e-phone under the front wheel of the landau where it congealed into smoking, toxic ooze. He dropped the envelope containing the referendum results onto the ooze, kindling a small flame.

Ruth wept violently. She pounded her fists on the road until her fists dripped blood. She screamed for someone to give her a spade. Jesse placed his hands on Normal's shoulders. He looked her in the eye with burning intensity. Ruth stopped screaming. She feared what he might do.

Jesse closed his eyes in concentration. Then he began to massage the base of Normal's skull. He sucked on the back of her head with his mouth for a several second. When he pulled away, a tiny, bloody microchip was fixed in his front teeth. He spat it out on to the road. Then he wiped Normal's wound with his sleeve.

"You didn't shoot Izzy, kid," Jesse said, pointing at the chip. "That damned thing did, and whoever owns it."

He stared at a security officer. The officer picked up the chip and placed it in an evidence bag. He led Normal to Izzy.

They wept together. The pelican stood at attention behind them. It had a bloodstain across its snowy breast. It had flown too close to the barbed wire fence on the roof of the *Office of Sovereign Interpretation*. It was dying.

Lucius looked at Izzy's broken head. He could see her aquarium shattering before his eyes, but this time from the inside. Now he was a fish, and she saved him with her cupped hands.

Then he saw his father rise out of a small drop of her blood, and look him in the eye. Richie winked and smiled and walked into the crowd, where his body burst into fine gold filaments.

The landau turned into a giant Monopoly token: an iron wheel. Parliament, the monuments, the statues and all of the buildings dissolved into grains of sand. The city was a nameless desert. Winds whipped the sand into a rage.

The world became a ceaseless storm. The storm blocked the sun. The world became dark. Lucius shielded his face with his arms. He knew he was alone inside the storm. And there was nothing outside it He feared a swirling chain would strike him.

The dark-eyed woman spoke.

"The stars, sun, moon, all shrink away

A desert vast without a bound,

And nothing left to eat or drink

And a dark desert all around."

Despite the roar of the storm, she only had to whisper to

be heard. She named the storm singularity, and the shoe friendship and the footprint life. She named herself servant. Then the pile of chains, manacles, and broken weapons she stood on was gone.

He opened his eyes. He looked at Normal.

"What's your name?" he asked. The girl looked terrified.

"Where am I?" she asked Lucius.

"We'll find her a name," Jesse said sternly.

Ottawa returned. The air was calm. The sun was bright. The parade was ruined. He saw sunbeams sparkle on Izzy's bloody wound.

He looked and saw Jesse and Ruth and the nameless girl walking away hand in hand towards the sun. He looked down. Izzy's body was gone. He saw the outline of her shoes left in her blood. The glare of the sun made it look almost like blood drops on snow. He took off his sock and slowly placed his naked foot in the outline. He felt new energy in his toes. But he had nowhere to go. He watched Jesse and Ruth and the nameless one disappear beyond the crowd.

A tear seemed to fall from the sky onto the blood. Lucius thought he saw a face in the tear for an instant. Then it vanished into the blood.

Parents pulled children away from a dead pelican on the road. The wheels of the landau collapsed in flames. Lucius suddenly had a mind to bring Izzy back to Alberta, to the lake where Noah and Simeon's ashes rested. The whole lake.

He felt a hand knocking on the back of his head. He turned, and saw a small boy holding a bag. "Want some of my McDonald's?" he asked. He pressed a wet fry on Lucius's chin.

"What's your name?" Lucius asked.

"Theo."

A small tear formed on Lucius's right eye. He let Theo put a fry in his mouth.

Epilogue

Rebirth Amid the Sound of Weeping, July 1, 2050

The teardrop fell for six thousand years.

When it landed on Wellington Street, a baby was born to two women in a place both near and far. Their names were Sanaz and Janika.

They were sheltering in the burned out ruins of a school in Damascus. They huddled together in what was once a principal's office. A gold cup lay on its side on the broken concrete floor. Some old, scorched Adidas soccer shoes lay in the corner beside a sandal that had no mate. They had no money and no food. They dwelled among the nations of Moloch and found no rest. So they decided to take in a young blind man who had no money and no food. They could not speak his language, but they wanted to help. His name was

Nuh.

Sanaz lay on the principal's metal desk with a plastic calendar under her back. Her water had broken. She was in labour.

Fire was raging around the room. Cries of maiming and mourning, lamentation and bitter weeping echoed from streets where voices go to die. Three of the G80's most underperforming economies – Liberia, Uganda and the Natural Republic of Penockyoh – had formed a military coalition to launch a pre-emptive strike against Damascus. The plan was to hit it hard while it was still rebuilding from decades of destruction. Special guest life coaches, sports psychologists, home decorators and television personalities from G80 nations offered helpful tips on strikes. The coalition named the strike *Operation Gracious Strikedown.*

The coalition was performing the gracious strikedown in central Damascus. Network drone-cams auto-censored the action. They edited the images to make blown up people look like empty buildings seen from a distant planet. The strike force employed heavy plastic artillery with biodegradable shell casings, reusable flame-throwing rockets and precision water bombers filled with highly flammable horse piss. The code name for the horse piss was *Chablis xox. Chablis xox* was a recent breakthrough in genetically modified animal-based weapons research. Ignited by precision lasers, *Chablis xox* was ten thousand times more corrosive than napalm meth. So the army diluted it with liquefied carbon emissions in order to lengthen the average duration of an urban firestorm. The Penockyoh government called it *Research Project Grapes of Wrath.* Penockyoh took advantage of the repurposed carbon emissions and the key role of horses to declare *Chablis xox* a green technology. Penockyoh lawmakers wanted decent folks to know that this was a green war. The coalition called today's attack not an attack at all but a green correction. Liquefied carbon gave the clear, urinous *Chablis xox* the look of a cloudy, brownish Merlot. So they trampled out the vintage of the grapes of endless war. Low-flying pilotless drones filmed the carnage for the G80's lucrative twenty-four-hour *Adult War Channel.* All this effort meant jobs, growth and pay-per-views back home. The promised economic recovery was underway.

On the ground, in the middle of the city, where young children faint with hunger at the head of every street, terrible men in black shirts and black balaclavas erupted out of deep, dry wells every hour like fevered ants. Their suits were literally black. They fired their guns into the air to strike fear into people, most of whom were already dead. The ant commander stood on the roof of a giant green pickup truck and shouted instructions from a training manual. The ant men shouldered their weapons and pulled out their phones. Filming themselves with phones in their left hands, shouting "death to language" in unison, the killer ants searched for small children to kidnap. The commander told the ant men to think of their guns as pens and children as words. Then he noticed the truck's glove compartment. His private stash of vintage porn was on fire. He quickly peed the fire out, rescuing all he could.

And young children and sucklings swooned in the streets of the city. Underneath an overturned truck lay one weeping and refusing to be comforted because her children are no more.

Sanaz and Janika had no countries, no citizenships, no passports. They became whatever religion or nationality the Network drones preferred. Some nations planned to charge them fees for their own executions or floggings or dungeons, if they found them. Sanaz and Janika had no credit cards and no savings. So Damascus had its appeal. Their baby would be born in a cracked, acrid, collapsing shithole of a room with no water, no food and no medicine, while thick dust and confusion reigned in the streets, and the dense smoke of hate and horror and death and droning and shelling clogged the earth and raped the sky and clung like glue to the lungs of a crying people. Nuh was a descendant of ancient princes but did not know it. He came to Damascus to look for a job as a cantor or a muezzin, preferably both. He had experience and references.

Now he was quiet, except when he coughed up dust. He feared the silence of the ant men more than the noise of the war that took his sight. A *Crusader Class X-70 Drone* killed one eye; a twelve-year-old ant man killed the other. Though blind, he could feel the darkness closing in on him and Janika and Sanaz. It was a darkness that had no outside, no beyond itself, no east or west. It roared negations of atomic epochs backwards into dissolution through the deafening throat of war.

Oh, for a voice of thunder to drown the throat of war!

He prayed for peace in whispers. Then he heard the sudden cry of birth. It was a cry the throat of war that cracked children on its larynx could not hush.

Nuh suddenly relaxed. A small, warm light circled his soul, like the ripple of dark pond holding a sinking diamond within itself, broadening surely through the equations of its empathy.

"Girl or boy?" Nuh asked his friends in song.

A bomb blasted outside the door smothered the answer. A fireball ripped through the window. The gold cup flipped over and rolled on its rim. Nuh felt scorched. He thought he was in a train wreck. He heard a scream and a cough.

There was a slow, fearful silence. Then the baby cried loudly. As a child, Nuh's hands had asked for bread. Now he smiled, breathed in, raised his hands, and fell to his knees.

THE END

Acknowledgements

Minister Faust, a celebrated Canadian writer of fantasy, science fiction, poetry, journalism and drama, gave me generous encouragement and valuable advice during his tenure as writer-in-residence at the University of Alberta in 2014-15.

44245260R00244

Made in the USA
San Bernardino, CA
10 January 2017